Season of Blessing

Season of Blessing

BOOK FOUR

BEVERLY LaHAYE
TERRI BLACKSTOCK

ZONDERVAN™

GRAND RAPIDS, MICHIGAN 49530 USA

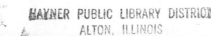

ZONDERVAN™

Season of Blessing
Copyright © 2002 by Beverly LaHaye and Terri Blackstock

Requests for information should be addressed to:
Zondervan, *Grand Rapids, Michigan 49530*

Library of Congress Cataloging-in-Publication Data

LaHaye, Beverly
    Season of blessing / by Beverly LaHaye and Terri Blackstock.
       p. cm.
    ISBN 0-310-23328-3
    1. Breast—Cancer—Patients—Fiction. 2. Cancer in women—Fiction.
3. Missionaries—Fiction. 4. Friendship—Fiction. I. Blackstock, Terri, 1957-
II. Title.
PS3562.A3144 S425 2002
813'.54—dc21
{B} 2002009097

This edition printed on acid-free paper.

Published in association with the literary agency of Alive Communications, Inc., 7680 Goddard Street, Suite 200, Colorado Springs, CO 80920.

Interior design by Melissa Elenbaas

Printed in the United States of America

---

02 03 04 05 06 07 08 /❖ DC/ 10 9 8 7 6 5 4 3 2 1

This book is dedicated to cancer patients everywhere,
and to those whose lives have been altered because
someone they love has fought this disease . . .
and to the Great Physician,
who sometimes cures here on earth . . .
and sometimes heals by taking us home.

Acknowledgments

Special thanks to Dr. Bobby Graham and Dr. Sharon Martin for being our consultants on this book. Your help was invaluable, and we couldn't have done it without you.

We'd also like to thank our agent, Greg Johnson, for the vision he had for a "Best Years" series, which ultimately evolved into these four books. He also had the vision to introduce us to each other in hopes of forming a partnership. That partnership has worked beautifully, and we've both been blessed by it.

And we must thank our editors at Zondervan—Dave Lambert, Lori Vanden Bosch, and Bob Hudson—for their tireless work to make sure these stories are the best they can be. And thanks to Sue Brower, who is responsible for letting our readers know that the books are out. This whole team does a wonderful job.

And finally, thanks to you, our reader, for giving us your time and attention as we spun these tales. Thanks for all your letters of encouragement, and for sharing tears and laughter with us as we've grown with Brenda, Tory, Cathy, and Sylvia.

May all your crises be blessings, and may you have many, many, many "best moments."

I will sing to the Lord all my life;
I will sing praise to my God as long as I live.

PSALM 104:33

CHAPTER *One*

Sylvia Bryan had always considered the words *early detection* to have more to do with others than herself. She'd never had anything that needed early detecting, and if she had any say in the matter—which apparently she did not—she would just as soon jump to the best possible conclusion, and proclaim the lump in her breast to be a swollen gland or a benign cyst. Then she could get back to her work in Nicaragua and stop being so body-conscious.

But Harry had insisted on a complete physical because of her fatigue and weakness, and had sent her home from the mission field to undergo a battery of tests that befitted a woman of her age. She had been insulted by that.

"I hope I don't have to remind you that you're a *man* of my age," she told him, "so you don't have to go treating me like I'm over-the-hill at fifty-four."

Harry had bristled. "I'm just saying that there are things you're at greater risk for, and I want to rule all of them out. You're not well, Sylvia. Something's wrong."

She'd had to defer to him, because deep down she'd been concerned about her condition, as well. It wasn't like her to be so tired. She had chalked it up to the brutal August heat in Nicaragua, but she'd weathered last summer there without a hitch. For most of her life she'd had an endless supply of energy. Now she had trouble making it to noon without having to lie down.

So he'd sent her home to Breezewood, Tennessee, to see an internist at the hospital where he'd practiced as a cardiologist for most of his life. After just a few tests, he'd diagnosed her with a bad case of anemia, which explained her condition.

But then he'd gone too far and found a lump in her breast.

She'd gone for a mammogram then, certain that the lump was nothing more than a swollen gland.

The radiologist had asked to see her in his office.

Jim Montgomery was one of Harry's roommates in medical school, and he came into the room holding her film. He'd always had an annoying way of pleating his brows and looking deeply concerned, whether he really was or not. He wore that expression now as he quietly took his seat behind his desk and clipped the mammogram film onto the light box behind him.

Sylvia wasn't in the mood for theatrics. "Okay, Jim. I know you want to be thorough and everything for Harry's sake, but my problem has already been diagnosed. I'm badly anemic, which explains all my fatigue. So you can relax and quit looking for some terminal disease."

Jim turned on the light box and studied the breast on the film. With his pencil, he pointed to a white area. "Sylvia, you have a suspicious mass in your left breast."

Sylvia stiffened. "What does that mean ... 'a suspicious mass'?"

"It means that there's a tumor there. It's about three centimeters. Right here in the upper outer aspect of your left breast." He made an imaginary circle over the film with his pencil.

Sylvia got up and moved closer to the film, staring at the offensive blob. She studied it objectively, as if looking at some other woman's X ray. It couldn't be hers. Wouldn't she have known if something that ominous lay hidden in her breast tissue? "Are you sure you didn't get my film mixed up with someone else's?"

"Of course I'm sure." He tipped his head back and studied the mass through the bottom of his glasses. "Sylvia, do you do self breast exams?"

She felt as if she'd been caught neglecting her homework. "Well, I used to try. But mine are pretty dense, and I always felt lumps that turned out to be nothing. I finally gave it up."

"Not a good idea. Especially with your history."

She knew he was right. Her mother had died of breast cancer when Sylvia was twenty-four. She should have known better than to neglect those self-exams. But she had been so busy for the last couple of years, and hadn't had that much time to think about herself.

"Well, I have tried to have mammograms every year since I turned forty ..." Her voice trailed off. "Except for the last couple of years when I've been out of the country."

"Well, it seems that the last couple of years were what really mattered."

She looked at him, trying to read the frown on his face. "But it's okay, isn't it? You can tell if it looks malignant ..."

He looked down at her chart and made a notation. "You need to get a biopsy tomorrow, if possible."

The fact that he'd averted his eyes alarmed her. "You just evaded my question, Jim. And you know Harry is going to want to know. Does it look malignant to you or not?"

He leaned back in his chair, crossing his hands over his stomach. The frown wrinkling his brow didn't look quite so melodramatic now.

She set her mouth. "Be straight with me, Jim. You see these things all the time. I want the truth."

"All right, Sylvia." He sighed and took off his glasses, rubbed his eyes. "It does have the characteristics of a malignancy."

For a moment she just stood there, wishing she hadn't pressed the issue. Malignancy meant cancer, and cancer meant surgery, and then chemotherapy and radiation and her hair falling out and pain and depression and hospice care and death.

Her mouth went dry, and she wished she'd brought her bottled water in from the car. She wondered what time it was. She had to get to the cleaners before it closed.

Her hands felt like ice, so she slid them into the pockets of her blazer to warm them. "Come on, Jim. I don't have cancer. I've been tired, that's all, and they already figured out it's from anemia. There is no possibility that I have breast cancer. None. Zilch."

"Sylvia, you have to get this biopsied as soon as possible."

"Okay." She looked down at her blazer and dusted a piece of lint off. "Fine. I'll get the biopsy, but I'm not worried about it at all."

"Good." But he still wore the frown that said it wasn't good. He turned and jerked the film out of the light box. "And you're probably right. But if it is cancer, you may have detected it early enough that you'll have an excellent prognosis."

As Sylvia drove home, she realized that, along with *early detection*, she hated the word *prognosis*. It was not a word she'd ever expected to have uttered about her own body. This was just a minor inconvenience, she thought. She did not have time to be sick. The Lord knew how hard she worked for him in Nicaragua, and how much the children in the orphanage there needed her. They were probably already grieving her absence.

The Lord surely wouldn't cut her work off when she'd been bearing so much fruit. He cut off barren branches and pruned those who needed to bear more. But when she spent her life giving and serving, wouldn't he want her work to continue?

So she determined to push the news out of her mind until she'd actually had the biopsy. She knew in her heart that the mass was benign.

And if the biopsy proved her wrong, she would deal with it then.

CHAPTER *Two*

Brenda Dodd wiped the white paint off of her hands and threw the rag across the plywood limousine. She hit Daniel—her sixteen-year-old—in the face.

"No fair! I wasn't looking."

He flung it across the prop and hit Leah across the forehead. She slung it at Rachel, her twin sister, leaving a smudge of paint across her cheek. Rachel tossed it at Joseph.

Preoccupied, twelve-year-old Joseph hardly noticed. He stood in front of his father, watching him sand the steering wheel that would go inside the car. "It seems like an awful lot of work to go to, Dad, if you're not even going to come to church and watch the play Wednesday night."

Brenda's smile faded, and she looked at her husband. David had that tight, shut-down look that he got whenever the subject of church came up.

"I don't mind."

"But, Dad, I'm the star. I play the Good Samaritan who drives into town in his limousine and helps the guy who got mugged. How can you not want to see that?"

David cleared his throat. A cool breeze blew through their yard, ruffling his wavy red hair, but he still had a thin sheen of sweat above his lip. "Son, you know how I feel about church."

"I know, Dad, but it's not like something terrible will happen to you if you come."

"I'm not a hypocrite."

"But I want you to see me. I've practiced so hard. And I'm good, aren't I, Mom?"

Brenda knew better than to get involved, but she couldn't let her child down. "He is good, David."

"It's not that he's good." Fourteen-year-old Leah slopped more paint on her shorts and bare legs than she did on the car. "It's just that he's such a ham. He's a terrible show-off."

"I am not."

"Are too." Rachel came to sit beside Leah. "I thought they were going to have to pry that microphone out of your hand the other night at rehearsal. They wanted you to sing one verse, but you sang three."

Joseph snickered. "Hey, I felt moved by the Holy Spirit, okay?"

Rachel laughed. "Yeah, moved to stand in the limelight just a little longer."

"Okay, guys." Brenda got up and went to the other paint can sitting on the picnic table. "Leave Joseph alone. He's a talented performer, which is why he was chosen to play the Good Samaritan."

Joseph struck a pose. "And Dad isn't even going to see."

"Enough, Joseph." David sanded the steering wheel, blew the sawdust off.

Joseph shrugged and grabbed a paintbrush and stuck it in the black paint.

Brenda winced as he dripped it across the lawn. "This paint's for the windows, Joseph, and we might not have enough. Be careful not to let it drip."

"I won't." With great care, he began to outline the windows. "But really, Dad. I know you don't want to come to church because you don't believe in Jesus, but I don't see why you couldn't just fake it every now and then."

David sanded harder. "I don't fake things, Joseph. You don't fake your feelings just to please other people."

"But *why* don't you believe? I mean, it's just so obvious to me."

David shot Brenda a look. "Joseph, could we drop it?"

"But why, Dad? You always say that we should ask questions when we don't understand."

Daniel turned to see his father's reaction. Rachel and Leah stopped painting. Brenda said a silent prayer that their son's probing would make David think. If anyone in the family could get away with questions like these, Joseph could.

David set the steering wheel down. He looked at Joseph, then at Leah, Rachel, and Daniel.

"Okay, here's the thing." He sat down on the bench and leaned his elbows on his knees. "Your mother is a believer, and I'm not. I'm a facts kind of guy. She's more . . . spiritual. Ever since she became a Christian a few years into our marriage, I've agreed that she can raise you guys in church. I figure if she's wrong, it doesn't hurt anything. And you guys seem to like it. But ever since I was a kid, I've hated church. It's just a personal thing."

That didn't satisfy Joseph. "But you wouldn't hate our church. It's a good church."

"I'm sure it is."

Brenda knew that David would never tell them that he'd been the son of a preacher who had run off with the church organist, or how the church had thrown his mother and him out of the parsonage—leaving them homeless—in order to take a moral stand against the divorce that resulted. He would never tell the children how the church members had insisted that he was demon-possessed when his anger about his broken family surfaced. His father had died with a shipwrecked faith, and just five years ago, his mother died without ever forgiving his father—or the church.

Brenda didn't blame David for being bitter about the church.

"But, Dad, if you're a facts man, then how come you can't see the true facts? It wasn't so long ago that I was dying, and Jesus healed me. Now I'm perfect," Joseph said.

"Perfect?" Leah grunted. "Get real."

"I mean my body is perfect. I'm healthy and normal, except for all the medicine I have to take. But I was dying, Dad. God didn't have to give me a heart transplant, but he did."

David met Brenda's eyes again. She knew Joseph had put him in a tight spot. They had agreed that he would never denigrate the children's belief in God. But how could he defend his own beliefs without doing that?

"Isn't that proof, Dad?" Joseph demanded.

David swallowed. "To some people it is."

"But not to you?" He went back to the paint can and got more paint on his brush. "Dad, it's like this. You know how I was dying, and I couldn't be healed without a heart transplant? Somebody had to die so I could live?"

"Yeah."

"Well, that's a lot like what happened with God. We were all dying, and we had no hope. So Jesus came and died in our place, so that we could have a new heart and a new spirit. So that we could live."

"I know how it works, Joseph." David's aggravation shone clearly on his face.

"But how could you not want to live?"

David gazed down at his son. "I think I am living, son. Don't we have a good life?"

"Well, yeah, but it's not just this life that you have to consider."

Brenda suppressed her smile and caught a black drip cutting down through the white paint. She doubted David had ever had the gospel presented to him in such a clear way. She knew that seeds had been sown, whether they took root or not.

Joseph was getting sloppier with his painting, but Brenda didn't dare interrupt. His words to his father hit dead center.

David reached out and tousled Joseph's hair. "I appreciate your concern, son. I really do. And I'm proud of you for being able to make your case that way. Someday you'll probably be a lawyer. If I ever have to face a judge, it's you I'd want speaking for me."

Joseph's face betrayed his sorrow as he looked up at his father. "When you face the Judge, Dad, I won't be with you. You'll have to answer him for yourself."

CHAPTER *Three*

Up. . . . down . . . up. . . . down . . ."

Tory Sullivan mouthed the words with Melissa, the physical therapist, as she moved Hannah's legs in an effort to tone her weak muscles. The small woman sitting on the classroom floor had become like a member of their family, ever since Hannah had been born with Down's Syndrome. Now, at twenty-two months, the child was just beginning to make the effort to stand on her own. Watching the other Down's babies at the Breezewood Development Center had been an encouragement to Tory, reminding her that these children did develop, even if they did it slowly.

But the struggle didn't get easier for Tory. A former Miss Tennessee, she had always expected near perfection from herself and her family. Her home was immaculate and decorated like something out of *House and Garden*. Brittany, her ten-year-old, was into frills and curls, ribbons and lace, just as Tory had been at her age. Eight-year-old Spencer was a textbook boy—

athletic, outgoing, and definite leadership material, even if he was sometimes a handful.

And then there was Hannah. It was almost like the Lord had declared Hannah the one to be imperfect in the Sullivan household, just to remind her that not everything could line up under her checklist of expectations. Everything didn't have order and logic. God's order often came without explanation.

Hannah had taught Tory to lean on God more than she ever had before . . . to lower her expectations . . . to exult in the unexpected.

Still she longed to know that Hannah would walk, talk, learn . . . That she would live a happy life without daily battles to function . . . That she would develop and grow and progress to her full potential.

The truth was, she wanted everything for Hannah that she wanted for her other two children. But Hannah had challenges that Spencer and Brittany would never have. She always would. But Tory considered it a miracle that the baby had come this far when just a few months ago she hadn't believed she would ever even sit up alone. She knew the walking wouldn't come for a while yet, maybe even a year or two, but the fact that Hannah tried to pull up now gave her great hope.

A knock sounded on the classroom door, and Mary Ann Shelton, the director of the school, stuck her head in. "What are you guys doing here so late? It's after five."

"My fault," Melissa said. "I had a dentist appointment this afternoon and had to reschedule Hannah."

Mary Ann came into the room. "I'm just glad I ran into you, Tory. I was going to call you. Can I talk to you in my office for a minute?"

Tory smirked at Melissa as she got up from the floor and dusted off her pants. "Oh, boy. Hannah hasn't been cutting class again, has she? Is that why I'm being called to the principal's office?"

Mary Ann laughed. "No, I just wanted to talk to you about a job we've had that just came open."

Tory couldn't imagine what a job opening had to do with her. Mary Ann knew that raising Hannah took up every moment of her time.

But the director led her into her office and sat down behind her desk. Tory sank onto the plush easy chair, feeling as if she had forgotten something important. She realized she had never been in here without Hannah on her lap.

"So what's this about a job?" Tory asked.

Mary Ann's eyes inspired excitement, whether she talked about school tuition or the janitorial staff. "We've had an opening for a part-time teacher's assistant in the older children's class, ages six to nine, and I was thinking that maybe you would be interested."

Tory frowned. "Oh, I don't know, Mary Ann. I haven't really thought about getting a job. I'm so busy at home with Hannah."

"Well, that's just it." Mary Ann set her hands palms-down on the desk. "You could bring Hannah with you and she could play in the nursery while you work with the older kids. I thought it would be an encouragement for you to see how these older children are learning. And I can tell from watching you with Hannah that you'd be a godsend for these children as well."

Tory had never considered working with the older kids, but the truth was, she spent a lot of time standing outside the door of that classroom, peering through the window at those older kids who could walk and dance and talk and sing.

"You wouldn't have to do any planning or preparation. Linda, our teacher in that room, would do all that. You'd just help two mornings a week, Tuesdays and Thursdays. I've gotten another parent to commit to three mornings, and we have a couple of teenagers who help in the afternoons."

"Two mornings a week," Tory repeated. "That wouldn't be so bad. Might even be fun."

"And of course, it wouldn't interfere with Hannah's class." Mary Ann caught her breath. "Oh, I forgot. It pays too. I don't want you to think it's a volunteer position. And it might be good for Hannah to play with some of the other babies without you around. I don't mean that in a bad way. It's wonderful to have you there. I wish we had more mothers as involved as you. I'm just saying that maybe she needs to start socializing a little and learning to separate from you."

Tory knew that was true. Even now she had a hard time leaving Hannah with a baby-sitter, even at church.

"I'll need to think about it." She got up, anxious to get back to the child. "I need to talk to Barry and pray about it some. Can I get back to you?"

"Sure," Mary Ann said. "Take your time. I will need to hire someone by the end of August. But you were my first choice."

Tory ran the possibilities through her mind as she drove home that evening, and wondered if taking the job would indeed be good for everyone involved.

CHAPTER *Four*

Cathy Bennet sat at her kitchen table, her patchwork family feasting on tacos, as if they had never been touched by divorce or remarriage or jail. Having her new family all together was a dream come true.

She didn't know why Mark had chosen to ruin it.

"What do you mean, you don't want to go back to school?" Her taco crumbled in her hand, and she threw it onto her plate. "Mark, I know you had school in jail, but you didn't finish. You still need a diploma. I want you to go to college. I thought you were finally getting your head on straight."

"I am getting my head on straight, Mom!" Mark chomped into his taco, and shredded cheese and ground beef avalanched out.

"Then what are you talking about?"

Mark swallowed the bite in his mouth without enough chewing. "I didn't say I planned to drop out altogether. I just want to get my GED, that's all. Then I can go to college *or* get a job."

"A job?" Steve leaned up on the table, studying the boy who sat across from him. "Mark, what kind of job do you think you can get without an education?"

"I *have* an education."

"A complete education." Steve wiped his hands on a napkin. "Mark, you have to think of what kind of money you could make without finishing school."

Tracy tapped her spoon to the side of her glass, drawing all eyes to herself. "If he quits school, I get to quit, too."

Steve shot his twelve-year-old daughter a disgusted look. "You can think again, buckaroo."

"Why? In some countries kids are finished with school before they ever get to my age."

Nineteen-year-old Annie pushed her food around on her plate. Since she'd come back from Nicaragua with Sylvia, she had gone on a health food kick and refused to eat anything that even looked like it had calories. "You should see the kids in Nicaragua, wandering the streets digging through trash for food. They'd kill to be in a school like yours."

Cathy turned her gaze back to Mark, her blonde ponytail waving with the movement. "Why don't you want to go to school, Mark? I thought after being in jail for a year you'd want to go back to normal."

Mark dropped his taco and wiped his hands on his jeans. "Don't you see, Mom? I can't go back to normal. I've changed. I can't go back to public school because the guys I got in trouble with still go there."

Cathy met Steve's eyes. "Well, at least he sees that."

Steve leaned up on the table. "So why couldn't you go back to home schooling with Brenda's kids? She's already said she'd take you back. And she needs the money we'd pay her."

"Man . . ." Mark propped his face on his hand. "I feel like I've grown up past that. Going to school with little kids and having her hovering over me. I don't have anything against her. I really like Miss Brenda. I do. But I just need to get on with things, you know?"

Cathy started to tell him that he wasn't as grown up as he thought he was, when Rick's cell phone rang, injecting life into the otherwise silent twenty-one-year-old who sat staring at his food. He pulled the phone from his belt clip.

"Hello? Yeah. What's up, man? Nothing much."

Steve met her eyes in silent encouragement to rebuke him.

Cathy touched Rick's arm. "Rick, could you please take that somewhere else? We're trying to have dinner conversation here."

He didn't answer, just got up from the table and strode to another room. She watched him leave, wishing she'd made him turn off the phone before they sat down to eat. Since he lived on campus for summer school, he seldom came home to eat with them, and she hated calling him down when he did.

She turned back to Mark. "Mark, let's say you did get your GED. You're only sixteen. You're probably not ready to jump right into college."

"I told you, I'm not sure I even want to go to college. I'm tired. I need some freedom after being locked up for a year."

Tracy started drumming her fingers on the table.

Steve reached out and stopped her hand. "But, Mark, there's no freedom in having to work without a college degree. It's hard. Why would you want to put yourself through that?"

"Steve's right," Cathy said. "Honey, school is the best place for you now."

"Okay, but where?" he asked. "Do you want me to go to public school or do you want me to go to Brenda's and study with Leah and Rachel and Joseph?"

"And Daniel," Cathy said. "Don't forget Daniel. He's exactly your age."

"But he's different, Mom. He's a good friend and all, and I'm glad to have him as my buddy, but he's basically clueless. I've been in jail for a year. I've been around people who are hard to get along with."

"Then this should be easy for you."

✗ "I don't want to be baby-sat all day and hovered over. I can take a GED course and get out of school and have some freedom."

Steve got up and took his plate to the sink. "Mark, you don't even have a driver's license yet. You're kidding yourself if you think this is going to give you extra freedom. And I think you need to define what freedom is."

"I know what freedom is," Annie piped in, flipping her dark hair back. "Freedom is just another word for nothing left to lose."

Cathy smirked. "Thank you, Annie, for bringing the wisdom of Janis Joplin into this conversation."

Rick came back into the room just then and took his place at the table. "Freedom? Oh, freedom. That's just some people talking." He broke into singing "Desperado," and Annie joined in. Mark threw his napkin across the table. Annie deftly caught it in the air and threw it back.

Cathy ducked. "Hey, not at the table. Come on, guys."

Tracy wadded one of her own and threw it smack into Cathy's face. Cathy caught it in her fist. The girl cracked up at the hit.

"Nice going, Tracy." Annie high-fived her. "Only I wouldn't recommend you repeat that."

Cathy waited for Steve to call Tracy down, but his eyes were still fixed on Mark.

"Mark, you must have given this job thing some thought. What kind of jobs are you thinking of?"

"I don't know. Maybe something like an electrician."

Steve came back to the table. "Electricians are trained. Some of them go to college. If they don't, at the very least they go to vocational school."

Mark shifted in his seat. "They need assistants, don't they?"

"Well, yeah, but that's a minimum wage job. And you've got a background, Mark. You've got a few strikes against you since you've been to jail. If you offset that with a college degree, people will forget about it and think that maybe you were irresponsible as a kid, but you grew up. But if you don't even finish high school and you get your GED and then try to get a job just a few months after getting out of jail, the chances are that you'll have to take some crummy job that you hate just to make a living."

"Well, it's not like you guys are going to throw me out in the street, is it? I can stay here for a while, can't I?"

Cathy took Mark's hand. "Of course you can, honey."

Steve crossed his arms. "You can stay here, Mark, as long as you're working toward something. If you're going to school . . . if you have a plan . . ."

Cathy turned to her husband, her eyes lashing him. "Steve, he's only been out a week."

"Yeah," Mark said. "It's not like I've been sitting around doing nothing."

"Honey, I think he's entitled to a few days of rest," Cathy said.

Steve looked as aggravated as she. "Of course he is, but now he's telling us he doesn't want to go to school, and if he doesn't, then we need to know what the plan is. There has to be a plan, Cathy."

Cathy turned back to her son. "Honey, he's right. You do need a plan."

Mark scowled. "I will have a plan, Mom. It doesn't have to be *his* plan."

Cathy winced and stole a look at Steve. His face had that hard, tight look it got when he was angry. "He didn't mean that the way it sounded," she said weakly.

"Yes, I did." Mark got up from the table and shoved his chair back. "I've already talked to my dad about this. He's all for it. He thinks the GED is a good idea."

Cathy bit her tongue. It wouldn't do to remind him that his father's ideas were usually bad. His involvement in Mark's life had left way too much to be desired. It didn't surprise her that the one time he advised his son on anything, he'd encourage him to drop out of school. Not certain how to proceed from here, she moved her gaze back to her simmering husband. He stared down at the table, the little muscle of his jaw popping rhythmically in and out.

Rick bottomed his can of coke. "Hey, Mark can come stay with me on campus."

Mark's face lit up. "Can I, Mom?"

"Of course not." Cathy pinned Rick with a look. "You're not helping matters."

Rick looked as if she'd slapped him. "Excuse me for trying to help. Excuse me for coming home for a nice family meal. Excuse me for daring to open my mouth."

Steve's teeth came together. "Don't talk to your mother that way, Rick."

Rick threw up his hands. "What way?"

Steve heaved a loud sigh.

Rick got up. "I'm finished eating. Can I go?"

Cathy wondered how long it would be before she could get him back again. "I guess so."

Rick got up and left the house, and Mark took off up the stairs. She heard his door close hard.

Annie and Tracy sat watching their faces, as if anxious for the next round.

"We need to talk about that door slamming," Steve bit out.

"He wasn't slamming it." Cathy rubbed her face. "He just closed it too hard. Boys do that. They walk harder, open cabinets harder, close doors harder."

"I used to be a boy." Steve grabbed Tracy's plate and dropped it hard in the sink. "I don't do that."

"Well, he's still learning." She gathered the rest of the plates and followed him to the sink. "You're used to raising Tracy, and she doesn't slam and make a lot of noise."

"One time I slammed my door," Tracy said, "and Daddy took it off the hinges for two weeks."

"You didn't slam it again, did you?" Steve pointed out.

Tracy grinned and shook her head.

Cathy followed him to the sink. "Please, Steve. Don't do that to Mark. He's had a rough year, and he came home to a changed family. I only want him to be comfortable here."

"And I'm making him uncomfortable?"

"No, that's not what I said. I just don't want you coming down hard with the rules. Give him some adjustment time. He's only sixteen. He's not supposed to have his whole life mapped out already."

Steve turned the water on full blast. "I'm not asking him to map it out. School is basic. You must agree with me on that."

"It is basic," she said, "but I can see where he's coming from. I can understand why he doesn't want to go study with Brenda's brood."

Annie rounded up the glasses and took them to the counter. "If you ask me, he's matured a lot since he got arrested. He's had life experiences . . . not good ones. It's got to be hard for him, coming back to his old life and everybody expecting him to be the same guy that went away. Only he's a year older and a year wiser. And he's a Christian now. And he just doesn't quite know how to fit his new self back into the old skin. You know what Jesus said, about putting new wine into old wineskins?"

Cathy just stared at her daughter. "I'm not sure exactly what you just said, but I understand the concept." She looked at Steve. "She may be right."

"Well, if that's true," Steve said, "it only means he needs a little more guidance. That's what we're here for. Not just to throw him out in the world to make more mistakes."

Annie folded her arms. "I'm just saying to cut him some slack. It's got to be frustrating coming back with everything changed. I know it is for me."

Cathy gaped at her. "Frustrating? Why?"

"Well, the house is different. The renovation changed everything. And you and Steve all chummy and romantic, like two peas in a pod, and before you were just dating . . . Rick gone and me getting ready for college in the fall . . . Tracy in your old bedroom. Mark was the youngest in the family when he left, and now Tracy is. The birth order has changed. I read all about that in an article."

Steve wasn't buying. "Amateur psychology notwithstanding, Mark Flaherty is still only sixteen. And if my parents had let me make my own decisions at sixteen, I'd be a fry cook alcoholic with children in every state."

Cathy couldn't picture it, but she didn't tell him so. She was getting a headache and didn't want to talk about it anymore.

CHAPTER *Five*

When Cathy crossed the yard to Sylvia's for the prayer time they had scheduled earlier, Tory and Brenda were already there, leaning against the kitchen counter as Sylvia bustled around making her favorite dip.

Tory, who seemed not to know what to do with her hands since Hannah wasn't on her hip, munched on a carrot. "So she asks me if I want to work there part-time two mornings a week, helping with the six- to nine-year-olds."

"You going to do it?" Brenda asked.

Cathy came and stood in the doorway, and Tory picked up the vegetable plate and thrust it at her. "Here. Eat."

Cathy shook her head. "Can't. We just had a family dinner. There were few survivors."

Sylvia looked up from the dip. "Oh, no. You didn't have a family squabble, did you?"

"Well, yeah . . . sort of. Long story."

Brenda slid up onto the counter. "We've got time."

Cathy grabbed a celery stick and bit into it. "But I want to hear what Tory decided."

"Haven't decided yet," she said. "Part of me wants to do it, but the other part feels like I'd be neglecting Hannah. But Mary Ann thought it would be good for me to work with the older kids. She thought it would encourage me about the things that Hannah will eventually be able to do."

Sylvia opened a jar of salsa and poured it into a bowl. "I think it's a wonderful idea. And you know Hannah will be cared for. She'll be right down the hall."

"I'm thinking about it." Tory took the vegetable plate and a bowl of chips to the living room, set them on the coffee table. Cathy followed with the dip, and Brenda brought the glasses.

Cathy plopped wearily down into an easy chair, and Tory and Brenda sat on the floor near the food. Sylvia came in, dusting her hands. "Okay, what am I forgetting?"

"Nothing," Brenda said. "Come sit down."

"Drinks!" Sylvia hurried back to the kitchen. "I forgot your drinks. Iced tea okay for everybody?"

The three agreed that it was, and she hurried back with a tray. "Now, that should do it."

Cathy watched Sylvia as she sat down. Her face looked tight and preoccupied, and dark shadows beneath her eyes spoke of her fatigue. "Sylvia, are you sure you didn't overdo it today?"

"I'm sure." But as she said it, she averted her eyes.

"So what did you find out at the doctor?"

Sylvia's smile faded. Pink blotches colored her neck. "Just a bad case of anemia. That's what's causing me to be so tired and weak."

"What do they do for that?" Tory asked.

"Iron and vitamins. I'll be all right in no time."

Cathy laughed. "Well, what a relief! I was worried it was something more serious."

Brenda looked as if she didn't quite buy that diagnosis. "Are they sure that's all?"

Sylvia grew quiet and looked down at her fingernails. "Well . . . not completely."

Cathy sat up straighter. "What is it, Sylvia?"

Sylvia snapped her face back up, forcing a smile. "Well, you know how doctors are. If they'd stopped at the anemia, it would have been just fine with me. But no, they have to keep looking until they find something else."

"What did they find?" Dread flattened Cathy's voice.

Sylvia picked up her glass and a napkin, wiped the dampness off of it. "It's probably nothing. I shouldn't have even told you. I'm not worried about it in the least."

Tory got off of the floor then and looked down at Sylvia. "And?"

"It's just that they found a lump in my breast."

"Oh, no." Tory's whispered words voiced what Cathy was thinking. But she told herself that it could be nothing. She'd had lumps in her own breasts, and they'd turned out to be nothing.

"Did you go for a mammogram?" Brenda asked.

"Sure did." Sylvia sipped her drink. "It's there, all right. I saw it myself."

"What are they going to do?" Brenda's voice held steady.

"Well, tomorrow I'm going for a biopsy. I'm really optimistic, girls. I mean, just think about it. I've got so much work to do in Nicaragua. The children need me so badly, and Harry . . ." Her voice broke off, and she swallowed back her emotion. "I don't believe the Lord would afflict me with breast cancer right now, so it's not even something I'm worried about. I'm going to go for the biopsy, find out it's benign, then go on back to my work. I refuse to worry about it until I get the results."

"I had a lump in my breast once." Brenda's voice was too quiet to inspire confidence. "It turned out to be just a cyst. No big deal."

Sylvia nodded. "See? That's exactly what this is. I guarantee you."

But Cathy wasn't satisfied. "What did the radiologist say?"

Sylvia looked at her as if she'd been caught.

Cathy leaned her elbows on her knees and locked onto Sylvia's face. "I know you talked to the radiologist. Harry knows every doctor in town, and if anyone would get personal attention it would be the wife of a cardiologist who worked in this town for twenty-five years. So what did the radiologist tell you?"

She shrugged. "He just showed me the lump, that's all. There it was, smiling at us, right from the X ray. It was really very creepy."

Cathy knew from her own experience with breast lumps that the doctor could tell a great deal from the mammogram. Cancer had specific shapes and characteristics ... She knew he would have an opinion.

But Sylvia stuck to her story.

"He just set me up for a biopsy and that was it. Now who wants a piece of pie? I'd like to say I made it myself, but I just went by Kroger and picked it up. My sweet tooth was really acting up, and I figured I'd lost enough weight that I could stand to stuff a few calories into me. I also bought some red meat so I could start getting the iron back into my blood. I cooked myself filet mignon for dinner."

Cathy looked from Tory to Brenda. They each had volumes written on their faces.

"Nothing for me, thanks," Tory said.

"Me, either." Cathy swallowed.

"Have you told Harry?" Brenda's question mirrored Cathy's thoughts.

Sylvia groaned. "I wish I could hold him off until I've gotten the biopsy back. But I guess there's no chance of that, because he knows I went to the doctor today. I really, really hate to make him worry."

"He's a doctor," Cathy said. "He can take it."

"Trust me. He's not that objective when it's his own family. I'll never forget when Sarah's appendix ruptured. You would have thought it was his fault somehow, that he should have seen it and prevented it. He hovered over her in the hospital for days, worried sick."

Sylvia got up and hurried to get the pie. "It looks good, girls. Sure you don't want some?" she called from the kitchen.

Cathy looked at Brenda, saw the worry in her eyes.

Tory's hand came up to her heart, and she sent a stricken look to both of them.

Sylvia fluttered back into the room with four slices. "You don't have to eat it. But one bite and you'll be a goner."

She took a bite and closed her eyes. "Mmm. This is the best thing I've ever put in my mouth," she said. "You girls don't know what you're missing. Cathy, come on and get a piece. Oh, I've missed American food."

Cathy took a piece, just to make Sylvia feel better, but as she ate, she couldn't help watching Sylvia and wondering what burden she hid behind her smile, refusing to share with them.

CHAPTER *Six*

It was eight when they finished praying together. Brenda walked out with Tory and Cathy, and all three seemed lost in thought as they crossed Sylvia's yard.

"She's keeping something from us," Cathy said. "I'm afraid the radiologist gave her some bad news."

Brenda locked her eyes on Cathy's face. "Would he really have been able to tell anything?"

"He could tell by the shape of the mass whether it looks like cancer. It's not one hundred percent accurate, of course, and in some cases it's nothing more than a guess, but it's an educated guess, and I know he told her something."

Brenda looked toward Sylvia's house, wondering if her friend sat in there, struggling with the fear and anxiety that she refused to share with them. "Why wouldn't she tell us?"

"Because she's Sylvia," Tory said. "She would think more of us than herself, and she wouldn't want to worry us."

Brenda felt helpless. "Wouldn't you think she'd need to talk?"

"Sure she does," Cathy said. "But she's not going to. Not if it gets us upset."

"Well, I hope she tells Harry."

Cathy shook her head. "She'll probably tell him as much as she told us. We really need to pray for her. And tomorrow, I'm going to close the clinic and go with her."

Tory nodded. "Good idea. She doesn't need to go through this alone."

As Cathy headed back to her house and Tory back to hers, Brenda stepped across her yard. David's light shone in the workshop, and she knew he was working late to make up for the time he'd lost working on the limousine. She opened the door and stepped in, smelling the scent of sawdust and lacquer. Her husband, with his red curly hair and freckled skin, stood over the cabinets he worked on, examining them with a critical eye.

"What do you think?" he said. "Is this my best work, or what?"

She ran her hand along the sandy wood. "I think your customer will be delirious."

"I think so, too. Maybe one of these days I'll make a set for us."

She laughed. "I'm not holding my breath. You've got too much paying work."

"Well, I can dream, can't I?"

She sat on one of the counters, watching him crouch down to screw the hardware onto the doors. "I was just over at Sylvia's."

"Nice having her home, isn't it? Too bad she can't stay. When's she planning to go back?"

"I don't know. She had a little disturbing news."

He looked up at her. "What was that?"

"They found a lump in her breast."

David unfolded from his crouch and stood up. "Oh, no."

"Yes. She's acting all upbeat about it, like she's not worried at all."

"But you know better."

"Yeah, I know better." Brenda slid off her perch. "The doctor says her fatigue and weakness are caused by anemia. But it worries me a little, David."

"Why?"

"Because if they're wrong, and anemia is not the thing causing her fatigue and weakness, then maybe she does have cancer, and if it's already affecting her that way, it could be really advanced."

"You're borrowing trouble," he said. "Who was it that said today has enough trouble of its own?"

She smiled. "Jesus."

"Oh." He turned around and fiddled with the tools behind him, got what he needed, and squatted back down. "Never thought you'd hear me quoting the Bible, did you?"

She didn't answer him. There was no point. "Well, I guess I'd better get inside and see if the kids did the dishes."

He got up and pressed a kiss on her lips. "You okay?"

"Yeah." She laid her face against his chest, and he closed his arms around her. "I'm a little concerned, that's all. But I'll pray for her tonight, heavy-duty prayers. God will listen."

He didn't respond, just turned back to his work as Brenda left the building and walked across the grass to her house. She whispered a quiet prayer that she knew was familiar to God's ears. "Take the veil from his eyes, Lord. Please help him to see."

The fact that God did not answer immediately didn't daunt her at all. He hadn't for the many years that she'd been praying for David. She knew one day the prayer would be answered. It had to be, in God's timing. God had promised that anything she asked according to his will would be done. Saving David would glorify the Lord, so how could it not be in his will? There were no ifs, ands, or buts about it. She only wished the Lord's timing was more like her own.

CHAPTER *Seven*

Later that night, Cathy found Mark sitting at his computer. She leaned in his doorway. "What are you doing?"

He looked at her over his shoulder. "He influences you too much."

"What? Who does?"

"Steve."

She sighed and pushed off from the doorway. "Of course he influences me. He's my husband."

Mark kept typing. "But he's not always right. Sometimes he could be wrong, you know."

She knocked some wadded clothes off the edge of his bed and sat down. "Mark, we're a team now. We're married. He's my husband. He's your stepfather."

"But he's not my real father." Mark kept his eyes on the monitor. "I have one of those, and he happens to like my ideas."

Again she restrained herself from making a deprecating comment about her ex-husband's wisdom. "That's fine, Mark, and we'll look into it, okay? I just need some more information. We need to think this through and pray about it."

"I have been praying about it," he said. "I really have."

"For how long?"

He finally turned away from the computer and faced her. "Since I've been home, okay? Since it's gotten so close to school starting." He got up and kicked his way through the clothes on his floor. He had only been home a week. She couldn't imagine how he'd already accumulated so much laundry.

"I really do want to have a plan, Mom. But there he is, telling you what to think, what to do ... and what *I* need to be doing. It's just not right."

"It *is* right," she said. "Mark, he's the head of this household now."

Mark grunted. "The head of the household? Mom, it was just you before. You were the head of the household, and we did just fine."

"That's because I didn't have a husband. But now that I do, he's the leader."

"But that doesn't even make sense, Mom, because he's not our real father. He's not supposed to be *my* leader."

Cathy wasn't sure how to respond to that. The Bible was clear on the marriage roles—it just didn't address stepfatherhood. "Mark, you know from all the time he invested in you while you were in jail that he cares about you. Don't you know that?"

"Well, yeah. But that's different. He can care without being so hard-nosed."

"He just wants things to go well for you."

"Things will go well for me, if he lets me get my GED and do what I want."

"Doing what you want is what got you in jail in the first place."

"But I'm not like that anymore, Mom! You know I'm not. I've changed. I'm a Christian now. I have a purpose. And I'll never get within ten feet of any kind of drugs again. I'm not ever going back to jail, and I can promise you that."

"I believe you, honey." She sighed and set her hands on her knees. "I don't want you to worry. It's going to be all right. We'll work all this out. We just don't want you to waste your life."

"You can be a worthwhile person without going to college, Mom."

"I just don't know why you're in such a hurry to grow up."

"I already *have* grown up."

He had a lot to learn, but Cathy didn't want to tell him so. Instead, she reached over and gave him a hug. "I'm really, really glad you're home."

"I am, too." He kissed her cheek. "And don't get me wrong. I do like Steve. I'm glad you married him. He's good for you. I just wish he'd stay out of it when we're talking about me."

"He's not going to stay out of it, Mark. He's a wise man and I admire him and trust him. I welcome his input. I wish you would, too."

"I do to some extent," Mark said, "but he's wrong this time. I'm trying to get my life back on track, but that doesn't mean I have to do it Steve's way."

Cathy got up and started back to the door. "I'll talk to him. We'll figure something out."

Mark followed her. "I think I might go and talk to Daniel."

She walked down the stairs with him, then stepped outside as he started through the garage. "Mark, are you sure you don't want to go back to home schooling with Brenda? Wouldn't it be fun to be learning with Daniel all day?"

Mark stuck his hands in his pockets and looked down at his feet. "Mom, the truth is that I'm too far behind. Daniel's way ahead of me academically, but he's way behind me in maturity."

"Why do you say that?"

"Because it's true. He was always smarter than me."

"Only because he's been home schooling all these years. You're smart too, Mark. You can catch up."

"Mom, I've been exposed to things that Daniel can't imagine. He's still just a kid, you know? But I'm not."

Cathy felt as if her heart had swollen too big for her rib cage, as the grief she'd struggled with for the past year ached inside her again. "I wish that wasn't so, Mark."

"I know you do. But it is. I've been in juvenile detention with kids who have been on drugs since they were four years old. Guys who've practically raised themselves. They've seen their dads and moms beat each other up. Most of them have been abused since they were toddlers. A lot of them are hard and they don't care about right or wrong. Some of them have killed people. You learn to tolerate different kinds of people . . . to get along with people you might have been afraid of before. It makes *you* different. And Daniel can't understand that. I mean, who could?"

She didn't want to cry in front of him. "But don't you think your experience could help Daniel? And his academics could sure help you."

"Mom, twelve-year-old Joseph is probably ahead of me academically. I never applied myself in school. I never listened. I was just a washout. I can't start it all over and do it right. I might as well just make the best of it and move on."

"Mark, you're settling. I don't like for you to settle. You have too much potential."

"Mom, I'm not settling. I'm just trying to find my place. Work with me on this, okay? Trust me."

She crossed her arms and leaned against the garage wall. "I trust you, Mark, but I don't trust your judgment, not yet. You're too young."

"Well, at some point, you're going to have to try my judgment out," Mark said. "I'll see you later."

She watched him, struggling to hold back tears, as he crossed the street to Daniel's house. Behind her, the screen door squeaked open.

Steve came out and slid his arms around her waist. "Is everything all right?"

She leaned back against him. "Yeah, I just think you might have been a little too hard on him."

He let her go and she turned around and saw the tension tightening through him. "Me, too hard? What did I do?"

"I think maybe you expect too much of him too soon. I think Annie's right. We need to cut him a little slack."

"I'm willing to cut him some slack. I just don't want him to make another mistake."

She slipped her fingers through his belt loops and drew him closer.

"Maybe we can't really keep him from doing that. I mean, as long as he doesn't go out there and ruin his life, maybe we need to let him make a little mistake or two."

"We're not talking about a little mistake or two," Steve said. "Dropping out of school could be a life-altering decision."

"Steve, a GED is not like dropping out. It's not that easy. He'll probably have to go to school and study for it. And he could still get into the community college here. Lots of colleges accept GEDs. If he does well in that, he could go on to a four-year college."

He picked up a weed eater leaned against the wall and hung it on its hook.

"I'm afraid he won't *want* to go to college. I have a bad feeling that if we let him drop out of school to get his GED, he's going to wind up getting a job and he's going to think he's making a fortune when he's only making a little above minimum wage." He set his hands on his hips. "And you know what worries me the most? I worry that he won't get a job at all, that he'll just want to hang around here all the time and do nothing."

"Well, what would be so wrong with that for a few weeks? He had a really bad year."

"But coddling him now is going to undo whatever jail did for him. I don't want to see you do that." He picked up Tracy's bike and took it to its assigned place on the other side of the garage.

"He's become a Christian, Steve. He's changed."

"But that doesn't mean he's all of a sudden going to have good judgment and wisdom coming out his ears."

She didn't know why he couldn't see things the way she did. Tears sprang to her eyes. "I know that. Don't you think I know that?"

"Well, you act like we need to do everything he wants."

She crossed her arms. "I'm just trying to show a little compassion. You remember that, don't you? Compassion?"

Her comment stung him, and she saw his face shut down. "That was low. Just because I'm the voice of reason, suddenly I'm devoid of compassion?"

"The voice of reason?" she asked. "Come on, Steve. What am I the voice of? Stupidity?"

"No. I'm just saying that you're thinking with your heart instead of your head."

"Which is exactly what *you* do when you're dealing with Tracy. It's a little different when it's *my* child involved."

Now he was insulted. "I don't do that with Tracy. I'm treating your kids exactly the way I treat mine."

She let out a sarcastic laugh. "Think again. I don't see that."

His face twisted with indignation. "What have I done? Give me an example."

"She threw a napkin and hit me in the face, and you didn't even bat an eye. If one of my kids had done that and hit you, you'd have been all over them."

He shook his head with disgust. "She was just playing. Give me a break, Cathy. What do you want me to do? Beat her?"

"I'm just saying that it's a double standard. You want to think that you're treating the kids the same, but you're not."

"Besides, Tracy wouldn't have done that if your kids hadn't started it. And while we're on the subject, it does concern me that she's picking up some of your kids' behavior. It's hard to punish her when she's seen your kids do so many of the same things."

"Oh, brother." She turned away. "This conversation isn't really going anywhere. I can see it going downhill from here."

He kicked a skateboard out of his way. "Not one of our better moments."

Cathy tried to keep her voice steady. "Maybe we'd better just cool down and talk later."

"Good idea."

Steve stormed into the house and slammed the door behind him. He headed for the bedroom.

"You do that again, I'm taking the door off the hinges!" Cathy yelled.

When he didn't respond, she burst through the screen door again and slammed it harder than he had.

But it didn't help her anger or her sense of injustice. And she wasn't sure if anything would.

CHAPTER *Eight*

Sylvia waited until nine o'clock to make sure that Harry was home from the clinic. León, Nicaragua, was on the same time zone as Breezewood, so she knew that he would be waiting for her call. He usually worked very late, treating all the poverty-stricken people who came to him for help. By now, he was probably unwinding, eating his dinner and reading his Bible, basking in the quiet. He also probably worried about her.

She dialed the number, listened for the ring, then heard Harry's voice. "Hello?"

"Hi, honey. How was your day?"

"Blessed," he said, as he always did. "Any better and I'd have to be twins. So tell me about your doctor's appointment. How did it go?"

"It was fine." She had practiced this phone call, and kept her voice level, just as she'd rehearsed. "Everyone at the hospital said to tell you hello."

Harry wasn't easily distracted. "What did he find, Sylvia?"

She drew in a deep breath. "Well, he found that I'm anemic. Said that was the reason for the fatigue."

"Anemia?" She could tell he wasn't satisfied with that. "I could have found that myself."

"Yeah, if you had a lab. And technicians to work in it."

"So that's all it was, huh?" He still didn't sound convinced.

Sylvia thought of saying yes, that was all it was, and switching the conversation from her defective body to the children she missed so much. But he had a right to know. "Harry, there was one other thing."

He got quiet, and she knew he braced himself. She wasn't sure if he needed to or not.

"When he was examining me, he found a lump in my breast."

Silence hung on the other end of the line. Sylvia hurried to fill it in. "He sent me for a mammogram. Jim Montgomery was the radiologist. He sends his regards. Says he's really missed you over at the golf course. His daughter's getting married next month."

Harry clearly wasn't interested in Jim's daughter's nuptials. "Sylvia, what did he say?"

"He showed me the lump, upper outer quadrant on the left breast."

"And?"

"And . . . I'm going for a biopsy tomorrow. No big deal. It's probably nothing."

Silence hovered over the line. "Honey, it's going to be all right. God's in control."

He cleared his throat. "I need to come home. I want to be there."

"That's ridiculous. Honey, I'll have the results in a day or two. It's probably nothing."

"Sylvia, I don't think I have to remind you that your mother died of breast cancer. You're at high risk. I should have seen it coming. I should have made you get mammograms while we were here. You could have gone to Managua to get one. It was important, but I just let it go."

"Harry, you are not responsible for my body. I'm a grown woman. I should have known to get mammograms, but we've been busy. The Lord understands that. I think I would know if my body was betraying me that way. I'd have some sense of it, you know? Some premonition or intuition that things weren't right."

"Sylvia, you know better than that. It's not like your body sends warning messages to your brain. Not in every case, at least. Not this way."

"I just don't think it's anything to worry about."

Harry's voice quivered slightly. "I would still like to be there. I could catch a plane tomorrow morning."

"Harry, I won't let you do that. I want you to stay right there and go on with your work, and in a few days I'll be there to join you."

Silence again. "You're not going to keep anything from me, are you? If I think that for a minute, I'll be on the phone calling every doctor who has anything to do with this."

Sylvia sighed. "You're going to do that anyway, Harry. You know that."

When he didn't deny that, she laughed softly. "I have a positive attitude, honey. Just like you've always told your patients to have. I'm not going to let this get me down. There's no reason for it. When we get the results, we'll find out it was no big deal. I don't intend to waste my time worrying. I'm having too much fun being back."

"I want to pray for you, Sylvia. Right now, before another minute passes."

"Okay, Harry."

She heard the silent prelude to the prayer, as Harry prepared his heart for speaking to the Lord. He always prayed the way the Israelites entered the tabernacle. He stopped at the bronze altar to deal with his sins, then washed in the cleansing water of the brass laver, then slowly approached the Holy Place . . .

"Lord, you know what's going on with my beloved bride ..."

Sylvia swallowed the tears in her throat, glad he couldn't see her. She listened as her husband lifted her up to God's throne, laying her on the mercy seat.

When he said amen, she could hardly speak. With great effort, she forced her good-bye to sound upbeat and normal.

But when she got off the phone, she sat there a moment, staring down at it, wondering what would happen if indeed this lump in her breast proved to be malignant, as Jim suggested it could be. Would she be able to have quick surgery to remove it, then return to her work in León? Or would their ministry have to be shut down altogether? She couldn't fathom the idea that God might want them to come back home, not after it took so much for her to leave in the first place. Not after she'd given her life so totally to the work God had given her.

As she got ready for bed, she walked through her house, thankful that they hadn't sold it in all the months that they'd tried. It was a comfort to be here, back on Cedar Circle, surrounded by people who loved her. Cathy had called after their prayer meeting tonight and insisted on driving Sylvia for her biopsy. What a worrier. Yet she was glad for the offer. It would make things easier.

No, she wouldn't worry, she told herself as she climbed into bed. She was too tired to worry. She could do that tomorrow.

Exhausted, she fell off to sleep, but she dreamed of doctor's offices and hospital gowns ...

At two A.M., she woke up and stared at the night. The clock ticked out its passing seconds, its red numbers glowing. She turned it around so she couldn't see.

Her mind wandered to the immediate future. Would she have to have surgery? She had planned on visiting her daughter and holding that grandbaby one more time before returning to Nicaragua. Would she have that chance now? She mentally tallied the commitments on her calendar. She had planned to meet with the realtor, to talk about lowering the price on the house, in hopes of making it sell. She wanted to be back in León by August fifteenth, when they planned the big work day to renovate the church that had been damaged in the hurricane. Until now, they hadn't had the supplies to do it, but recent donations had made it all possible. She'd planned to take some of the older children from the orphanage and let them help paint. They were all looking forward to it.

Maybe if she did have to have surgery, she could fly back to León for the work day, then come back and have the surgery done afterward.

But would it be wise to wait? If she did have cancer, was it growing with every passing moment? Should she get it ripped out of her before it spread?

She lay her hand on the offending breast, mashed it, and tried to feel the lump. Had her breast betrayed her? Was it her enemy now? Would she have to have it removed to keep it from killing her?

What would that kind of surgery mean? Pain ... difficulty lifting her arm ... emotional upheaval ... frustration at having to find a prosthesis to wear over a healing wound, so she wouldn't be lopsided and call attention to herself ... self-pity and anxiety about her husband's disappointment that one of his favorite parts of her body would be gone? And if the truth were known, it was probably one of *her* favorite parts, too.

Or would that be the least of it? Surgery on other organs? Chemotherapy?

Would the surgery be the beginning of her death, or the start of her cure? Would she go downhill from here, through a form of hell, before she came out on the other side?

She thought of getting up, turning on the light, and beginning her day, just to banish these thoughts from her mind. But she wanted ... needed ... to sleep, so that she could cope with the day ahead of her. She didn't want to be tired and emotional and fall apart when the doctor told her the results.

It looks like it's malignant.

She turned to her side, fluffed her pillow, and pulled the covers up to her chin. Would she handle his answer with dignity and faith, or would she fall apart and feel sorry for herself and whine to everyone who would listen? She'd always been fairly healthy. How would she behave as a sick person? Would she get angry and bitter, or would she accept this as one more of the human trials God warned us of, another offshoot of the Fall? Would the Lord allow her to get well so that she could continue to bear fruit, or did he intend to bear fruit through her death?

Finally, she did get up and went into the kitchen, flicking on lights as she went. She poured herself a glass of cold water, then sat at the kitchen table, staring down at it.

She recalled the Scripture about having not because you ask not, and asking with wrong motives. Did she have wrong motives? Would those hinder her prayers?

She started to examine them, desperate to find any unrighteous reason for her prayers not to be heard. Why did she ask God to take this from her? Was it because of the inconvenience and pain and illness it would bring to her life? Was it because she loved this world more than him? Was it because she tried to hold herself out of God's reach, refusing to trust him with her life, whatever happened?

Was it because she wanted to see her children grow into mature adults? Wanted to attend her grandchildren's school plays? Was it because she didn't want her children to suffer?

Or was it because of the children at the orphanage, who had so few people in the world who loved them? Was that a selfish motive?

Or was it because of Harry? Didn't she trust God with her children, her husband, her life?

She examined those motives, wearily trying to find some fault within them. They were human, normal motives, borne of uncertainty. Didn't God understand?

She asked the Lord to show her what lay in her heart. She asked him to forgive her for the selfish motives, the ones that were more for her than for God's kingdom and his plan. Then she asked him to let the tests come out negative for cancer.

"Let it be a wake-up call," she whispered. "I'll get my annual mammograms from now on, and exercise and eat better and give up Nutrasweet and sugar and flour and whatever else I have to."

But she still prayed without confidence, because she understood God's sovereignty, that his ways were not her ways.

"Not my will, but thine be done," she made herself say. Then she added quickly, "But please don't have it in your will to do this to me."

She went back to bed, curled up under the covers that gave her some comfort, and tried to put these things from her mind.

Be anxious for nothing . . . She knew better than to let herself wake up worrying in the wee hours of morning. But knowing better didn't always make it so. Sometimes fear came in before the morning. It was fear of the unknown, mostly. Fear of what lay beyond the certainty.

Finally, as daylight seeped in through the window blinds, she checked her alarm. One hour before it would go off. Slowly, she drifted back into sleep, before she had to get up and face what the day held.

CHAPTER *Nine*

I don't need the hand-holding, but I appreciate the company." Sylvia smiled at Cathy as she drove. "We can have lunch afterward."

"Sounds good to me. And I'm not coming to hold your hand. I want you to hold mine."

Sylvia laughed. "You're not worried about this, are you?"

Cathy shrugged. "A little. What did Harry say?"

"Oh, he wanted to drop everything and fly home. I told him not to, that there's no reason to panic until we get the results of the biopsy. Then I'll be flying to him."

Her bravado seemed to lighten Cathy's spirits, but when they reached the doctor's office, Sylvia's own spirits began to flag. She looked around at the others in the waiting room, wondering who there might have a tumor, who was having a biopsy, who had already gotten the results, whose life would be forever changed. Her hands felt ice cold again, so she slipped them under her thighs.

Cathy seemed to have thoughts of her own swirling through her mind, for she didn't bother to pick up a magazine or strike up a conversation.

This was craziness, her pretending not to worry, when she wasn't fooling anyone. She needed to come clean, she thought, and be honest with Cathy. "Have I ever told you that my mother died of breast cancer when she was about my age?" she said in a low voice.

The alarm in Cathy's eyes was unmistakable. "No, Sylvia, you've never told me that."

"She did. I don't bring that up because I think that it means I have it. I feel sure that my body would have told me if I had something terrible like that, but it does seem relevant, doesn't it?"

"You've told the doctor, haven't you?"

"Yes." She breathed in a deep breath, let it out hard. "The thing is, I've known I was at high risk for getting it myself. I don't know why I let it go for the past couple of years."

Cathy took her hand. "You're cold."

"Freezing."

"It's nerves, you know. You're not as tough as you act."

Sylvia started to laugh, and Cathy joined her.

Sylvia closed her other hand over Cathy's. "Let's talk about lunch. Something beyond this biopsy."

"Okay. Where do you want to go?"

Sylvia thought for a moment, trying to picture herself and Cathy relaxing over a chef salad. "Alexander's. I've been wanting to go there."

"Alexander's it is. And you'll have to have steak, you know."

"Why is that?"

"Well, we need to build your blood back up, get some iron pumping through your veins."

Sylvia nodded.

A nurse came to the door and Sylvia looked up. "Sylvia Bryan," the woman called. Sylvia didn't move. She looked at Cathy, and Cathy gave her a reassuring look and patted her knee. Finally, she leaned over and grabbed her purse.

"Guess I'll see you in a little bit."

"I'll be praying."

A little while later, Sylvia returned to the waiting room. "That was easy," she said.

Cathy looked up at her. "Any results?"

"No. They said tomorrow."

Cathy grabbed her purse. "Okay. How do you feel?"

"Fine right now. The local anesthetic hasn't worn off yet."

"And emotionally?"

Sylvia examined her own heart. "Well, I can't say I won't think about it again until the results come . . . but let's just have lunch and not talk about it."

"Okay," Cathy said. "Whatever you say."

At the restaurant, Cathy accommodated Sylvia's wish to avoid the subject of cancer, and told her instead of the fight she and Steve had had last night. "It's not like the marriage is going badly." She stirred more butter into her potato. "I'm really happy with Steve. I love him and I love Tracy, and I think things are going well . . . basically . . . but I can't help wishing that he'd go easier on Mark. He's trying to be Mark's father, but Mark doesn't appreciate it much. He's having trouble adjusting to coming home to a different family, and all of a sudden having to do what Steve says. I'm in the middle, you know, like I'm being torn in two."

"Nobody said it was going to be easy." Sylvia set her fork down. "Marriage never is. And a blended family is a lot harder than a normal marriage."

"Tell me about it." Cathy took a bite, shaking her head. "The thing is, Steve expects me to make my kids act just the way he wants them to, but then he overlooks the things that Tracy does. Don't get me wrong, she's not bad. But occasionally he needs to call her down, or punish her even. But he doesn't even notice it. It goes right past him. Yet he notices *everything* my kids do. He knows how Mark has changed and he knows what a struggle he's going through since he got out of jail. He knows that Mark is trying to decide exactly where he fits back into this world. It's not easy for him. But he just doesn't seem to understand that I need to give Mark a little more time. And he got his feelings hurt last night when I asked him to go a little easier. I don't know why it has to be so hard. Why can't we just love each other's kids the same?"

"Because you're not really Tracy's mother and he's not really your kids' father."

Cathy studied her potato. "I wish there was some magic key to having a happy second marriage, but if there is, I don't know what it is."

"Oh, there is one." Sylvia dug into her salad. "It's the same key to having a successful *first* marriage."

Cathy set her fork down and leaned back. "Okay, hit me with it."

Sylvia smiled. "It's easy. Die to yourself."

Cathy's eyes narrowed. "Die to myself?"

"That's right. Die to yourself. As soon as you and Steve each figure that out, your marriage will be a success."

"Well, what does that mean?" Cathy asked. "How do you die to yourself?"

"You decide that the other person's needs are more important than your own. If there's ever a question between your doing what you want and your doing what *he* wants, you do what *he* wants."

"Wait a minute. That doesn't sound like happiness. It just sounds like a lot of sacrifice."

"Well, sure, it's sacrifice. That's what marriage is about."

Cathy opened a pack of butter and dropped the square onto her plate.

"All right, sacrifice, maybe. But it's not supposed to be martyrdom. I mean, how far do you go in fulfilling his needs? Do you not eat or sleep or buy anything for yourself?"

Sylvia dabbed at her mouth with her napkin. "Cathy, you know better than that. I'm not talking about lying down like a doormat and inviting him to walk all over you. The fact is, you married a man who is not going to do that anyway. But he is the head of your household, biblically speaking, and when there's a question of your will against his will, you need to let him win."

"What if he's wrong?"

"Well, you pray for him every day," Sylvia said. "You pray that God will guide him, that he'll have a heart that's fertile and teachable, and that he'll listen to God's prompting."

Cathy crossed her arms and tipped her head. "That didn't answer my question. I asked you what if he's wrong? How do I submit to him . . ." Her voice was rising, and she looked around, wondering if anyone had heard. Quickly, she lowered it. "How do I submit to him if he's flat wrong?"

"Easy." Sylvia took a drink of her iced tea and brought her eyes back to Cathy. "Watch Brenda. She's been submitting to David for years, and he's often wrong. Most of the time she lets him lead. But when it comes down to doing his will or God's will, she goes with God. It's really simple."

"But I can't say that Steve's going against God. He's just mistaken. Misguided. *Wrong*." She took a few more bites, as she thought through what Sylvia was telling her. "That dying to yourself stuff is hard, Sylvia. Who wants to die?"

"No one does," Sylvia said, "but I'm telling you, that's the key. You have to die to yourself if you want to be happy in a marriage. Period."

The advice only frustrated Cathy more. She tried to visualize what the advice meant, but it evaded her. She told herself it didn't matter.

The important thing was that she had gotten Sylvia's mind off of her biopsy, at least for a little while.

CHAPTER *Ten*

The night of the church program came with a flurry of activity at the Dodd house. Brenda lined Joseph, Leah, and Rachel up in her bathroom, and applied the heavy makeup that would make their fair skin look less pale under the harsh lights.

Joseph had a strange look on his face. "I'm nervous. I might throw up."

"You're not going to throw up." Brenda wiped her makeup sponge under his eyes. "You're going to do it just like you've done at rehearsal, and you'll be wonderful."

Leah stood in front of the mirror, spraying her spiked hair. "This is so embarrassing," she said.

David stood, grinning, in the doorway. "What is?"

"That Rachel and I have to be Spencer's entourage. Like we'd really follow around some eight-year-old kid like we were in love with him."

"He's dressing like Elvis," Brenda told David. "He's so cute. And Leah and Rachel have to follow him around like groupies."

"Okay, you've got to videotape this for me," David said.

Brenda shook her head and went for the blush. "David, I can't. I'm helping backstage."

"Then let Daniel do it."

"He's working the lights. I'm sorry, honey, but if you want to see it, you'll have to come." She brought the blush brush to Joseph's cheeks, but he jerked away.

"Huh-uh, Mama! You can't put that on me!"

"Why not? I'm just trying to give you a little color."

"I'll look like a girl!"

"Joseph, all actors wear makeup."

"Not me," he said. "This mud all over my face is bad enough, but I do not want all that pink stuff on my cheeks."

Rachel gave Joseph an assessing look. "Mama's right. You need contour, Joseph. Here, let me do it."

Joseph grabbed the brush out of his mother's hand so Rachel couldn't get it. "I'm finished, Mama. I have all the makeup I need. Please don't let her touch me."

Brenda laughed and took the brush back. "All right, Joseph. Go put on your suit, and be careful not to get the makeup on your white shirt."

She left the girls primping in the bathroom and grinned up at David. "This is going to be some kind of night."

"I can't believe there's no one who can tape this. What about Tory and Barry? If Spencer and Brittany are in it, surely they'll be videotaping."

"They might. But Tory's helping backstage, too. And I think Barry is helping with the props."

She stuck her head in Joseph's room and saw him carefully unbuttoning the white shirt on its hanger. He already had his pants and shoes on, and she saw the thick scars from his heart transplant on his chest. Stepping into the room, she helped him get the shirt on without getting makeup on his collar.

"I can't wait to get this stuff off my face."

"You can go right from your curtain call to the sink," Brenda said.

David grew quiet as the activity grew more frenzied, and by the time she had loaded everyone into the van, she could see the dejection creeping over him.

He'd made his choice not to come, she thought, and as she backed out of the driveway and left him standing alone on the porch, she tried to silence the yearning in her heart. He was missing some of the major moments in his children's lives. Their baptisms, their choir solos, their testimonies, their Bible drills, their plays . . . All because they happened within the walls of a church. In the interest of upholding his principle not to participate in church events at all, he had violated his principle to support his children in the most meaningful events of their lives.

But he didn't see it that way.

As she drove the chattering children to church, she prayed that the Lord would work in David's heart tonight, and help him to realize what he was missing.

David made himself a sandwich and tried to watch a ball game, but his mind kept drifting to his children.

The blueprint of the limousine lay on the coffee table, and he picked it up and wondered how it would work. Would it roll the way it was supposed to? Would it hold together? Would it add to the program, or detract from it?

He set the picture down and thought how excited the kids would be when they came home tonight. Daniel's pride at a job well done, Leah and Rachel's giggles at the way the congregation would probably respond to Spencer's Elvis impersonation, Joseph's funny stories about everything that went wrong on stage. They would remember this night for decades. When they came home years from now, with their spouses and children, they would sit around the table talking about tonight's event with fond memories.

One of those memories would be that their father hadn't been there.

He hated being a disappointment to them, and he hated even worse disappointing his wife. But he was an honest man, and he didn't believe in pretending to be something he was not. For him to walk through the doors of a church, when he'd vowed years ago never to do it again, would be like betraying himself.

He thought of how cruelly his own church had treated his mother and him, when his father, the pastor, had run off with the organist. Instead of loving them through it, helping them, and praying for them in their grief, the church had treated his mother like she had somehow caused her husband's infidelity. They had asked them to leave the parsonage to make room for a new pastor.

He and his mother had taken a garage apartment, and his mother had gone back to work. He'd spent many long, angry hours alone in a stuffy apartment, praying for his father to come back. But those prayers had never been answered.

When his mourning played out in anger and childish rage, the church had proclaimed him "possessed." They'd insisted on casting the demons out of him. That, too, had failed according to them.

He remembered those tragic, mixed feelings of fear that they were right, that hateful demons occupied his mind and heart, that God had turned away from him for some unknown reason, just as his father had abandoned him.

Those feelings fed him for the next couple of years, until he finally reached the point of not believing anymore. The God of his father, his mother, and his church did not exist, he had decided. And if he didn't believe in God, then he didn't have to believe in the demons, either. In some ways his atheism had set him free from the burden the church had placed upon him. But he'd never been able to fill the void left in his soul.

He'd vowed never to return to church—any church—and when Brenda became a Christian, he held to his vow. When she'd convinced him to let her raise their children in the church, he'd remained faithful to that vow.

Now he wondered if keeping that promise was such a noble thing after all.

He hated being left out. He wanted to see his son star as the Good Samaritan. He wanted to see Leah and Rachel following Elvis across the stage. He wanted to see Daniel doing magic with the lights.

He wanted to be a part of this memory.

He took his plate to the sink, set it down, then headed back to the bedroom. Quickly, he changed his clothes, then got his keys.

His hands trembled as he drove to the church. The parking lot was full, so he parked on a side street. The small sanctuary would be packed, he thought. Parents and grandparents had probably come to laugh and applaud at their own children's roles.

He hurried to the front door, hoping he hadn't missed too much. He opened the door, and heard the opening song that Joseph, Rachel, and Leah had sung for weeks around the house.

He stepped in and saw the colorful set and all the children in their various costumes. Leah and Rachel stood behind Spencer, who was hamming it up in a white sparkly Elvis jumpsuit, while Joseph stood on the other side of the stage, dressed like a businessman. He glanced up at the landing at the back of the room, where Daniel sat, flicking switches and moving spotlights.

He slipped into the back pew and grinned as the play began with a boy on a skateboard, gliding across the stage, and gangsters coming along to beat him up and leave him for dead. The story of the Good Samaritan began.

David was glad he had come.

Brenda watched the show from behind the curtains on the side of the makeshift stage. The children were in top form. The butterflies in Joseph's stomach seemed to have settled, and he was hamming it up.

When the opening scene ended, Joseph rushed toward her. "Mama! Dad's here. He really came!"

Brenda was sure Joseph was mistaken. The lights made it difficult to see the audience clearly. "Are you sure, honey?"

"Yes! He's sitting at the back."

Brenda peeked around the curtain, but the church was too dark.

The audience laughed raucously as Spencer strutted across the stage, Leah and Rachel prancing behind him, at least two heads taller than the small Elvis.

When Leah and Rachel's scene ended and they came behind the curtain, they both began to jump up and down. "Mama! Dad's here."

It must be true, Brenda thought. *Please let it be true!*

Tory scurried backstage to congratulate her son. He high-fived her, then accepted her fussy hug.

"Don't mess me up, Mommy. I have to go out for the end."

Tory laughed and let her son go. "Brenda, you didn't tell me David was coming."

Brenda swallowed the emotion in her throat. "He didn't tell *me.*"

"Well, he's out there laughing his head off."

As Tory hurried back to her seat, Brenda touched her chest and whispered a heartfelt prayer of thanks. God had managed to get David through that door.

Maybe it was just the beginning.

CHAPTER Eleven

Sylvia was up before dawn, three hours before the doctor's office would open. Even after that, it could be hours before they called.

She made her coffee and took it outside.

Sitting on her back porch, she watched as the sun came up over the mountains, first in a gray light that slowly gave way to a pale blue, then to a bright blue, then to a burst of orange as day exploded. A cool breeze blew through her brown hair. She had let it grow too long in León, and the frosted color she had left with had slowly evolved into the brown she'd had growing up. It was easier to color over her gray with a solid color than to highlight it every few weeks. Sarah, her daughter, had sent her the L'Oreal products from the States every month or so. Getting her hair cut was one of the items on her agenda before she went back.

She swept it behind her ear and pulled her thoughts back to God's art. Whatever man tried to do was a poor imitation.

Everyone needed to see at least one Smoky Mountain daybreak to appreciate true art.

She went back in and refilled her coffee, checked the time. Only seven o'clock. She had to stop this. She couldn't sit here and wait . . .

She went to the front window and looked out on the driveway. That phantom paperboy who only communicated through an envelope in the Sunday edition had already left today's paper. Though their subscription had been canceled long ago, he'd left her one since she'd been home, no doubt hoping she'd resubscribe.

She went outside, up the lonely driveway, and retrieved it. She heard a door close and looked around, waiting to see who might be coming out.

Annie strode out of her house in a baggy shirt and a pair of shorts. Barefoot, she headed up her own driveway and grabbed the paper.

"Up early, Annie?" Sylvia called across the yard.

Annie started. "You scared me. I didn't expect anybody to be out here."

Sylvia crossed the grass. Annie's long brown hair looked as if she'd just gotten out of bed, and her eyes were sleepy and unadorned. She had seen Annie that way every morning for the year they'd been together in León. Her heart burst with love for the girl.

"I've missed you." She reached out and hugged her.

"Me too," Annie said. "I got so used to getting up early down there that I can't sleep late to save my life. It's just not right, you know? People my age are supposed to sleep till noon."

Sylvia laughed. "Well, since you're up, you want to go for a walk with me? Or did you have your heart set on reading that paper?"

Annie glanced down at the paper and raked her hand through her tangled hair. "No, I can read it later. Just let me go get my shoes on."

"I'll be on my back porch."

Sylvia watched as the girl ran back into the house.

"Thank you, Lord," she whispered. Annie was just what she needed today.

Annie bounced around the house a few minutes later, her hair brushed back into a ponytail and her tennis shoes on.

Her face was brighter than it had been moments before. "I'm ready. Where do you want to go?"

"I thought we'd walk out to the barn. I haven't been back there since we sold the horses. Then we can walk through the woods, unless it starts getting too hot."

"Hot?" Annie laughed as Sylvia came down from the porch. "This is nothing compared to where we've been. I can't wait for winter. I missed snow. Imagine if we could gather up all our kids from León and bring them here for the winter. Wouldn't they get a kick out of the snow?"

"Oh, that would be so much fun. I'd love to watch little Juan build a snowman. I read him *Frosty the Snowman* once. He was captivated."

Annie reached the barn before Sylvia and opened the door. "I wonder what they're doing today. It's Thursday, so they have art."

"Yeah, and music. They're working on their program. It's just a few days away."

Annie shook her head. "Man, I hate missing that."

Sylvia stepped into the barn and looked around at the empty stalls. It still smelled of horses and hay, even though the place hadn't been occupied for almost four years.

She went to the stall where Sunshine, her favorite horse, used to be.

"Do you miss the horses?"

"Sometimes." She rested her arms on the stall door. "But we sold them for a good cause."

"For Joseph's transplant." Annie's voice was soft, nostalgic.

"We would have had to sell them eventually, anyway, when we left the country."

Annie got quiet, and Sylvia realized that melancholy was setting in again. "Let's go walk and see what's in bloom."

They followed the old path where Sylvia used to ride her horse. The sun had grown bright, and dusty rays cut through the tree branches and cast a golden light on the path ahead of them.

"Look at that," Sylvia said. "'A light unto my path . . .'"

"'A lamp unto my feet,'" Annie finished. "Maybe it's a sign."

Sylvia glanced over at her. "A sign?"

"Yeah." Annie broke off a branch and began peeling off its leaves. "For today. You know. The phone call you're waiting for."

Sylvia stopped and faced the girl. "How did you know I'm waiting for a call?"

"Well, I knew you were getting the results today. *I'd* be waiting." She dropped the stick and dusted her hands on her shorts. "I just meant that maybe God lit up our path like that to tell you something."

Sylvia smiled. "What, Annie? What is he telling me?"

"That whatever happens, you won't go into it alone. You won't be groping through the darkness. He'll light your way."

Sylvia looked at the path again. "Thanks, Annie. I think that's just what he's saying."

"I mean, I'm not expecting the news to be bad or anything," Annie said. "Not at all. It's probably going to be good news. I've just been a little nervous because you've been feeling so bad lately . . . Bad enough to come home."

"It's anemia, Annie. That's probably all."

"Yeah, I know." But Sylvia knew she didn't believe that for a moment. Annie turned away, scanning the trees. She knew the girl was hiding tears, and for the first time she wondered if her worry for Sylvia was what had gotten her up so early today.

"Whatever the news is, I'll be okay," Sylvia said. "You know that, don't you?"

Annie still didn't look at her. "I know." She wiped her eyes, then quickly looked back toward the house. "Shouldn't we go back? It's probably almost eight by now. They could call."

Sylvia looked at her watch. Annie was right. "I guess so. The sooner I get that call, the sooner we can all breathe a sigh of relief and I can get back to León."

Annie's smile was strained. "Wish I could go."

They started walking back, slower than they'd come. "Are you excited about school, Annie?"

"A little. I'm looking forward to it, but I feel like I've left so much undone back in León."

"I know the feeling."

"I want to go back again," Annie said. "I'm going to start saving now."

"We'd love for you to come back."

"I would have just stayed, you know, but I missed my family and my friends. And I figured I'd never meet a guy if I stayed there. I really want to marry an American, and I wasn't likely to meet one there, unless I happened on a tourist."

"No, Annie, you did the right thing. You have plenty of time for the mission field if the Lord calls you to it."

Annie's grin was back as they emerged out of the woods. "Since I've been back, though, I've realized that I don't really like any of the guys I used to date. They're not right for me. I wonder what I ever saw in them."

Annie was growing up, Sylvia thought. She had learned to see her life through more mature eyes.

"I want a godly man, like Dr. Harry," she said. "Like Steve. A man who answers to God. That way I'll know he'll never cheat on me."

Sylvia knew Annie had a hard time trusting men because of her father's infidelity. Her family had been torn apart because of that.

But Annie would be okay. She was too precious to fall through the cracks, and Sylvia would never stop praying for her.

They got back to Sylvia's porch, and Annie hung back. "Well, I'd better get home before my mother starts wondering where I am. If she notices I'm not there, she'll think I was abducted by aliens or something."

Sylvia smiled. "I enjoyed our walk. Thanks for coming with me."

"Anytime." Annie gave her a hug. "I'll be praying for you today."

"Thank you."

Sylvia watched as the girl tromped across the yard and headed home.

Somehow, she didn't feel the heaviness she had felt earlier that morning. She felt equipped now for the wait that lay before her, because she knew that one of God's favorite children was praying.

It was after lunch before the phone finally rang. Sylvia snatched it up. Her hand trembled as she tried to punch the "on" button. "Hello?"

"Mrs. Bryan, this is Dr. Phillips' office." The woman spoke in a flat monotone. "Dr. Phillips would like to speak to you. Could you hold a moment, please?"

"Of course." She held her breath as her doctor came to the phone.

"Sylvia, hi." His voice was low, serious.

She swallowed. "Hi, Al. Any news?"

He sighed. "I'm afraid the mass in your breast is malignant."

It was as if she sat in an echo chamber, and that word reverberated around her. *Malignant. Malignant. Malignant.*

She tried to center her thoughts back on his words. Something about getting her an appointment with the surgeon, about possible mastectomy, about radiation and chemotherapy, but none of it registered. The word still rolled around in her head trying to plant itself. *Malignant. Malignant. Malignant.*

"Sylvia, are you listening?"

She cleared her throat. "Yes. What's my next step?"

He seemed to understand that she hadn't heard a word he'd said. "I'm making you an appointment with Dr. Jefferson. You remember Sam, don't you?"

"Yes, I remember him."

"He specializes in breast cancer surgery, Sylvia. He's the best in town. I'm going to try to get you in for tomorrow. As soon as I tell them who you are, that you're Harry Bryan's wife, I'm sure they'll get you right in."

"Yes. Thank you."

"Sylvia, I recommend that you go to the bookstore and get some books on this, try to understand what your different options might be so that when Sam recommends them you'll understand. And remember that breast cancer is usually pretty slow-growing, so you have time. You don't have to make a decision in the next few hours. You have time to get Harry home and to talk things over with him and get some second and third opinions."

The thought of telling Harry snagged her mind. He would have questions. He'd want details. What would he want to know? "Al, can you tell how bad it is?"

"I can tell you that the tumor looks to be about three centimeters. That's larger than I would have liked. It has poorly defined margins, which is also not a very good sign. I'll know a lot more when we get a pathology report on the tumor itself after it's removed, and Sam will probably want to take some lymph nodes." He paused. "Sylvia, are you all right?"

She ran her fingers through her hair, trying again to focus. "Yes," she said, "I'm fine. Thank you for calling, Al."

"No problem. Sylvia, I'll call Harry if you want me to. I can explain things to him."

"No, that's all right. I'll do it. I just don't want him to rush home. His work there is so important."

"Sylvia, he needs to come home. How much surgery you have is up to you and the doctor, but I wouldn't go through this alone. Harry wouldn't want you to. Tell him everything, Sylvia. Don't hold it back."

Her eyes stung with tears by the time she got off the phone, and she sat there staring into the air. Moments ticked by, and she didn't move.

The phone rang again, startling her.

"Hello?" It didn't even sound like her voice.

"Sylvia, it's Al again. I just wanted to let you know that Dr. Jefferson's office had a cancellation this afternoon. You can go at three o'clock if you'd like."

She nodded, as though he could see. "Yes, I might as well get this over with."

"I'm sure you'll have a lot of questions," he said. "I'd recommend that you take a tape recorder with you so you can remember everything later. You might take a friend, too, just to be there with you."

Her hand trembled as she brought it to her forehead. "I'm not ready to tell anybody yet. I'm going alone."

"Whatever you think is best. And, Sylvia, call me if you have any questions. Harry, too."

"I will."

She hung up the phone and decided that she didn't have time to stare into space. Her problem was in her breast, not her brain. She had a tumor, and it could be removed. She might not even need a mastectomy. Lumpectomies were just as successful these days. Maybe they could quickly pull it out on an outpatient basis, and she wouldn't have to have radiation or chemo or anything. The sooner she took care of it, the sooner she could return to Nicaragua and pick up with her work as if nothing had ever happened.

But as she prepared for her appointment she realized that that probably wasn't the case. *Poorly defined margins.* She knew what that meant from dealing with her mother's cancer. It meant that the cancer wasn't contained in a bubblelike wall. It had seeped out, into the tissue. It wouldn't be as easy to remove as it would if the margins were well-defined.

The phone sat on the desk before her, like a live being challenging her. She needed to pick it up and call Harry, but she knew he would panic and drop everything to come home. No, she needed more information before she called him. She would wait until after the appointment with Sam Jefferson. She looked in the mirror, struggling with the surprising anger that her body had betrayed her in such a way. Her intuition had failed her.

Pulling herself together, she drove her rental car to Radio Shack and bought a little handheld recorder to take with her.

The doctor's office felt like Montreal in January. Though it was August, and the thermometer outside read eighty-five degrees, Sylvia wished she'd worn her coat.

Sam Jefferson seemed pleased to see her. "How have you and Harry been?" he asked as he ushered her into his office.

"We've been fine." She took a chair while he settled behind his desk. She tried to keep her voice level, polite. "Working hard, though."

"Yeah? Harry practicing cardiology down there, or has he branched out?"

"He's more of a general practitioner now. He has a medical clinic that takes care of everything from sore throats to gangrene. He puts in about twelve hours a day. We've really come to love the people."

The doctor smiled and looked down at her chart. "Well, you guys really have guts doing what you're doing. I've thought of doing a medical mission trip. It sounds really rewarding."

"I'm sure Harry would love to have you come to León for a couple of weeks if you ever want to."

She was stalling. She knew that, but she wasn't sure she was ready to jump into this discussion. What if she couldn't handle the truth?

But they couldn't go on making small talk forever.

Finally he got around to the subject at hand. "Sylvia, I've looked over your X rays and your biopsy report, and as I see it, we have several options."

She got out her recorder, switched it on, and set it on the chair next to her.

"With many of my patients I offer the option of a lumpectomy or a partial mastectomy to preserve as much as we can of the breast. That's certainly an option for you, but because of the irregularity of your tumor's margins and the type of cancer cell it is, I can't recommend that. I would recommend a mastectomy."

Her stomach sank like lead. "My mother had a mastectomy over thirty years ago," she said.

"Well, the good news is that it doesn't have to be as bad as hers was. Back then, we did radical mastectomies, where we took the breast, lymph nodes from the armpit, and the muscles in the chest. Today we can do a modified radical mastectomy, where we leave the muscles alone. That makes the surgery less disfiguring and easier to recover from." He handed her a couple of books and pamphlets about mastectomy surgery. "These will explain the procedure in more detail and answer your questions."

"If I have a mastectomy, will that take care of all of it, or will I have to have chemo?"

"I'd recommend that you follow up with chemotherapy, especially if it's spread to your lymph nodes."

She thought of her mother with her bald head and paper-thin skin, suffering through intense nausea and weakness.

"You said options. What are the others?"

"Another option I'd recommend you consider is a bilateral mastectomy."

"Both breasts?" Her ribs seemed too small for her lungs, and she tried to catch her breath. "Why?"

"The fact that your mother died of breast cancer causes me some worry," he said. "A bilateral mastectomy would virtually ensure that you don't get future tumors in the contralateral breast."

Tears sprang to her eyes, but she fought them back.

"It's not absolutely necessary," he said. "As I said, it's just an option. Some women choose to do that to be safe, to prevent recurrence, or to prevent a new cancer from growing. But it's your call."

"Do you think the cancer has spread?"

"The undefined margins mean that it's spread into the tissue around it, but it could be confined only to the breast. The lymph nodes will tell us a lot."

Sylvia cleared her throat. "If I have a lumpectomy, it might get it all. Right?"

"Possibly. But you're not a good candidate for that, Sylvia. You'd be taking a chance."

"But if we found out it didn't get it all, we could always go back and do a mastectomy, couldn't we?"

"That's possible. Again, I don't recommend it."

Sylvia felt herself shrinking back into her chair. She suddenly wished she had waited until Harry could be with her. She tried to prop herself back up and sat straighter.

The room seemed to be moving, and Sam's face blurred.

"I don't know what I want to do yet," she said. "I have to think."

"Of course you do," he said, "and you can take a week or two to decide."

Sylvia got up and walked to the window, looked out. In the hospital courtyard, she saw children playing while their mothers sat and smoked cigarettes, the smoke rising on the breeze and disappearing.

"This is not a decision you need to make quickly. It's your body and your life. But my main concern right now would be trying to get as much of the cancer out of your body as possible so that any additional adjuvant therapy is easier and most successful. You need to talk it over with Harry and decide what you want to do. And if you'd like to get a second and third opinion, my secretary will help set those up for you."

She glanced back at the doctor, trying to remember what it was she'd wanted to ask. The questions just whirled through her mind and she couldn't settle on one.

"If you choose the mastectomy, we need to decide whether you'd like to have reconstruction surgery at the time of the mastectomy. Or you may want to wait until later when you're finished with your treatment, and then go back and do the reconstruction. You may even decide you don't want the reconstruction at all. Some women prefer to have their battle scars to remind them how hard they fought and how much they've overcome."

Sylvia had once believed that if anything like this ever came up in her life she would know quickly what to do. But everything seemed muddy and unclear.

He leaned forward on his desk, crossed his hands in front of his face. "I have to tell you, Sylvia, that the biopsy report shows that these are aggressive cancer cells."

"Aggressive?" She turned back from the window. "Really?"

"Yes."

Her hand came up to her breast. "But you said I had time. Two weeks, you said."

"You do. But we shouldn't wait longer than that."

She rubbed her face. "Well, I'd like it out now. Right this minute. Can you do it now?"

He smiled. "Take a little time, Sylvia. Get Harry home."

She wondered how she would sleep that night knowing that this monster called cancer moved aggressively through her body, conquering new territory, staking its claim.

The doctor gave her some books on breast cancer and instructed her to read them thoroughly before she made up her mind. She walked in a haze back to the secretary, her arms overloaded with the books and her purse and the legal pad she hadn't used and the tape recorder clutched in her hand. The woman started talking about second and third opinions, plastic surgeons, possible operation dates.

But Sylvia couldn't make her mind focus. She wished she had followed Al's advice and brought a friend with her today. Someone who could think clearly while her thoughts rollercoastered out of control.

Failing to make any appointments at all, she left the building and went to her car.

CHAPTER
Twelve

Sylvia didn't go straight home to call Harry or share her news with her friends. She had errands to run. She had to go to the post office, the bank, the cleaners. She had to get things done.

The post office wasn't busy, so she went right up to the counter and bought her stamps. As she walked back to the car, she breathed in the sweet mountain air. The breeze felt like freedom on her face, but she was anything but free. She got into her car and drove to the cleaners. *Malignancy, mastectomy, aggressive cancer cells . . .*

She shoved those words out of her mind and told herself that she wouldn't fall apart until she got home. She would finish her errand list.

She went to the counter at the cleaners, and the college girl behind it asked, "Name, please?"

"Sylvia Bryan," she said.

The girl checked her slips for Sylvia's name one by one under the B's, then turned the spinning rack and checked some more.

"Bryan?" she asked. "B-r-y-a-n?"

"Yes," Sylvia said. "Sylvia Bryan."

"I'm sorry. I don't find a Sylvia Bryan."

"I brought them in Monday." *After I found out I might have cancer*, she wanted to add. "You told me they'd be ready today."

"Just a minute. Let me check." The girl went to the back, then reemerged and punched on the computer. "What's your phone number?"

Sylvia gave her the number and waited, tapping her fingernails on the Formica surface. The girl disappeared for five minutes while Sylvia waited. *Malignant . . . mastectomy . . . aggressive cancer . . .*

The girl finally came back. "I'm sorry, Mrs. Bryan, but we seem to have misplaced your clothes. Could you tell me what they were?"

"A green dress, a black skirt, a pair of white slacks." Her voice broke off and she desperately tried to remember what else she had brought, but she couldn't concentrate on her wardrobe. Her mind kept lunging back to reconstructive surgery, chemotherapy, death. Her mouth started to tremble and her eyes filled with tears.

Horrified, the girl caught her breath. "I'm so sorry, ma'am. I'll go look again."

But Sylvia couldn't wait. She turned and ran from the building, got out to her car, closed and locked the door, and humped over her steering wheel.

She screamed out her rage and fury, then wept loudly for several moments. Finally, she pulled herself together enough to start the car.

She couldn't stop railing as she drove. "Lord, what are you doing? This wasn't part of the plan. I didn't even *want* to go to the mission field but you changed my heart, you made me want to go, and now that I'm there, now that it's my life, why would you take it from me? Why would you stop us in our tracks and bring our work to an end like this? I don't understand."

She wept as she drove home, praying all the way, and when she pulled into the cul-de-sac, she prayed that none of her neighbors were waiting outside. But that prayer wasn't answered either.

Cathy stood in her driveway. Sylvia drove past her, gave her a quick wave, then pulled into her garage and closed the door behind her.

CHAPTER
Thirteen

Cathy knew something was wrong when she saw Sylvia close herself in the garage. She never did that. Whenever Sylvia saw that anyone was out, she would get out of her car and walk down the driveway and spend at least a few minutes talking.

Cathy's stomach plummeted. She was certain Sylvia had gotten bad news.

She ran back into the house and called upstairs. "Annie? Annie, come down. I need you."

Annie bounced down the stairs. "What is it, Mom?"

"I need for you to come with me and baby-sit Tory's kids. I need to gather her and Brenda up, so we can go see what's wrong with Sylvia."

Annie's face changed. "Did she get her results?"

"I think she must have. She looked upset."

"Oh, Mom, you don't think it's cancer! Tell me it's not cancer. It couldn't be cancer."

"I don't know, Annie, but I need to get over there."

Cathy bolted out the door, Annie close on her heels. "Mom, please let me come with you. I've been praying so hard for her."

Cathy crossed the street and ran up Brenda's porch steps to ring the bell. "Annie, please. Tory will need a sitter so she can come without Hannah. She trusts you."

The door came open, and Joseph took one look at Cathy's face and yelled out, "Mama!"

Annie hadn't given up. "Mom, if it is cancer, what will happen?"

Brenda dashed to the door. "Cathy, what is it?"

"Something's wrong with Sylvia," she said. "She drove right past me and closed her garage. I think she got the results."

"Oh, no."

"We need to get over there. Annie's going to baby-sit for Tory."

Brenda burst out of the house. "Let's hurry."

As they crossed the empty lot between the Dodds' and the Sullivans' houses, Cathy glanced back at Annie. Tears were rolling down her face. Cathy stopped. "Oh, honey."

Annie came into her arms. "Mom, I'm scared. Nothing can happen to her. She's too special."

Cathy held her and stroked her hair. "It's going to be all right. Look, if you really want to, you can come with us. Tory could just bring Hannah with her . . ."

Brenda touched Annie's shoulder. "I could get Leah and Rachel to sit for Spencer and Brittany."

Annie considered that, then stepped back and wiped her eyes. "No. I'll do it. She really needs the three of you. I'd probably turn into a basket case and get her even more upset." She dried her hands on her jeans.

"Thank you, sweetheart. I'll come tell you the minute I leave her."

They headed into Tory's garage and knocked on the kitchen door.

She answered quickly—Hannah on her hip—and stared at the looks on their faces. "What is it?"

"We have to go to Sylvia," Brenda said.

Tory brought her hand to her mouth. Annie took the baby, and the three of them hurried on their way.

CHAPTER
Fourteen

Sylvia knew who it was the moment the doorbell rang, but she wasn't up to talking to anyone. She tried to ignore the bell, but her neighbors weren't going away.

Finally she grabbed a Kleenex, blew her nose, dabbed at her eyes, and decided that she might as well get it over with.

She opened the door, and Cathy, Brenda, and Tory stood there looking intently at her as if they already knew the verdict. Unable to utter a word, she reached out to hug all three of them. They came into her arms and clung.

For the moments that they embraced, Sylvia was sure that they were the only thing holding her up, keeping her from collapsing completely.

"Have you told Harry?" Cathy asked as they each let go and stepped back to look at their friend.

"Not yet. I wanted to tell him first but I dread it so much. I'm going to have to have surgery in the next week or two. I've got so many decisions to make. This ruins everything, you know."

"What does it ruin, honey?" Brenda asked.

Sylvia walked away from her and started flipping through the mail that sat on the counter.

"Our mission work. Harry's going to want to rush home, and what's going to happen to the people who need him? And the children are expecting me back. I don't understand this." She threw the mail down and flattened her palms on the counter. "What is God doing?"

Her voice broke off and she pulled a chair out from the kitchen table, lowered into it. Her friends sat down, Tory and Cathy across from her, Brenda next to her.

"Sylvia, what exactly did the doctor tell you?" Cathy's voice was soft, careful.

Sylvia propped her forehead in her hand. "Cancer in the breast," she said. "Poorly defined margins. Aggressive cells. I have to decide whether to have a lumpectomy or a mastectomy, and what *kind* of mastectomy, or even a bilateral mastectomy ..." She hated that they'd come when she was so upset. She'd wanted to be stoic, philosophical, gracious. "I'm sorry, girls. I don't mean to get you all upset. I handled myself really well in the doctor's office. I really did. And then I went to the post office and the cleaners." She hadn't handled herself well at the cleaners, but she didn't tell them so.

"You know, this really makes me sick, the way I'm responding. It's not at all what I would have envisioned."

"What in the world did you envision?" Tory asked.

"I pictured myself being tough and godly, taking it all with some sense of divine power working in my life. I thought I was grounded enough in my faith that I could accept whatever God decided to throw my way, that I wouldn't fall apart."

Brenda hugged her. "Honey, you haven't fallen apart. You've just been given the worst news of your life. You're supposed to cry."

Cathy took her hand. "Sylvia, what would you say if it was me, if I had just come home with a cancer diagnosis and I was crying? Would you think I was weak?"

Sylvia lifted her chin and took in a deep breath. "Of course not. I'd probably cry with you, and say something totally inane. I'd probably give you some platitude like 'This, too, shall pass,' or quote you Philippians 4:13: 'I can do all things through him who strengthens me.' And I'd tell you that God will never leave or forsake you, that I wouldn't either." Tears assaulted her again and she wiped them away. "But, please, I'm begging you—don't say any of those things to me."

Tory smiled. "They're all true, you know."

"I know," Sylvia said. "I know they're true, and I'll hold on to them as this progresses, but right now I'm angry and confused, and I have too many options, and I don't know what to do."

"Well, let's break it down," Cathy said. "One thing at a time. First, you need to call Harry."

Sylvia nodded. "I know. But this is going to be the hardest thing I've ever done. How will I convince him to stay there?"

Brenda got up and looked down at her. "Stay there? Sylvia, you *can't* convince him to stay there. He needs to be here with you."

"But his work is more important," Sylvia said. "Don't you understand? Some of those people would have died without him. They can't do without him."

"Somehow they can," Tory said. "Sylvia, they can do without him because God put this in your path right now. He didn't do it so you could go through it alone while Harry works for the Lord. There are times when our work has to stop and we have to deal with things that come into our lives. This is one of those times."

"You know he's going to want to come." Brenda handed her a box of Kleenex. "Don't give him a hard time about it. Just let him do what he needs to do."

Sylvia knew they were right. She tore a tissue out of the box. "Oh, I hate breaking Harry's heart. And I hate not being there to comfort him when he hangs up the phone."

Sylvia blew her nose again and grabbed another one to wipe her eyes. "Who would have thought? When I came home feeling tired and weak, who would have thought I had cancer?"

"Maybe Harry did," Brenda said. "He sent you home for tests, didn't he?"

"Harry never suspected cancer," she said. "Not in a million years. And it turns out that the fatigue and the weakness are not even about the cancer. It's stupid anemia."

"Well, be thankful for it," Cathy said. "It was what got you back here so they could discover the breast cancer. God is working."

Sylvia got up, putting distance between them. "I know I should be thankful. It's just hard right now. I guess I've got to call him. I can't put it off any longer. I know he's waiting to hear."

"Honey, do you want us to stay or go?" Cathy asked.

Sylvia stared at them all for a moment. Part of her wanted to deal with this alone in a dark closet where she could curl up on the floor and scream out her anger and misery and confusion. But she knew it was better for her if they were here to walk her through this.

"Why don't you wait in here and let me go call him in the bedroom? I might need you when I come out."

The three women nodded and sat where they were as she headed into the bedroom.

Harry picked up on the first ring. "Hello?"

"Hi, honey." She forced her voice to sound upbeat, but feared that her stopped-up nose would give away her distress.

"Sylvia, what did you find out?"

She tried to draw in a breath and cleared her throat. "It's malignant, Harry."

Silence followed, and she pictured him covering his face, struggling with tears, trying to clear his own voice. "How big is the tumor?"

"Three centimeters," she said. "And the margins are poorly defined, and the cancer cells are aggressive." There. It was all out.

Harry didn't say a word. She knew he was letting it sink in, running it through his database, lining it up with all of his medical knowledge. She knew he was shaking, rubbing his face, frowning, and struggling with tears.

"Have you told the kids?"

"No, not yet. I don't want to, Harry. It'll scare them to death. I'd rather wait until some things are decided. Then I can give them more information, and maybe it'll soften the blow."

His sigh was shaky. "That's my Sylvia. Always thinking about others."

She could hear in his voice that he was taking it hard. "Harry, we have some decisions to make." Oh, she didn't want to cry right now, but her throat grew tight and she felt that emotion creeping up, waiting to ambush her. "It's so confusing. He recommended a modified radical mastectomy because of the size and nature of the tumor. But I'm thinking about maybe having a lumpectomy and radiation, and then if that doesn't get it all, I could go back and have a mastectomy later."

"Sylvia, that's not wise. You'd be giving this cancer the chance to metastasize."

She squeezed her eyes shut. "He also suggested that I could opt for a bilateral mastectomy just to keep from taking any chances with the other breast. Harry, I want to do the right thing, but this is all so unreal. I feel like I'm watching a Monday night movie."

"I don't," he said. "I feel like my bride is in serious jeopardy, and I want to get home to her as fast as I can."

She longed to tell him that he didn't need to come, but she knew it was all in vain. He was probably throwing things into his suitcase even as they spoke.

"Harry, what's going to happen to the mission work, to the clinic, and to the orphanage?"

"Sylvia, it was God's plan to send us here in the first place. Do you think he doesn't have a plan now that we're leaving?"

"But why would he get us there only to make us come home?"

"He knows what he's doing. And he's got replacements for us. We've got to trust him. But right now I've got to get home to you."

"Harry, my biggest wish is that you would stay there and keep doing the work and let me handle this. The girls will take care of me. I can handle it."

"Sylvia, I can't think of anything more torturous than to be here while my wife is suffering at home. God doesn't require that of me."

"I'm not suffering. I'm doing just fine. I don't have any pain."

"You will after the mastectomy. You're part of me, Sylvia, and when we suffer, we suffer together. That's all there is to it. I don't want to hear another word about it."

She closed her eyes. Tears streamed down her face. "When will you be here?"

"I'll get the first flight out of Managua tomorrow," he said.

"You don't have to rush. You can take a day or two."

When he spoke again his voice wobbled. "They said it was aggressive, Sylvia. I want it out of you as soon as possible. I'll see you tomorrow. Until then, honey, I want you to relax and not worry."

"How do I do that?"

"Call on the girls. Get them to come over and have popcorn and watch a funny movie."

She shook her head. "No. What I really need to do is read about breast cancer. I need information, Harry. I think I'll feel better if I know what I'm doing."

"All right, whatever you need to do. But I'm here, okay? If you need to talk tonight, just call me." His voice broke off and she knew he was crying. Anger surged through her again.

Lord, why would you break his heart like this?

"I love you," she whispered.

"I love you, too. I'll see you tomorrow, honey."

She hung up the phone and grabbed up his pillow, mashed it against her face, and wept into it, hoping her friends in the living room didn't hear. She sat there like that for a long time, spending her tears, venting her anguish. Finally she went into the bathroom and washed her face. Quickly, she reapplied her makeup. Then, taking a deep breath, she went back into the living room.

Cathy, Tory, and Brenda had been crying. Their eyes were red and puffy. They were all huddled together on the couch, and she sensed they had been praying.

She stood in the doorway, her hand on the casing. "Harry's coming home tomorrow."

"Good." Cathy's smile was overbright. "That will help a lot."

Sylvia nodded and averted her eyes.

"So what do you want to do to get your mind off of this?" Brenda asked.

"I don't want to get my mind off of it," Sylvia said. "I want to keep my mind on it. I want to read the stuff the doctor gave me, and go to the bookstore and get every book I can find on the subject. And I want to stay up late tonight reading until I feel like I have a better handle on this. I know that God is in control. There's no doubt about that. And I know that he's faithful. I'll hold onto that as I go. But I feel like a certain amount of this is under my control, and I need to know more to make the right decisions."

"Okay," Cathy said, "then let's go."

Sylvia looked around at them. "All four of us? What about the kids? What about Hannah?"

"Annie's got the kids," Tory said, "and she's great with Hannah."

"She'll be fine," Brenda added. "You trained her well in León."

So they headed off to the bookstore on a mission to find the information that could help save Sylvia's life.

CHAPTER *Fifteen*

Harry's hands trembled as he sat at his old desk at the back of his clinic and dialed the number for the airline. When they put him on hold, a screaming sense of injustice shivered up inside him. Jeb Anderson, one of the other missionaries who ran the orphanage, stepped into the doorway. Noting the sweat on Harry's brow and the expression on his face, he asked, "Harry, you talked to Sylvia, didn't you?"

Harry nodded quickly, as if he didn't have time to answer.

Jeb stepped closer. "Was it malignant?"

Harry raked his hand through his hair. "Yes, it was. I'm going home tomorrow, Jeb." He looked up at his friend and saw the dread on his face.

"Of course you are." Jeb crossed the room and looked into Harry's face. "Harry, don't worry about anything. I've been talking to Carlos Gonzales, and he thinks he can run things here while you're gone. He's been on the phone with some churches back in the States, and he's trying to get some doctors to come here on medical mission trips to fill in while you're gone."

Harry's eyes widened as he looked up at Jeb. "You were anticipating the worst."

"We know how bad Sylvia's been feeling."

"It's not supposed to have anything to do with the cancer. But if they're wrong and it does, then it's more advanced than we think."

The airline clerk finally answered the phone. "_Le puedo ayudar?_"

"Yes. Uh . . . I need to get the first flight for the United States out of Managua tomorrow morning," he said in Spanish. He fumbled through his wallet for his credit card.

When the flight was finally booked, he hung up and leaned back.

"Harry, are you all right?" Jeb asked.

Harry evaded the question. "I've just got a lot to do tonight. I need to put things in the clinic in a little better order so that anybody who comes in here can take over. I need to check on Mrs. Hernandez and make sure she has enough antibiotics to get her through her infection. And I'd probably better go by and see baby Maria. She wasn't doing well and I was worried she wouldn't even make it through the week." His voice broke off and his shoulders began to shake.

"They'll be all right, Harry," Jeb said. "I'll go see her every day and make sure they're giving her the medicine."

"They sell it, you know." Tears began to stream down his face. "They sell it to buy food. And can you blame them? But they don't seem to understand that without it she could die."

"I'll make sure," he said. "In fact, if you want me to ration it out and take it daily one dose at a time, I will."

"Could you do that? That's what I've been doing. It was the only way."

"Of course. Harry, if you'll make a list of what needs to be done, I'll do everything that doesn't require a doctor. You need to be with Sylvia. You don't have to feel guilty about it." He came and sat down next to him, put his hand on Harry's back. "The Lord is still in control, you know."

"I know," Harry said. "I know he is. I would never want to suggest that he isn't. But my wife . . ."

He was going to lose it. He was going to break down right here in front of Jeb. He couldn't handle that, so he got up and headed for the door. "I've got a lot to do, Jeb. I have to get home and pack."

He took off without another word, walking as fast as he could to the old Fiat parked out beside the clinic. He realized that he had just contradicted himself. He'd said that he needed to organize supplies so that the medical missionaries could come in and take over, then he'd headed off to pack.

Jeb would understand.

He got to his house and went in, looked around at all the things that screamed Sylvia's name. The smell of her lingered on the air, and he suddenly felt a sense of deprivation, as if she'd already been snatched from him and he didn't know why. He went to the bedroom, pulled her pillow out of the bed, lay down and curled up with it . . . and began to weep. After a while, he got off the bed and knelt beside it to pray.

"Please," he begged his almighty God, "heal her. Please don't let this be the end. We've tried to be obedient, Lord. We've tried to do everything you've said. Father, please don't take her. I'm begging you. I've never asked you for a lot, not anything really big. This is the first time, Lord. Please save my wife."

He fell prostrate on the floor, pleading and crying for God's help and mercy.

CHAPTER *Sixteen*

It was eight-thirty the following night when darkness began to dominate the sky. Steve had finished mowing just before daylight gave up its ghost. Cathy took a glass of cold lemonade to him in the backyard. His sweaty T-shirt stuck to his chest and back. He grabbed the towel that hung over the lawn mower handle and wiped his face, then took a long swig of the drink.

"I like a wife that brings me lemonade."

She smiled. "I like a husband who mows the lawn. I haven't done it since you moved in."

"See? Marriage does have its perks."

"Lots of them." She lowered to the chaise lounge chair under the covered patio and looked up at him. Steve touched her neck. "You've been quiet today. Have you talked to Sylvia?"

"No, she made herself scarce, said she wanted to read and think about the decisions she had to make. And I think she's out picking Harry up at the airport now."

"You didn't sleep much last night."

"Hope I didn't keep you awake. So many things were going through my mind. Sylvia and Mark . . ."

He took another drink. "What about Mark?"

"Well, I've been thinking a lot about this GED thing. We're getting down to the wire. School registration is the end of the week, and I found out that a new GED class is starting up next week. He would have the choice of going nights or mornings."

"If he went nights, he could work during the day."

Cathy sighed. "Yeah, but I don't know if I want him doing that. Working all day and going to school at night? That's a lot of stress."

Steve nodded. "It is, but I thought it might be beneficial for him to work like a dog for a few months, and find out how valuable that college degree is."

"You have a point," she said. "Only you realize, don't you, that if he's doing a full-time job with other high school dropouts, he could be influenced by them? I mean, kids usually drop out because they hate the rules, want to party all night, take drugs and drink . . ."

"That's true," Steve said. "But haven't *all* those in the GED classes dropped out of school? Morning or night, it doesn't really matter."

"You're right." Cathy rubbed her forehead. "And I know there is something to having him work really hard. I do want him to realize how much he needs his education."

"Cathy, why not just make him finish school the traditional way?"

"Because I've been trying to put myself in his place. I understand why he doesn't want to go back to high school. That's where he met the kids he started doing drugs with in the first place. And I can understand why he doesn't want to study with Brenda anymore. I think he's insecure and feels stupid, because her kids are so advanced."

"But that would challenge him. And you know Brenda needs the money."

"She's done without it for a year. I'm not even sure she wants him back. We haven't really talked about it. And, Steve, he may be able to get his GED *now*, even without the class. I mean, he has gone to school straight through. Brenda put him a few steps ahead, and then he had school at River Ranch. He may very well know enough to pass it."

Steve finished his glass and set it down next to him. "I don't like it much, Cathy, but if you have peace about it, go ahead and let him. The goal is to get him to go to college, and the GED shouldn't hurt in that area, not if he plans to go to the community college first."

"All right," Cathy said, "I'll let him. Now all I have to decide is whether he should go to the morning or night class."

"And he has to start looking for a job."

"Right. A job." Cathy held his gaze for a moment. "Do you really think that making him take the class at night and work during the day is the right choice?"

"Depends on what you want to accomplish."

Cathy smiled. "I want him to hate the kind of work he can get and go to college."

"Then let him work his tail off for the next few months," Steve said. "Guaranteed, he'll be in college by the next semester."

CHAPTER
Seventeen

The moment Harry stepped off the plane Sylvia felt as if the parallel planes of her life had finally converged. She could get through this now.

He started to cry as he walked toward her, and she took him into her arms and held him as if he were the diseased and she were comforting him. They stood there like that for a long moment, him weeping into her hair, her weeping into his shirt, while the hustle and bustle of the airport life moved around them. Then she took him back to the house he hadn't seen since they'd left it to go to the mission field.

The "For Sale" sign still sat in the front yard. Harry got out of the car, and instead of going toward the door, he headed to the sign.

"Harry, what are you doing?"

"Taking the sign down." He moved it in the dirt, loosening it so he could pull it up.

"No, don't. We have to sell the house, Harry."

The sign came up. "Not until this is resolved. Honey, God is obviously working here. He didn't let us sell it because he knew we'd need it. We can put the sign back up when the time is right."

She watched as he laid it on a shelf in the garage—one more reminder that their plans and dreams had been derailed.

Harry went back to the car and got his suitcase. He carried it into the kitchen and looked around. "Home," he whispered. "I didn't even know how much I'd missed it. Isn't God good for not letting us sell?"

Sylvia put her arm through his and led him through the house. "The Gonzaleses did a great job of taking care of it. Since they left, Brenda and Tory have come over here every now and then to keep it dusted."

She led him into the bedroom, and he set the suitcase down and sat on the bed. "Are you tired, Harry? You could rest and we could talk tomorrow."

"No." He got up and fixed his eyes on her. "I want to see the pathology report and the X rays. You brought them home, didn't you?"

"Yes," she said. "They knew you'd want them."

"And I don't want to waste any time. We need to go for second and third opinions."

"I've already got the appointments booked," Sylvia said. "I called today and Dr. Jefferson's secretary set it all up. Monday we see Dr. Thibodeaux."

Harry nodded. "The oncologist?"

"That's right," she said. "And before that appointment I've got an appointment with Dr. Simon, the plastic surgeon. Then a second-opinion appointment with Dr. Hartford."

He stepped into the dining room and saw the breast cancer books spread out across the table. "You've been studying."

"Yeah, I've learned a lot," she said. "I at least have a little better understanding than I did yesterday."

He sat down and read the pathology report. His face betrayed his tension and strain as he flipped through the pages the doctor had sent home for him. Finally he looked up at her.

"Sylvia, I don't want any more talk about a lumpectomy. I want you to have a mastectomy. If it weren't such an aggressive cancer and if the margins of the tumor were more defined, I might not say that. But this report convinced me."

She closed her eyes. "They'd be cutting off a part of me, Harry. I don't know if I can deal with that."

"Don't think of it like that." He took her hand and made her sit down. "Think of it as them cutting out the enemy."

She met his eyes. "But my body will be different. That will change *us*."

He leaned forward and looked hard into her eyes. "It's not your breasts I'm in love with. It's you. It's going to be all right, Sylvia. Every time I look at that scar, I'll remember how close I came to losing you. If that scar is what saves your life, it will be beautiful to me."

"Let's just see what they say in the other opinions," she said. "I'm not ready to make up my mind just yet."

"Okay." He pulled her onto his lap and held her for a long moment. "We need to tell the kids, honey. Sarah and Jeff need to know."

"Not yet," she whispered. "Not until we've made some decisions. They'll take it so much better if they know what we're going to do about it. Please, Harry. Let's wait."

He nodded, his mouth straining to hold back his weary, raw emotions. "Whatever you think."

They went to bed soon after, Sylvia exhausted from the hours of study she'd put in that day, and Harry wiped out from a sleepless night and the trip home from Nicaragua. He reaffirmed her body and his love of it before falling off to sleep.

Sylvia lay next to him, watching his face in repose. She touched her breast, the offending one, and let her hand cup over the shape of it. In just a few days it would be gone. But if she could exchange it for the peace of mind she lost the day she found out she had cancer, she supposed it would be worth it.

Finally she drifted off into a sweet sleep, curled up warm next to her husband.

CHAPTER *Eighteen*

Some of the heaviness lifted from Sylvia's heart as she sat in the plastic surgeon's office looking at the before and after pictures of breast reconstruction.

"We have several reconstruction methods," he was saying. "We can reconstruct using your own tissue from other parts of your body. With the TRAM flap we pull up fat, muscle, and tissue from your abs."

"Ouch." Sylvia turned a page in the photo album. "That sounds painful. Does it look real when it's finished?"

Dr. Simon took the album from her and flipped through its pictures. He found one and pointed to it. "You tell me."

She studied the picture. "So you get a tummy tuck as part of the package?"

"That's right. Or we can take the tissue from your gluts."

Harry wasn't impressed. "What are the risks?"

"Well, there are some. Sometimes the flap develops necrosis."

Sylvia looked up at him. "What is that?"

"The tissue dies," Harry said. "They'd have to remove the flap then, and that could cause you to be in worse shape than you were before the reconstruction."

"We could do a LAT flap, where we take muscle and tissue from the upper back and move it to the breast area."

"Still sounds painful. I'd have incisions in front *and* back." She looked at the picture the doctor offered her.

"We supplement this procedure with an implant."

Harry still wasn't satisfied. "What about not doing any of the flaps and just doing a synthetic implant?"

Dr. Simon nodded. "Yes, we can put an expander bag under her skin." He picked one up and showed it to them. "It has a valve at the bottom, and every week or two you come in and let me inject saline into it. Slowly, it will stretch your skin into the shape of your other breast. When the skin is properly stretched, say in six months or so, we can put in the permanent implant."

Sylvia liked the "after" pictures of that one. She showed them to Harry. "What do you think?"

He stiffened. "I think reconstruction isn't that necessary. That maybe we need to cross one hurdle before we move on to that one."

Sylvia shook her head. "But I'll have more hope if I think my breast is someday going to look normal again."

"It's just a lot of extra pain to go through, when you're already struggling."

"But, Harry, if I wait I may never do it. I'd rather get it all done at once."

Harry got quiet.

The doctor leaned forward on his desk. "When we get the permanent implant in, then we can do some skin grafts to finish the cosmetic appearance. It actually looks very good."

Sylvia looked at the "before" picture of the woman with an incision that cut from her sternum around to her back, leaving a flap. She swallowed the lump in her throat. Then she saw the "after" picture. The reconstructed look was more than she could have hoped for, but she knew better than to expect the best-case scenario.

She frowned. "I want to see a picture of one that didn't turn out like you hoped."

"I understand what you're saying." He flipped through the pictures, then brought out one that was a little less symmetrical. Even that looked better than she thought it would.

She glanced at Harry. "If this is the worst it will be, I think I can live with it. It's a lot better than not having anything at all."

Harry leaned forward. "Bob, I want you to tell us something honestly. Don't these surgeries and implants increase the risk of infection during the chemo?"

"That is a risk," the doctor said. "But it's minimal."

"What about recurrence? Would an implant keep us from being able to see new tumors?"

"Not at all."

Harry wasn't finished. "So you'd have to be there at the time of the mastectomy. Would this delay the surgery date at all? Coordinating your schedule with the other surgeon, I mean?"

"When are you planning to have it?"

"Early next week," Harry said.

Sylvia shot him a look. They hadn't talked about that. She hadn't even told the children yet. She hadn't prayed about it enough. She wasn't ready.

"Yes, I can work it into my schedule. If we choose an autologous tissue reconstruction, it'll take an additional five or six hours of surgery. The expander implant takes less time. But I'll need to know as soon as possible so we can schedule it."

Sylvia swallowed. "Can we schedule the surgery before I know for sure what I'm going to do?"

"Yes. We could hold the time for you. I'll check with Dr. Jefferson, and by the time we work out the time, maybe you'll know what you want."

As they drove away from the office, she recognized the tension on Harry's face. He was going to require some convincing, but she already had her mind made up. She reached across the seat and took his hand. "Honey, it's going to be all right."

He smiled. "I'm supposed to say that to you."

"But you're not sure it's true, are you?"

He focused on the car in front of him. "Of course I am."

"I'll probably have the mastectomy, but I want the reconstruction, Harry."

"I know you do. And it's your body."

She watched the way he worked his jaw, and knew that he still had serious reservations. "What's your main concern?" she asked.

"The unnecessary pain you'll be in, wherever they take the grafts, when you're already suffering from the mastectomy. Possible infection. Longer surgery. Harder recovery."

They were all valid concerns, she thought. She had always deferred to him in matters of medicine for their family. But there was something else here that she couldn't quite explain. She was losing a part of her body, and she needed to know she could get it back. Even if it was a poor facsimile of the real thing, just the shape and the contour would do so much for the way she felt about herself.

But she had to think of Harry's needs, too, and she didn't want to cause him unnecessary anxiety.

But that anxiety was impossible to hold at bay as they went for her appointment with her oncologist. He explained the process of chemotherapy to her, how necessary it would be to kill any cancer cells left in her body after the surgery. The strength of the chemo and the number of treatments would depend on how many lymph nodes were involved.

The only good news she could filter from his words were that she'd have a four-week period to recover from her surgery before starting the chemo treatments.

Their visit didn't make her decisions any simpler.

There was still so much to think about. It ought to be easy to decide these things. You had cancer, so you had it cut out. Took medicine to prevent recurrence. Took measures to cope with the side effects. But none of what she'd read or heard in the last couple of days made the choices easier.

She let her gaze drift out the window as they wound their way back up Bright Mountain. She didn't know why she was so adamant about reconstructing her breast, when there were so many more important things to think of. What if she didn't survive this? How would her children take it? They weren't ready to be motherless, even though they were both grown and out of the house. Even in Nicaragua she e-mailed them every day and spoke to them often. Sarah still called her for recipes and baby-raising tips. Jeff still wanted her advice on the women he dated.

And there was the grandbaby. She'd been so thrilled to have her, and now to know that she might not live to see her start school, star in her school play, accept Christ as her Lord.

There was no more frightening feeling than that of leaving her children behind. Death would be fine—absent with the body was to be present with the Lord, according to Paul. This was not her home. But she couldn't help the bonds that held her so tightly to her kids.

And her husband.

"You're awfully quiet." Harry's voice was raspy, hoarse.

"I was just thinking about the kids."

He nodded. "We have to tell them."

"Yes," she said. "I'll call them when we get home."

CHAPTER
Nineteen

Sylvia employed the three-way-calling feature she'd never used in her life, and got Sarah and Jeff on the phone together. When she told them the news, they both sat silent for a long moment.

Finally, Sarah spoke. "Mom, I'm coming home tomorrow."

"Me too." Jeff's voice was heavy, thick.

"No, you're not," she said. "Sarah, you've got the baby. And, Jeff, what about your job? I don't even know yet when the surgery will be scheduled. It's foolish to come here now. I'm going to be fine. I'm having surgery sometime next week, and then, according to the oncologist, I'll have four weeks before my chemotherapy starts."

"Chemotherapy?" Sarah sounded as if the breath had been knocked out of her. "Oh, Mom."

"Oh, Mom, what?" she asked her. "Honey, don't you realize that chemo is a blessing? What if they didn't have it? I know it's going to be hard, but I'm ready for it. I want to do everything possible to kill the cancer." She sighed. "Guys, it's going to be okay. Really."

"How's Dad?" Jeff asked.

"He's fine. Preoccupied, as you can imagine. We have a lot of decisions to make about the surgery. But we'll make them."

"But I want to do something!" Sarah cried.

"You *can* do something. You can pray."

"Mom, as soon as you know when the surgery is, let me know. I'll come so I can help Dad take care of you when you get home."

"How long before they'll know if it's spread?" Jeff's question rippled over the line.

"I won't know right away. Probably a couple of days."

"I want to be there when the results come back," he said.

She closed her eyes and tried to think of those results coming. If the cancer hadn't spread to the lymph nodes, they'd have a wonderful celebration. But if it had . . .

She didn't want her children there hurting that way. She didn't want to see the fear on their faces . . . the dread of her demise.

On the other hand, she didn't want them hearing about it on the phone.

"All right, you can come after the surgery," she said. "But only if you bring the baby, Sarah. And, Jeff, I don't want you missing more than a couple of days of work."

"Mom, are you sure you want me to bring her?" Sarah asked. "You won't be feeling well. Her crying and fussing might make you feel worse. I could leave her with Gary."

"Absolutely not," Sylvia said. "I have to have something to look forward to, don't I? If you bring her, I won't have time to feel sorry for myself. I'll have a little treasure to keep my mind off those results."

"All right," she said. "I'll bring her."

"And Jeff, no long-term absences from work, okay? I can't wait to see you, but your father and I didn't put all that money into your education to have you run off and leave your job."

"I hear you, Mom."

"So you'll call us when you schedule the surgery?" Sarah asked. "The very minute?"

"You know I will."

When she finally hung up the phone, she felt as if the last vestiges of her strength had drained right out of her. She got up and went into the living room and found Harry sitting in his favorite chair, staring out into the air.

"I told them," she said. "They insisted on coming after the surgery. Sarah's going to bring Grace."

Harry only looked at her. "Something to look forward to," he whispered. "How did they take it?"

"Just like you'd expect."

He nodded and reached for her hand. She went to him, and he pulled her into his lap. There, she curled up in his arms, holding him and loving him, and praying silently that God wouldn't bring too much pain into the heart of this beloved man who had been such an obedient servant of God, and such a precious husband to her.

"There's something we have to do," he said, "before we go another day."

"What?"

"We have to call for the elders of the church and get them to pray over you, just like the Bible says."

Sylvia looked down at his serious face. "Are you sure? Do they still do that? I never hear of it." She got up and moved to the chair across from him.

"No, it isn't done that much in churches like ours, though if someone asks for it, they do comply." He got up and got his Bible, opened it to James 5, and read verses 14 and 15. "The Bible tells us that if anyone is sick he must call the elders and let them pray over him ... that they should anoint him with oil ... and that the prayer offered in faith will restore him. But there's a dispute as to whether the Greek word that's translated 'sick' really means 'sick.'"

"I don't understand. Isn't it clear?"

"Not really. The word translated 'sick' is *kamno*, which means 'to tire . . . faint, sicken, be wearied.' So it *can* be translated 'sick.' But it could also mean someone who is weak in conscience or weak in faith. And the problem is what we've seen. People who are prayed over by the elders don't always get well. Some of them still die, no matter how strong their faith is. This would imply that everyone who has strong faith and prays will have perfect health. But that's not so."

Sylvia was more confused than ever. "So why should we do it?"

Harry looked down at his Bible again, then brought his eyes up to her. "Because what if they're wrong? What if it really does mean 'sick'? What if God really does assign some extra power to prayers prayed by the elders? What if God wanted to heal you that way?"

Sylvia lifted her chin. She didn't need any more convincing than that. "Then we'll do it. But when? I've always wondered at what point it should be done. If you hurt your back, should you do it then? If you have the flu? If you break your leg? Or is it just for terminal illness? And even then, do you do it at the beginning of the illness, when there's a chance that modern medicine could cure you, or do you wait until there's no hope left?"

Harry shook his head. "I don't know the answer to any of those questions, honey. I really don't. All I know is that now is the time for us. And I'm going to call the elders tonight, and ask them to meet us tomorrow."

Sylvia took the Bible from him and read over those verses again. "It says that 'the prayer offered in faith will restore the one who is sick.' Does that mean that we trust in the healing and don't follow with the surgery or the treatments?"

"No, of course not. That would be like demanding that God heal you, not taking no for an answer. In that case, if he chose not to, it would shake our faith and make God the bad guy somehow. No, God doesn't want us testing him or demanding things of him. He simply wants us to pray. I have total faith in his ability to heal you this way if he chooses."

"Then how will we know if he healed me, or if the surgery or chemo did?"

"If you're healed, Sylvia, it will be God who did it, regardless of how he chooses to."

The hope in his eyes was intense, and she could see the pleas his mind and heart were already sending up on her behalf.

"After the surgery," Harry said, "if there's no cancer in the lymph nodes, I think we can assume that the elders praying over you really worked."

"And if it is in the lymph nodes?" she asked.

He cleared his throat and looked down at his hands. "If it is in the lymph nodes, then we assume that God heard the prayers of the elders, and has chosen to answer it according to his will. Whatever that will is."

Her eyes filled with tears again. He stood up and pulled her to her feet, framed her face with his hands, and gazed into her wet eyes. "Whatever happens, Sylvia, we know that God loves you more, even, than I do."

She nodded. "I know. And whatever he chooses, it's for some great purpose that we can't even imagine."

A tear rolled out of Harry's eye and ran down his cheek. "We'll pray that we can accept that, whatever it is."

"Yes," she whispered. "And that we'll be thankful, even if it means suffering."

It was more than she had the power to do . . . more even than Harry was capable of offering. But she was sure that they wouldn't have to rely on their own power to do that. God would give them what they needed, as they needed it. Comfort when it was needed, and healing if it was part of his plan.

CHAPTER
Twenty

After a couple of hours of having the elders pray over her, Sylvia told Harry that she felt the peace of mind to make the right decision. She had weighed every possible choice carefully, and she chose a modified radical mastectomy of only one breast, and reconstruction using the expander implant. Once the decision was made, Harry pulled every string he had and finally got a surgery date of the following Wednesday.

On the day of the surgery Brenda, Cathy, and Tory assembled in the waiting room at the hospital with Harry, and waited for word on how things had gone. They prayed and paced and worried until the surgeon finally came back out and took Harry aside.

Harry was silent as he followed his old friend into a consultation room. He sat down, studying the surgeon's face as he took the chair across from him. "Be straight with me, Sam."

Sam Jefferson met his eyes. "Harry, the surgery went well. You know I'd tell you if anything had gone wrong. They sent the tissue to the pathologist. We also took out ten lymph nodes and we should know if any of them are positive within the next seventy-two hours. But the surgery went very well. The incision looks good, and Bob did a fabulous job on the reconstruction."

"How did the tissue look?"

"Like cancer, just as we thought. But there's no way of telling whether it's spread until we get the results back."

Harry had never been particularly good at waiting. "When can I see her?"

"Probably in the next thirty minutes or so. We'll let you know."

Harry headed back to the waiting room. All three faces turned to him. "She's fine," he said. "Surgery is over. Everything went well."

"And the cancer?" Tory asked.

Harry shook his head. "We won't know anything for seventy-two hours or so."

Cathy got up. "Why so long?"

"It takes a while to get the pathology reports back," he said. "Meanwhile, we'll just help her recover from the surgery and not borrow any trouble until it comes."

"Harry, what's the best-case scenario?" Brenda asked. "Is it that they got all the cancer and it's not in the lymph nodes?"

"That would be good news to me. If it is in the lymph nodes we'll have more to worry about."

Cathy slapped her hands on her thighs. "Well, it won't be. I just know it."

But Brenda and Tory grew quiet as he gathered his things and headed to the recovery room to see his wife.

Sylvia slept peacefully on the bed in the recovery room, and Harry stepped up to her and kissed her forehead. She looked pale and lifeless, but the warmth of her skin reassured him.

He saw the bandage on the left side of her chest and under her arm, the flat place where her breast had been . . .

His heart sank at the grief he knew she would suffer.

Her eyes fluttered open, and he whispered, "Hello, sweetheart. How do you feel?"

"Fine. Is it over?"

"It's over. You came through it great."

Her voice was hoarse from the tube that had been in her throat. "Do they know anything yet?"

"Not yet, honey."

She brought those tired eyes up to his. "How do I look?"

He leaned over and kissed her dry lips. "You're still the most beautiful gal in the joint."

Sylvia didn't seem to buy that. She looked down at herself, saw the bandage over her incision.

"When did they say we'd know about the lymph nodes?"

"Seventy-two hours. It's going to be a long wait."

Sylvia swallowed and closed her eyes, then opened them again. "Then let's just pretend they got it all, Harry. Let's pretend that the worst is behind us."

"Okay, sweetheart," he whispered against her face. "That's what we'll pretend."

CHAPTER
Twenty-One

When Tory dropped Brenda off, she saw that Leah and Rachel sat on the front steps, playing jacks. The moment they saw her, they launched from the steps and ran toward her.

"Mama!"

Joseph came out the front door and waited on the porch, and Daniel came around from the backyard.

"How is Miss Sylvia?" Leah asked.

"She's okay. She came through the surgery fine."

Leah blocked her way up to the front, a dramatic look on her face. "Is she gonna die?"

Brenda sighed and put her arms around her twin girls. "Now why would you ask a thing like that? She had surgery so she wouldn't die."

Rachel laid her head against her mother's shoulder. "We studied about cancer, Mama. It kills people."

"But not all of them. We have lots of new drugs that can fight it. Lots of people survive the kind that Miss Sylvia has. So don't you worry."

She looked at Daniel, who stood near the driveway, and Joseph, who leaned against the post on the porch. Both boys had somber looks on their faces. "Come on into the house, kids," she said. "Let's talk."

David was in the kitchen when she came in, painting mustard on the corn dogs that had just come out of the oven. They sat around the table, and Brenda looked at each face, moved by how seriously they were taking Sylvia's illness.

"Miss Sylvia's going to be okay," she said, "at least for now. They took her breast off hoping to get all the cancer, and we won't know for a few days if they did or not."

"Why not?" Leah asked. "Couldn't they see it and make sure?"

"They can't always see it. Sometimes it gets into the bloodstream. We're waiting to see if it has, but we're hoping for the best."

Joseph blinked back the mist in his eyes. "We've been praying for her, Mama."

"I know, sweetheart." She touched Joseph's flaming red hair, tried to stroke it into place. "You keep praying. The same God who healed you is hearing these prayers, too."

Satisfied that Sylvia was not in immediate mortal danger, the children took their corn dogs outside to eat them at the picnic table.

Brenda and David were left in the kitchen alone.

He took her hand. "You sure you're okay?"

Renegade tears burst into her eyes. "No, I'm not okay. I hate it when someone I love is suffering."

"She's not suffering," David said. "She's going to be all right. It may be better than you think. There's no need to worry."

Brenda got up and put the pan that had held the corn dogs into the sink. "We're totally out of control, you know. I feel as helpless as I did when Joseph was sick. It's completely in God's hands." She wiped her tears and came back to the table, her wet eyes fixed on her husband.

"What can I do to help?"

She shook her head. "It would be so great if I could pray with you. Two or more gathered in prayer ..."

"Brenda ..." The word had that long-suffering sound, like an admonition, and it closed the discussion. He got up and grabbed some napkins and got his glass. "Let's go out with the kids."

"Okay," she said. "I'll be right there."

She watched him as he headed out, but she made no move to go. Instead, she cried into her hands for a few minutes, partly for Sylvia, and partly for David ...

Then finally, she cleared the evidence from her face, and joined her family outside.

Three gathered that night in prayer—Tory and Brenda and Cathy—sitting on Brenda's porch where they'd prayed as a foursome so many other times in their lives. They all wept as they prayed, asking God to spare Sylvia's life.

As they brought the prayer to an end Brenda wiped her face, but the tears kept coming.

Cathy reached for her hand. "Honey, are you okay?"

Brenda shook her head. "Just ... seeing Harry and Sylvia's approach to this disease has made me long for the day when David wakes up ... and sees the truth about Jesus." She dabbed at her eyes. "I've prayed for him for years. It seems like it's never going to happen."

"You have to trust the Lord for it," Cathy said. "You just have to claim it."

Brenda rolled her eyes. "Oh, Cathy, trust the Lord for what? I trust him with everything, my life, David's salvation, *every-thing*. But he never *said* he was going to save David, so I don't know why people think all I have to do is expect it and it will happen. God's ways are not our ways. I don't believe in name-it-claim-it."

"Well, neither do I," Cathy said. "But I'm just saying that you need to believe God for it."

Brenda's face twisted in anger. "What does that mean, 'Believe God for it'?"

Tory looked uncomfortable at Brenda's response and reached out to touch her arm. "Brenda, she didn't mean anything."

"No, I'm serious," Brenda asked. "Cathy, I need to know what you mean by 'believe God for it.' That's like a demand of God, a presumption on him, that he has to keep some bargain he never made."

Confusion shone on Cathy's face. "You don't think God wants to see David saved?"

"Of course he wants to see David saved," Brenda said, "but he's not going to force him into it. He doesn't bang the door down. He just stands at it and knocks. There's nothing in the Bible that says that I can believe God for anything I want and it will come true."

"It does say ask and you will receive. That anything you ask in his name will be given."

"Yes, it does, but that's according to the will of God and his timing. I can't order God around with my prayers. I can't just believe he's going to do something because I asked him to, and think that it somehow obligates him to do it. Jesus asked God to take the cup of suffering and death from him, but he didn't. Paul asked him to remove the thorn from his flesh. He said no. They didn't just 'believe God for it' and expect it to come true."

Cathy leaned forward, her face soft as she looked at Brenda. "I guess you're right, Brenda. All I meant was that you have to have faith and keep praying."

Tory nodded. "Jesus said, 'You have not because you ask not, and when you ask you do it with wrong motives.' Brenda, the Lord knows your heart, that you're not asking with wrong motives. And we know that it's not his will that anyone should perish. So why wouldn't he eventually answer this prayer? You're praying right, according to his will, with pure motives. God will hear you and answer you, Brenda."

Brenda knew she'd never shown this side of herself to her friends before. Even when Joseph was sick, she'd had such strength and faith. But as serious and frightening as that was, she considered David's eternity to be at much greater risk.

"It's just that, after all these years of praying, it hasn't happened yet. And I want it to happen now." Her voice broke off. She rubbed her hands through her hair and sank back onto her chair. The cool wind from the Smokies blew up, ruffling it into her face.

"I'm sorry, Cathy. I'm sorry, Tory. I just want so much to have the kind of intimacy with David that Sylvia and Harry have. And you, Tory, and Barry. And Cathy and Steve. To be able to hold his hand and pray with him and know that we are agreeing in prayer and that God's hearing us."

"He hears you anyway," Cathy said. "He hears when you pray alone, and he hears when you pray with us."

"I know he does, but sometimes I just need that support, you know? I need a spiritual leader. Up until now it feels like it's been Sylvia. My mentor. My spiritual mother. But what if something happens to her?" Brenda wiped her face. "Oh, that's so selfish. I can't believe I'm saying these things. She's up in that hospital fighting for her life, and I'm sitting here worried about me."

"We're all worried about us." Tory put her arm around Brenda, leaned her head against hers. "We've all wondered what it would be like without Sylvia. Even when she was in Nicaragua, we still had her. We could e-mail her anytime, pick up the phone if we wanted to."

Brenda's face twisted. "But if anything happens to her . . ."

"It can't," Cathy cut in. "Nothing is going to happen to her. God wouldn't do that. She's too important to his kingdom. Trust me. He's going to keep her alive."

Brenda turned her sad eyes to Cathy. "Honey, God takes people all the time. Death is a part of life. It's a part that is hard for us to accept, but it is. And sometimes he takes them when they're young, and sometimes he takes them with disease. And sometimes we don't know the reason."

Cathy's eyes flashed. "He's *not* going to take Sylvia, and that's all there is to it. You mark my word. He cherishes her."

"All the more reason to take her home," Brenda whispered.

CHAPTER
Twenty-Two

Harry, sit down," Sylvia said two days later as Harry ran around the room arranging the flowers that had been sent. "You haven't gotten a moment's rest since my surgery. Please sit down. You're wearing me out just watching you."

"Well, what else am I going to do?" Harry asked. "That's what I'm here for."

"You're not here to wait on me hand and foot. You're here to hold my hand. That's all I want from you, Harry."

He came to the bed and leaned over her, took her hand. "You look beautiful, you know."

Sylvia rolled her eyes. "You don't have to appease me with compliments, Harry. Nobody looks beautiful two days after surgery."

"I know. You're an enigma. I'm thinking about writing you up for a medical journal. It's probably a first or something."

A knock sounded on the door and they both turned to it. It cracked open and their daughter, Sarah, stepped inside. "Mom?"

"Sarah!" Sylvia sat up in bed. "Oh, honey." She reached her good arm out for her, and Sarah came to her and gave her a careful hug. "How are you, Mom?"

"I'm great, now that you're here. Where's that baby?"

"They wouldn't let her come up."

Sylvia gasped. "So you left her alone?"

Sarah laughed. "Right. She's fourteen months old, and I left her toddling around in the lobby. What kind of mother do you think I am?"

"Well, where is she then?"

"She's with her daddy, downstairs."

Another knock turned her attention to the door, and her son ducked in.

"Jeff! I didn't think you were coming until tomorrow! Come in! Oh, sweetheart, you didn't have to take off work on a Friday. You could have just come for the weekend."

"Like I'd just go on with things and forget that my mother is laid up in the hospital?" He leaned over and kissed her on the cheek. She recognized the way he avoided looking at her chest. "How you feeling, Mom?"

"Better than I expected." She reached up to hug him, and winced as the incision on her left side pulled.

They both went to their father and hugged him tight and hard. Neither of them had seen him in over a year, not since the baby had been born. Sylvia saw the emotion on his face.

"Okay, that's it. I'm going to get my grandchild," he said. "I need to see her, and your mother needs to see her."

"Oh, can you, Harry?"

"Of course I can. I know people. I can pull strings."

He rushed out, looking for his son-in-law and grandchild.

Sarah watched her father go, then turned her serious face back to her mother. "Are you sure you're all right, Mom? You look a little pale."

Sylvia tried to look shocked. "And your father told me I looked beautiful."

"Pale in a good way," Jeff said. "Like one of those porcelain-looking women in those antique paintings."

"Antique?" Sylvia swung at him. "Give me a break." Again, the incision pulled, but she wouldn't let herself wince.

"So have you heard anything yet?" Sarah asked.

"No, not yet." She took her daughter's hand. "We don't expect any news until tomorrow. But since tomorrow's Saturday, it might have to wait until Monday. Until then, we just assume that the cancer hasn't spread, that they got every bit of it in the surgery, and that I've already been through the worst part of this."

"Okay, Mom," Sarah said, but Sylvia didn't miss the look that passed between her children.

Chapter *Twenty-Three*

Sylvia hated eating in front of an audience, but the next morning as she ate her breakfast, Harry, Sarah, and Jeff watched. Dr. Jefferson came in before she'd even finished her yogurt.

She set her spoon down and stared up at him. His face was somber, and she didn't like it. Harry introduced him to their children, then asked him point-blank, "You have the results?"

"That's right," he said. "Maybe we should talk alone . . ."

Jeff started to get up, but Sarah was more stubborn. She stood her ground, wanting to hear.

"That's okay." Sylvia held out a hand to stop Jeff from leaving. "I want them to stay. You can talk to me in front of them."

With all her heart, she hoped she was doing the right thing. They couldn't be sheltered from this. They were adults, after all. And they needed to know the truth. Keeping it from them would serve no purpose.

"Very well." He pulled up a chair and sat down next to the bed. Harry stood up, jingling the change in his pocket. He didn't even know he was doing it.

Sarah and Jeff didn't move a muscle. They didn't even seem to breathe.

Sylvia was glad she'd taken the time to put on makeup and fix her hair this morning. She didn't want to look sick when the verdict came down.

"Let's go ahead," she said. "Be blunt. I want the truth."

He shifted in his seat and opened her chart, as if seeing the results for the first time. Sylvia knew better. "It turns out that six of your lymph nodes are positive for tumor cells." He said it matter-of-factly, as if it held no particular significance. It was the way surgeons had of cushioning the blow.

She would have expected to start screaming out "no!" She would have pictured herself demanding that he run the tests again. Tears, at least.

Instead, she sat there numbly, staring at his face, wondering if that scar over his lip had happened in childhood, or if it had been recent. Had stitches been involved, or plastic surgery, or just a Band-aid?

Harry cleared his throat, shaking her out of her rambling thoughts. He was beside her now, taking her hand. It felt like ice, though she wasn't sure if it was his or hers that needed warmth.

"Six positive lymph nodes," she repeated. "What does that mean?"

"It just means that the cancer cells have spread. That we have to be a little more aggressive with treatment."

Sarah moaned and covered her face, and Jeff took her hand.

"Let me see the report," Harry said, and the doctor handed it to him.

"The cancer cells are also hormone receptor positive," the doctor went on.

Sylvia's mind groped awkwardly for the information she'd gathered. She had read about the hormone part of this, but for the life of her, she couldn't remember it now. "What does that mean?"

Harry rubbed his eyes and handed the report back to Sam. "They look for a particle of protein on the surface of the cancer cell to see if it's sensitive to estrogen," he said. "If it is, the cell is triggered into growing and dividing when it's stimulated by estrogen. Most women over fifty have that. Isn't that right, Sam?"

"That's right. That means that we'll have to treat it with hormones after the chemotherapy."

"For how long?" Sylvia asked.

"For at least five years, but possibly the rest of your life."

She swallowed, wondering how long that would be.

The doctor explained, "The hormone therapy will keep the hormones from triggering the cells into growing."

"What about the breast tissue?" Harry asked. "Can I see that report?"

The doctor flipped through the file and found the pathologist's report on that. "He determined that her breast tissue is poorly differentiated. No surprise there. The tumor is three centimeters, as we thought."

Harry took the report and studied it. His face was pale, and she felt his hand tightening over hers. He didn't realize how strong he was. Often, when they prayed together, he would hold her hand so tight that it would go numb. He did that now.

"As we told you going in, Sylvia, your cancer cells are very aggressive," Sam said. "That means that our chemo treatment is going to have to be aggressive, too. It's not going to be a picnic."

Sylvia thought of her hair falling out, her eyebrows bare . . .

Tears stung the backs of her eyes, but she told herself she would not cry in front of her children. She wasn't finished teaching them lessons, even in early adulthood. They were learning from watching her. Everything she did, every expression, every word, would be forever etched in their memory.

So she rose to the occasion. "I'm up for it, Sam. Bring it on."

He smiled weakly.

"What do we do next?" Harry asked. The paper in his hand trembled as he handed it back to Sam.

"I'm going to send Sylvia for scans of her head, chest, abdomen, and bones to determine if there's cancer anywhere else in her body. That should give us a good indication of what we're dealing with."

"More tests," Sylvia said. "How long does all this take?"

"We hope to get all the scans done today."

She nodded and looked at her children. Sarah had tears running down her face. Jeff's face was red and as serious as she'd ever seen it.

"When will I be able to start killing this cancer?"

"We can't start chemo until a month from now. We've got to give your body time to heal from the mastectomy."

She didn't like that answer much. "I know the oncologist warned me of that, but it seems like we need to do it sooner. Those cells are dividing and growing."

"It's okay," he said. "Even with aggressive cancer you have time to heal."

She looked at her children again, saw the terror on Sarah's face and the rock hardness on Jeff's.

"All right," she said, "I'm ready for those scans anytime you are."

"We'll schedule them for this afternoon." He closed her file and got up. "My secretary is making you an appointment about two weeks from now with your oncologist, so that you've had a little time to heal and we've gotten all the results back."

He patted Sylvia's hand. "Don't worry. We're going to be walking alongside you in this. We wouldn't mess up for anything, knowing Harry the way we do." He chuckled, and Harry forced a smile.

He started to leave, but Sarah came to her feet. She looked like a child lost at the mall. "Doctor?"

He turned at the door.

"Is my mother going to be all right?"

"We'll know more after the scans," he said. Without offering any more in the way of commitment, he headed down the hall.

CHAPTER
Twenty-Four

By the time Sylvia had finished all her scans, the kids had gone home to give the baby a nap. Sylvia tried to sleep, but the pain in her chest and under her arm was so great that she couldn't relax.

But it wasn't the pain keeping her awake. It was the fear. She'd already had bad news once today. If the scans showed tumors in other organs ... Well, she couldn't even think past that.

Harry had gone to see the film and gather the reports. Once again, she thanked God that he had pull in this hospital, and that she didn't have to wait through another long night.

When he finally came back into her room, his eyes were bright and dancing.

She caught her breath. "Good news?"

"Yes," he said. "The cancer doesn't seem to have spread to any other organs."

"Oh, thank you, God." She brought her hand to her forehead and gave in to the tears that had threatened her all day. "Thank you."

Harry's eyes were wet as he bent over her bed. "You're going to be fine, sweetheart," he said. "What the surgery didn't get, the chemo will."

She reached up and framed his face with her hands. "Oh, Harry. Are they sure?"

"They're sure and I'm sure."

She sat up, slid her feet off the bed. Wiping her eyes, she said, "Okay, then that means I can get on with this. I need to go home, Harry. I need to shop for a prosthesis to wear under my clothes. I need to look for a wig for when my hair falls out. I need to start physical therapy so I can move my arm again. I need to spend time with my grandbaby. I need to get on with things."

"I already talked to Sam about releasing you. He told me you can go home tomorrow."

She got up and pulled Harry into a one-armed hug, and melted against him. "You're going to be all right, sweetie," he whispered again. "You're going to be all right."

But the good news didn't outweigh the bad, and that night, as she tried to sleep one more night in the hospital room, with the bright night-light over her head and nurses coming in and out to take her blood pressure and temperature, she thought about those cancer cells that had already gotten past the filters of her lymph nodes. Where had they gone, and where were they headed? Would they take up residence somewhere in her body before the chemo could nuke them out?

Once again, she kicked herself for thinking this way. There was so much to be grateful for. How could she overlook the blessings of the normal scans and only concentrate on the negative?

But as hard as she tried to banish them, the thoughts wouldn't go away. She almost wished she hadn't insisted that Harry go home tonight. He was exhausted from sleeping on the sofa next to the window, and with Sarah's family and Jeff in the house, he needed to be home.

Besides, she was a big girl, and the uncertainty had passed. She knew where she stood now, what to expect, what would come next. It could be so much worse. People recovered from breast cancer all the time. It was treatable, and she had the best doctors anyone could want.

Yes, she told herself. She had much to be grateful for.

She reached for the Bible that Harry had left on her bed table, and turned to the Psalms. There would be comfort there, she knew. There always was.

She turned to Psalm 42 and began to read. When she reached verse five, she knew the Lord was speaking to her.

Why are you downcast, O my soul?
*   Why so disturbed within me?*
Put your hope in God,
*   for I will yet praise him,*
*   my Savior and my God.*
My soul is downcast within me;
*   therefore I will remember you*
from the land of the Jordan,
*   the heights of Hermon—from Mount Mizar.*
Deep calls to deep
*   in the roar of your waterfalls;*
all your waves and your breakers
*   have swept over me.*
By day the LORD *directs his love,*
*   at night his song is with me—*
*   a prayer to the God of my life.*

She hung on the last words of that passage . . . His song would be with her tonight . . .

Yes, she thought. She should sing that song. She should praise him, even from her despair.

Softly, tentatively, she began to sing about entering his courts with thanksgiving in her heart . . .

She sang it slowly at first, haltingly, in a quiet voice that belied the words of the song. But then her heart lifted, and she sang in a faster rhythm . . . over and over . . . until joy did fill her heart like a prayer.

When she finished the song, she smiled and snuggled under her bedcovers. Yes, that was what she needed, she thought. The words of Psalm 104:33 whispered from her lips. "I will sing to the LORD all my life; I will sing praise to my God as long as I live."

Sweet sleep wrought from the Lord's presence fell over her, and in spite of the light and the cold and the pain and the intrusions, Sylvia slept better than she had in days.

CHAPTER
Twenty-Five

Sylvia was home two weeks when she decided to lead a Bible study of the book of James for the ladies of Cedar Circle. Tory couldn't have been happier. Since Hannah's birth, she'd spent so much time obsessing over the child that she hadn't taken enough time for Bible study.

The late August heat hung heavy over Breezewood, so they met in Sylvia's cool air-conditioned living room.

Tory sat at Sylvia's feet as her friend taught her about "considering it all joy" when you encounter trials. Sylvia was still weak from the surgery, and Tory could see the pain on her face when she moved a certain way. But she seemed to be doing well.

As she taught from James, Tory realized that the choice of books was as much for Sylvia as for them. They had all gone through trials of one kind or another, but Sylvia's was one of the worst of all. Tory couldn't imagine how she had the energy to concentrate when so much uncertainty hung over her.

But the study gave Tory comfort, and she could see that it was helpful to Cathy and Brenda, too. When they ended with prayer, Tory sighed. "You know, the more I learn about the Bible, the more I realize I don't know."

Brenda laughed. "Isn't that the truth? I feel the same way."

Cathy, curled up with her stocking feet beneath her on Sylvia's couch, waved them off. "You guys are way ahead of me. I came into this Christian thing too late."

"Don't be ridiculous," Sylvia said. "It's never too late."

"But I don't know *half* of this stuff."

"Well, you will. We're going to work through it together. It'll keep me going."

"Yeah," Cathy said. "Every time you get discouraged and don't want to teach us, you'll realize what heathens we are and decide that you've got to keep going."

Sylvia laughed. "That wasn't what I meant."

Cathy moaned and dropped her feet. "But it's true. I feel like a downright pagan when I start studying. All these things start coming up that I've never even heard."

Tory laughed. "And the worst part is that you're accountable for the things you know. So in a way, ignorance is bliss, right? If you don't know it, you're not accountable?"

"Hey, you're accountable, all right." Sylvia held her Bible up. "Everything you need to know is right here. You're accountable because all that information is available to you. There's no excuse for having it and not reading it."

"Ouch," Tory said. "You can be so brutal."

Sylvia's laughter lilted through Tory's heart. It was music.

Sylvia led them into her kitchen where she'd baked a cake earlier that day. They cut it and took their saucers to the table. "So, Tory, what have you decided about the job?"

Tory shrugged. "I haven't decided yet. But I do need to let Mary Ann know by the end of the week. She's got to hire someone else if I don't take it." Never one to eat much of anything with calories, Tory picked at her cake. "I just feel like I need to stay at home with Hannah. I don't like the idea of putting her in a nursery."

"But it's not just any nursery," Sylvia said. "It's a nursery that challenges her and helps her grow. She needs that, Tory. I wouldn't feel guilty about it at all."

Cathy dug into her cake with gusto. "And think of the benefits to you, getting to work with the older kids. You'll have so much hope about what Hannah is going to do eventually. I think Mary Ann sounds like a genius. You were the perfect choice for that."

Tory cut the icing off and took a small bite of cake. "The truth is, I'd really like to do it. And Barry wants me to."

"Then what are you waiting for?" Brenda's question sounded so reasonable. "I don't even know what's making you hesitate."

Tory smiled. "Do you really think I should?"

"Of course I do," Brenda said. "What's the downside?"

"Well, I wouldn't have as much time for Bible study with you guys. If I have Hannah in the nursery in the morning, I don't want to leave her again at night."

Sylvia wasn't satisfied. "You'll only be working Tuesdays and Thursdays. This is Monday. It's doable, Tory."

Tory considered the passion on Sylvia's face. She needed this study to get her mind focused for her upcoming chemo, and Tory needed it to have the strength to go on with her mothering of Hannah. "I'll probably take the job," she said. "And I'll try to keep up with the study. But the homework you're giving us is pretty substantial, and I'm not sure how much time I'll have to do it. There are some pretty complicated concepts in James."

"Well, you can't let the complicated concepts make you forget that the salvation message is very simple," Sylvia said. "'Believe in the Lord Jesus Christ and you will be saved.' That's all there is to it."

"But there's so much more," Tory said. "We know that works can't save you. Only faith can. But then James says that faith without works is dead. So there's more than just 'believe on the Lord.'"

"There's not more to salvation," Sylvia said. "Just to growth and sanctification."

"Holiness," Cathy said, pointing her fork at Tory. "Now that's the hard part."

"It is hard," Sylvia said, "but when we stay in the Word we can figure out how to be holy. And the great thing is that it's not our holiness that we need, but Christ working in us."

"Amen," Tory agreed.

That night, with her decision made and the Bible still fresh in her heart, Tory snuggled up to Barry.

"I think Sylvia's going to be all right," she said. "She's already back to herself. She's visiting the oncologist tomorrow but she doesn't even seem to dread it."

"I think she'll be all right, too," Barry said.

"And I'm looking forward to my job. I guess I'll start Tuesday."

He kissed her. "I'm excited for you. I think it will be good for you to think about someone other than Hannah for a change."

CHAPTER
Twenty-Six

Harry went with Sylvia to her first post-surgery visit with the oncologist the next day. They sat across his desk, a stack of books and articles on the table next to them.

"What's her chance of recurrence?" Harry asked.

Martin Thibodeaux, the oncologist, drew in a deep breath and thought for a moment. "I'd say fifty percent."

Sylvia gasped. "Fifty percent? I thought my chances were better than that!"

He shook his head. "We'll fight the recurrences if and when they come, Sylvia. But the number of lymph nodes involved raises the stakes."

She felt herself wilting in her chair. Harry's hand closed over hers.

"I'm recommending six months of chemo," the doctor said, "with treatments every three weeks."

"Which chemo?" Harry asked.

The doctor told him the name of the drugs they'd be using.

Sylvia saw by the look on Harry's face that the choice didn't please him. "What is it?" she asked.

"It's a really harsh chemo." The lines of his face deepened. He looked as if he'd aged ten years in the last few days, despite his attempt to keep her positive.

"We need to be harsh," the doctor told her. "Like you've already been told, it's a very aggressive cancer."

Sylvia closed her eyes. "I don't even feel sick. I feel like I've had surgery, but I don't feel like I have cancer. Not the kind that needs the big guns."

"Just keep in mind that we're only doing it for six months. And then because we had six positive lymph nodes, I recommend radiation to begin six weeks after the chemo has ended and the hormone therapy has begun."

Sylvia felt as if facts flew around her head like debris in a tornado, threatening to crash her skull if she didn't duck at the right time. "Harry, I'll never remember all this," she said. "I hope you're getting it."

"I am." She realized that Harry's knowledge of what she was about to embark on made it even more stressful for him than her. Maybe it was good that she didn't know all the horror stories that he knew.

"So when does she go for her first treatment, Martin?" he asked.

"Two weeks. I'm going to go ahead and set up her appointment. She should have healed well enough by then."

The doctor handed her one of the books off of his stack. "I want you to be sure and read this before you come. The first chemo treatment probably won't be quite as bad as you've read. But the effects will accumulate with each treatment. Your hair probably will fall out. And you probably will have a hard time tolerating the drugs. You'll probably have nausea. You might get sores in your mouth. You might get headaches. You'll probably feel pretty rough for a week after each treatment, then you'll have a couple of weeks to get your energy and your blood count back before we do it again."

Sylvia just stared at him and wondered if she was really ready for this. What if she just let it go? Took her chances? Left the chemo to those who could handle it?

"Honey, are you all right?" Harry was stroking her hand, watching her face.

"I just don't know . . . if I'm up to this . . ."

"You are." He put his arm around her shoulder and pulled her close. "Honey, you are. You're strong and brave, and you can do this."

Her mind reeled through pictures of herself pale and sick and bald, sitting on the bathroom floor waiting for the nausea to move her again. Funny how the very drugs that were supposed to make her live would make her sicker than she'd ever been in her life.

But it was the provision God had given her, and somehow, she had to search her soul and find gratitude for that.

Chapter Twenty-Seven

When Tory, Cathy, and Brenda came over that night to hear what the oncologist had said, Sylvia tried to put on a happy face again.

"I was just thinking about my hair," she said. "Since it's going to fall out, I'm ready to shop for a wig."

The girls were silent, just watching her, and she knew they were on the brink of tears.

"I want you all to come with me Saturday," she said. "There's a wig store in Chattanooga that specializes in wigs for people with cancer. I want you guys to come with me and help me pick one out. I don't want to look like a hag while I'm retching my guts out."

No one laughed.

Brenda touched her arm. "Sylvia, are you sure you don't want to do this alone?"

"I'm absolutely sure," she said, "and Harry's no help. He'll just tell me everything looks great. I want some serious help on this. I know you three will tell me the truth. Besides, it'll be fun. We can go first thing in the morning, then stop for lunch on the way back. It'll be a girl trip. We've never had one of those."

Cathy smiled. "Count me in."

"Me, too," Brenda said.

Tory had to think a little longer. "If Barry can keep Hannah, I'll come," she said. "I would sure hate to miss a day with my three best friends."

"Come on," Sylvia said. "When's the last time you went hair shopping? It's the chance of a lifetime."

That Saturday, they all gathered for breakfast at Sylvia's, then took the short drive to Chattanooga, chattering all the way about anything but cancer. But as they went into the store with wigged Styrofoam busts on shelves around the walls, they all grew quiet.

Sylvia was first to break the silence. "It's a little creepy, isn't it?"

Cathy began to laugh. "It's just hair."

A plump woman popped out of the back, wearing a hot pink crepe dress and a black Cher wig. "Hi, girls! I'm Trendy. Are you looking for wigs?"

Sylvia tried to keep a straight face at the name. "Hi, Trendy. Actually, I am. I'm starting chemo in a couple of weeks, and I'd like to be ready."

"Of *course* you would." Trendy had a little-girl voice that lilted with enthusiasm. "And you'll be so glad that you took care of this before you started it. Trust me. After the hair falls out, most women get desperate and hit that wig store at the mall— you know, the one with all that synthetic hair? And they put it on their bald little heads and, besides having a perpetual bad hair day, they might as well have 'I have cancer' written across their foreheads, because it's obvious they're wearing a wig, because real hair doesn't really look like that. Our hair is one hundred percent real, and it *looks* real. You'll love it."

She led Sylvia to a dressing room with mirrors all around, and sat Sylvia down at the dressing table. She pulled chairs up close for Tory, Cathy, and Brenda.

"So, is your color out of a box, or are you one of those lucky gals who never grays?"

"Box." Sylvia glanced with amusement at her friends' reflections in the mirror. "Definitely a box."

"Great. Then we can use the same color to dye the wig you choose. That is, if we don't have the style you like in your color." She stood behind Sylvia, looking at her in the mirror. "Now do you want to keep this style, or do something different?"

Sylvia sighed. "Well . . . I'd kind of like to look like myself. But then again, it might be fun to have something different. Maybe one of those new styles that's bigger on the top and thin around the neck."

"Oh, honey, we have those. I'll bring a few of each."

"Or . . . maybe I could go longer. I've never been able to let my hair grow out. Maybe I could have a big head of hair. You know, the kind that hangs down around the elbow. Maybe like yours."

Trendy snatched her wig off of her head, revealing a short cropped pixie underneath. Cathy howled with laughter and fell against Tory. "Here, try this while I gather up several more choices."

Sylvia looked horrified. "I didn't mean to take the hair off your head!"

Trendy waved her off. "Oh, honey, I have plenty more. I was itching to pull a Nicole Kidman today, anyway."

Sylvia's eyebrows popped up. "Nicole Kidman? Red and curly? I might like to try that, too!"

Brenda's mouth fell open. "Sylvia, you really want to go red and curly?"

Sylvia thrust her chin out. "Maybe."

"Bring one of those," Cathy called. "And do you have a Meg Ryan like she was in *Sleepless in Seattle*?"

"Do I ever!" Trendy said.

Tory and Brenda leaned into each other, giggling. "Sylvia, you're crazy."

Sylvia winked at them in the mirror. "Hey, it doesn't hurt to try them."

Trendy spun around, her dress flowing behind her. "You girls come try some, too. You never know when you might need them. And it's the only surefire way not to have a bad hair day, ever. You may just want to take one home your own self."

The girls scooted their chairs closer to the table as they caught the dream. "I want to be a blonde," Tory said. "Marilyn Monroe."

Brenda ran her fingers through her hair. "I've always wondered how I'd look with short hair. One of those new styles, maybe, that flips up?"

"Got it," Trendy said. "And what about you?" She looked at Cathy.

Cathy thought for a moment. "Got any dreadlocks? I've always wondered how I'd look in dreadlocks."

Sylvia loved it. She laughed hard and loud, and the others joined in.

"I can't believe we're trying this stuff on," Tory said. "It's not like we'd buy it in a million years."

"Really?" Sylvia feigned disappointment. "Didn't you hear about the little boy who had chemotherapy and his hair fell out and everybody in his classroom shaved their heads so that he wouldn't feel bad about the way he looked?"

Cathy narrowed her eyes. "You're not expecting us to shave our heads, are you?"

"You mean you're not willing to? Not even for me?"

Tory couldn't hold her giggles back. "Sorry, Sylvia. I love you, but not that much."

Cathy cleared her throat. "See, I have to keep hair so the animals at my clinic won't get scared of me. Plus there's that pesky law that vets have to have hair."

"Oh, yeah," Sylvia said. "I've heard of that law." She looked at Brenda. "Et tu, Brenda?"

Brenda wiggled her shoulders. "I'll shave. But I don't want a wig. I just want a tattoo of a butterfly right on top."

The four of them screamed at the image.

"Oh, forget it," Sylvia said finally. "I can't have that much change in my life. Just try on the wigs, but keep your own hair."

Within moments the saleslady had come back with about twenty wigs on Styrofoam stands. The women set about putting them on their heads and making fun of each other in the mirror. Sylvia had brought a camera, just to help her remember what she'd bought if she couldn't bring it home today.

She got a shot of Tory in a blonde Marilyn Monroe, Cathy in her Jamaican dreadlocks, Brenda in a short cropped wig.

By the time they had gotten the silliness out of their system and chosen a serious wig for Sylvia, three hours had passed. She'd finally picked a style that was more modern than her own hairstyle. It was blonde now, but she would leave it for Trendy to dye to match her color. This wouldn't be so bad, she thought. She would look younger and perkier as she suffered through her chemo. Already she felt better about herself as she and her friends headed out to have lunch.

CHAPTER
Twenty-Eight

The morning Tory was to start her new job, she set her alarm for 6:00. Waking up wasn't a problem, since she hadn't really slept much at all. She had lain in bed listening to the rhythm of Barry's breathing and wondering if she was doing the right thing by taking Hannah to the nursery for several hours at a time. Of all the people in Breezewood, she trusted the lady who would be caring for Hannah. But she still worried.

She'd be right down the hall. If Hannah got upset or sick or hurt herself, Tory would be just feet away. It wasn't as if she was leaving her at all. And she needed this.

Despite her trepidation, she'd been a little excited about working with the older children who had the same affliction as Hannah. She wanted to hear how clearly they could speak. She wanted to see what concepts they could grasp, how much they could learn, whether they had skills of reason and logic.

"Why are you up so early?" Barry's sleepy voice sounded slightly irritated.

"I'm sorry," she whispered. "I didn't mean to wake you up. I just have to get ready for work."

"You don't have to be there till nine."

"Yeah, but I thought I'd run a couple of miles first, read my Bible, do a couple of loads of laundry, make the kids a good breakfast . . ."

"Tory, are you gonna do this every day?"

"Nope. Just the days I work. I refuse to neglect my family for an outside job."

Barry sat up and turned on the lamp. "You're not neglecting your family, honey. Brittany and Spencer will be at school. They'll never even know you're gone. And you can do the laundry on your off days."

She slipped on her shorts and sat down on the bed to pull on her running shoes. "I just want to start out right."

"You'll be exhausted by the time you get there."

"Don't worry about me." She came around the bed and kissed him, then turned the lamp back off. "Go back to sleep. Your alarm doesn't go off for another hour."

He pulled the covers up over him again and settled back on his pillow.

Tory scurried out of the room.

She went to the laundry room and started a load, then hit the floor and began her stretching.

When she was finally warmed up enough to run, she took off out the door. The dark morning air was full of dew, but summer still hung on, making it warm. She left the cul-de-sac and headed down the mountain road, easily making the distance she had marked off so long ago. She ran hard and fast, and when she reached the one-mile point, turned around and headed back uphill.

The run back was more punishing than the first half had been, but it was important to her to stay fit and slim. She couldn't stand the thought of getting plump and lumpy. It wasn't vanity. It really wasn't. She just expected more of herself, had a higher standard than most. She wanted to be her best.

By the time she got back home, it was 7:00, and she was soaked with perspiration. Barry had already gotten up and had put in a second load of laundry. Scrambled eggs and bacon fried on the stove.

"You're cooking," she said with a grin.

He nodded. "Not the kind of thing you eat, but the kids'll like it."

She kissed him. "I promise not to wake you so early every time I work."

"It's okay. You're nervous."

She got a towel out of the laundry room and wiped her face. "Am I? You think this is nerves?"

"I know it is."

She leaned against the doorway. "So why am I nervous?"

"Because you're not sure you're doing the right thing."

She smiled. He knew her too well. "Am I?"

"Yes." He grabbed the waistband of her shorts and pulled her close, until her nose touched his. "You're doing the right thing, Tory. I want you to say that fifty times while you're in the shower."

She grinned and brought her sweaty arms around his neck. "If you say so."

"I do. And you'll see."

She felt better as she got into the shower. Barry was on her side, Brittany and Spencer wouldn't know the difference, and Hannah . . .

She heard Hannah crying as she woke up, and Barry called out, "I've got her!"

As the warm shower rained down on her, soothing her jitters, she smiled. It was going to be okay.

Class was already going full tilt when Tory finally left Hannah in the nursery and went to her classroom. The children, age six to nine, all with Down's Syndrome, sat at a table, already hard at work. Their teacher, a woman named Linda Shelton, sat with them as they shaped Play-Doh blobs into things only they could identify.

"Hi, Miss Tory," the teacher called out in a singsong voice as Tory came into the room. "Children, say hi to Miss Tory."

The children looked over at her while still molding their Play-Doh and muttered things that sounded a little like "good morning."

"Good morning, boys and girls." She wondered if Linda called them "boys and girls," or if they even knew that they were boys and girls.

Then she told herself to stop obsessing. These children were forgiving. If she made a teacher faux pas, they probably wouldn't notice.

She pulled a chair up to the table and sat down. Ten children sat around two tables. Two of them sat in wheelchairs, and three others had braces on their legs.

But the other five she had often seen running down the hallway on their way to lunch or recess.

"Thank goodness for your help," Linda said. "We'll get so much more done with you here. And frankly, I was thrilled when Mary Ann told me you're a Christian. It's not a requirement for working here, you know. But I love the fact that most of the teachers here are. And I like for the kids to have that kind of influence. Some of their parents aren't believers. But they really need Christ, I think. Don't you?"

"Of course," Tory said. "But I didn't think we could talk about Christ in the classroom."

"Sure we can," Linda said. "This is a private school. And even though it isn't a Christian school, the people who run it are believers, too. So they're just fine with our passing our faith on to our precious children."

Tory looked at the children working so hard on their blobs, and wondered if they even had the capacity for faith, but she didn't say so. It seemed to make Linda feel better to think she had an impact. And who was she to say Linda didn't?

The little boy next to her tore off a glob of Play-Doh and thrust it at her. "Thank you," she said. She looked at the teacher. "What's his name?"

"Ask him," Linda said. "He'll tell you."

She asked him his name, and the boy said, "My name Bo."

"What are you making, Bo?"

"Haws."

"A horse?" she asked, delighted that she'd understood.

"I make a ball," one of the other ones said, and she oohed and aahed over the ball. A couple of the others muttered things that she could not understand, but the teacher managed to translate as she helped them work on their Play-Doh creations.

Already, she tried to picture Hannah sitting at this very table in this very room hammering on a piece of Play-Doh and explaining what her vision for it was. Would she be one of those in the wheelchairs or have braces on her legs, or would she walk and talk like Bo? Tory didn't know, but just being here gave her peace that she hadn't had before. Sylvia and Barry had been right. She was glad she had taken the job.

CHAPTER
Twenty-Nine

Sylvia grew more serious as the day of her first chemotherapy treatment approached in the second week of September. She'd been warned that the treatment would be given intravenously and could take three hours.

When the day came she packed a couple of novels, her Bible, and some magazines, and Harry drove her to the Cancer Center.

The place looked different than she'd expected. Decorated in warm shades of green, with accent lighting in strategic places around the room, it looked more like someone's living room than a sterile hospital room. Recliner-like vinyl chairs were spaced about three feet apart in the large room, and soft classical music piped through the sound system.

Several other cancer patients occupied those chairs, their own medication dripping into their veins. A couple had on Walkmans, and leaned back with their faces pale and sunken eyes closed. Would she look like that a few months from now?

The nurse led her to a chair next to a woman who stared in front of her with dull, lifeless eyes. The woman's hair had already begun falling out, and thin, lifeless wisps hung into her face. She had a yellow cast to her skin, and dark circles hung under her eyes.

Sylvia tried to get comfortable as the nurse drew blood to check her count. When she disappeared to take it to the lab, Sylvia shivered, and wondered why they kept it so cold in here. She didn't know what it was about doctor's offices, but it seemed that the moment she stepped over the threshold, her circulation cut off, and her extremities flirted with frostbite.

The nurse returned with her IV pole. Sylvia trembled as they inserted the IV needle into her arm and began the drip of the poisonous fluid that would kill the cancerous cells in her body. She looked over at the woman next to her and saw that her eyes were closed. She wasn't asleep, though, for she had a frown on her face. Sylvia could see that she was already beginning to get sick. Sylvia reached over and took the woman's hand. Her eyes flew open.

"Are you okay?" Sylvia asked.

"No," the woman said. "I hate this. It's going to kill me."

Compassion welled up in Sylvia's heart. "No, it's not. It's going to save your life." She smiled. "My name's Sylvia."

The woman's frown melted. "I'm Priscilla."

"Hi, Priscilla. How many treatments have you had?"

"Three before this one." The woman glanced at her hair. "Is this your first?"

Sylvia nodded. "I'm very nervous."

The woman let go of Sylvia's hand and touched her balding head. "I would have worn my wig, but my skin feels so irritated during the treatments ..."

Sylvia swallowed. Would she have three whole treatments before her hair started falling out? "It's cold in here," Sylvia said.

"They'll bring you a blanket if you need it. I don't. This stuff has brought on early menopause for me, and I seem to live in a perpetual hot flash."

Sylvia had been taking hormone replacement therapy since her own menopause, but the doctors had taken her off of it after they detected the breast cancer. She'd struggled with those symptoms herself, and Harry had warned her that they would likely get worse.

She looked at Priscilla. The woman was probably in her early forties. "What kind of cancer do you have?"

The woman sighed. "Breast, but it's metastasized to my lungs. You?"

"Breast, too."

Priscilla shook her head. "I have three kids. I have to beat this. But cancer can make you feel out of control. All my efforts still might not work."

"God's in control," Sylvia said.

Priscilla started to cry then, as if she wished that were true but didn't quite believe it.

Sylvia's head was starting to hurt, so she laid it back against the seat. Her stomach churned, and a nauseous feeling seeped through her. *Focus*, she told herself. *Think about something else.*

Slowly, she started to sing. "Jesus, Jesus, Jesus ... sweetest name I know ..."

Priscilla looked over at her.

"Do you know the song?" Sylvia asked.

"Yes."

"Sing with me," she said. "Come on. It'll get your mind off of it."

Sylvia started to sing again, and finally her new friend joined in with a weak, raspy voice. Sylvia watched the woman's countenance lift.

Priscilla's treatment ended an hour before Sylvia's. By the time her new friend was gone, Sylvia needed all her energy to get through her last hour.

When it ended, she found that she wasn't as ill as she'd expected. Headachy and queasy, she checked with the appointment nurse to see when the woman's next treatment was and scheduled hers at the same time. Maybe they could help each other again, she thought. Then she returned to Harry, who'd waited patiently in the waiting room.

He sprang up the moment he saw her. "How are you, honey?"

"Better than I expected," she said. "Just a little headachy, but that's all."

He took her shoulders and looked into her eyes. "Are you sure you're not feeling sick? You have this way of putting on a happy face for everybody, but I don't want you putting one on for me."

"You don't think I can hide it, do you? I mean if I start throwing up, I can't very well pretend that I didn't. And don't start wishing bad symptoms on me, Harry. When I say I'm okay, believe me."

As they drove home, she felt the fatigue seeping into her bones. She needed a nap, she thought, but that was all. She had much to be thankful for. But she didn't delude herself into thinking that it wasn't going to get worse. She knew that the next treatment might not be so mild.

CHAPTER Thirty

The second chemotherapy treatment seemed to have come too soon. Three weeks had passed way too quickly. Priscilla looked pleased to see her.

"My new friend," she exclaimed as Sylvia got comfortable in the seat next to her. "God is good for sending you to help me through this."

But it was Sylvia who needed help this time, and as her head began to ache and she began to feel that desperate, nauseous sense rising up into her throat, Priscilla started to sing. Sylvia joined in and tried to concentrate on the words and the concepts therein, praising the Lord and keeping her eyes on him as she grew sicker and fainter. By the time they got the needle out of her arm she was retching into the bowl they had brought her.

Harry had to walk her out to the car and into the house. She lay in bed curled up in a fetal position for the next few days, concentrating on feeling better.

The neighbors brought food that she couldn't eat. Friends brought books on alternative treatments, information they got from web sites, tapes on positive thinking, and diets that helped fight cancer.

Strangers she couldn't place for the life of her called her to see how she was doing. She didn't feel like talking to any of them, but on the rare occasion that she answered the phone, she felt as if they were only looking for gossip.

"That's not true," Harry said when she voiced that to him one day. "They just want to know how to pray for you and offer their support."

"Some of them, maybe," Sylvia said, "but people I've never talked to on the phone are calling, people who hardly even speak to me at church. People who didn't even realize we'd been gone to Nicaragua. It's like I'm a celebrity now, and people want to get to know me. Where were they when we were trying so desperately to raise money for our mission work?"

Harry didn't argue, but part of her knew that her attitude wasn't very charitable. People did, indeed, care. She just didn't have the energy to deal with them.

She began to feel better the next week and her sweeter nature crept back in ... as her hair began to fall out. When she woke in the mornings, strands lay on her pillow. She found it sticking to her clothes, collecting on her furniture, gathering on her carpet.

"I feel like a dog that's shedding," she told Harry. "I think it's time to bite the bullet and shave my head."

Harry looked stricken. "You're not going to do that, are you? Not really!"

"Why not?" She ran her hand through her hair and pulled out a wad. "Look at this. By the end of the week it'll all be gone, anyway. If I shave I'll at least feel like I have some control. And I won't have to vacuum six times a day to get it all up. Then I can start wearing my wig and stop obsessing over my baldness."

She called Cathy as soon as she saw her car home from work. "I need you to come over with your grooming shears," she said.

Cathy laughed. "For what? You don't have a dog."

"I want you to shave my head."

There was silence for a moment. Then Cathy said, "Oh, Sylvia!"

"Don't sound so shocked. My hair's falling out so fast that one good tug would just about do the trick. I have to do something. I'd rather just get it all over with."

"Sylvia, I've never shaved a human head before."

"I promise to be a lot more compliant than your usual subjects. Oh, and call Brenda and Tory. We might as well make a party of it. And tell them to bring a camera. I'm making a survivor scrapbook, and I want a picture of this. Someday when I'm well I'll look back and remember how far I've come."

Cathy hesitated a moment. Then, in a voice packed with amusement, she asked, "This isn't a trick, is it? You're not going to shame us into shaving our heads, too, are you?"

Sylvia laughed hard. "That, my dear, is up to you. Just get over here, and let's get this show on the road."

By general consensus, the three decided again not to shave their own heads for Sylvia.

"There are other ways to support you, Sylvia," Tory said as she bounced Hannah on her lap. "I'll walk ten miles in a walkathon to raise money for cancer research. I'll bring you food. I'll take you for your treatments. But I will not shave my head."

Sylvia gave her a look of mock disgust. "Some friend you are."

The shears over her head began to buzz. She swallowed hard and clutched the arms of her chair.

Brenda sat on the porch swing, her hand gripped around the chain from which it hung. "Sure you want to do this?"

"Absolutely." Sylvia looked back over her shoulder. Cathy stood there, holding the buzzing shears and staring down at her hair.

"Oh, Cathy. Don't look so nervous. You can't mess this up!"

Cathy tried to smile. "Okay. But you won't hate me for this, will you?"

"Of course not."

Sylvia turned back around. The buzz moved closer to her head. Cathy lifted the hair at her neck . . . and began to mow through.

Brenda covered her eyes. "I can't look."

"You have to," Sylvia said. "I want you to take pictures. Cathy, give me a mohawk before you shave it all off."

Tory screamed. "A mohawk? Sylvia!"

"Just for a minute," Sylvia said. "For one picture. I'll send it to my kids. Heaven knows they need a good laugh."

Sylvia held her breath as Cathy buzzed off one row after another. She watched as the breeze blew it off across the yard.

"The birds'll love it," she said. "It'll cozy up their nests."

A strand blew past Hannah, and the baby laughed. But Tory's face was red as she stared at Sylvia.

"Okay," Cathy said. "Just let me lengthen the clip so the mohawk will stand up." She buzzed again.

"Oh my gosh," Brenda shouted.

"It's you," Tory said. "Quick, take a picture!"

Sylvia struck a pose and Brenda snapped the picture. Cathy handed her the mirror.

A demented stranger stared back at her, and she howled out her laughter.

When the laughter had settled, she sat back down. "Okay. Finish it off."

Cathy cut off the last row of Sylvia's hair, then buzzed around her head trying to find places she had missed.

"There," she said in a quiet voice. "It's all done." Brenda and Tory's faces grew more serious as Cathy handed her the mirror.

Sylvia raised it and looked at her reflection. The sight startled her, jolting her heart. She looked . . . awful. Not stylish or trendy . . . not even particularly brave. Just sick and pale and bald.

She tried to think of something funny to say, but nothing came to mind. It didn't seem that funny anymore.

"So that's what my head looks like. I've always wondered what it was shaped like. You know all those times when you see *Star Trek* and see those bald-headed women with the perfectly shaped heads? I always had a feeling that mine was probably egg-shaped and lumpy."

"It's not." Tory's voice was weak.

Sylvia kept staring into the mirror. "No, it's not, is it? I should have done this years ago."

Brenda laughed again, but it was a forced, strained laugh, and it didn't fool Sylvia. She stared at the shape of her head and at the soft, smooth, peach-fuzzy feel of the buzz cut.

"Put the wig on," Brenda said softly. "You haven't tried it without a mane of hair underneath."

But Sylvia couldn't speak. She felt the tears rising up in her throat, her voice getting tight. "Why do I feel such shame?" she asked. "It doesn't even make sense."

"Shame?" Cathy asked, coming around to face her. "Honey, what are you ashamed of?"

"I don't know. I guess it's just that I *look* like I have cancer now. It announces it."

Tory got up. "Where's the wig, Sylvia?"

"On that Styrofoam head in my bedroom."

Tory headed in. "I'm going to get it."

She came back a few moments later sporting the wig they had spent so much time choosing. Still serving as the designated hairdresser, Cathy put it on Sylvia, straightened it, finger-combed her hair. Sylvia raised the mirror and examined herself.

"Not too bad, is it?" she asked.

"Sylvia, it looks beautiful," Brenda said. "When your hair grows back, I think you should style it like this."

Sylvia's tears backed out of her eyes, and her throat relaxed. "I do like it. It's just hard to get used to."

"Pretend you just had a makeover," Brenda said.

"And think of the bright side," Cathy added. "No more hair drying, no more rollers."

Tory shifted Hannah. "Like Trendy said, no more bad hair days."

"No more dandruff," Cathy added. "Or can you get dandruff when you're bald?"

"You wouldn't think so," Sylvia said, "since you can put lotion on your scalp. That's a good thing."

"Think how much less time it'll take you to get ready in the mornings," Brenda said.

Sylvia sighed. "Okay, Brenda. Take a picture of the alien Sylvia." She pulled off the wig.

Brenda held the camera up to her eye. Sylvia smiled, showing all her teeth, as Cathy snapped the picture.

"Now on with the wig." She pulled it back on, straightened it with her fingers, then posed up at Brenda. "Not bad for a sick woman, huh?"

"Not bad," Brenda said. "Sylvia, I think you look even better than before."

"See? Chemo becomes me."

The others laughed, but she knew that it was hard for them. Once again, tears threatened the backs of her eyes and hung in her throat. But the wig really did look good. Things could be so much worse.

She suspected they soon would be.

CHAPTER
Thirty-One

The image of Sylvia's shaven head, and the pale yellowish color of her skin, implanted itself in Brenda's mind. She remembered seeing Joseph looking that way, weak and shaky and not quite right. The knot that seemed to tighten in her chest every time she saw her dearest friend had grown bigger today.

Instead of going into her house, she went out to the swing David had hung on a tree on their back lawn, and looked out at the trees that lined their yard. She hadn't wanted to cry in front of Sylvia, not loud and hard like she'd needed to. Now she let the tears come.

She prayed for Sylvia, that the chemo was doing its job, that there wouldn't be any trace of cancer left in her body. She prayed that her friend wouldn't have to suffer or grow weaker before her eyes. She prayed that Sylvia would have the strength she needed to get through this.

"You all right?"

She looked over her shoulder and saw David. She wondered how long he had been watching her. "Yeah, I'm fine. Just a little down."

He grabbed a lawn chair and set it in front of her. Sitting down, he looked into her eyes. "Bad time with Sylvia?"

"No, actually, it was a good time. She made Cathy give her a mohawk. You should have seen it." She laughed, but more tears rolled down her face. Finally, she gave in to the tears and let them twist her face. "Oh, David."

He slid his arms around her and held her, and she wept against his shoulder. "You're really scared, aren't you?"

"Not scared, so much," she said. "Just upset that she has to suffer."

"Is she really suffering already?"

She thought about that, and realized that she wasn't. Not yet. "She just looks weak and pale. And her hair . . ."

"If she's okay about her hair, then you should be."

"That's just it," she said. "I don't think she is okay. She's just so . . . Sylvia. Putting on a happy face. Trying to make everybody think she's just having fun. But she shaved her head today, David, because the chemo was making it fall out. She shaved her head!"

She wilted against him again, and he held her quietly. She was thankful that he didn't accuse her of overreacting. She hadn't expected to feel like this. She wondered if Cathy and Tory were crying somewhere, too.

Finally, she got up, and David walked her into the house. He was gentle with her for the rest of the day, helping with the kids and the house and the laundry, as if she was the one with cancer, and not her friend.

But she couldn't get the sight of Sylvia's bald head out of her mind.

CHAPTER
Thirty-Two

Sylvia stood in front of the mirror Sunday morning a week and a half after her second treatment, trying to adjust the prosthesis so that she wouldn't look lopsided or call attention to what wasn't there. Her incision was still a little sore, but it was worth the discomfort to look normal.

When she was satisfied that it looked fine, she adjusted her wig. She had ventured out a few times since she'd started wearing it, and the few people who had seen her commented on her new haircut and how good it looked. She wasn't sure if they were being kind, or if they really meant it. She'd rather they didn't mention it at all.

"You sure you want to go to church?" Harry asked.

"I'm sure," she said. "I need to worship. I can't hide forever."

He came up behind her and slid his arms around her. "You've never needed to hide. You're still the best-looking dame in the joint."

Sylvia found herself sitting in the service next to a pleasant young man in his early twenties. He looked like a soap opera star, with dark hair and brown eyes behind a pair of intelligent wire-framed glasses. Just the kind of young man Annie would like. He greeted her politely during the greeting time, and she made note of his name, Josh Haverty, and learned that he was a medical student. With delight, she realized he was the son of a couple she'd known for years.

From time to time throughout the sermon, she glanced to her side. Josh kept his Bible open and took copious notes.

As they started out of the sanctuary, Sylvia nudged Harry. "That young man is perfect for Annie. He's George and Sally Haverty's son. I've got to come up with a scheme to get them together."

"Sylvia, no matchmaking," he said. "Come on. You've got better things to do. Besides, Annie probably already knows him from youth group."

"I doubt it. He told me he'd been away at Vanderbilt for the last four years. But he's going to medical school here. I love Annie, and I want to make sure she marries well. Introducing them is the least I can do for her."

"Let Cathy worry about marrying Annie off."

"Well, I'll sure let her in on it. But can't you just see the two of them together? I was thinking we could have a get-together, invite both of them, and see what happens."

Harry rolled his eyes. "Sylvia, you're not up for a get-together."

"Yes, I am," she said. "You just watch."

The weekend before her third chemo treatment Sylvia had a dinner party. She invited Annie, Cathy and Steve, Tory and Barry, Brenda and David, and Josh and his parents. The young man came into the house completely oblivious to the fact that the whole thing had been arranged for this meeting between him and Annie, but she noticed the amused, accusing look in Annie's eyes as the fact dawned on her.

"Miss Sylvia, tell me you didn't," she whispered in the kitchen.

"Didn't what? Honey, would you grab that tray of hors d'oeuvres?"

Annie grabbed the tray. "You had this party to set me up with that guy!"

"Who?" Sylvia asked. "Oh, Josh? He *is* close to your age, isn't he?"

Annie popped one of the hors d'oeuvres into her mouth. "You are incorrigible."

"But isn't he cute? He's a med student. And he's very polite, and he took notes like a madman during church last week."

Annie's mouth fell open. "That's why you picked him for me? Because he took notes in church?"

"No, because he seems like a godly young man. The kind you deserve. Just give him a chance, Annie."

Annie groaned, but Sylvia knew she wasn't mad. "What if *he* doesn't like *me*?"

Sylvia put on a shocked face. "Well, that's the silliest thing I've ever heard. Why on earth wouldn't he like you?"

Annie grabbed a napkin and dabbed at her mouth. "You're good for a person's ego, you know that? Do I still have lipstick on?"

"Yes, you look lovely. Now get out there and talk to him."

Sylvia watched Annie walk around with the tray, offering hors d'oeuvres to everyone in attendance. She saved the young man for last, then stood talking to him in the corner as the conversation went on around her.

Sylvia brought the tangy citrus drinks out and passed them around, and tried to listen in to Cathy's conversation.

"So we figure the first step is helping Mark learn to drive, so he can get his license," Cathy was saying. "But I have to tell you that I dread it with all my heart. Remember what happened when Brenda was teaching Daniel to drive?"

"Oh, yeah," David said. "He wrecked our van and my parked truck the first time he pulled into the driveway."

Brenda started to laugh. "Not one of our better moments. Cathy, you could hire one of those private teachers to come and teach him."

"We thought of that," Steve said, "but Mark balked. Said he didn't want to sit in the car with some stranger yelling at him."

"I'd rather be beaten than teach my strongest-willed child how to drive," Cathy said.

"Well, let me teach him," Harry said.

Everyone looked at Harry.

"Well, don't look so shocked," he said. "I taught Rick how to drive, didn't I?"

"Well, yes, but that was a while ago. Mark's got a little more edge."

"I can handle Mark," Harry said. "Can't I, Sylvia?"

Sylvia chuckled. "You'd better let him do it. He needs a project."

"Guaranteed, I'll even teach him to parallel park, and that's no picnic."

"They don't require that on the driver's exam anymore," Cathy said. "But I require it. I told him no license until he has enough skill to do that."

"Good call." Harry was getting excited. "Come on, let me do it. I would consider it an honor."

"Well, all right." Cathy looked at Steve. "You didn't have your heart set on it, did you?"

Steve laughed. "No, I didn't. Harry, you're a lifesaver."

Harry chuckled. "I've been called that before."

"Yeah, but in your medical hat. We're talking real life-saving here."

As the dinner party went on, Sylvia watched the two kids out of the corner of her eye. They seemed to be getting along well. Everyone there was having a good time. She only hoped that her efforts were not in vain.

CHAPTER
Thirty-Three

A week after Sylvia's third chemo treatment, when she felt human again and was able to ride in a car without getting sick, Harry decided to take her along on a driving lesson with Mark. He'd already taken Mark out numerous times, starting with country driving, then moving into city driving and even highway driving. Today was the day he'd teach Mark parallel parking. For fun, Daniel, Brenda's son, rode along next to Sylvia in the backseat.

Harry instructed Mark as he drove the streets of Breezewood, then braved the interstate. When he was satisfied that Mark knew what he was doing, it was time to teach him the art of parallel parking, to satisfy Cathy.

"All right," Harry said in a calm voice as Mark drove gently along the street heading to the coliseum's parking lot. "That's not bad. Now I want you to make a right turn up here. Put your blinker on. Easy. Easy. Slow down. All right, now turn. That's great, Mark. You're a natural."

Mark grinned and drove like he was the king of the road. They got to the parking lot of the coliseum, and Harry got out and set up an obstacle course of two-liter pop bottles he'd filled with sand. Mark wove through them as adeptly as if he'd been driving in the Daytona 500.

When he'd woven through them several times, Harry was satisfied. "I think you're doing fine, Mark. You'll get your license in no time. Now all we have to do is learn to parallel park."

He got out and set up another obstacle course with bottles a car's width apart, then he got back in. "Now, Mark, I want you to pull up to half a car's length in front of the spot you're trying to get. Half a car's length now. There you go."

"I can do this," Mark said. "Piece of cake."

"Now start backing up slowly. Now cut your wheel hard to the right. There you go. Now let your rear end go all the way in, then cut hard back to the left and straighten it out."

They heard a pop, and Mark slammed on his brakes. "What was that?"

Harry got out and looked. "You hit three of the bottles, Mark. If that had been a car . . ."

"I can do it," Mark said. "Let me try again."

He pulled out, straightened the car, and began backing up again.

"Cut hard now," Harry said. "Pull in . . ."

Another two pops, and Mark stopped again. "Man, those bottles are too close."

Sylvia started to laugh, and Daniel did, too.

Mark grinned. "Don't make me turn this car around."

Sylvia fell against Brenda's boy, raucous laughter coming from both of them.

"Hey, I can do better." Mark pulled the car back out and started over again. This time he didn't turn quite so sharply. He pulled into the parking space, then tried to slam on the brakes. His foot accidentally hit the accelerator and he mowed down the cones. Sylvia yelled.

"Hey," Mark said, "that was an accident, okay? I realize that if that had been a real car I would have totaled it. But it wasn't a real car, and now I'm sure of the difference between the accelerator and the brake. Man!"

Harry shot Sylvia an admonishing look. "If you can't stop laughing, we'll have to put you out of this car."

Sylvia dabbed at the tears in her eyes. "I'll be good. I won't laugh." She looked at Daniel, her lips closed tight. They both spat out their laughter.

By now, Mark was laughing too. "Is this hopeless?"

"No, it's not hopeless," Harry said. "It just takes practice. Nobody can do it on the first try." He got out of the car and righted the mangled plastic bottles. He got back and put his seat belt on. Bracing himself, he said, "Okay, Mark, try it again."

Slowly, Mark made it, this time slipping into the parking space without killing any hypothetical others.

"Now let's try it about twenty more times," Harry said, "and then maybe you can convince your mom to let you get your license."

CHAPTER
Thirty-Four

When Mark got back from practice driving, he got Annie to take him to the local grocery store. She waited in the car while he went in and found the manager.

As soon as the man came to the front, he rolled his eyes. "Mark, I told you I'm not going to hire you."

"I know." Mark held up both hands. "But I wanted to try again. October's almost over and I still haven't found a job. I thought I'd have one by now. I've applied just about everywhere."

"That happens when you've been to jail, Mark. It limits your choices."

"But I can bag groceries!" Mark said. "My brother worked here for years, and my best friend works here now. You know my mother. I made a few mistakes, but I've changed, and I really need a job."

The man shook his head. "I don't hire kids with records. I've kept that policy for years, and it's worked well for me. I have enough problems with the good kids."

Mark swallowed. "I'm a good kid. I know you wouldn't know it from my past. But if nobody ever gives me a chance, how can I prove it?"

"I'm sorry, Mark."

Giving up, Mark shuffled back out to Annie's car and slammed into it.

"No luck?" she asked.

"Nope."

"Bummer."

"Annie, don't be cute. This is my life, and it's not going very well."

"Mark, you'll get a job soon. It's no big deal."

"It is to Steve. Every single day he asks me where I looked and what my prospects are. I'm getting sick of telling him how many times I've been turned down. I'm starting to feel like a loser again."

"Well, you're not one, okay?" Annie pulled out of the parking lot. "Maybe God just wants you to concentrate on getting your GED."

"Yeah, well, that's another thing. I took the test as soon as my class started. I didn't tell Mom or Steve because I wasn't sure I'd pass. And I was right."

"You failed?"

"Yeah. So I'm stuck taking this class until I can try again. This isn't turning out like I hoped."

She shook her head. "You should have gone back to school, Mark."

"No, I shouldn't have. I still think this could work out, if I could just get a stinking job. Isn't there anybody out there with compassion? Somebody who messed up once himself, and understands that one stupid act shouldn't mean a life sentence?"

Annie pulled back onto Cedar Circle and whipped into their driveway. "There is somebody like that, Mark. Just keep looking. And pray. God'll work things out."

Mark was quiet as he went into the house and hurried up to his room to start studying before class.

CHAPTER
Thirty-Five

Though she wasn't feeling her best, Sylvia continued with the Bible study she'd started in her home. The effort of keeping it going had been good for her. It had forced her to stay in the Word when her instinct might have been to wallow in her own problems and forsake the very book that gave her strength.

It also gave her a reason to see her friends. It seemed that the only time they came around now was on Bible study night, and before they did, they always called to make sure she was up to having company.

Of course I'm up to it, she thought. Did they think that she enjoyed being a hermit? She thought back to the day when she'd shaved her head. It was the last time they'd really laughed and shared together. Since then, they seemed to walk on eggshells around her, like they feared they would say exactly the wrong thing to send her over the edge.

She leaned back on the couch, trying to get comfortable, and looked at Tory who sat next to her. "So tell me about your job," she said. "You haven't talked much about it."

"Well, it's great," Tory said. "The kids are sweet. They keep me busy, but I like it."

She looked at Cathy. "And what about your family? How's the whole stepfamily thing going?"

"Good," Cathy said. "Great."

Monosyllables, Sylvia thought. Why couldn't they answer her in paragraphs instead of sentence fragments?

"And Brenda? What's new at your house?"

"Just the same old thing," she said. "Nothing new, really."

She sighed and opened her Bible and flipped to the page they'd be studying tonight. For a moment she just stared down at the page, feeling the grief of lost friendships.

But that was crazy. She knew they were still her friends. They weren't sharing their lives with her for one simple reason. They didn't want to burden her. They felt that her problems were so huge that she couldn't handle the weight of theirs too.

She knew all that, but it didn't make it easier. So many things had changed. She hated the cancer that had altered her world so drastically. Oh, for the day things would be normal again!

She started reading the passage they were studying, and silently asked God to clear her mind and make her stop feeling so sorry for herself. And slowly, moment by moment, she got over the hurt of being shut out of her friends' lives, and concentrated on the Word of God.

CHAPTER Thirty-Six

Days after her fourth treatment, Sylvia curled her body more tightly into the fetal position she'd been in for the last five days. She lay still, focusing on the backs of her eyelids, hoping that if she didn't move, the room wouldn't begin to sway and she wouldn't have to launch out of bed like a toilet-seeking missile.

Vaguely, she remembered the days in León when she'd worked from daylight until dark helping out in the orphanage, a surrogate mother to the broken and abandoned children. She'd hardly ever given a thought to her balance or her equilibrium, her energy or her metabolism. Health had been a given. She'd never even thought of it as a gift.

How she longed for that now! She would never again take it for granted.

Sores bubbled on her lips and in the soft tissue inside her mouth, making it hard to eat or swallow. Yet somehow she'd still managed to gain weight. How could that be? She could hardly stand anything in her mouth other than ice chips or water, and almost inevitably, whatever she did swallow came right back up. So how was it that she'd gained almost ten pounds since her treatments had begun?

Just another perk of cancer, she thought. She doubted the disease was going to kill her, but she felt certain the treatment would.

When the doorbell rang, she pulled herself tighter into a ball and tried to figure out what day it was. Monday, she thought, but she wasn't sure. Visitors didn't often come on Mondays.

She hoped Harry would send them away. She had no strength to be on display for anyone who'd come to get a first-hand glimpse of her suffering. The grapevine was going to have to be adequate for anyone looking for gossip.

You've grown bitter, Sylvia.

The self-admonishment was no more welcome than the ringing doorbell. She didn't care if she was bitter. She had every right to be.

But the moment that thought crossed her mind, she took it captive. How dare she be bitter? She had always claimed to trust in God, whatever he brought her way. Now he had brought her something difficult, something challenging. Was she going to spit in his face now?

She heard Mark's voice in the living room, laughing and talking as if he'd just won the lottery. He must have gotten a job, she thought. He must have passed his GED.

Then she heard "driver's license," and she carefully lifted her head to hear more.

"The guy testing me said I was the best he'd ever seen."

She heard Harry laughing. "You've got to be kidding me. Let me see that license." More laughter, and she realized Daniel was with Mark.

"I told him not to smile," Daniel said, "but he stretched up like that monkey on that commercial and showed all his teeth."

"Hey, I was proud."

Sylvia smiled.

"We wanted to tell Miss Sylvia. Does she feel like visitors?"

"Uh . . ." His voice dropped. "Sylvia's not really feeling well right now, guys. Maybe you should come back later."

But she didn't want them to come back later. Mark was excited *now*. As sick as she felt, she didn't want to miss one of the boy's best moments.

She raised up on her bed and straightened the robe she'd been wearing. "Harry," she yelled out with as much strength as she could muster. Harry stepped into the doorway.

"I want to see them," she said. "Give me a few minutes, then let them come back."

She forced herself to get off the bed, grabbed her wig, and pulled it on. She straightened her robe, then sat down on the mattress. "Come in, guys," she called, "and let me see that license."

Mark looked around the doorway and stepped in tentatively, and Daniel followed. Mark brandished the license as if it was an FBI badge. "You believe this, Miss Sylvia? I'm a licensed driver."

"We've got some celebrating to do." Sylvia took the license in her shaking hands, and started to laugh. "Mark, the teeth—"

"I was just kidding," he said. "I didn't know they were about to snap the picture. But they're tricky. They make you think they're not ready yet, so you sit on that stool and look around, and then they tell you to look at the camera. They wait for, like, the stupidest expression you could make, and then they snap it. I was trying to get a laugh out of Daniel while they were setting up, but next thing I knew they were herding me off the stool."

Daniel joined in. "Mark begged and pleaded for them to give him another chance, but they felt they'd gotten the dumbest expression he had, so they kept it. I'd say they were right."

Sylvia hadn't felt like laughing in days, but now her shoulders began to shake with the joy of these kids.

"Yeah, Miss Sylvia. I'm like, 'Nobody's gonna recognize me in this picture.' I look like that chimpanzee in that pager commercial. It's cruel, I tell you. Cruel."

Sylvia handed the license back. "But the instructor said you were . . . what was it you told Harry? That you were the best he'd seen?"

"Well, not the best, exactly," Mark said. "But really good."

Daniel shoved him. "What he really said was, 'Fine job, kid.'"

"Yeah, well, he doesn't say that to everybody, does he? He urged me not to stop with my private license. He said I was so good I should get my commercial license and drive for a living. He practically handed me a commercial license."

"Practically?" Sylvia asked.

"Well, almost."

Forgetting her nausea, Sylvia pulled her feet up on the bed and leaned back on her pillows. "This fish is getting bigger and bigger, Mark."

Mark threw his head back and laughed. "Okay, so he just said, 'Fine job, kid.' The important thing is that he passed me."

"That's right. What does your mother say?"

He shrugged. "She kind of turned white when I asked her if I could use the car tonight. I don't think she's real keen on me being out there on my own behind the wheel yet, but she'll get over it." He slid the license into his wallet. "Hey, Miss Sylvia, I really like your hair."

Sylvia grinned at him. She wasn't sure whether he was pulling her leg again. It was quite possible that Cathy hadn't told Mark about her shaved head. "Thank you, Mark," she said.

"No, really. It looks great. I thought you were supposed to, like, lose your hair or something when you had chemo."

Sylvia smiled, and Harry stepped into the room behind them, watching for her reaction. "Some do, some don't. Maybe I'm one of the lucky ones."

Mark seemed satisfied with that. "Well, we'd better go. We just wanted to show you."

"I'm glad you did, guys. I'm so proud of you. Even if the DMV man didn't say you were the best he'd ever seen, I'm sure he thought it."

When the boys were gone, Harry came back into the bedroom and sat on the bed next to her. "See? I told you no one knows it's a wig. It looks great."

She smiled. "Why is it that young people can lift my spirits so when no one else can?"

"You miss the kids in the orphanage, don't you?"

She nodded. "I wonder what they've been told about me."

"They've been told that you're sick and won't be able to come back until you're well. They're praying for you. I e-mailed Julie with the dates of your chemo, and they're praying hard on each of those days."

"I don't want them worrying about me," she said. "I think if I feel better tomorrow, I'll go buy them all something and send them a big box from Mama Sylvia. I was thinking about Beanie Babies."

"They'll love them."

"That way they'll know I'm still kicking." She sighed. "I wish I could go visit them between treatments."

"Sylvia, there's no way. Your immune system is too weak. And look at you. You haven't gotten out of bed for days."

"I know." She slipped back under the covers and curled up. "But it's terrible to be without them for so long."

"They're being well cared for. You're not the only one who loves them."

"Thank God for that." She laid her head back on the pillow.

"Do you think you might be able to eat now?"

She thought about it. "Maybe. I'm not making any promises."

"Okay. I'll bring you some soup."

"Not too hot," she said. "My mouth is so sore."

He started out of the room, and Sylvia closed her eyes and wished she had the energy to sit at the table with him. But the room was beginning to spin again.

Still, she was thankful for those two silly boys who had come by to lift her spirits. It was the first time in five days she'd seen hope that she'd emerge from under this pall of sickness. Maybe by tomorrow she could actually get out of bed.

Cathy was in the kitchen when Mark came in, closing the back door softly behind him.

"Mom, is Miss Sylvia going to die?"

Cathy turned around, startled to see tears in her son's eyes. "Why do you ask that?"

"Because I was over there," he said, "and she looks awful. Her face was so pale, and she's got these sores on her mouth, and her hands were shaking."

Cathy abandoned what she was doing and pulled a chair out from the table. Mark sat down across from her. "We just have to pray, Mark. We just have to hope that God will spare her."

"And why wouldn't he?" Mark asked. "I don't get it. I thought God blessed his children. Why would he let them suffer like that?"

Cathy sighed. Hadn't she asked the same question herself a million times? "God doesn't just take the lives of the ones he doesn't like. He takes those he loves, too. Sylvia is not immune to death by disease. None of us is. But I think she's going to live, Mark. I know five or six people who've survived breast cancer just fine. It's highly curable. The chemotherapy is the worst part, but she'll get through that."

Mark was quiet for a long moment. "Mom, I know you're uncomfortable with my driving by myself yet, but have you decided yet if I can borrow the car?"

Cathy stared at Mark, amazed at how fickle a teenager's mind could be. One moment they were talking about death, and the next he was thinking of going for a joyride. She sighed. "What for?"

"I want to buy a box of Popsicles before I go to class tonight," he said. "I was thinking that Popsicles might be something Miss Sylvia could eat. Those sores are bound to hurt."

So he wasn't thinking about joyriding, after all. He wanted to do something for their neighbor.

Tears misted her eyes as she leaned over and pressed a kiss on his forehead. "Yes, Mark. You can borrow the car. Go buy Miss Sylvia Popsicles."

CHAPTER
Thirty-Seven

That evening when Steve came home from work Cathy hit him up with what had been on her mind for several days.

"Steve, I've decided I want to buy Mark a little car so he can get to his GED classes and to work as soon as he gets a job. That way we won't have to keep taking him everywhere he has to go."

Steve dropped his keys on the counter. "Cathy, that's not a good idea."

"Why not? He needs one, and I got one for Rick and for Annie when they started driving."

"I know, but I've always thought a kid should save up at least half the money before he gets a car."

"Do you know how long it would take Mark to save that kind of money? And it's an endless cycle. He can't get a job unless he has transportation, and he can't get transportation unless he has a job. I want to help him. He *needs* some help."

"Cathy, we can get him to class. But how are you going to teach him about the drudgery of minimum wage work if he's not having to pay any bills of his own?"

"He's sixteen, Steve. I don't want him to have bills! Besides, it's not fair for me to buy a car for Rick and for Annie, then when it's his turn tell him that I've changed the rules."

"What rules? You have a rule that you have to buy him a car?"

"You know what I'm saying. It's not fair if he doesn't get one, when they did. He shouldn't get passed over just because I remarried!"

Steve stared at her for a moment before his face shut down. He turned to the refrigerator, opened it, and scowled inside. "Fine then. You've got your mind made up. I don't even know why you asked me."

Cathy rolled her eyes. "Come on, Steve. I asked you because I care what you think."

He slammed the refrigerator door, knocking the bottles inside against each other. "Only if I think what you want me to. Go find him a car, Cathy. I won't say another word about it."

"Steve, you don't have to get mad. I wanted to talk about this. Am I not allowed to make my case?"

"Of course you're allowed. But you already have your mind made up, and you're not going to take no for an answer."

"Well, why would you *say* no? I can understand your position if we were starting when Mark was ten years old, and he knew ahead of time that he'd have to save for his own car. But you don't come up when he's sixteen and say, 'Oh, by the way, I may have gotten cars for your brother and sister, but you're going to have to save for yours.'"

"So even if what you're doing is wrong, you do it just to be fair?"

"Why is it wrong?"

"Because Mark needs to learn responsibility."

"He will. Rick and Annie have responsibility. They both work and make good grades. Mark will too."

Steve breathed a derisive laugh. "Are you kidding? I don't even think he's looking for a job. He's been home three months, and all he does is sleep till noon and watch television all afternoon. Then he pulls himself together and goes to class."

"He *has* been looking, Steve! You're not here all day. You don't know how he's spending his time."

"Where has he looked? Name one place."

"I don't know, but he has. He does want to work, Steve. But his record is getting in his way. He'll get a job soon."

"I'll believe it when I see it."

She tried to calm her voice before she set him off again. "Would you just come and look at this car I found? I'm not sure if it's reliable enough."

"So you didn't really need my opinion at all. You've not only made up your mind, but you've found the car."

"No, I haven't found the car. I found *a* car, and I wanted your input."

"Fine." He grabbed up his keys. "Let's go."

Cathy had hoped to change out of her jeans and tennis shoes and the baggy shirt she'd been wearing to pull weeds out of the backyard. But she knew better than to detour Steve now. She followed him out to the car and got in.

He brooded as they drove to the car lot. She didn't like him when he brooded. It reminded her too much of her ex-husband, when he would use his passive-aggressive silence to keep her in line.

Steve rarely did it, so when he did, it had a greater impact.

She brooded back, not willing to give him the satisfaction of melting into a rambling idiot trying to make up with him.

When they got to the car lot, she led him to the little Civic she had chosen. For Mark's sake, she broke the silence. "It seems to be in great condition. It's four years old. I thought he'd like it."

Steve was quiet as he looked under the hood, examined the belts, and checked the engine for leaks. He got under the car and checked its underside, as if he would look until he found something wrong.

Cathy bit her tongue and waited patiently for him. Finally, he stood up and brushed his hands off.

"It looks like a good enough car," he said. "How much is it?"

She told him and he rolled his eyes. "Cathy, don't you think that's a little expensive for a kid's first car?"

"It's not like it's a Cadillac. I just want him to have something reliable, okay? I don't want him breaking down somewhere."

"You could probably get an older model that might not be in perfect condition for a whole lot less money."

For a moment, Cathy wondered what this moment would be like if Steve were Mark's real father. Would he want the same thing she wanted for Mark? Would he be more interested in seeing the joy on their son's face than in grinding out some lesson on responsibility?

Or did original parents bicker over these things, too?

She supposed she would never know. "I want to get him this one," she said. "This is the one I like."

He breathed a frustrated laugh. "Then why did you bring me here? I thought you wanted my opinion."

"I did want your opinion," she said, "about whether it was reliable or not."

"Oh, I see. You wanted my opinion about its reliability but not about the wisdom of buying him the car."

"I thought we'd already been through this!"

"We have," Steve told her. "I'll be waiting in the car while you do your business. You let me know what you decide."

She stood there at the car, hands on her hips, as the salesman strode toward her.

"So, you want me to write it up for you, ma'am?"

She felt as if the wind had been knocked out of her, and crossing her arms, she shook her head. "No, I think I'm going to have to come back."

"He didn't like it?"

She shot a look at the car. Steve had a look of granite on his face as he stared out the side window. "No," she said, "he didn't."

"Well, what didn't he like about it? Maybe I could show you something else."

She shook her head. "No, he doesn't want to see anything else."

Without another word she headed for the car, got into it, and slammed the door. She snapped her seat belt into place and crossed her arms.

He looked at a spot on his windshield. "Are you going to buy it?"

"No, I'm not."

"Why not?"

"Because I don't want to have to deal with your attitude."

"My attitude?"

She ground her teeth. "Before I married you, Steve, I could buy anything I wanted for my children. I didn't have to ask anybody's permission."

"Well, you knew when you married me that we were pooling our finances *and* our children. That was the plan, anyway. I thought you valued my input." He started the car and pulled off of the gravel lot.

"I do value your input, Steve, except when you're wrong."

"Oh, that's just beautiful." He set his mouth, and she was glad she couldn't read his thoughts.

But she spoke hers out loud. "I don't know why you have it in for my children."

His eyes flashed as he turned to her. "I can't believe you would accuse me of that."

"I'm not accusing you. I'm just pointing out the truth."

"The truth is that I have it in for your children? Give me a break, Cathy. I've been nothing but good to your children. Even when Mark was in jail I was the one who was mentoring him. I thought you appreciated that."

"I do." She knew he was right. He had made such a difference in Mark's life. "I really do, Steve. But why can't I do things for my children? You do things for Tracy."

"I'm not going to buy her a car."

"Well, why not? When it's her turn I'll be just as generous with her as I am with my kids. I don't understand why I can't buy my son a car."

"Because it builds character to have them pay their own way."

"Well, that's fine," she said, "except for the last few years Mark hasn't been interested in paying his own way. And for the last year he's been in jail so he couldn't possibly have saved for his car. He got out with a new attitude, Steve, and he's trying to change his life. I want to help him. Is that so wrong?"

His face softened as he stared at the road in front of him. "No, it's not wrong, Cathy, and I do understand your intentions. And if you want to buy him a car, go ahead. I don't want to stand in your way. I just think that one is a little bit too expensive."

"I'll pay for it," she said. "Come on, Steve. I earn plenty of money, and you earn plenty of money. Together we don't have financial problems to speak of. Why can't I splurge a little bit with my son?"

"Okay, now we're down to it." Steve set his mouth again. "I should have known we weren't really pooling our resources. It comes down to yours and mine. The first time I balk at something you want to buy, you all of a sudden want to take your half back. Is that how it's going to be?"

She grabbed her ponytail and tugged on it. "No! I'm just saying that if I work hard and earn my share, why can't I spend it on my son? I don't know why everything has to be so hard."

"Everything is hard?" he asked. "I thought we'd done pretty well, Cathy. For the last six months we've done really, really well. Until Mark came home."

"Are you saying that Mark has caused all this trouble? Because he hasn't done anything. He's been a perfect angel."

"He's been a good kid," Steve conceded. "I'm not saying he hasn't. I just think that maybe we were sailing along too smoothly until we had more kids in the house, and now that we've got Annie back home and Rick dropping in and out at all hours . . ."

"And Tracy," Cathy added. "Don't forget that you have a child in the mix, too."

"I know that," he said. "It's just that we have different parenting styles and different philosophies on what a kid needs as they grow older."

"Well, we're going to have to find some common philosophies," she said. "We're going to have to agree on some things before Tracy gets any older. But right now I can't go back and undo everything I've done with my children."

He banged his hand on the steering wheel. "But you can change a few things now."

"What if I don't think things are wrong?" she threw back.

He got quiet then. "Look what we're doing to each other."

"What?" she snapped.

"We're turning on each other, all because of the children. All that premarital counseling, and we thought we could beat those blended family problems they warned us about. But we haven't. They're sucking us under, too."

"You're changing the subject." Cathy looked out the window. "I want to buy Mark the car."

He leaned his head back on the headrest. "Then go for it."

"I will."

They didn't say another word for the rest of the way home.

When he went into the house she got behind the wheel, backed out of the driveway, and headed back to the car lot to make a deal on the car.

Chapter *Thirty-Eight*

Cathy surprised Mark with the car the next day before he went to GED class. Steve had made himself scarce since he'd come home from work, and now he busied himself washing his truck. He'd hardly said a word to her since the night before, and each of the children had noticed and mentioned it at least once. The house was tense, for all of the kids had noticed the strain between them.

When she blindfolded Mark and led him out to the driveway, Steve looked at her across the roof of his truck. His eyes accused, indicted, punished. But they did not convict her.

Mark's excitement shivered through him. "Can I open my eyes now?"

"Just a minute." She positioned him in front of the new car. Annie and Tracy came out behind him and gasped at the sight of the car in the driveway.

"Open your eyes," she ordered.

Mark's eyes opened, and for a moment he stared at the car as if he didn't quite understand.

"It's for you," Cathy said. "I bought it last night."

Mark gaped at her. "The car? The whole thing?"

"No, Bozo." Annie shoved him. "Just the steering wheel."

"I don't believe it. Mom, I love it!" He laughed and threw his arms around his mother, then danced to the car and opened the door. "It's beautiful. I never expected anything so nice. I figured you'd get me a clunker like you did Annie and Rick."

Annie turned on her. "Yeah, Mom. What's up with that?"

Steve shot her another look and went to turn off the hose.

"Well, I figured you deserved a nice car. I wanted you to have something reliable."

"Mom, it's fantastic." He got behind the wheel and cranked it up, listened to the engine. "Listen to it purr," he said. "It's beautiful. Look, and it's got a CD player. Oh, man."

"Way to go, Mom." Annie gave her a high five.

Tracy jumped up and down and ran around to get in the passenger's side. "Take me for a ride, Mark!"

Drying his hands off, Steve came around the truck. "Not yet, Tracy. Let's let Mark get a little more practice under his belt before he starts taking passengers."

"I'm a good driver," Mark said. "You should see me."

"I know, but I just prefer that Tracy didn't ride with you for a while."

"Well, he can take me, can't he?" Annie said. "I'm a licensed driver. I can correct him when he messes up."

"I'm not going to mess up," Mark said. "It's like I've been driving for years. I can parallel park and everything, can't I, Mom?"

Cathy smiled. "He did a knock-up job at the driver's test. The instructor was sure impressed."

Steve didn't say anything. He turned back to the truck and began drying it off.

When Mark drove off with Annie, and Tracy had gone back into the house, Cathy stood in the driveway and regarded her husband across the truck. He seemed to be intent on polishing it to perfection. The silence screamed at her, and she hated it. She'd hated it last night when he'd gone to bed without a word, and she'd stared at his back all night. Several times she had almost touched him and tried to make up. But to do that, she would have had to give in to him, and Mark wouldn't have gotten his car.

But now that the deed was done, she didn't feel as thrilled as she thought she would. If she could consider today a victory, it was a hollow one. Mark was happy, but she was left feeling alone and shut out.

She watched Steve drying his truck, and wondered if he hated the silence as much as she did.

"Can we be friends again?" she asked him.

He breathed a laugh. "We're friends, Cathy. We're husband and wife."

"But you're not real happy about it right now."

He just kept drying.

She went around the truck. He was bent down now, drying the lower part.

"Honey, I'm sorry for all this," she said to his back. "I still don't agree with you. I don't think I've done anything wrong, but I don't like us being mad at each other."

He straightened. "I don't like it either, Cathy, but your attitude the last couple of days has been really hurtful. You've accused me of being mean to your children, of not wanting them to have things, of standing in your way of parenting them. And you've tried to take back your part of our money, separating it out like I have nothing to do with it. That really hurt, Cathy, because when we got married I thought we were two becoming one. You said we were joined at the heart. But it doesn't feel like we're very joined at all right now, and I don't know what to think about that."

She took the wet towel out of his hands and slid her arms around him. "I love you, Steve. I didn't want to make you mad. I'm just a mother bear trying to protect her cubs."

"I'm not a threat to your cubs, Cathy."

"I know, but I want so much for Mark right now. I want to encourage him. I want to give him things to give him a head start. I don't want him suffering anymore. It's done now. Can we get past it?"

"Is that how it's always going to be? You're just going to do it and then I'm going to have to accept it?"

"No." She pulled back. "I'll try to be more sensitive to your feelings from now on. Please. I love you. I don't want us to be mad at each other. It's hard on the kids and it's especially hard on me."

He looked at her for a long moment. Finally, his expression softened. "I'll try to get over it, Cathy. I don't want to be mad, either, but it doesn't go away just like that. It's hard to shake off the things you said. Once they're out of your mouth, you can't really take them back."

"But can't I be forgiven?"

"Sure you can be forgiven," he said, "but I just don't think you're very sorry."

She backed away, crossing her arms. "What do you want me to do, Steve? Get down on my knees and beg?"

"No."

"Well, do you want me to snatch the car back out from under Mark and take it back to the dealership and tell him that I was wrong, that I don't want it?"

"Oh, that would really make me look like a hero," Steve said. "I've tried to be a good stepfather, and somehow I've wound up being the bad guy. It didn't start out that way."

He was right. Cathy dropped her arms and looked down at the water under the car. "No, it didn't," she said. "You don't deserve that."

"Well, thank you for that."

She looked up at him and saw the love in his weary eyes. He reached out for her. She went willingly into his arms and held him, thankful that his love was strong enough to survive these storms. But in her heart she knew that he wasn't completely over it.

That evening when they went to bed, she could tell that he was still tense, still upset about the things that had occurred between them, and she wasn't sure that she could make it right. She couldn't undo what had been done. Mark had the car now, and Steve didn't want to be the bad guy by making him give it up.

And after all was said and done, she still didn't feel she'd been wrong.

With that hovering in her consciousness, she fell into a deep sleep . . . but the space between Steve and her on the king-size bed seemed wider than it ever had before.

CHAPTER
Thirty-Nine

The drugstore was crowded, full of shoppers with coupons, and the line at the photo counter was almost as long as the line at the pharmacy. Brenda fidgeted as she waited to talk to the pharmacy's cashier. While she did, her mind clicked through calculations of her checking account balance, the checks about to clear, and the cost of Joseph's medication. Getting the medicine was critical. Transplant patients couldn't do without it. But how would she pay this time?

She went through this every month, when she came to get his drugs refilled. Sometimes David's work had netted enough to pay outright. Those were the good months. But other months she juggled between paying by credit card or adding to her store account. This month both were almost maxed out.

She got up to the cashier, said Joseph's name, and the woman scurried away and came back with a bag of medicine. She scanned each bag. "That'll be $553. Cash or credit card?"

Brenda's hands trembled as she fumbled with her checkbook. "Uh, is there any possible way you could put this on my account? I know I already owe a lot, but . . ."

The woman punched her up on the computer, studied the account like a million-dollar banker disgusted with the riffraff. "Can you pay any of it at all?"

Brenda wondered why they kept it so hot in here. "I can pay $300 if you could put $200 on my account."

"Okay, we could do that," the woman said, "but you really need to make a payment pretty soon."

Brenda drew in a deep breath and started writing the check. "I know. I will. We don't have very good insurance because my husband is self-employed."

The woman wasn't interested. Brenda tore out the check and handed it to her. "Thank you so much."

"Uh-huh." The woman chomped her gum and typed into the computer. Then looking past Brenda to the next customer, she asked, "May I help you?"

Brenda went back to her car and sat behind the wheel, staring at the windshield and trying to decide what she needed to do. She couldn't go another month like this. At some point the drugstore would insist on being paid for the tab she had run up. She couldn't take the risk of having them cut off Joseph's supply of medication.

Once again, the idea of getting a job loomed in her heart. Not just any job, but a good one, one that had insurance benefits and paid well. Always before when she'd thought of getting a job she had looked for things that were small and insignificant, part-time work that she could squeeze around her home schooling. The job she'd had as a telemarketer at night had been an ordeal and she didn't relish the idea of repeating it. When she had home schooled Mark, Cathy's payments had helped with the medication, but even that hadn't been quite enough.

Always before, she had found it critical to stay home with her children. But the fact was that Joseph, their youngest, was twelve now, and David was home working in his workshop all day long. It wasn't like the children would be unattended or unsupervised. She could get a normal job with normal work hours, and give them assignments to do during the day. Then she could home school them at night when she got home.

It wasn't ideal, but it was necessary. Sometimes sacrifices had to be made.

She had never stopped trusting God to provide for her, but she realized that sometimes God provided by leading you to work. Maybe it was time for her to do just that.

She started the car and pulled out of the parking lot. Her mind drifted to Sylvia's plight, and she wondered what Sylvia and Harry would have done without adequate insurance. Thankfully, their denomination had offered that when they'd gone to the mission field. What if cancer struck the Dodd family? How would they ever pay? In a family of six, someone would get sick, someone would need surgery. There would be tonsillectomies and appendectomies. She and David could be struck with disease, or there could be an accident. They had to be ready.

But David would never go for it.

How would she convince him of the wisdom in her going to work?

And if she did convince him, would he urge her to put the children back into the school system? They would balk at that for sure. Besides, they'd be bored to death because her schooling had gotten them way ahead in their studies. Rachel and Leah were probably already two years ahead of their counterparts in school, and Daniel probably could have graduated by now and headed off to college. Joseph had almost caught up with Leah and Rachel.

No, they needed to stay home and keep studying in the way that worked for them. It would just be more challenging now, but they could do it.

She drove home, holding back the tears in her eyes, trying to psyche herself up for her talk with David. If he saw any trepidation or dread in her face, he would put his foot down and kill himself trying to work even longer hours than he already did.

He'd start talking again about going to work for someone else, where there were benefits and a steady income.

But David loved what he did, and she liked having him home. No, it made more sense for her to work. Somehow she would convince him.

She got home and took the medicine inside, then stepped out the back and found David in his workshop. She went inside.

David didn't hear her. His power saw buzzed through a flat piece of lumber, and Brenda waited until it came to a stop.

"Hey there," she said.

He pulled his safety glasses up to his forehead. "Hey. I thought you were at the drugstore."

"I'm back." She picked up one of the pieces he'd just cut, and blew off the sawdust. "Listen, I need to talk to you."

"Shoot." He pulled the safety glasses completely off. "What is it?"

"David, I had an epiphany."

"Uh-oh."

She smiled. "I want to get a job. But not a part-time job like I've tried before. Not a night job. I want to work full-time at a place that has benefits."

She saw the distress darkening his pale features. "Brenda, we've talked about this."

She tipped her head to the side and softened her voice. "No, we haven't. Not really. We've never considered a serious job. David, I haven't had any income since I quit teaching Mark fifteen months ago. There's no reason I can't work."

"There are *four* reasons," he said. "Daniel, Leah, Rachel, and Joseph." He crossed his arms and sat down on one of his sawhorses. "Brenda, is this about Joseph's drugs?"

There was no use denying it. "David, it's getting harder to pay for them. Even the most affluent family would have a hard time paying a monthly drug bill like ours with no drug coverage."

"We could get another credit card," he said. "Or change drugstores and open a new account somewhere else."

"David, we don't *have* to go deeper into debt. I could help. I've figured it all out. I could give the kids assignments in the mornings, and you could look in on them all during the day. When I get home, I could do the one-on-one teaching. It could work."

"The kids would be unsupervised most of the day, Brenda. I'd rather put them back into school than do that."

She crossed the room and stood in front of him. "David, they're good kids. If I gave them enough to keep them busy . . ."

"Brenda." He said it in that tone that brought a halt to the conversation. "I don't like the idea. It won't work."

She felt tears pushing to her eyes, tightening her throat. Staring down at the floor, she said, "David, I want to do this for Joseph, and for the rest of the family. I *need* to do this. It can work if we make it work. When have we ever backed down from anything just because it's hard?"

He stared at the jigsaw hanging on the wall, his teeth set. "I'll figure something out, Brenda."

She had heard that before, but there wasn't anything to figure out. The answer was obvious. "Honey, I know that you have a hard time with this. But it's not your fault. You've been working out here fourteen hours a day. You're a wonderful provider. But who could have expected us to have a child who needs hundreds of dollars' worth of medication to stay alive? You're not the only one who has to make sacrifices, David. I need to make some of them, too."

David set both palms on his worktable and let his head slump down. "You're great at what you do, Brenda." His voice was barely audible. "Ours are the luckiest kids in the world. I want you to keep doing what you do best."

That did it. The tears rushed her eyes, stung her lids, trembled in her throat. She crossed the room and slid her arms around him.

"That's so sweet," she said. "But they're older now."

"They're not grown. They still need you."

"And I'll still be here at night and on weekends. And you'll be here too. We could try it, David. Just to see. If it doesn't work out, we could find a Plan B."

"That is Plan B."

"Okay, then, Plan C or D . . . on down the alphabet. We Dodds can handle a challenge. All of us."

David held her, and after a moment, he kissed her hair. "All right, honey. Go ahead and look for a job. It doesn't hurt to look. We'll see what comes up."

She rose up and kissed him. "Thank you, David." She touched his face. "It'll be okay. You'll see."

He nodded silently, then put his safety glasses back on. The saw buzzed behind her as she stepped out of the workshop.

CHAPTER Forty

Friday afternoon, Cathy was in the middle of administering heartworm medication to one of her regular patients, a German shepherd she'd treated since he was a pup, when her secretary came around the door.

"You have a phone call from a Harry Bryan."

Cathy finished with the dog, then hurried to the phone.

"Harry?" she asked when she picked it up.

"Hi, Cathy. I hope I haven't bothered you."

She closed her office door with her foot and sat down. "Is everything all right?"

He didn't answer. "I wanted to talk to you about Sylvia."

"Sure." She leaned forward on her desk. "How's she feeling?"

"Pretty bad," he said. "That last chemo treatment really did her in. She's getting her energy back now, but she's been depressed. And she told me yesterday that she feels left out of your lives because nobody's talking about themselves. You come over and you're totally focused on her. I wanted to ask you if you would gather up Brenda and Tory and come over and visit her after work today. She needs some company."

"Well, of course." Cathy swept a strand of hair behind her ear. "We've been trying to stay away because she's been so sick. We thought it took too much energy for her to have us over."

"She needs a reason to get out of bed," he said. "So come over and tell her all your problems, tell her what's going on with Mark and with Rick and Annie, tell her how the marriage is going. Get Brenda to tell her what's going on with the family, and let Tory update her on Hannah. In fact, tell her to bring Hannah with her."

"Harry, we really don't want to burden her."

"You're not burdening her," he said. "You'd be helping her."

She sighed and pulled on her ponytail. How many times over the last few days had she wished she could run to Sylvia for advice? "Well, I can sure give her an earful tonight."

"Good," he said. "Just come whenever you're ready."

"How about seven?"

"All right. I'll tell her so she'll be ready."

Sylvia sat in the living room when the trio came in. Cathy hesitated at the door as a rush of emotion tightened her throat. She looked worse than Cathy had ever seen her. Her skin had a yellow cast to it, and her eyes seemed sunken in. But the moment she saw Hannah on Tory's hip, she reached for her.

"Give me that baby."

Tory set her in Sylvia's lap. Sylvia laughed as Hannah smiled up at her. "Oh, you sweet thing."

"How do you feel, Sylvia?" Tory asked.

"Better than I look. Aren't you glad?"

"You look great." Brenda's weak statement didn't ring true.

Sylvia waved her off. "I feel like I've aged twenty years in the last two weeks."

Cathy sat down next to her. "Is it the chemo?"

"Yes. The cancer and I were getting along fine until they started shooting that stuff into my veins. But I don't want to talk about that." She sat back and put her feet on the ottoman. Hannah settled her head comfortably against Sylvia's chest. "So what's going on with you girls? Cathy, how's Mark settling in?"

"Oh, all right."

Sylvia gave her a knowing look. "That doesn't sound good. He's not getting into trouble, is he?"

"No," Cathy said. "It's just that Steve and I don't exactly agree on everything about Mark. In fact, we've been at each other's throats."

Sylvia's eyes speared her. "Tell me everything, Cathy. What's going on?"

Cathy looked from Brenda to Tory, and realized that they were watching her with great interest.

"Well, let's hear it," Tory said. "I thought you two were the happiest couple in the cul-de-sac. What gives?"

She sighed. "Steve's really mad at me."

"About what?" Sylvia asked.

"I bought a car for Mark," she said, "and Steve didn't think I should. He thought I should make him save up for half of it. But the thing is, he can't get to work if he doesn't have a car."

"Where's he working?" Brenda asked.

"Well . . . nowhere yet. That's another sore point between Steve and me. But he will have a job soon."

"So you bought him the car," Sylvia said, "against Steve's will?"

"Not really. I mean, he says he's not upset that I bought the car, but that I bought the one I did. He thought it was too expensive."

"Was it?"

"No," she said. "I earn good money, Sylvia. I work hard. I should be able to buy my son something if I want to. Mark's been through a rough year. I wanted to do this. I don't know why he wanted to stop me."

"It doesn't sound like Steve to sulk over something like that."

Cathy took off her shoes and pulled her feet beneath her. "He says he's mad because of the way I did it, because I told him that he was interfering with my parenting of my children. And then when I started talking about how I earned enough money to be able to do things for my children, he felt like I was splitting our finances down the middle and taking my half back."

"Sounds like it to me too." Sylvia's calm declaration shot through Cathy.

"That's not true. Sylvia, I know all about submission and everything, but Steve was off base."

"It's like I told you before, sometimes he will be. But the Bible didn't say submit to your husband when you're sure he's doing the right thing. I doubt if Steve would have pressed the issue if he knew how you really felt. He probably would have gone out and bought Mark a car himself, if I know him."

"Well, it didn't seem like he was heading in that direction, Sylvia. Trust me."

"I'm just saying that maybe you jumped the gun. Maybe there would have been a meeting of the minds if you'd just waited a little while."

"But I wanted to buy him the car now."

"I know you did," Sylvia said. "And look where it got your marriage. Honey, when are you going to learn that you've got to die to yourself to have a happy marriage?"

The baby started to squirm, and Tory took her back. "She's right, Cathy."

Cathy turned on Tory. "How can you say that after what you went through with Barry during your pregnancy? When he wanted you to abort Hannah? You didn't submit to him then."

"That was different," Tory said. "I wasn't willing to sin against God to make my husband happy. But you're talking about a car, Cathy. Not a life."

Cathy turned to Brenda. Surely she was an ally. "What do you think?"

Brenda smiled. "I can understand how you feel, Cathy. But I think Sylvia's right, too."

Cathy got up and set her hands on her hips. "I have a problem with dying to myself when it comes to my children. I'm not doing this for me, Sylvia. I'm doing it for Mark. Don't you agree that he deserves a car, that he needs something to help him get a head start so that he can get a good job and get his GED and get on with his life?"

Sylvia shook her head. "That's not the point, Cathy. It's like I told you. Steve probably would have come around and it wouldn't have been a bad thing then. But now you've got a strain between you. That's not going to help Mark in any way."

Cathy just stared at Sylvia, then Tory, then Brenda. "All right. When I get home I'll die to myself so hard that you'll have to plan my funeral."

Sylvia laughed. "That's my girl."

Cathy plopped back down and propped her feet on the coffee table.

"So, Tory, how's your job?"

"I love it," Tory said. "It's the greatest decision I've ever made. You should see the kids. They're so precious. They celebrate every victory, from washing their hands in the sink to scribbling on paper."

"I'm so glad you like it," Sylvia said. "Has it changed your perspective about Hannah's future?"

"Some. But mostly it's changed my perspective about me. They have no self-consciousness at all. They don't have the same critical tapes playing in their heads that I have. Nothing inside them is censoring them or scolding them. They just go for it. If they can't do it, fine, but if they can, you should see the joy on their faces."

"We could all learn from that," Brenda said.

"Really." Tory got on the floor and set Hannah down. "There's this little guy named Bo who loves to learn. And he loves for me to teach him. He always wants to sit by me. When we go outside he wants to hold my hand. He has the sweetest heart."

Sylvia's eyes glistened at Tory's enthusiasm. "Do you think they might let me come when I'm feeling better, and read to them or something?"

Tory looked up at her. "Well, sure. We always need help."

Brenda set her elbow on her knee and propped her chin. "Are they hiring, by any chance?"

Tory glanced up at her. "Maybe. They have all the teachers they need, but they might need some part-timers."

"Too bad." Brenda straightened. "I need full-time."

"You?" Cathy's question was too blunt. She'd known that Brenda and David were on a tight budget, but she didn't know Brenda was looking for full-time work.

"Yes, I'm looking for a real job with benefits."

Sylvia leaned forward and got a pretzel out of the bowl Harry had put out. "Brenda, are you sure you want to do that?"

"Yes, I am." Brenda got a pretzel of her own and seemed to examine it. "I've got to find a way to pay for Joseph's drugs. Most part-time jobs don't have benefits, so I'm going full-time."

Cathy couldn't picture David going along with that. "How does David feel?"

"Well, he wasn't thrilled about it at first. But he knows it's necessary. I'll be giving the kids assignments to do while I'm gone, then I'll home school at night."

Sylvia shook her head. "Honey, you'll wear yourself out."

"I'll be fine."

Tory slid Hannah back onto her lap. "Have you found anything yet?"

Brenda ate her pretzel. "No, not really. I've put in applications at about a dozen places. Since I've been at home for the last sixteen years, they act like I have no skills."

"No skills?" Sylvia laughed. "Brenda, that's ridiculous. You have more skills than someone who's been in the workforce for twenty years."

"That's right," Cathy said. "You have medical experience, lots of it."

"True," Brenda said.

"And you're a teacher," Tory added.

"Yeah, but not a licensed one. Home schooling momhood doesn't count."

"You can type," Sylvia said.

Brenda nodded. "Yes, I'm a really fast typist."

"You could be an office manager," Tory said. "You've organized your family for years."

"Or a bookkeeper," Cathy said. "Aren't you the one who handles the finances?"

"Some of them."

Sylvia took another pretzel. Cathy watched her, wondering if she'd been able to keep much down for the last few days.

"Looks to me like you're a candidate for just about anything out there," Sylvia said. "I just hate to see you doing it. Maybe you could find something you could do from your home."

"I'd love that," Brenda said, "but it wouldn't pay benefits. That's the main incentive. I have to have insurance."

Sylvia stared into the air for a moment as if she was thinking, then ate another pretzel. "We need to pray about this," she said finally. "God has something just right for you."

"I'd appreciate those prayers," Brenda said.

Cathy saw through Brenda's smile and knew it was a facade. Her friend didn't have much peace about this, but she was doing what she had to do. Cathy wished she could help her, but she had offered her money before, and Brenda had been insulted. She wished Mark were still home schooling with her so she'd at least have that income.

But it still wouldn't solve the problem of the insurance.

"I'll put some feelers out," Cathy said. "Maybe I'll hear of something."

"Me too," Sylvia said.

Tory nodded. "I'll check at the school."

"Don't worry," Cathy said. "You'll be gainfully employed before you know it."

"Maybe," Brenda said. "But I don't think it's the best time to look for a job, right before Thanksgiving and Christmas."

"In God's timing," Sylvia said. "By the way, what are you all doing for Thanksgiving?"

Tory pulled some plastic keys out of her diaper bag and handed them to Hannah. "We're going to have dinner with Barry's mom and brother."

Cathy shrugged. "I think we're going to stay home. It's getting kind of complicated. Mark can't decide whether to have it with us or with his dad, though Rick and Annie both want to stay home. And Steve's parents want us to come see them, but my kids don't really want to do that . . ."

"Nothing's easy with you guys, is it?" Tory asked.

"Nope. Never is."

Cathy looked at Brenda. "What about you, Brenda?"

Brenda smiled. "We're having our traditional pilgrim dinner. The girls dress like pilgrims, and the boys are Indians, like the first Thanksgiving."

Sylvia laughed. "You never stop teaching, do you, Brenda?"

"Oh, it's fun. Sylvia, why don't you and Harry join us?"

Sylvia shook her head. "Can't."

"Why not? Are you going to Sarah's or Jeff's?"

Sylvia's smile was weak. "They're coming here, just for the day."

Cathy's heart swelled, and she took Sylvia's frail hand. "If you need help with the meal, let us know," she whispered.

"It's all under control," Sylvia said. "It's going to be a good day."

CHAPTER
Forty-One

As Cathy walked home from Sylvia's, she thought about what her friends had said about dying to herself and submitting to her husband. She was tired of the tension between Steve and her. Someone was going to have to break it, and she knew it had to be her.

When she got inside, Steve sat in the living room watching a ball game on television while he folded a load of towels. Steve rarely just sat back and relaxed. If he allowed himself the time to watch television, he always tried to accomplish something else while he did. Cathy was thankful for the help he gave her in running the household.

Tracy sat at the kitchen table behind him, trying to polish her nails. So far, she'd gotten more polish on her cuticles and fingers than she had on the nails themselves. Cathy touched Tracy's hair. "How's it going there?"

"Not too good," Tracy said. "I think I'll have to take it all off and start over."

"Why don't you let me do it for you?"

"Would you?" Tracy looked up hopefully at her.

Before Cathy pulled out the chair to sit down, she looked at her husband. They had talked some since their fight about the car, but she could still see the tension in his back and neck as he kept his eyes on the game.

She went over to him and pressed a kiss on the back of his neck. He glanced back at her and forced a smile. "Sylvia okay?"

"Yeah, all things considered."

"Good." He folded another towel, set it on the stack.

Cathy sat down and helped Tracy take the polish off, then slowly, painstakingly, began her manicure.

"You do a good job," Tracy said quietly as she watched each stroke down her nail. "I don't know why I can't do it."

"It's hard to do it to yourself," Cathy said. "Sometimes a girl just needs someone to help her."

"But my friends all do it themselves, and they don't look like freaks when they're finished."

"Just takes a little practice."

They both got quiet as Cathy finished up, blowing on them to dry them. "Now," she said, "how's that?"

Tracy looked proudly at her nails. "Much better."

Cathy propped her chin on her hand. "Time to get ready for bed."

Tracy moaned. "But can't I watch TV awhile? I'm not tired."

"Tracy, it's late."

"But I'm twelve. I should be able to stay up."

Cathy sighed. She needed to talk to Steve and couldn't do it with Tracy sitting here.

"Besides," Tracy added, "it's Friday. I don't have school tomorrow."

"But you said you were coming to work with me in the morning. You need to earn some money, remember? I don't want to have to scrape you off of the bed. So go on, kiddo. Hit the sack."

"Okay. In a minute." Tracy went around the couch and plopped down.

Cathy looked at Steve. He still watched the game and folded the towels, as if he hadn't heard the exchange at all. If he had, he certainly wasn't going to rebuke his daughter.

So she tried a different tact. "Steve, can I talk to you alone?"

"Sure." He finished the towel he was working on, and handed Tracy the remote control. Taking the stack of towels, he headed for the bedroom. Cathy followed him.

"What is it?" He put the towels away, then sat down on the bed and started to take his shoes off.

Cathy stood, watching him. He didn't meet her eyes—she tried to remember if he had even once since their fight. "Steve, I was talking to Sylvia and the girls tonight about the car and everything . . . and I just realized that I've made a lot of marital mistakes lately. I should have waited and given you time about the car. I should have tried to compromise and maybe come to some kind of agreement with you. And I shouldn't have expected you to get over it with my belated apology."

He put his shoes in the closet, then leaned against the door. "I accept your apology. Again."

Could it be that easy, she wondered, or were his words only one of those lip-service things that wouldn't pan out in his behavior?

But then he crossed the room and pulled her into a hug. "I miss you when I'm mad at you," he said.

All her tension and anger melted away. She laid her head against his chest. "I miss you, too. That bed is so big when we're mad. You're a good-feeling husband."

He smiled. "You're a good-feeling wife." He kissed her, then looked into her eyes. Really looked. That distant gaze was gone. "I hope you know I wasn't trying to make Mark's life hard for him."

The truth was, she didn't know that. She released him and stepped back. "I think sometimes you do want things to be hard for him so he'll be tougher or have more character. I'm just not sure you're right."

It was the wrong thing to say, and suddenly, Steve's soft look hardened. "Wait a minute. I thought you just apologized. What was it exactly that you were apologizing for?"

"For overriding you. For doing it when you didn't agree that I should."

He nodded, like he just now understood. "Okay. So you're sorry you did that, but you still stand behind your reasons for doing it."

"Not exactly."

He breathed a laugh and shook his head. "Well, excuse me for being dense. It's just that an apology doesn't sound very heartfelt when it's followed with more argument."

"I'm not arguing, Steve. I'm just asking if it could even be possible that I'm right for once?"

He narrowed his eyes and stared at her. "Did you think you were going to apologize, and that would lead me into saying, 'No, no, *I'm* the one who's sorry. I should have jumped on board with the car, because you were absolutely right'? Is that what prompted the apology?"

"No. Of course I didn't expect that. And the apology was prompted because I don't want you mad at me."

He sat back down on the bed and stared at his knees. "Good, because that's not going to happen. I still think that *you* were wrong. You think you have to make it up to Mark for the year he was in jail. But you're wrong when you start trying to spoil him and make things easy for him. He still needs structure and firmness. He needs to have to strive for things and know the satisfaction of achieving them. It's not good for him to just lie around the house when we've told him he needs to get a job."

"He's looking, Steve. You know that. And he's studying."

Cathy heard Nickelodeon blaring from the living room, and she stepped to the door and peered out into the living room. Tracy still hadn't turned off the television. Instead, she sat on the floor in front of it.

"Tracy, I told you to turn off the television and go to bed," she called out, then turned around to Steve. "Why are you so tough on Mark but you let Tracy get away with murder?"

"Get away with murder?" he asked. "What are you talking about?"

"She's disobeying this very moment, and you haven't said a word about it."

Steve sprang off of the bed and headed to the doorway. "Tracy, turn off the television now and get to your bed!" he yelled.

Cathy hadn't expected that. She watched Tracy turn around with startled eyes. "What did I do, Daddy?"

"You didn't mind Cathy. Now do what I said."

She turned off the television and headed quickly up the hall.

When he turned around, he looked like the wind had been knocked out of him. "Are you happy?"

Cathy grunted. "See how it is? You hate disciplining her, but you don't mind being hard-nosed with my kids. I understand your points about Mark, but Tracy's disobedience goes right over your head. You treat my kids differently than yours."

He started to protest, then caught himself and sank down on the bed. "It shouldn't be different," he said. "I don't mean for it to be."

"Well, it is, and it's normal. I do it, too. I'm soft with my kids, but less tolerant with Tracy. There's grace involved when you're parenting your own child. But there's more law between the stepparent and the child. God is a lot like our parent, and the law is like our stepparent. When we have the Holy Spirit it's pure grace, but when we're under the law, it's hard-nosed and objective . . . but without grace."

He got quiet and tried to process that. "Grace versus law. That's an interesting perspective."

Relieved, Cathy wondered where her words had come from. She'd never thought of the situation exactly in those terms before, and yet the words had spilled out of her mouth. But there was wisdom there, she thought. And it might be the key to learning how to make their stepfamily work.

"Think of it," she said. "Think of it from Tracy's perspective. I told her to go to bed, and she didn't. You didn't see any reason why she couldn't stay up. So I get mad at you for not taking action . . ."

"I just didn't see any harm in letting her watch TV when it's Friday night."

"And I didn't see the harm in buying Mark a nice car. It's grace, Steve. You give grace to Tracy, and I give grace to Mark. I'm not suggesting that you get tougher on Tracy. I'm just saying that if we could treat each other's kids with more grace and less law, we'd have a happier family."

He looked down at his sock feet. "You may have a point."

"I'm trying to learn, Steve." Tears shone in her eyes, and she went to sit next to him. She slid her arm across his shoulder. "I'm really trying to understand about dying to myself and submitting to you. It just doesn't come easy, not for a woman who's been going it alone for so long."

He reached for her hand at his shoulder, and laced his fingers through it. "It's okay. We're both still adjusting. We're going to make it. We've just got a few glitches to work out."

"Do you think so?" she asked. "Are you sure we aren't going to be mad at each other for the rest of our lives?"

He smiled and looked at her. "I couldn't be if I tried. You're just too irresistible."

Grace instead of law. It was the nature of their marriage, too.

CHAPTER
Forty-Two

Sylvia woke soaking wet. The hot flashes had been almost debilitating for the past few weeks, even when she was having her good days after the treatments.

She got out of bed, careful not to wake Harry, and went into the bathroom. Her clothes needed changing again. Exhausted from her constantly interrupted sleep, she turned on the shower, shed her clothes, and got into it.

The cold water ran over her body, washing away the perspiration and cooling her off. Despair rolled over her too, threatening to pull her under. She leaned against the shower's wall, letting the water spray into her face.

And softly, she began to sing. "A mighty fortress is our God . . ."

It wasn't a magic formula that made her symptoms stop, cured her cancer, or solved her problems. It just made her feel better to adore her God and remember that he was her defender and her refuge against the enemies assaulting her. It got her mind off of herself and onto him.

It didn't happen right away, and as the depression hung on, she told herself that she didn't feel like singing. But she sang anyway.

Finally, by the third verse, she felt the depression dripping away like the sweat that had awakened her. Her spirits lifted, and hope seeped back into her bones.

She got out and dried off and tried to focus ahead. She would probably feel all right by Thanksgiving, just six days away. The kids were all flying home just for the day, because Jeff and Gary, Sarah's husband, had to work the Friday after. Harry had insisted on letting a local restaurant cook the dinner, so they'd just have to warm it up before the meal. She hoped she'd have more energy to put into Christmas. Her sixth treatment date fell just three days before Christmas, but her doctor had agreed to postpone it until the following week, so that she would feel good. She was thankful for that.

Breanna would be eighteen months by Christmas, and Sylvia couldn't wait to see her toddling around their house, fascinated by their tree, tearing into the presents.

It was dreadfully important to have the best Christmas she'd ever had this year. But to do it, she would have to start now.

With thoughts of decorations and food and family coming to visit, she went back into the bedroom.

Harry had the lamp on and was changing the sheets.

"Harry, I didn't mean to wake you."

"It's okay, honey. I wanted to change the sheets for you."

"They were soaking wet," she said. "Another hot flash."

He smoothed the fresh sheet out. "All dry now."

She sighed. "Until the next one."

"We have more sheets," he said. "Plenty of them."

She crawled back into bed and curled up next to her husband. Gratitude filled her heart again for the man who had chosen to be her life partner and had never faltered in fulfilling that promise.

She had much to be thankful for.

As hard as Sylvia tried to put on her best face for Thanksgiving Day, she realized that her children saw her as a sick, possibly dying woman. The look on Sarah's face when Harry brought her in from the airport spoke volumes.

"Oh, Mom ..." She burst into tears and threw her arms around Sylvia. Sylvia held her, rocking back and forth. Sarah just cried.

And then Jeff came in, and she saw the startled look on his face. He quickly rallied. "Hey, Mom. You look great."

She hugged him. "Don't give me that. I must look awful, judging by the looks on your faces. Come on, I spent all morning fixing up for you. Now where are Gary and Breanna?"

Sarah wiped her eyes. "Gary's getting her out of the car seat." She touched Sylvia's face. "Mom, are you sure you're all right?"

"Yes!" she said. "Chemo is no picnic, but I'm doing fine. It's not the cancer you see, honey, but the side effects of the medicine. I've gained a little weight, so I might look a little puffy. And my skin color would make Elizabeth Arden cringe. But it's temporary, guys. It's going to be okay."

Harry burst through the door, carrying the baby in his arms, and Gary came in behind him with the suitcases. Sylvia gasped and reached out for the child, and as she got to know her grandchild, the seriousness faded, and the joy of Thanksgiving filled the house.

When they sat down for the meal, Harry asked them each to tell what they were most thankful for in the past year. Sarah muttered something about her child and marriage, Jeff said he was thankful that they could all be together today, Gary said he was thankful for Sarah and Breanna, and Harry said he was thankful for all the opportunities the Lord had given them to serve him.

When it was Sylvia's turn, she hesitated a moment and looked from her daughter to her son. They watched her, waiting to see if she could truly be thankful for anything in this state. So she surprised them.

"I'm thankful for my cancer."

Sarah's face twisted. "Mom, how can you say that?"

"It's easy," Sylvia said. "God gave it to me as an opportunity ... a gift. I can use it. I'm not sure how yet ... he hasn't revealed all that to me. It might be to support other cancer patients when I've gotten through this. Or it might be just to prove his faithfulness. But whatever the case, he's going to use it to bear fruit through me. I know he is. And that's what I'm here for, isn't it? To bear fruit. If I can do that better because of my cancer, then why shouldn't I be thankful for it?"

Her words didn't bring a smile to either of their faces. Gary reached over and took Sarah's hand, a silent gesture of support as she struggled to hold back her tears. Harry patted Jeff's shoulder, as her son stared at the turkey at the end of the table.

Breanna began to bang on her tray, demanding attention and food. It broke the ice and made them all laugh, and she became thankful for that, too.

As they dug into the meal, she silently asked the Lord to make her even more thankful. The cancer *was* a gift, she knew. She just needed the courage and strength to use it fully.

Thanksgiving came and went, and Sylvia felt good about the facade she'd shown the kids. They had put them back on their planes that night with smiles on their faces, and promises to see them next month for Christmas.

But her fifth treatment knocked her out again.

Still, as soon as she was able, Sylvia forced herself out of bed. She had too much to do to get ready for Christmas, and she wasn't going to let her cancer ruin it.

She made her way through the woods at the back of her property, a garbage bag in one hand and a pair of pruning shears in the other. Now and then she would spot a tree that was perfect for trimming branches that could be made into garland, or the wreath that she had made every Christmas for years.

Harry trudged through the woods behind her with his own garbage bag and shears, but she knew he wasn't interested in the live wreath that she planned to create. He had come just to make sure she didn't fall in the woods.

"Honey, you know this isn't necessary," he said. "We could go to one of those craft stores and buy a bunch of fake garland this year. Everybody else in the world does it. Some of it is really beautiful."

Sylvia shot him a disgusted look. "I do real garland, and I've been known to make the most beautiful wreaths in Tennessee. I'm not going to stop now."

"But I'm not sure you're up to this. I don't even know how you've made it this far out here."

"I'm fine." The truth was, she wasn't fine. She had spent the night throwing up, and she hadn't been able to eat a thing this morning. Her legs shook with each step, but she was determined. "I want the house to look just like it always looks at Christmas. The kids are scared enough. I want normalcy, joy, excitement this Christmas."

"They would understand this time. In fact, they'd probably love to help decorate."

"By the time they come for Christmas, it's going to be done. We have a grandbaby this year. I want her to walk in and see the wonders of Christmas."

Harry didn't argue anymore. She found a stump and sat down, tried to catch her breath. A feeling of nausea rose up over her, but she fought it until it was gone. The brisk air against her face made this a little easier.

When she had gotten all she needed, she went back to the house for a nap. She would rest for a while, then get up and wire the garland together and make her famous wreath. In fact, she might just make one for each of her neighbors.

She heard Harry in the garage, pulling out boxes of lights. She knew he did it just to please her. Usually, she had to beg and plead with him to get it done by the second week in December. December was still two days away, but Harry was getting it done.

In bed, she prayed that the Lord would give her uncanny strength to make this a wonderful Christmas for her children and her grandchild, because she knew he had given her no guarantees that there would be another one for her.

Chapter *Forty-Three*

What're you doing, Dr. Harry?"

Harry turned from the lights he was hanging on the bushes in front of their house and saw Joseph standing with his hands in his pockets.

"Hanging lights. Wanna help?"

"Sure." Joseph unwound the spool on which Harry had wrapped them the last time he'd taken them down, and fed it to Harry. "It's early for Christmas lights, isn't it?"

"Sylvia has her heart set on getting it done early. I think she's worried she won't have that many good days, so she's giving herself plenty of time."

"I know what her problem is."

Harry turned back to the boy. "You do?"

"Yes. She's not having any fun. She needs to have fun. When I was sick, my mom tried to make me have fun, and it helped. It gets your mind off of your problems."

Harry finished the bush and plugged it in to test it. The lights came on. Satisfied, he unplugged them again. "So what do you suggest, Joseph?"

"Well, what's the most fun she's ever had?"

"She likes playing with our granddaughter. And all the kids back at the orphanage in León."

"But they're not here." Joseph kept unwinding the lights. "Miss Sylvia used to have a lot of fun when she rode your horses."

Harry smiled and took the strand of lights from him. "Yes, she did. But that was quite a few years ago."

"She'd still like it, I bet." He got to the end of the strand and handed it to Harry. "I wish you hadn't had to sell them for me."

Harry turned back to the child. "Joseph, everyone in town was trying to help out with your transplant expenses. It was the least we could do, especially when we were about to go to the mission field."

"Yeah, I know. And I appreciate it. I really do. But maybe you could get another horse for Miss Sylvia, just until she's better."

Harry wrapped the lights, letting that idea filter through his mind. "I don't know, Joseph. She might be too weak to ride."

"But it would get her out into the fresh air, because she'd want to talk to it and pet it and feed it and stuff. And I could help, you know. When you two didn't feel like feeding it or cleaning the stables, I could do it. I remember how."

Harry crossed his arms and looked down at Joseph. Brenda had always said that Joseph had an uncanny wisdom that few children his age had. Now Harry believed it. "You know, you could be right, Joseph. Maybe it would be good for her. Give her something else to love. Something to take care of."

Joseph nodded, his round face very serious. "Because she had to give up so much, leaving Nicaragua and all. She's probably mourning for all those kids and stuff. And if you got her a really good horse, she'd fall right in love with it."

"But what about when she's well and we go back to Nicaragua?"

"You could sell it," Joseph said. "Maybe I could buy it. I could start saving now . . ."

Harry grinned. "What about riding it? Do you think you could ride it for us if Sylvia didn't feel like it? Just to give him exercise?"

"Sure." Joseph's whole face grinned. "I'd love to do that."

Harry had caught the vision. He pictured Sylvia sitting out on the back porch, instructing Joseph in brushing the horse, cooling it down, putting on the saddle and taking it off. It would go so far in getting her mind off of her illness. She might even bounce back faster from her chemo if she got the fresh air and exercise she needed.

"Joseph! Supper!" Brenda's voice cut across the yard.

"I gotta go," Joseph said. "Sorry I couldn't help more, but I can come back after supper."

"No, I'm almost done," Harry said. "Besides, you did help a lot. I'm going to think about what you said."

They slapped hands, then Joseph took off running across the yards. Harry watched, moved, at the exuberance and health in the boy, when he'd come so close to death not so long ago.

Maybe he did, indeed, know what Sylvia needed. But if he got her a horse, would she be strong enough to ride? Maybe if he found a gentle mare, she'd be able to do it. It would certainly give her something else to think about.

Boxing up the leftover decorations, Harry went into the house to search the classifieds for a horse.

CHAPTER
Forty-Four

Full-time job openings were sparse this time of year, and Brenda wondered if she'd have to wait until January to find work. That would make Christmas awfully tight, and she dreaded that next trip to get Joseph's refills. She sat poring over the want ads at the kitchen table, when Daniel came in.

"Mama, I've got a plan," he said. "I want to see what you think."

David, coming in from his workshop, went to the sink to wash his hands.

"Dad, you need to be here, too. I was telling Mama about my plan."

David gave Daniel a look over his shoulder. "Shoot," he said. "We're listening."

"Okay, here's the thing."

Whenever Daniel started anything with "here's the thing" they knew that it was going to be good. Brenda closed the paper and put her pen down.

Daniel's eyes danced with excitement. "You know how Mark is taking the GED course? He'll be literally out of high school soon, and then he can go to college or get a job or do whatever he wants to, right?"

Brenda looked at David. "Well, something like that."

"Well, I was thinking that since Mama plans to go back to work, and she doesn't have so much time for home schooling, that I could take the GED test, too. Then I'd be finished."

"Why do you want to do that?" Brenda asked. "Why don't you just want to finish school and get your diploma?"

"Well, what difference does it make? I'm home schooled. It's not like I'm going to put on a cap and gown and walk through the high school."

"We do have a home schooling graduation, Daniel. You know that."

"Yeah, but that would be another whole year and a half, and I don't want to do it. I could be finished now."

David chuckled. "Daniel, is this about Mark getting out of school before you? Are you jealous or something?"

"No, I'm not jealous." Daniel's ears pinkened. "But it's not fair. I'm a better student than he is. It's like he's getting rewarded and I'm not."

"You'll be rewarded when you finish school the way you're supposed to," Brenda said. "Lots of people get GEDs and it works out fine, but you don't have to do that. You're too close to graduating."

Daniel turned his pleading eyes to his father.

"No," David said. "I agree a hundred percent with your mother. You are not going to finish early."

"Great." Daniel threw himself back into his chair. "It's like I'm being punished because I never went to jail."

"What?" Brenda's mouth fell open. "How can you say such a thing?"

"Well, look what's going on with him. I mean, he spends a year in jail. He gets out and they throw this great big party for him. You've never thrown a party for me. And then he doesn't have to go back to school. He gets his GED. And they hand him a car on a silver platter when I have to work like a dog to pay for mine."

David bristled. "Son, I paid for part of yours."

"I know, and I'm glad, Dad, but sometimes it just seems like he's getting a better deal."

"You think it was a good deal when he had to spend a year locked up?" Brenda asked. "Come on, Daniel. You're not thinking clearly."

He drew in a deep breath and let out a sigh. "It's not fair, that's all. He gets out of school before I do, and he didn't even apply himself. He didn't even try."

"He's trying now," Brenda said.

"Not very hard," Daniel threw back. "And if he'd come back to home schooling with us, we'd have more money and you wouldn't have to go to work."

Brenda met her husband's eyes. "That's not true. I'm going to work for the insurance benefits." David's expression was somber, and she knew his pride ached that his wife was joining the work world.

"We need more money than I could have made with Mark, anyway, Daniel. Don't you understand that?"

He propped his chin on his hand, sulking. "Yeah, I guess. Joseph has all that expensive medicine to take."

"Well, that's right," she said, "and it's a small price to pay to keep him alive. I'm willing to go to work to do that."

"Well, I'm just saying if I got a GED then I could go to work and get some insurance and I could pay for it."

"It doesn't work that way, Daniel. They don't let you put your brother on your insurance. Or your parents. It's a sweet thought, but we'd rather have you at home studying so you can get scholarships to college."

David patted his shoulder. "You're going to be fine, Daniel. You'll go at the normal pace, and you'll be in good shape for college entrance exams. You'll probably qualify for all sorts of scholarships. College is going to be a breeze for you."

"Well, maybe I don't want to go to college," Daniel said.

Brenda gasped, and David sprang up from his chair. "Young man, I don't want to hear that again. You *are* going to college."

"But you didn't, Dad."

David gritted his teeth. "Son, that's the worst mistake I ever made."

"But you've made a good living as a carpenter."

"I love being a carpenter, and I probably would have been had I gotten a degree or not, but I don't have the options that I would have had if I had gone to college. And I want you to have better."

"But Mark isn't going to get better."

"That's up to Mark," Brenda said. "We have a different plan for you."

"Well, what if it's not the plan I have for myself?" Daniel asked.

Brenda could tell he'd been talking this over with Mark. She rubbed her temples. "Daniel, quitting school and skipping college is not a plan."

David shook his head. "Daniel, when you become an adult you can make up your own mind about what you're going to do, but for right now we're going with our plan. You will finish school. Do you understand?"

Daniel scraped his chair back and got up. "Yes, sir."

"And you will go to college. Is that clear?"

He hesitated, then muttered, "Yes, sir."

"Fine. I'm going back to work." David headed out of the room, ending the conversation.

Daniel turned his eyes to Brenda. She took his hand. "Your father is right, Daniel. Do you understand why?"

"No, ma'am, but I'll do it."

"Good," she said. "You're a very wise boy."

Chapter Forty-Five

The snow that covered the ground infused Sylvia with a burst of energy the week of Christmas. The kids would be home Thursday, the day before Christmas Eve, and she needed to get ready for them. Harry had gone to run some errands. Left to her own resources, she went up into the attic and found Jeff and Sarah's old crib. Knowing she couldn't get it down herself, and unwilling to wait until Harry got home, she called Cathy's house.

"Hello?" Mark's voice was soft across the line.

"Mark, this is Sylvia. How are you?"

"Hey, Miss Sylvia. I guess I'm okay. How are you?"

"I'm great. Nothing like the last time you saw me. By the way, thanks for the Popsicles."

"Sure. Did they help?"

"They sure did. In my book, you're a downright hero."

"Cool," he said. "Too bad I can't put that in my resumé."

"Still no job, huh?"

"Not yet. Man, you'd think I was a convicted killer or something. I'm never gonna get away from my record."

"Yes, you will, Mark. You'll see. As a matter of fact, that's why I'm calling. I want to hire you myself, just for the afternoon. I need someone to come get some things out of the attic for me."

"Sure, I can do that," Mark said. "Only, I can't take money for it."

"Then I'll have to find someone else. Maybe Daniel's available."

"No, I can do it." Mark laughed. "Man, you drive a hard bargain."

"Is Annie there?" Sylvia asked. "I could use her help, too."

"Yes, ma'am. She just got home from school. Do you need us now?"

"As soon as you can get here."

"Okay," he said. "We'll be right over."

In moments, Mark and Annie stood at her door. She welcomed them in with hugs. "Mark, I think you've grown a few inches since you've been home."

He stood straighter. "I think I have, too. I'm five-eight now."

"You are not," Annie quipped. "I'm five-five, and you're not that much taller than me."

Sylvia turned to the girl who was so special to her. "Annie, you just grow more beautiful every day. Look at you." She took her face in her hands and kissed her cheek. "So tell me about that boy Josh. Has he called you?"

Annie cocked her head and crossed her arms. "Miss Sylvia, you *were* trying to fix me up with him, weren't you?"

"Of course I was," Sylvia said. She led them through the house, to the attic stairs. "Why wouldn't I? When I meet a wonderful boy, wouldn't I want him to meet the most precious girl I know?"

Annie grinned and shot a look at Mark. "I told you."

"You should listen to her," Mark said. "I'm getting to know Josh at church. He helps out with the youth group. He's pretty cool."

Sylvia started up the ladder. "So has he called you or not?"

"Not." Annie followed her up. "Big bummer. I thought we hit it off, too."

Sylvia waited until Mark was up, then led them to the crib. "Well, maybe I need to get creative. Have another party or something."

Annie laughed. "No, Miss Sylvia. It's okay. If he doesn't like me, he doesn't like me. I'm okay with it. There are other fish in the sea."

"Sharks, you mean." Mark snickered. "The guys you pick are more like great whites."

"I'm only nineteen," Annie said, ignoring him. "I'm in my first year of college. I'm not looking for a husband, okay?"

"Okay," Sylvia said. "But you should know that I met Harry in my first year of college. We didn't get married until four years later, but I knew."

"I like Josh, but not that much, Miss Sylvia. I didn't go out shopping for a wedding dress the day after we met."

Sylvia shook her head and grinned at Mark. "They're not cooperating with me, Mark. What's a woman to do?"

"I don't know," he said. "But if you see any cute girls and want to fix me up, I promise to cooperate."

When they had gotten the crib down, she had them bring down the boxes of baby things that she had put up so many years ago. When it was all down, she paid Mark and sent him back home. Annie stayed behind to help her decorate one of the bedrooms for the baby.

As they sat on the floor digging out motherhood memorabilia, Sylvia got misty-eyed. She pulled out a threadbare homemade doll and gazed down at it. Sarah had carried it around until it had fallen apart. Sylvia had completely reconstructed it three times.

She reached into the box and pulled out a tiny baseball cap. Jeff had never wanted to take it off. Most nights, he'd fallen asleep in it, and they'd slipped it off without waking him. It seemed like so long ago.

"Don't rush your life, Annie," she whispered. "It goes by so fast. You just have to hang on to every single moment."

Annie smirked. "Hey, you're the one trying to marry me off. I'm not in any hurry."

She set the doll down and pulled out a worn-out blanket that had covered both her babies. "When your kids are young, you're tired and busy, and you just think they'll be that way forever. And then one day, you find yourself sitting on the floor looking through all the stuff that had so little meaning before ..."

She looked up at Annie and saw the tears in her eyes. "Miss Sylvia, are you sure you want to do this?"

She tried to rally. "Yes, I'm sure. I want to fix this room up for little Bree. Last time she was here, she had to sleep in a playpen. This time I want her to have the crib. They're coming for Christmas, you know."

Annie looked around at the decorations she'd already arranged. Small Christmas trees in every room, real garland strung all over the house ...

"Miss Sylvia, how did you get the energy to do all this? It would make Martha Stewart proud."

Sylvia knew she was right. She had done a good job this year. "My kids are really worried about me," she said. "I don't want them coming home to a sick house. I want them to be excited here, happy, like they were so many other Christmases. I want them to forget about my cancer."

Annie's soft eyes fell on her. "How long are they staying?"

"Until the day before my next treatment on the 27th. I'm so blessed that the doctor let me postpone my next treatment until after Christmas. I'm at my best this week. Isn't God good?"

Annie's face sobered. She pulled some blocks out of the box, stacked them up on the floor. "Yes, he's good." But her face belied the statement.

Sylvia pulled the crib bumper pads out of the box. They were wrapped in a garbage bag, carefully preserved so they wouldn't yellow and collect dirt. "Look at these. They look as fresh as they did the day I packed them up."

Annie wasn't listening. She hugged her knees. "Miss Sylvia, do you ever just get mad at God and ask him why?"

Sylvia set the pads down and looked fully at her young friend. "Why would I be mad?"

"The cancer." Tears filled the girl's eyes. "Because sometimes I do. It just seems like you're supposed to be blessed when you're serving God. Not cursed."

"So you think my cancer is a curse?"

"Don't you?"

She smiled and recalled her declaration to her children on Thanksgiving. She had meant it then ... and she meant it even more now. "No, I don't think it's a curse, Annie," she said. "I think my cancer is a gift."

"A gift?" Annie wiped a tear as it rolled down her cheek. "How?"

"It's a gift that gives me new opportunities. Think about it. If I'm healed, then I'll have a testimony about how God brought me through a fatal disease. I'll be able to help others with terminal illness. I'll know how to relate to them, in a way that others can't possibly know."

"And if you're not healed?"

The question was blunt, but Sylvia knew that Annie didn't mean it maliciously. She had grown so close to her over the year she'd spent with her on the mission field. And Annie wasn't one to hold much in.

"If I'm not healed, if this disease takes me, then I can guarantee you one thing. I'm not going to go without taking a lot of people with me."

Annie frowned. "What do you mean?"

"I mean that if I'm going to leave people behind, I'm going to make sure they'll be coming to join me someday. I'll make up my mind to win every single soul I can to Christ before the

Lord takes me home. A woman who's ill is taken a little more seriously when she talks about matters of the soul, don't you think?"

Annie nodded. "So you really think it's a gift?"

"Yes, Annie, I do. It is a gift. And I need to be thankful for it."

Later, when the crib was up and the baby's room was decorated, and Annie had gone home, Sylvia sat out on the swing on her back porch, watching the sun set over the Smokies. Yes, she thought. Her afternoon with Annie had given her clarity. While she planned to fight her cancer with everything she had in her, she also planned to use it. She had always said that the Lord doesn't give gifts that he doesn't equip one to use.

That meant that the Lord would turn her cancer into a tool. A tool for winning souls.

She heard Harry's car pulling into the garage and suddenly realized how very tired she was. But it was a good kind of tired. She had accomplished much today. And there was much more to do.

CHAPTER
Forty-Six

 Sylvia managed to pull off the Christmas she'd planned for her family. Within a couple of days of being home, both Sarah and Jeff seemed to forget their mother was ill. They stopped walking around with somber faces, trying to keep the baby quiet, and watching every word they said to her.

By Christmas Day, the family had relaxed completely, and it felt like old times. Sarah helped her in the kitchen while Harry played with Breanna, and Jeff and Gary watched a ball game in the den.

By the time the dinner was served and eaten, chemo exhaustion was pulling at her. Harry insisted on cleaning the dishes so that Sylvia could lie down for a nap, while the kids went to visit high school friends from town.

That night, as her children continued to visit with friends, Sylvia joined the neighbors at Tory's house for her annual Christmas night celebration. The Christmas paper had all been thrown away and the presents were no longer new. It was the perfect time to gather and relax from the harried pace of the season.

They sipped eggnog and munched on Chex mix and watched Tory's Christmas morning video of Spencer and Brittany and baby Hannah tearing into their presents. Harry read the Christmas story from the Bible, while David sat quietly, tolerant of the observation. Sylvia sat with baby Hannah on her lap, and Joseph leaned next to her on the couch, patting her arm in a quiet affirmation that he knew what she was going through.

All seemed right with the world. Her abundant blessings were too many to count.

That night as Brenda and David and the kids headed back to their house, David put his arm around Brenda and kissed her on the cheek. "I love you," he whispered.

Brenda smiled up at him. "I love you, too."

"Watching Harry and Sylvia made me think," he said. "You can just see how much they love each other. He's worried about her."

"He is going through a rough time."

"Yeah, but I'm just amazed at her attitude." David stopped in the yard between the two houses, and grabbed the chain to the big porch swing he'd built to hang beneath the arbor. As he always did when he passed it, he tested it to see if it was safe. Joseph, Leah, and Rachel horsed around just ahead of them, their cheeks and noses red in the cold night air.

"Joseph seems so drawn to Sylvia," David said.

Brenda sat down on the swing. "He's never forgotten how close he came to death. But Sylvia does have a good attitude. She has her down moments, but mostly she just has a lot of hope."

David sat down next to her. "What if she dies?"

Brenda tried to picture Sylvia facing death head on. "I'm sure she's hoping for a cure, David. But if it turns out the other way, if she's going to die from this cancer, I think she'll be ready for that, too. She has a lot of faith."

"Faith in what?" he asked. "I mean, if she's going to die anyway, wouldn't that faith be misplaced?"

Brenda looked at her husband, and felt his breath warming her face.

"This life is temporary, David. I wish you understood that. There's a lot more on the other side."

"Let's see if you feel that way if Sylvia dies."

She knew he didn't mean to be cruel. In a way, she suspected his words were a kind of plea. Whether he admitted it or not, she was pretty sure he relied on the stability of her faith.

"You've seen me suffer over impending death before," she said. "I got to the point where I thought we were going to lose Joseph, and so did you. Did I ever despair?"

Tears misted his eyes and he shook his head. "No, you didn't."

"I won't this time either, but I'm still hoping that Sylvia is almost out of the woods."

David looked down at his feet. "Yeah, me too. I'm really hoping that."

He took her cold hand, pulled her to her feet, and snuggled her against him as they went into their house to get warm.

Chapter
Forty-Seven

That night after the party, Steve and Cathy felt the warm sense of contentment that Christmas night brings, when all the work and celebrating are done. Annie and Tracy had gone home from the party with Sylvia to help her make a pot of soup for her family. Both Rick and Mark had signed up with their church to work at the local soup kitchen tonight, cooking for and serving those who didn't have Christmas dinner.

While Steve started a fire in the hearth, Cathy curled up with a cup of hot apple cider. When the fire was going strong, Steve joined Cathy on the couch.

Propping his feet on the coffee table, he said, "Ah, this is one of the nicest parts of Christmas."

"Yeah," she said. "No deadlines, no food to prepare, no gifts to wrap. When it gets quiet and slow."

Steve pulled her close. "You sure you're not upset that the kids aren't here tonight?"

She smiled. "They were here all last night and most of today. It's nice to have quiet, especially when I know they're doing something good. Can you believe Rick signed up to work at the soup kitchen?"

"Sure I can," Steve said. "He's got a good heart. The miracle is that Mark is doing it. A year ago, would you have ever imagined it?"

"No," Cathy said. "God has done amazing things."

She heard a car door slam, then another.

Cathy got up and looked out the screen door, and saw Mark coming toward the door. Someone else walked behind him, but he was taller than Rick.

"Looks like we're about to have company," she told Steve.

Mark opened the door into the kitchen, and as his companion stepped in behind him, Cathy recognized Josh, the young man Sylvia had pegged for Annie.

"Josh, hi," she said. "It's good to see you."

"Good to see you, too, Mrs. Bennet."

"Josh gave me a ride home from the Stewpot." Mark winked.

Cathy only looked at him, wondering what the wink meant. Was Mark telling her that he had set this up for Annie's sake?

"Where's Rick?" she asked.

"He wanted to stay and help clean up," Mark said. "Josh was leaving, so he offered to bring me home."

Cathy grinned, wishing Annie would hurry home. "Did you have a nice Christmas, Josh?"

"Yes, ma'am. Did you?"

"Wonderful," she said.

Steve came and shook his hand. "So how was the Stewpot?"

"Great," he said. "My parents and I have been there all afternoon. We served five hundred people today. Mom and Dad are still there, closing the place down."

Mark brandished the Blockbuster movie he held. "I invited Josh to come in and watch a movie. I figured Annie and Rick and Tracy might want to hang out."

Cathy doubted that the twenty-two-year-old had accepted the invitation to spend time with sixteen-year-old Mark. She hoped that meant he wanted to see Annie.

"Annie and Tracy are next door. They should be home any minute."

Mark shot her a look that spoke volumes. *Call her and get her home, Mom. I didn't do this for my health.*

She slipped into the bedroom, and Steve followed. "I'm calling Annie," she said.

"I was just going to suggest that." Steve grinned. "Do you believe Mark did that?"

"Guess it's just a little belated gift for his sister." She punched out Sylvia's number.

"Hello?"

"Sylvia, it's Cathy." She kept her voice low. "Would you tell Annie that Josh is here?"

Sylvia gasped. "Really?"

"Yes. He brought Mark home from the Stewpot. He's in the living room watching a movie."

"She'll be home in two minutes," Sylvia said. "I'm throwing her out right now."

Cathy laughed as she hung up the phone.

Annie hurried Tracy out the door and across the yard. Back home, Tracy ran straight for the new computer the family had gotten that morning, but Annie gravitated to the living room. "Hey, guys," she said. "What you watching?"

Josh came to his feet. "Hi, Annie," he said. "Remember me?"

She grabbed a handful of the popcorn the guys had between them, popped it into her mouth. "Sure I remember. From Miss Sylvia's dinner party."

"That's right."

"We're watching *Monty Python and the Holy Grail*," Mark said. "And don't hog our popcorn, okay?"

Annie ignored him. "I love this movie." She came around the couch, picked up the popcorn, and plopped down between them on the couch. "Oh, good. I didn't miss the part about the rabbit."

Josh threw his head back and laughed. "I love the killer rabbit."

They started trading off lines they'd memorized from the movie, and before long they were laughing and chattering, and rewinding bits of it so that they could act it out again.

As the movie came to an end, Annie realized she owed her brother big.

She and Josh had a lot in common, and she enjoyed being around him. Maybe once again, Miss Sylvia had been right.

It was almost midnight when Josh got up to leave, so she walked him to the door.

"Thanks for the ride home, man," Mark said from the couch.

"Sure," Josh said. "Thanks for the movie."

"Bye, Josh," Annie said as nonchalantly as possible.

"See ya," he said. "Uh, could I get your phone number, by any chance?"

Annie grinned, but Mark spoke up. "Mine?"

Josh chuckled. "Either of yours."

"Same number," Annie said. "And either of us would be glad if you called."

She wrote it down for him, hoping she'd hear from him soon.

When Josh was gone, Annie turned back to her brother. Grinning, he lifted his hand, and she slapped it.

"Merry Christmas, sis," he said.

Annie leaned over the couch and kissed him.

CHAPTER
Forty-Eight

The week after Christmas Mark learned that he'd flunked his second GED test. His instructor had warned him that he still wasn't ready to take it, but he had insisted. Now he saw that he was going to have to finish his entire class in order to get it.

Trying to revive his sagging ego, he set his mind to applying for jobs. A guy in his class had told him that the building contractor he worked for was hiring, so he called ahead and made an appointment, then got dressed up and drove to the site.

"I'm looking for advancement," he told the builder. "I'd like something I could grow into, maybe work my way up."

The contractor rubbed his mouth. "You're how old?"

"Sixteen, but I'm mature for my age."

"Well, Mark, I'm not really hiring for any executive positions today. I'm looking for people willing to work hard for minimum wage."

Mark sat straighter. "Well, you have to start somewhere. But it's pretty cold out. What do you do when it rains?"

The man leaned back in his chair and propped his feet on his desk. "We don't work. And I don't pay you when you don't work."

Mark thought that stank, but he didn't say so. "How would you be able to pay your rent if it rained a lot that month?"

"That's your problem," the boss said. "Besides, you live at home, don't you?"

"Yeah, but I don't want to forever. But it's okay. I think I'd like construction work."

The man dropped his feet and looked back down at Mark's application. "Tell me about this year of incarceration."

Mark cleared his throat. "I sold some marijuana to an undercover officer. It was stupid to smoke the stuff, much less sell it to somebody else. I served a year, but it changed me. It really did. I'm a different person now."

"Yeah, I've heard that before." The man closed his file and got to his feet. "Well, thanks for coming by, Mark. I'll let you know."

Mark left the office discouraged and headed for the mall. He went around and put applications in at several different stores. He had made up his mind not to lie about his conviction, but now he wondered if that had been a mistake.

He felt whipped by the time he got back home. Steve was home early and sat at the kitchen table reading the paper. He looked up when Mark came in. "What's up, Mark?"

Mark shook his head. "Not much. No jobs, that's for sure."

Steve put down the paper and looked fully at him. "You've been looking?"

"Yeah, but no luck."

"Where have you been applying?"

"You name it. I've been there." He poured a glass of milk and sat down across from Steve. "I was honest on all my applications. Told them about my year at River Ranch. But maybe that was stupid. Maybe it wouldn't have hurt anything to keep that to myself."

"Honesty never hurts, Mark. I'm proud of you for telling the truth about it."

Mark took a drink, set the glass down hard. "Even if one of them does hire me, it'll be for a minimum wage grunt job. But I'm looking for something a little more permanent."

"Why? What's wrong with getting something temporary for now, even part-time?"

"Because you can't make a living doing that," he said. "And I don't want to go to college. I'd like to get a job I could grow into."

"Well, the problem is that unless you do go to college, you're not going to have as many choices."

"I know, but I want to do something a little more substantial than working an hourly job for minimum wage. I can do it. I'm a hard worker. I worked hard at River Ranch. I'm not afraid to get my hands dirty. But nobody will give me a chance."

Steve picked up the newspaper and flipped to the employment section. "Let's see. Maybe between the two of us we can come up with some ideas."

When Cathy got home from working at the clinic, she stepped into the kitchen and saw Steve and Mark huddled over the paper.

Her mama bear instincts kicked in, and she imagined that Steve had been lecturing the boy about pounding the pavement for work. "What are you guys doing?"

"Hi, honey." Steve rose up and gave her a kiss.

"Hi, Mom." Mark's voice was flat, and she could see that something was wrong.

"We were just talking about Mark getting a job," Steve said. "Trying to figure out places he could apply."

"Oh." Just as she'd thought. Mark had probably walked innocently in, and Steve had hit him with the classifieds.

She took off her coat and hung it up. "Steve, could I speak to you alone for a minute?"

He looked up at her, puzzled. "Sure."

Mark took the list they had been working on and began to study it as they headed for the bedroom. When they were alone, she turned on Steve.

"Why are you riding him about getting a job? He's been looking. I happen to know that for sure. He's applied at dozens of places."

Steve gave her a stunned look. "Why do you assume I'm riding him?"

"Because I can see what's going on. You're sitting there lecturing him and he looks like he's been hog-tied."

"Well, that would be your impression. And it's just possible it could be wrong."

"I don't think I'm wrong."

Steve's lips thinned, and he sat down on the bed. "Cathy, for your information, Mark came home after applying to about twelve places today and getting rejected at every one, and he was upset. He sat down with me and I started trying to offer him some suggestions. He's listening. It's not a pleasant experience for him because he hasn't had good luck so far. But he's not in a bad mood because of me."

She stood there a moment, letting the information sink in. "Oh. Guess I was wrong."

"Yeah, guess you were wrong." He got up and grabbed his keys off of the dresser.

"Where are you going?"

"Out," he said. "I think I need to put a little distance between you and me for a few minutes while I cool off."

"Cool off?" she asked. "I didn't mean to make you mad."

He swung around. "I know you didn't mean to, Cathy. It just comes naturally these days. I don't like being accused of riding your son. It makes me angry."

"I'm sorry."

"You *should* be sorry. This isn't the first time, and I know it won't be the last time. But I am not Public Enemy Number One to your son." With that, he strode through the living room and kitchen, and headed out to his car.

"Hey, where'd he go?" Mark asked. "We were in the middle of something."

Cathy stared at the door. "He had to run to the bank before it closes."

Mark got his list and took his glass to the sink. "I guess I have enough leads to keep me busy tomorrow," he said. "Man, I've *got* to get a job."

He headed up the stairs, and Cathy stood in the kitchen, realizing she'd made a terrible mistake. Once again, she had failed to give Steve the benefit of the doubt. She had shot first and asked questions later.

She didn't blame him for being so angry.

When Steve hadn't come back after twenty minutes, Cathy started getting angry again. They needed to talk this out, but if he didn't come home, how could they?

She didn't know why things had been so hard for them lately. When they were dating, it seemed that they had worked all of these things out. But now, only months into their marriage, it was as if the seams were coming unstitched.

She needed to talk to Sylvia.

Crossing the yard, she knocked on Sylvia's door. When no one answered, she checked the garage. The car was there, so they must be home. She knocked again.

Finally, Harry answered the door. "Oh, Cathy." His hair was tousled and his face looked tired and aged.

"Harry, what's wrong?"

"It's Sylvia. She's really sick. She had her treatment today."

"Oh, I forgot."

"Come in." He left her at the door and ran back into the house. She stood just inside the foyer for a moment, not certain whether to stay or go.

Finally, she stepped back toward the bedroom and saw Sylvia on the bathroom floor, retching into the toilet bowl. Harry bent over her, wiping her face and neck with a cold, wet rag.

He looked to see if she was there and called out, "Cathy, get me a couple more wet washcloths. They're in the linen closet."

She got them and held them under the faucet, squeezed them out, and brought them back to him. He set them on Sylvia's neck and forehead.

"If you wouldn't mind, go get her a Popsicle. She's got terrible sores. Maybe it would help."

Cathy grabbed a Popsicle and stuck it into a cup, then got some crushed ice out of the little dispenser at the front of the freezer.

Sylvia was retching again when she came back. When she stopped, she lay on the floor, her bare cheek against the cold tiles.

"Here, honey," he said. "Some ice chips. Just suck on these." Harry put them into Sylvia's mouth.

She lay there curled up on the floor, unable to move. He lifted her head gently and put it onto his lap.

Cathy stood speechless just outside the door, tears stinging her eyes. For the first time, she sensed the pall of death that seemed to hang over Sylvia. Rage rose in her chest. How dare death stalk her this way? How dare it torment her?

Harry seemed to have forgotten she was there. She watched as tears rolled down his face and plopped onto Sylvia's cheek.

Cathy started to cry and decided to let herself out. As she pulled the front door shut behind her and launched out across the yard, she saw that Steve's car was back in the driveway. Weeping harder, she realized that this petty argument she had come to tell Sylvia about was worthless. It was hardly a blip on the screen of a lifelong marriage that she hoped she would have with Steve. But here she was being petty, accusing him of things that he hadn't done, looking for the worst in him when she had married him because he was a precious, wonderful man just like Harry—a man who would sit on the floor next to her in her darkest hour and hold her head while she vomited.

Why had she attacked him in the way she had?

Die to yourself. Sylvia's words reeled through her brain. She *hadn't* died to herself. Instead, she still clung mercilessly to herself, feeding her own feelings of paranoia and suspicion and anger ... but Steve didn't deserve any of it.

She went through the garage to the door into the house. She stumbled into the kitchen and saw that Mark was back at the table, studying his job prospect list and scoping them out on a map.

"Where's Steve?" she asked.

Mark looked up at her. "You okay, Mom?"

She sucked in a sob. "Yes ... just ... where's Steve?"

"In the bedroom, I guess."

She headed back to the bedroom and found Steve sitting on the bed staring into space.

"Oh, Steve!" She stood at the door, her face twisted and red.

He saw her grief and got up instantly, reached for her. She fell against him, clinging with all her might. "I'm so sorry, Steve," she wept. "I'm so sorry."

"It's okay, baby," he said. "It wasn't that bad. Why are you so upset?"

"Because I'm so stupid," she said, "and so catty. And Harry and Sylvia are over there struggling for her life. Harry's so afraid he's going to lose her, and here I am, picking at you. Just picking, picking, picking."

He touched the back of her head and pressed her closer to him. "It's okay, honey. It's okay."

"I promise I'm not going to accuse you anymore. You're the best thing that's ever happened to me or my children."

Steve held her and let her cry until her tears subsided. Then together they sat on the bed and prayed for Sylvia.

CHAPTER Forty-Nine

A week after her sixth treatment, Sylvia lay curled up on the bed, wondering when she would ever get her energy back. Each chemo treatment seemed worse than the one before it, and took longer to recover from. And what if it was futile? What if she was putting herself through these grueling treatments, and the cancer grew in spite of it?

Harry came and sat on the edge of the bed. "You want to go for a walk?"

"No, I'm too tired."

"But you love the snow. And your favorite place in the world is the woods behind our house. Maybe it would be good for you to get some exercise, breathe some fresh air, get your mind off of how bad you feel."

"I can't, Harry. Not today."

But Harry didn't give up. "Sylvia, I've got a surprise out there I want to show you. A late Christmas present."

She rubbed her eyes. "I don't want any surprises. I don't have the energy for them."

"Come on. You'll love this one." He pulled her up, helped her to her feet.

She didn't want to go. Within a few days, she knew she would be back to herself, except for the debilitating fatigue. But right now . . .

He pulled her up, got her coat, pulled it around her shoulders. She didn't have the energy to fight him as he took her by the hand and led her out into the backyard.

Harry couldn't wait to show her his surprise. Ever since Joseph came up with the idea, he'd been looking for a gentle, older horse that would be right for Sylvia. If she had something to take care of, something that needed her, he knew she would feel better sooner after each treatment. He'd found the horse through a friend of a friend. Its owner had died, and the family needed to sell it.

Before he made an offer, he'd consulted with her oncologist. He'd told him it was okay for her to ride as long as she didn't overdo it.

He took her hand and walked patiently beside her, one step at a time. When he put his arm around her, he could feel her body trembling with weakness. He hoped he was doing the right thing.

"I've missed having the horses," he said as they headed slowly for the barn. "Haven't you?"

"Yeah, I really do."

He grinned. "Wouldn't it be nice to have one again?"

"Sure it would," she said. "But if we got one, we'd just have to sell it again when we went back to León."

That positive proclamation did him good. For the last few weeks, he'd worried that she was giving up.

"Well, I was thinking that this time if we got a horse, when we left we could just donate it to somebody."

She looked at him with dull, distant eyes. "Somebody like who?"

"Somebody like Joseph."

Sylvia stopped and looked up at him.

"Wouldn't that be like coming full circle?" Harry asked. "We sold the first horses to raise money for his transplant, and this one we'd give to him because he's so healthy he can ride."

"But Brenda and David could never afford to keep a horse for Joseph."

Harry shrugged. "We could work something out."

Sylvia smiled. "I like that idea."

He laughed and pulled her into the stable, and she heard something over in the corner where Sunshine, her favorite horse, used to live.

She frowned. "What's that? I heard—"

His grin was giving him away. "You'll see." He led her to the stall, where a tall, beautiful mare looked over the door.

She caught her breath. "Oh, Harry, what have you done?"

He laughed. "I bought you a new horse," he said. "Isn't she beautiful? Look at her." He opened the door and grabbed the horse's bridle, which he had put on a little while earlier. He pulled her out of the stall so that Sylvia could have a good look.

She started to cry and stroked the horse's chocolate coat. "Oh, Harry. I love her."

"I've been looking all over for just the right horse. I thought it would be good therapy for you to ride again. It's your favorite thing to do in the whole world, and you haven't done it in years."

The horse nuzzled her neck and she rubbed her face against it. "What a sweetie," she said. "Oh, Harry. Are you sure we can afford it? We don't have that much left in savings."

Their finances had been drained by their mission work. They'd funneled all of their savings and much of their retirement into medical supplies and food for the people of León.

"Sure we can," he said. "I've decided to go back to work at the hospital part-time. Joe Simmons wants me to join him in his practice, and I told him that I might be able to do it on non-chemo weeks."

Sylvia turned away from the horse and regarded him. "Does he understand that you're only going to be there a few months?"

"He understands," he said. "I'm not planning to take any long-term patients."

She hugged the horse as if he were a long-lost member of her family. "Can I ride her?"

"Of course you can." He grabbed down the saddle that had hung there for over two years, dressed the horse as Sylvia watched. Already he could see the energy seeping back into her, and her countenance had changed completely.

"Take it easy now the first time," he said. "I don't want you breaking any bones."

With his help, she got on the horse, sat for a moment. He saw the perfect peace passing over her face, as if she was finally home.

Her laughter was like a symphony. "Oh, Harry, you're a genius," she said. "I'm already feeling better."

"Now take it real, real easy," he said again as the horse walked out of the barn and into the fresh air. Big snowflakes floated down around them. "Don't underestimate your weakness."

"I won't," she said. "We're just going to get to know each other. What's her name?"

"Midnight," he said.

She patted the horse's neck. "Let's go, Midnight."

Then she walked the horse off to her favorite path.

Harry stood watching, and said a silent prayer that she would not hurt herself. But the surprise had accomplished his goal to get her out of bed and her mind off of her problems. She only had two more treatments. They were sure to get worse and more draining. Then, as she built her strength back, she would have Midnight to nurture and pamper.

It was the perfect plan. Harry just hoped God would go along with it.

CHAPTER *Fifty*

A week into the new year, Mark got up early to beat the bushes for a job. He went to each business on the list that he and Steve had forged. Some of the managers were not in, and he was only able to fill out applications. When he finally found one that would see him, he felt as if he had hit pay dirt.

It was a roofing company and paid a little bit more than minimum wage. It sounded like a good job, at least according to Steve, and Steve knew the guy who ran the company.

The interview was going well until Mark told him what he had done with the last year of his life. The open look on his face closed, and he leaned back in his chair. "You should have told me that up front, Mark."

Mark shifted in his seat. "Why? You wouldn't have even seen me if I had told you that."

"Well, I needed to know. It's kind of pertinent."

Mark felt his cheeks burning. "It's really not. I did a stupid thing a year and a half ago and I paid for it. But I'm different now. I don't do drugs anymore."

"Still, I don't hire ex-cons." The man got up and stuck the file back into the file cabinet behind him.

Mark knew he was being dismissed. He got up, slid his hands into his pockets. "It was River Ranch juvenile delinquent center." He kept his voice low, steady. "It's not like I was serving time in the federal penitentiary. Besides, I'm a Christian now. And if the almighty God of the universe can forgive me, then I don't see why somebody like you can't."

He turned and started back to the door.

"Wait a minute," the man said.

Mark stopped and turned around.

"Come back in here and sit down."

Mark slid his hands into his pockets again and came back.

The man sat back down and leaned his elbows on his desk. "I'll tell you what. I can see that you're a passionate young man, and that maybe you really do have it in you to change. And since you're Steve's stepson, I guess I can help out with that a little."

Mark started to tell him not to do him any favors, but thought better of it.

"If you're here tomorrow morning at seven o'clock, you can start working. Just report here and fill out all the paperwork, and then Myra, my secretary, will tell you where our work site is for the day. You can come over and we'll put you to work."

Mark slowly unfolded from his slump, and a grin crept across his face. Had he heard right? Had the man hired him? The man got up and held out a hand to shake. Mark got to his feet and shook. "Thank you, sir. You won't regret it."

"Let's hope not."

CHAPTER
Fifty-One

Cathy hadn't seen Sylvia since her treatment just after Christmas, but one day in early January she spotted her sitting out on her horse, staring out at the hills behind her property. Something was wrong. Sylvia didn't move, and the horse beneath her stood motionless. Cathy hurried across the yard to see if she needed help.

As she grew closer, she saw that the color of Sylvia's skin was a grayish-yellow. She looked sick now, not just weak or frail. The systemic effects of the chemo were taking a terrible toll on her.

Sylvia didn't seem to hear as she approached. "Sylvia, are you feeling all right?"

Sylvia turned slowly and looked down at her. "Hey, Cathy. I was just going to ride, but I think my legs are too weak. Can you help me off?"

Cathy gave her a hand, and felt Sylvia's body trembling as she stepped to the ground. "How did you saddle the horse?"

"Joseph did it, then I sent him back home to study. I didn't realize I was still so weak."

Cathy let her lean on her and led the horse back to the stall. "This last treatment must be hanging on, huh?"

"Yes, but there are only two more."

Cathy wondered if those last two would completely do Sylvia in. It seemed cruel, injecting such a harsh drug into a cancer patient's veins, when there were no guarantees that it would even work.

But she supposed the alternative was even more deadly.

Sylvia took measured steps. The horse walked slowly beside them as if it understood that she was ill and could not hurry. Cathy took the horse into the stall and pulled the saddle off.

"Poor Midnight," Sylvia said. "She was all dressed up and ready to go."

"Well, you'll have plenty of time to ride when you're stronger. Won't you be glad to get these treatments behind you?"

"I guess."

Cathy set the saddle down and gaped at her. "You guess? What does that mean?"

Sylvia leaned her face against the horse's neck. "It's hard to explain, but I kind of feel like I'm doing something as long as I'm taking the chemo. When it's over, I won't be doing anything. What if the cancer's not gone?"

"It will be," Cathy said. "You know it will be. I mean, they probably got it all in the mastectomy. The chemo was just because of the lymph nodes, right? It hadn't metastasized anywhere."

"No."

Cathy took off Midnight's blanket and hung it over a rail. "Sylvia, I just know you're never going to have to deal with this again. When you finish, you'll be home free."

Sylvia sat down on a tack box and watched as Cathy started to brush the horse.

"Oh, I've got some good news for you," Cathy said. "Josh called Annie, and they went out on a date. They really seemed to hit it off."

Sylvia's countenance lifted. "We've got to help it along. Maybe I could have another dinner party, invite them both over."

"Sylvia, I don't think you can get away with that. Come on. It was weird enough for you to invite them both the first time. I think we should just let God do the rest. I'm not so sure I want Annie in a relationship right now, anyway."

"Well, I can understand that," Sylvia said, "but you know Annie. She's going to wind up in one before long. I just want to make sure it's with the right person."

"No arguments from me," Cathy said.

CHAPTER
Fifty-Two

January went by in a blur as Sylvia struggled through her seventh chemo treatment. Sarah came with Breanna to visit, and Jeff was able to come for a long weekend. Though she still had a few good days the week before her treatment, she was too exhausted to ride. Most days, Joseph rode Midnight for her as she sat out on her porch and watched. She carefully taught him how to groom and care for the horse and hired him to clean the stables.

The child gave her comfort when he was around, and since Brenda was spending so much time in a hunt for a job, she didn't feel she was taking him away from his schoolwork.

On the days after her treatment, when she could hardly crawl out of bed, Joseph cared for Midnight without her help. They'd given him permission to ride anytime he wanted without asking, and he kept the horse in shape.

At last in early February the day of her final treatment arrived. Sylvia was quiet as Harry drove her to the Cancer Center.

"Eight times," she whispered. "I can't believe I did this eight times."

"Six months," he said.

"I wouldn't wish it on anyone. I just hope it helped."

"It did," Harry said. "It had to." He took her hand, squeezed it as he drove. "Are you excited?"

She hesitated and looked out the window. "I'm a little scared."

"Scared? Why?"

"Because after this treatment, I go for all the scans. That's when we'll know for sure if it worked. And they said there was a fifty percent recurrence rate. I hate the chemo, but I hate the cancer worse. And without the chemo, the cancer could take a foothold."

"It won't though. You're going to be fine. After this treatment, you'll feel bad for a couple of weeks, but then you'll start feeling better, your strength will come back, your hair will grow back, the color will return to your face . . ." He pulled into the parking lot of the Cancer Center. "And the radiation and hormone therapy will still be battling the cancer."

Harry walked her in, and she took her place and waited as they put the needle into her vein.

An hour into her treatment, her head began to ache, and she dipped some ice chips out of the bowl on her lap and put them in her mouth to keep the sores from forming. Vertigo taunted her, and she felt slightly nauseous.

She closed her eyes and, quietly, started to sing. "Amazing grace, how sweet the sound . . ."

A woman's voice beside her joined in, and she opened her eyes and saw Priscilla, the woman she'd sung with during her first couple of treatments. Priscilla had been finished with her chemo for some time now, and her hair had begun to grow back in. She stood over Sylvia with a smile on her face and a vase of roses. "Hi there," she said softly.

Sylvia smiled, though dizziness wobbled over her again. "Priscilla."

"I knew this was your last treatment day," she said. "I wanted to bring you flowers to celebrate." She put the vase on a tray.

Sylvia touched her hand. "You're so sweet. How are you?"

Priscilla pulled up the rolling stool that the nurses used, and sat down facing Sylvia.

"I'm great. I seem to be in remission. We're very optimistic."

"You look great. Your hair is wonderful. You should keep it that short."

She ran her hand over the inch-long strands. "I'm tempted."

A wave of dizziness seemed to turn Sylvia's stomach, so she closed her eyes again.

"Sing with me," Priscilla whispered. "Come on, honey, sing. Just like you made me do those times. Amazing grace . . ."

Sylvia sang along, trying to get her mind focused on the amazing grace of a God who sent a compassionate friend who'd suffered through the same thing, on the day that she needed her the most.

Priscilla stayed through the whole treatment, then helped her back out to Harry, and hugged her good-bye.

"We both made it through," Priscilla said. "We survived. The worst is behind us now."

Sylvia started to cry. She hadn't expected it, and didn't really have the energy to do it. Yet the tears came—deep, soulful, blubbering tears. "It's over," she whispered to Harry. "It's over."

Harry and Priscilla cried with her, as the joy of her release from the bondage of chemotherapy finally began to dawn on her.

CHAPTER
Fifty-Three

Several days after Sylvia's final chemo treatment—when she was finally able to get out of bed—she went to the hospital for CT scans of her head, chest, abdomen, and bones.

She prayed while she waited for the scanners to move over her body, searching for any more signs of cancer that had spread to other organs or bones. At the end of the day, she went for her blood test and prayed as they drew the blood that the tumor markers would not be elevated.

The results wouldn't be in until the next day.

Still tired and weak, Sylvia went home and tried to get her mind off of the tests. Cathy, Brenda, and Tory came over that night, and they watched *Harvey* on video and munched on popcorn and jelly beans.

But as Harry slept next to her later that night, Sylvia lay awake, praying for remission. She didn't know what she'd do if the test results showed that cancer had taken up residence somewhere else in her body.

So this is what Gethsemane felt like, she thought. Stark fear, heartbreaking dread. She'd heard her pastor say that Gethsemane was the word for "olive press," where they crushed olives to get the oil. In the garden of the olive press, Jesus had been crushed.

Tonight she felt as though she was being crushed, too.

As morning dawned and she gave up trying to sleep, Sylvia came to the place where Jesus had ended up that night.

Not my will, but thine.

She only wished she had more peace about it.

Harry took her back to the oncologist's office for the results. They waited, jittery, in the waiting room until he could see them in his office.

"Good news," Dr. Thibodeaux said as he hustled into the room. "Everything looks normal."

Sylvia gasped so hard it made her choke. "No. You're kidding."

"Not kidding," he said. "It looks like the chemo was successful."

Harry started to laugh, and she saw the tears glistening in his eyes as he hugged her. She threw her head back and laughed like a hysterical woman.

"You're not out of the woods yet, though," Dr. Thibodeaux said. "You still have to go through radiation and hormone therapy. But the chemo was the worst of it, and for right now the results look as good as they could possibly be."

Sylvia felt as if the olive press had been lifted off her back. "Thank you. Oh, thank you, Lord!" She almost danced. "Doctor, isn't there some way that I can have the radiation in Nicaragua so we can get back to our work?"

Harry shook his head. "Honey, that's not a good idea."

The doctor frowned. "Harry, I agree. I don't recommend that at all. I'd prefer she waited here until she was finished. There's a lot of danger of infection in the hospitals there, and the equipment is not up to par. León, Nicaragua, is not an environment that will help this process at all."

Harry gave her an apologetic look. "Sylvia, we can't go back to the field just yet."

She wasn't going to let that news get her down. "It's okay. Only a few more months."

As they walked out of the office with Dr. Thibodeaux, Harry stopped him. "Could I get a copy of her records to take to the plastic surgeon? It's time for her to have her expandable implant replaced with a permanent one, and he'll want to see where we are in the process."

Dr. Thibodeaux nodded. "Sure. I can give you all the records of the test results, but my dictation won't be back for a month or so, so you won't have my notes. It takes that long to get it transcribed."

Harry laughed. "The test results will be fine. You should try doing your notes the old-fashioned way like I do. Write them yourself."

"I see too many patients," he said. "It slows me down to handwrite them, and I tend to abbreviate my comments. I can be more thorough if I dictate. It just takes so long to get them typed. Our transcription service handles most of the doctors' offices in town, so there's a terrible turnaround time on them."

The germ of an idea planted itself in Sylvia's mind. "Have you ever thought of hiring your own typist for the office? That way you could have a one-day turnaround."

The doctor shrugged. "We haven't really given that any thought. We just do it the way we always have."

"You should think about it," Sylvia said. "If you made someone a full-time employee with benefits and everything, you could hire someone of quality. They could even work from home. Show up once a day to return the notes they've typed and pick up what you dictated that day . . ."

Dr. Thibodeaux gave Sylvia a knowing look. "Sylvia, you're not looking for a job, are you?"

Sylvia laughed. "Me? Heavens, no. I'm no typist. But I have a dear friend who would be perfect for a job like that. All you'd have to do is create it, and I bet I could convince her to take it."

His smile faded, and he stared at her for a moment as the wheels seemed to turn in his mind. "Tell you what. This might be an excellent idea. Let me talk to my partners, and then I'll give you a call. Maybe we could set up an interview with your friend."

"You'd better hurry before someone else snaps her up," Sylvia said.

She laughed as they walked out to the car, and all the way home she chattered and planned the party she was going to have for the neighbors that night to celebrate her good news. As she made her plans she felt as if the worst of her disease was behind her. What lay ahead was going to be easy in comparison. Soon cancer would be a distant memory in her life, and she would be able to get on with her work.

She decided to hit the ground running to prove to everyone that the old Sylvia was back.

CHAPTER
Fifty-Four

Since the weather was unusually warm, the neighbors had a picnic in the open lot between Tory's and Brenda's houses that night to celebrate the good news. The Dodd kids decorated the trees with toilet paper and balloons, and Cathy brought her karaoke machine.

Spencer tried to monopolize it, doing the Elvis impersonation he had become known for, but Leah and Rachel managed to get the microphone away from him to do a few numbers of their own. Brenda didn't remember when she had ever laughed more.

As darkness fell and the early March evening grew cool, they grabbed sweaters and turned up the grill and kept celebrating long into the night.

When Brenda got home that night, her excitement over Sylvia's remission left her floating on a wave of energy. As soon as the children were in bed, she hurried to her computer. David sat at the desk in the small room, working on the checkbook.

He looked up at her as she began to type. "What are you doing?"

"I decided to write a proposal to give to Dr. Thibodeaux at the Cancer Center."

He stopped working and turned his chair to her. "What kind of proposal?"

"A proposal of what I could do as the office transcriber. Sylvia said this would be a new job that they create. I don't want to rely on Dr. Thibodeaux's memory or imagination for this. I want to paint them a picture of what they could have if they hired me. Something Dr. Thibodeaux can take to his partners, so they can all catch the vision."

David smiled. "Good thinking. You're a genius."

"No, Sylvia is. It was all her idea. Can you imagine? She'd just gotten news that her body was clear of cancer, and what does she do? She starts campaigning for a job for me. And not just any job, but a job that doesn't even exist, a job that would be perfect for me and allow me to work from home and still have full-time pay and benefits . . ."

Her voice broke off as tears filled her eyes, and she brought her hand to her mouth. "Oh, David . . . do you realize what a blessing this could be?"

He leaned forward, putting his face inches from hers. "It will be, honey, but I hate for you to get your hopes up. What if it doesn't pan out?"

Brenda blinked back her tears and slapped her hands onto her knees. "I've thought of that. If they decide not to take advantage of my offer, then I'll submit the same proposal to every doctor's office in town. And in the proposal, I'm going to offer to do two days' worth of transcribing for free, just so they'll see that I can do it. And hopefully, they'll love the speed and the way it works, and hire me."

He grinned. "It could work."

"It will work, David. It has to."

CHAPTER
Fifty-Five

The final step in Sylvia's breast reconstruction was a minor surgical procedure that needed to be done before her radiation, since the X rays were known to inhibit healing and rob the skin of its elasticity.

She scheduled it for a couple of weeks before her first radiation treatment, then checked into the hospital, anxious to get her body back to as close to normal as possible.

Sylvia stood in front of the hospital mirror, assessing herself with a critical eye. Her hair had begun to grow in and it felt like peach fuzz on her head, much like her grandbaby's hair. Though it was gray, it was new, soft and fine, and it looked like it might have a slight curl as it grew. She hadn't had a curl before.

The breast implant had already been expanded to the size of her other breast—through her monthly saline injections—and under her T-shirt it looked as if she'd never had a mastectomy. Today they would remove the expandable implant and replace it with a permanent one, then make a few cosmetic adjustments to make it look more real.

But she couldn't help the delight surging through her at the idea that she was cancer-free and rebuilding her body. It made her feel that she was on her way to full and complete recovery. She would have the chance to watch her grandchild grow, see Jeff get married someday, and rock all the other grandchildren born into their family . . . and the ones she'd left in León.

A knock sounded on the door. "Come in."

Harry stepped into the bathroom. "They're ready to prep you for surgery," he said.

She nodded. "I'll bet I'm readier than they are."

He gave her a hug and kissed her on the lips, then sent her on her way.

The phone call Brenda had prayed for came Wednesday, the same day as Sylvia's outpatient surgery, less than a week after she'd sent the proposal to the Cancer Center. She'd been dissecting a video on calculus, in an attempt to help Daniel with his lesson, when the phone rang. She dove for it.

"Hello?"

"Mrs. Dodd?" It was a woman's voice.

"Yes."

"This is Sheila Morris, office manager at the Cancer Center." Her heart jolted. This was it. This was the call.

"Dr. Thibodeaux asked me to set up an appointment for you. He said to tell you that he and the other doctors in the clinic had reviewed your proposal and were very interested in talking to you."

Brenda groped for a nearby chair and made herself sit down. It was happening. It was really happening. "Yes, of course. When would he like for me to come?"

"He was wondering if you could come in at 5:30 this afternoon, after the clinic is closed. The doctors have a meeting scheduled for that time anyway, and they thought it would be a good time to talk with you."

"Yes," Brenda said. "That sounds perfect."

When she got off the phone, she let out a whoop, then ran into the room where the children were working, and began laughing and dancing around. "I have an interview! It's really happening!"

Joseph got up and began to dance with her. "Mama, what kind of job is it?"

"It's the one I wanted, where I can work at home."

Leah and Rachel caught the excitement then, and they sprang up and began to jump up and down. Daniel just sat at his desk and grinned.

She heard the back door open, and David came in. "Hey, what's all the commotion?"

"Mom's got an interview!"

Brenda abandoned the children and threw her arms around David. "The Cancer Center, David! They called! They liked my proposal and want to talk to me today!"

David threw his head back and laughed then, and picked her up and twirled her around.

Brenda had calmed down by that afternoon, and with the assurance from Cathy and Tory that they would be praying for her, she dressed in a skirt and blazer and went for the interview.

It went better than she could have imagined, and within half an hour of arriving, she headed back to her car with a medical dictionary and each doctor's tapes for that day's transcription. If she delivered as she'd assured them she could, she could come in Monday morning to fill out all the paperwork, making her a full-time employee.

There was no doubt in her mind she could pull it off.

She sang praise songs as she drove home, filled with joy that the Lord had answered her prayers even better than she'd hoped or imagined.

She immediately set to work transcribing the tapes, and had them all finished by noon the next day. At the end of the day, she returned them to the clinic, and picked up another day's work. When she returned them at 5:30 on Friday, the office manager shook her hand. "Congratulations. Dr. Thibodeaux told me you're hired. You can come in Monday morning to do all the paperwork to get you on the payroll."

Brenda didn't need gas to get home that day. She could have made it on pure joy.

CHAPTER
Fifty-Six

Within a week of the reconstruction surgery Sylvia felt ready to resume her life. The children came home for a visit, and when they were gone she and Harry decided to start a class at their church, a Bible study for those who wanted deeper discipleship. Sylvia decided that they should do a study of Jesus in the Old Testament, so she and Harry had set about to design a curriculum.

They showed up at the church the night of their first meeting, hoping and praying that someone would attend. By fifteen till seven, the room was already full. Some of the men went out and began bringing in extra chairs.

Sylvia's heart soared as she saw Annie come in with Cathy and take one of the back row seats. A little while later, just after seven, Josh slipped in and took a seat across the room.

Harry started teaching, and Sylvia threw things in whenever something occurred to her worth adding. Together they managed to hold the class's rapt attention.

"That went well," Harry said as they drove home that night. "Who would have thought we'd have that big a group? Almost made me feel like we were doing as much good as we did in León."

"Me too," Sylvia said. "I've felt so unproductive for the last few months. This revived my need to be used. I want to do more than a once-a-week Bible study."

Harry grinned as if that didn't surprise him at all. "What do you have in mind?"

"I've been thinking about what I could do during the day," she said. "I was thinking that maybe I could volunteer at the Breezewood Development Center, where Tory works. I could teach the wordless book to the children with Down's Syndrome."

Harry studied the road. "Are you sure, honey? The radiation might take a lot out of you. You don't really want to commit to anything until you know how it's going to be."

"Well, it can't be as bad as the chemo," Sylvia said. "Besides, if I'm a volunteer I can not show up once in a while and it won't hurt anyone. But while I'm able, I want to bear as much fruit as I can."

"Do you think Down's Syndrome children that age would be able to understand the wordless book?"

"Sure they could," she said.

He stopped at a red light and leaned over to kiss her cheek. "I'm proud of you," he said. "Most people in your shoes would be finding ways to indulge themselves to make up for the last few months, but here you are, trying to think of ways to fulfill the Great Commission."

"That's what I'm here for. I'm going to go ask Tory as soon as we get home. She's probably got her children in bed by now."

Tory's garage was still open, so Sylvia knew it wasn't too late to knock on the door. They usually closed the garage as their last task before going to bed at night. She knocked on the door, waited, and after a moment Barry opened it.

"Hey, Sylvia. How's it going?"

"Couldn't be better," she said, stepping inside.

"How was your Bible study?"

"Just fabulous," she said. "You should have been there."

"Well, we were going to, but you know how hard it is for Tory to leave the kids with a sitter. So we've decided that maybe we'll take turns going starting next week. I'll baby-sit and let her go, and then the next week she'll baby-sit and let me go. Maybe we can keep up in the meantime."

"Sure," Sylvia said. "I was thinking about taping it anyway. Whoever doesn't come could hear the tape."

"That's a great idea," he said. "Come on in and I'll get Tory."

Sylvia walked into the spotless living room and sat down on the couch. Tory was a perfectionist and never left anything out of place. But tonight she saw that a few toys lay out in the living room. Tory was loosening up a little, and Sylvia was sure that benefited the whole family.

Tory came out of the back of the house. "Hey, Sylvia. How did the class go?"

"It was fun, and it just thrilled me to be able to do something again. And it sort of started me thinking."

Tory plopped down on a chair near the couch. "Thinking about what?"

"About what you're doing at the school, the children you work with. I'd love to meet little Bo."

"Well, come on up there," she said. "That'll be fine. We invite visitors."

"Well, what about volunteers?" Sylvia asked. "I was thinking about coming up there and reading to the children."

"Well, sure, we'd love to have you. And I know we're always looking for help. The only problem is they have very short attention spans and they're not very good listeners."

"Well, I had another idea," she said. "I have some special books that I used to use for the Nicaraguan kids, and I was thinking maybe it would be a good tool to use with your kids. Since it's a private school, they won't mind if I teach them about Jesus, will they?"

"No, they'll love it. The director's a Christian, and so are most of the teachers. Let me just clear it with the administration tomorrow and I'll get back to you. But I know it won't be a problem. If somebody volunteers to do something they don't have to pay for, they're going to be thrilled. They're constantly having budget problems. I was shocked that they offered to pay me."

"Well, I was just thinking I could come every morning at the same time and work with the children. And on my bad days I could skip and no one would be any worse off for it."

"I think it's wonderful," Tory said. "But, Sylvia, are you sure you want to do that? I mean, if I were you, I'd probably be focusing all my energy on getting well."

"I am getting well," Sylvia said. "It's all in God's hands. Besides, we're supposed to bear fruit in every season of our life. I don't plan to take this season off."

Tory looked down at her hands. "Sometimes I wonder if I bear any fruit at all."

"Of course you do," Sylvia said. "How can you think such a thing? Look at all the work you do with your children. That's bearing fruit. Some day they'll grow up and bear fruit of their own. You're doing your life's work right now. This is what you're called to."

Tory got up and started picking up the toys on the floor. "Remember when I wanted to be a writer?"

"You're still a writer," Sylvia said. "You write better than anyone I know. And those days are not over. But right now you're called to take care of Hannah and Spencer and Brittany, and the children at the school. If that isn't bearing fruit, I don't know what is."

Tory dropped the toys into a basket beside the couch, then hugged Sylvia. "When I grow up, Sylvia, I want to be just like you."

CHAPTER
Fifty-Seven

Sylvia got permission to read to the children at the Breezewood Development Center, so she ordered the wordless books she would need, and took them to the school the Monday after they came in.

Tory and Linda, the teacher, spent the valuable time planning their activities for the rest of the day, while Sylvia sat in a circle with the children. She started off trying to teach them "Jesus Loves Me." A few of them picked it up, but most of them only hummed and muttered words that sounded nothing like the words in the song.

Then she gave them each a wordless book, and began teaching them what each page meant.

"Red is for Jesus' blood," Sylvia would say, and the children would stare blankly at her. "And black is for the bad things we do, all the sin in our hearts. And white is for how clean we are when Jesus washes us."

On their way home, Tory voiced her skepticism that Sylvia's work would do any good. "It's hard for them to grasp concepts like Jesus' blood washing away their sins," she said. "I'm not even sure they understand sin at all."

"Oh, they'll get it before you know it," Sylvia said. "Within a few months I'll bet we have every one of them asking Jesus into their hearts."

Tory turned into Cedar Circle. "I don't know, Sylvia. That might be a little optimistic."

"Optimistic? Why?"

"I just sometimes feel that salvation isn't even a message that *needs* to be brought to these children. They're never going to reach the age of accountability, because they're mentally handicapped. They're already God's children. Their minds never really grow into mature adulthood. Don't you think that they're already saved by virtue of being perpetual children?"

Sylvia regarded her for a moment. "I'm sure that's true. But it never hurts to teach them the truth. And the best truth in the world that we can teach them is about Jesus' love for them and what he did to prove it."

Tory pulled into her driveway and let the car idle for a moment. Hannah slept in the back, so there was no hurry to get out. "I just think the concept of salvation is very complicated. They can barely even learn 'Jesus Loves Me.' Can they ever really grasp that Jesus died on a cross, and was raised from the dead?"

"Don't you want Hannah to?"

"Well, yes, of course. But I don't have much hope that she will. I think God will make a special provision for her."

"Of course he will. But I think you need to raise your expectations. Jesus said to come to him just like those little children. He wouldn't have said that if he meant it to be complicated. It's the adults who make it complicated."

Tory frowned. "You really think so?"

"Of course I think so. We teach them that we did bad things and God decided to send his Son to take our punishment, that when he died on the cross he bought our way into heaven. That's simple, Tory."

Tory looked back at Hannah, sleeping soundly in her car seat. "I know. But there's so much more, even beyond that. All the things I'm learning in the Bible about sanctification and obedience and bearing fruit."

"Those children can understand it on their own level. God isn't some phantom that hides from the innocent. He'll reveal himself to them. And it's good for us to share him with them. It grows *us* when we bear fruit."

As Tory took Hannah into the house, those two words rolled over and over in her mind. *Bear fruit. Bear fruit.* It was the main focus of Sylvia's life. Yet Tory wasn't sure it was a focus at all for her.

Hannah woke up as she started to put her down, so Tory got the wordless book Sylvia had given her. She had never tried reading to her before, never even thought it would have any effect, but maybe Sylvia was right. Maybe she could teach little Hannah about the love of Jesus. The result was completely up to God.

CHAPTER
Fifty-Eight

Mark slammed into the house in late March, sweating from head to toe, an angry scowl on his face. He looked as if he'd been dipped in tar. "This is absolutely the worst day I've ever had in my entire life!"

Cathy flipped the hamburgers she was frying and glanced at Steve, who leaned against the counter. "What is it, Mark?"

"It's a crummy job, that's what. I almost fell off the roof today, and it got so hot out there I thought I was going to die. Eighty degrees in *March?* It's some kind of record or something. And I couldn't take my shirt off because yesterday I took it off and I got so sunburned that I'm blistered. They work us daylight till dark and the money's crummy."

Steve winked at Cathy. "You'll get used to it. People always do. There are people who have been in that business for most of their lives."

"Yeah, but they don't do what I'm doing all those years. They advance to management, and the management guys don't even get up on the roof. They just go from site to site overseeing."

"Well, maybe you can work your way up to that."

Mark dropped his keys on the counter. "I don't even want to *be* in this business."

Steve cleared his throat. "Well, you know, it takes a lot of brains to do construction work, Mark. Reading and interpreting blueprints, making everything come out all right. And roofing is not a small thing. The roof protects the whole house . . ."

"Maybe so, but all I'm doing is hammering and getting tar under my fingernails." He stretched. "Every muscle in my body hurts."

"You'll build your muscles up," Cathy threw in. "After a while, you won't notice it anymore."

"There are better ways, Mom."

She turned from the stove. "Well, Mark, what would you like to do? It was your idea not to go back to school."

"I know. I'm just thinking maybe I need to look for a different job. The problem is, I don't have time because I'm so busy working at this one. By the time I get off I'm filthy and exhausted. I don't have time to go do anything else. Besides, nobody wants to hire a guy with my record. Even when I get my GED, it'll be practically worthless when it's balanced against the conviction."

Annie came into the room, munching on a celery stick. "Told you you should go to college. It's a breeze, Mark. Practically like a day at the beach compared to what you're doing."

Cathy shot Annie a look. "Annie, stop snacking. We're about to eat."

"Seriously, Mark. You'll have your GED in the next month or so. You should sign up for the summer term at the college. You'll have fun, especially after all this."

"I don't want to go to school," Mark said. "I just want a decent job, where they don't treat me like some kid."

"Well, you are a kid," Annie threw back. "Mark, you're only sixteen. Give me a break. What do you think they're going to do, let you become a stockbroker?"

Cathy grinned. "She's got a point, Mark." She got out the buns and put one on each plate. "The fact is, you're trying to grow up too soon. You need to slow down and take your time, do the things that a sixteen-year-old is supposed to do, like go to school and work for the grocery store bagging groceries. Take your time planning what you want to do for the rest of your life. You can do that, Mark."

Mark went to the sink and washed the filth off of his hands. "But I don't even know where to start. What if I can't even get into the community college?"

"I think you can, Mark. And if you make good grades, I'm sure you could get into a better college when the time came."

Steve handed Mark a towel to wipe his hands on. "Mark, I know you think your sentence will always hang over your head, but the truth is, if you have four good years of college with good grades and good behavior and no more trouble, people will forget that when you were in high school you made a few mistakes."

Mark slumped over the counter. "You think so? Because right now that's all they care about, like I'm some kind of drug dealer who's wanting to get on their payroll."

"People will forget," he said. "It's a lot easier to overlook a year at River Ranch when you've got four good years of college and good behavior."

"I'd definitely have good behavior," Mark said. "I'm not so sure about the good grades part. I've never been a very good student."

"But you're more mature now, Mark," Steve said. "You can do it. You've got it in you now. Look how much you've learned about the Bible on your own in just a few months."

"Well, that's true," Mark said. "I guess when I'm interested in something I can apply myself."

"Well, maybe you could make yourself be more interested in English and history and science when you realize that it's your alternative to getting up on a roof every day in the hot sun and hammering shingles."

X Mark thought that over for a moment. "I don't know," he said. "I'll have to think about it."

"Why don't you run up and take a shower?" Cathy said. "We'll hold supper until you're finished."

"Good," he said. "The sooner I can get this filth off of me, the better."

They watched as Mark trudged up the stairs.

Cathy turned around, grinning, and Steve raised his hand for a high five. "It's working," he whispered.

Annie's mouth fell open. "You two planned this."

Cathy swung around. "What? Us?"

"Yes," she said. "You knew all along he'd hang himself with his own rope."

Cathy laughed. "Harsh image, Annie. We just hoped it would work out this way."

"Boy, you guys are slick."

Cathy almost danced as she set the table.

It started to rain about lunchtime the next day, and Mark was sent home from work. The house was empty when he got there, so he took a shower, cleaned up, and then decided to go to the local community college. Something had to give, he thought, and this hard manual labor was for the birds. It wasn't that he was too good for it. He wasn't. The other guys on the crew were hardworking men who did what they had to do to make a living. And there was something satisfying about working with his hands and coming home exhausted at the end of the day.

But he wanted more. His mind needed stimulation. He wanted to stretch it somehow, the way he'd done when he'd home schooled with Brenda. His GED test was this coming Saturday, and he felt confident that he'd pass it this time. Then he'd be ready to move on.

He drove over to the community college, found the administration building, and went in and got a catalog. Then he sat out in his car and flipped through it, wondering if he did go to college, what in the world he would study. He liked computers, he thought, and he liked to draw. Years ago before he'd gotten too cool to do it, he'd even been pretty good at it. He'd once considered being a graphic artist. His father had suggested architecture, but that seemed like a lofty goal, too far out of his reach.

He flipped through the catalog and looked up graphic art, then architecture, and saw that some of the basic courses were the same. Maybe he could have a broad target and start with both of those, then narrow it as his focus cleared.

Whatever he did, he felt an urgency to sign up for the summer term.

Man, he hated it when his parents were right.

CHAPTER *Fifty-Nine*

Sylvia floated along for the months of March, April, and May, taking her radiation treatments and her Tamoxifen, volunteering at the school, teaching the Bible study with Harry at her church, and writing letters to the children in the orphanage in León. In the afternoons, she rode her horse, visited her neighbors, and prayed for those around her.

When her lower back began to ache, she told herself that she had pulled a muscle, and went on with her life.

She threw a neighborhood party for Mark when he got his GED, then celebrated again when he got into college for the summer term.

Though she was tired from the radiation and still had frequent hot flashes from the hormone pills, she felt as if the cancer was just a part of her past. She began counting the days until the radiation would end and she could return to her work in León.

But then the oncologist ordered blood tests at her three-month checkup. Her tumor markers were elevated, so he sent her for more scans.

And a sense of dread began to fall over her again.

The doctor's face was grim as he came into the office to deliver the results. "We've got some bad news, I'm afraid. The scans showed that the cancer has metastasized to your lower spine."

Sylvia sat frozen, not certain she had heard right. The cancer that had been cut out of her breast, blasted with chemo, burned with radiation, had now conquered her bones? She turned her stricken eyes to Harry.

She heard the groan that seeped out of him as he pulled her into his arms. "Honey . . ."

"Please don't panic," the doctor went on in a calm voice. "The skeleton is not a vital organ. This is still treatable."

Sylvia gaped at him. Was he crazy? Not a vital organ? Did he equate her bones to tonsils or appendixes? "Not a vital organ? We're talking about my skeleton. How can you say it's not a vital organ? I can hardly live without it."

"He's right." Harry's voice trembled. "The truth is, the prognosis can still be pretty good with this kind of cancer. If it were in your liver or your brain or your lungs, we'd have a bigger challenge."

So she should be grateful that it had only attacked her bones? All that time that she'd thought she was out of the woods, had it been laying ambush to her spine? Would it begin to attack her joints, her skull, her limbs? She didn't want to think about what was to come. She'd felt so good knowing the cancer had disappeared, that she had fought it back valiantly, and that it had fled. But now it was back, hunkering down in her body, waiting to attack other cells and organs. "What does this mean?" she managed to ask.

"Well, for right now I think the best approach is to change your hormone therapy," the doctor said. "We'll see how the cancer responds to that. Meanwhile, we'll just continue with the radiation and pray."

Sylvia was quiet all the way home, and so was Harry. She'd believed she was out of the woods, but now she felt so deep in them that she couldn't see her way out. The cancer could still kill her, despite her efforts to fight it.

She thought of her grandbaby, little Breanna. Would she watch her grow up after all? Would she be around when Jeff found the right girl and married? Would she hold any more of Sarah's babies?

And would she ever be able to return to her work, and hold little Juan and the Nicaraguan children who were so much like her own? Was all that behind her forever?

When they got home, Harry sat down. "Honey, talk to me."

She paced across the room, her arms crossed. "I can't," she said.

"Yes, you can."

"No. I just want to read. I want to get all the books I have about cancer and dig into your medical journals, and try to find out what my chances are."

"They're good, Sylvia. Very good. You can't give up yet."

Tears glistened in her eyes. "But I thought I was cured. I know they tell you not to think that until you've been cancer-free for five years, but I still thought it. I'm not prepared to fight metastatic disease. I'm afraid of this cancer, Harry! It's so aggressive, nothing can kill it."

"It can be stopped," Harry said. "Honey, you just have to have faith."

Sylvia finally sat down beside him. "I've presumed on God," she whispered. "All this time I've been sure that he would send us back to the mission field, let us resume our work, allow us to bear more fruit. But he's got other plans, hasn't he?"

Harry's mouth quivered at the corners, and she saw him struggling with the tears in his eyes. "Maybe for now."

"His ways are not our ways." She breathed a humorless laugh. "That makes me so mad. What is he doing?"

"I don't know." He pulled her forehead against his, and started to cry.

She touched the tears on his face, and pulled back to look into the agony in his eyes. "Oh, Harry." She hated seeing him so sad, and she knew that her own pain provoked that sadness. She had to pull herself together. If not for herself, then for him.

They wept together for a few moments, then finally, she dried her tears. "I'm gonna be okay," she said, drying his face with her fingertips. "I am, Harry. I'm going to fight and do everything that the doctors tell me to do, and I'm going to trust the Lord, whatever he chooses to do."

Harry swallowed and nodded. "That's my girl."

"We can't live in fear," she told him. "That's no way to live. We'll have to figure out a way to live life without constantly thinking about it."

He made a valiant effort to wipe the emotion from his face.

"Remember when I said that cancer was a gift God had given me?" she asked.

"Yes."

"I said that, believing it would go away. But it's still probably true. If God gave it to me, then it's a gift. An opportunity. I have to find a way to think of it as that again. Would you pray that for me, Harry?"

He didn't wait until he was alone. Instead he just held her, and began to pray.

CHAPTER *Sixty*

That night when she had her bearings, she called her children and each of her neighbors individually and told them the news. They were each crushed and quiet, and had little to say in the way of comfort. But Sylvia hadn't expected otherwise. They were as shocked as she, and it would take a few days to sort out all these emotions and figure out what to think.

That night as she and Harry lay in bed next to each other, neither tried to fool the other into thinking they were sleeping.

"The thing I hate most about all this," Sylvia whispered, "is that I've always hoped that if I ever came to a place like this where I had a terminal disease and was going to die . . ."

Harry cut in immediately. "You are not going to die."

"But you know what I mean, Harry," she said. "I hoped that if I ever had a terminal illness, I would handle it as a godly woman with a positive attitude and a cheerful heart. I hoped I would focus more on the people around me than on myself, that I'd worry more about whether their spiritual needs were being met than I would about my own physical needs. But that's not how I am."

He touched her face. "How can you say that? You're the most godly woman I know. Anyone would agree."

"But *anyone* doesn't know what's going on inside of me," she said. "I feel so angry and so out of control. I want to scream and holler at God and ask him what in the world he thinks he's doing. I want to yell at everybody who's healthy, that they'd better enjoy it while they can because it could be snatched out from under them at any moment. And I want to scream at all those complacent Christians sitting in the pews on Sunday mornings and doing nothing with their lives, wasting their talents and gifts God has given them when they could be out sharing the love of Christ."

"I feel the same way. Honey, it's not ungodly to feel all those things."

"But that's not what I want to feel," she said. "I want to be someone that God would be proud of. If I'm going to die, I want to go out with a bang, you know? And don't say I'm not going to die again because we're all going to die someday. Whenever it is, I want to do it right."

He wiped the tears off of his face with the top of the sheet. "Honey, God's going to give you whatever you need to get through this. You can believe that. The one thing we've learned over all these years is that God is faithful. Haven't we learned that?"

"Yes, we have." Sylvia let the tears run down her temples and through her hair onto her pillow. "I wonder if I'll live to see my hair grow all the way back in."

"Of course you will," he said. "It's long enough now that you could go without your wig."

She was quiet for a moment, trying to picture herself as she'd been before the surgery, with her body whole and her hair just the way she'd chosen to wear it.

"It's strange, going from thinking of myself as being healthy and healed, to realizing that my fight is not over."

"No, it's not over," he said, "but you don't have to worry, Sylvia, because you're not fighting it alone." He slipped his arms around her and pulled her close, and they wept together long into the night.

Instead of slowing Sylvia down, the news of her recurrence spurred her onward, faster, with more fierce urgency to do the things that she felt God had called her to do. Since the Breezewood Development Center didn't close for the summer, Sylvia spent more hours than ever at the school, working with the children. Little Bo began to meet her at the door each morning. "Miva," he would call her, in his own special combination of "Miss" and "Sylvia."

As if the Lord wanted to show her that her work did please him, the children had all managed to learn their own version of "Jesus Loves Me." The tunes varied, but the sounds of their awkward words hit close to the real words. Even their attention spans seemed to have broadened. Sylvia had a calming influence on them, and they loved to hear her read. She had advanced from the wordless book to reading actual stories. Still, each day she went over the wordless book again, until each child considered it his favorite book, the only one that some of them could "read."

Sylvia didn't stop with the children. In the afternoons, she spent time teaching Bible to Brenda's kids, while Brenda did her typing.

On Wednesday nights, she and Harry kept teaching the Bible study at church. And on Thursday nights she and her neighbors gathered to pray.

In between all her work, she wrote the children in the orphanage in León individual letters letting them know she loved them and missed them.

There was little time for self-pity, even though her back had begun to ache constantly as the cancer sank its teeth deeper into her bones. There was no kidding herself that the new drug was working.

She knew from deep within that the cancer was growing, occupying more territory, overthrowing her body.

But there was little that she could do, except press on, and trust that God had things under control.

CHAPTER
Sixty-One

The meteor shower that only occurred every thirty-five years or so was scheduled to happen at the end of May. Brenda suspended school that day and let the kids sleep late, so they could stay up late enough to see the heavenly display. At ten o'clock they took blankets outside and went up to Lookout Point at the peak of Bright Mountain.

Stars shot across the sky, delighting the children as they lay on their backs, clapping and cheering for each burst of light.

Brenda lay next to David, praying that the beauty and majesty of the shower would cause him to acknowledge his Creator. But he had made his salvation so complicated that the doorway was not only narrow, as Jesus had warned, but it seemed locked and bolted shut.

Still, she prayed and hoped. With every star that flew across the sky, she asked the Lord to let this miracle be the one that opened David's eyes.

"Isn't God cool?" Joseph asked, his head pillowed on David's chest.

Brenda laughed. "Very cool."

David's silence became his answer, but Joseph didn't let it lie.

"Dad, how could you not believe in God after you've seen this? It's just so obvious. All this stuff didn't happen by accident."

David expelled a long sigh. "I'm just not the kind of person who can have faith in what I don't see, Joseph."

Joseph sat up. "But you did just see it. It would take more faith *not* to believe than it does to believe."

David didn't answer.

"Wish we could have videotaped this," Daniel said from his place on the ground. "This is the most awesome thing I've ever seen."

David nodded. "It is amazing."

They lay quietly for a moment, listening to the music of the wind as it scored the spectacular showing in the sky. After a moment, Leah sat up and looked at her mother.

"Mom, is Miss Sylvia going to die?"

Brenda shivered. Forgetting the display overhead, she got up and went to snuggle between her twin daughters. "I don't think so, sweetie, but we're not sure yet."

"Do you think she's scared?" Rachel asked.

"Nope," Joseph said. "Not Miss Sylvia. She's not scared."

"How do you know?" Daniel asked. "Did she tell you that?"

"She didn't have to," Joseph said. "I just know, 'cause I was there once. How can you be scared when you know you're going to be with Jesus?"

Brenda met David's eyes, but he looked away. He slid his arm around his youngest son's shoulders and pulled him close. Once again she said a prayer for her husband to believe.

CHAPTER
Sixty-Two

When Annie called Sylvia to ask if she and Josh could come over to ride the horse, Sylvia welcomed the opportunity to spend time with the two kids she had chosen for each other. The horse needed riding, but her back ached too badly to ride today.

She met them out at the barn that afternoon and helped them saddle her and get her ready to ride. Josh had ridden for most of his life, so it all came easily to him.

They rode double on the horse, and headed off to the pasture beyond the trees. Sylvia sat on her swing and watched, smiling at how well things were working with them. She thought of herself and Harry, when they had first fallen in love. Every touch, every look, every smile had carried special significance. In so many ways, that hadn't changed today.

She thought of the way Harry had stood beside her during this illness, even though his own dreams had been interrupted.

But she knew he would have it no other way. How blessed she was to have him.

Lord, whether it's Josh or someone else, bring Annie a soul mate like that. Someone to stand by her for her whole life. Someone like Harry.

She heard footsteps and turned to see Cathy coming toward her. "Hi," Cathy said.

"Hi yourself."

She sat down next to Sylvia, making the chains creak. "How you feeling?"

"Not bad."

Cathy got quiet. Sylvia knew she was keeping a respectful distance from the subject of Sylvia's cancer. It was clear that she tried hard to let Sylvia set the parameters of their conversations.

"Looks like Josh and Annie are getting along really well," Sylvia said.

Cathy nodded. "Yeah. They don't need much help from us."

"I just think they'd be a wonderful couple."

"Well, don't rush them. You know Annie's still young."

"I know," Sylvia said, "but she's a precious young woman and she deserves the best."

She looked at Cathy and saw tears misting her eyes. "You know, there was a time when I didn't hold out much hope for Annie being a spiritual person."

"I know that. But God surprised you, didn't he?"

"Yes, he did."

"That's the thing with God. He always has surprises for us. He has so many plans and so many layers, and they're so rich in our lives . . . if we just had enough faith to trust in them." She'd said too much, she thought, and now they were back on the subject of her cancer. She wished she'd kept that thought to herself.

"You have enough faith, Sylvia."

Sylvia frowned into the wind. "I don't know if I do or not. People tell me I'm brave, that they admire me for such a valiant effort, but the fact is, I don't have any choice. What do they think I'm going to do, just roll over and die?"

The wind was the only answer. It whispered through their hair and hung between them. Cathy looked down at her knees. "You're going to beat this, Sylvia. I know you are. So many people are praying for you."

"I know they're praying, but I'm not sure if they should be praying for healing."

"Why not?" Cathy asked. "Why would we pray for anything else?"

"Because it may not be God's will. He may have a whole different plan. And, you know, just because he takes one life and leaves another doesn't mean that one person is blessed over another, or that one person's prayers are more important to God. He's just got these ways that are so mysterious. Who can understand them?"

Her voice broke off and she looked up at the leaves over her head, focused on them as if she might find some answer there. "I just want to be faithful," she went on. "When I get to heaven, whenever that day may be, I want to hear those words."

Cathy smiled. She knew what those words were. "'Well done, my good and faithful servant.' You'll hear them, Sylvia. I know you will."

"The thing is, it's easy to stop running the race. Sometimes I feel like just resting on the fact that I worked in Nicaragua, that I helped a lot of people there. I feel like if I just curl up in a closet somewhere, never to be heard from again, it won't really matter. But that's not what the Bible teaches, is it?"

Cathy just looked at her.

"The Bible teaches that we should run the race until the end. And I'm not at the end yet."

Tears stung Cathy's eyes. She laid her head on Sylvia's shoulder. "Sylvia, how could you ever doubt that God is pleased with you?"

"Because I have all these conflicting emotions raging through my heart, and I don't feel very holy sometimes. I'm not the way I thought I would be if I ever faced a crisis like this."

"God asks us to be holy," Cathy said. "He doesn't ask us to be superhuman. Within your humanity, I think you're as holy as you can be. Don't forget that even Jesus prayed that the cup would be taken from him."

Sylvia sat there for a moment, taking that in. "He did, didn't he?"

"Of course he did. He wept and he railed and he sweat great drops of blood."

"I understand that," Sylvia said. "I've been there myself."

"If you're supposed to take this with all the stoicism of a statue, then why would God let us see the Gethsemane Jesus?"

Sylvia nodded as that truth became clear to her. "I guess he did it for me. Seems like I've been going through my Gethsemane for an awfully long time. Maybe I'll eventually come out on the other side and be able to do whatever it is God has for me to do."

Even if it's to die.

Chapter *Sixty-Three*

Sylvia's Gethsemane didn't end for several weeks. During her times of serving others she managed to smile and laugh and get out of herself and forget those anguished pleas she sent up to heaven at night when she faced her illness head-on. But the pain intensifying in her back and hip told her the hormones weren't working. And when she started feeling pain where she knew her liver to be, fear overtook her again.

For several days she failed to tell anyone about it because she didn't want to be an alarmist. She had learned that when dealing with cancer, every pain had significance. If she got a headache, she assumed that the cancer had spread to her brain. If her wrist ached, she was certain it had gotten into that part of her bone. If her blood sugar was off, she was sure that it had advanced to her pancreas.

But finally when the pain grew more intense, she decided it was best to tell Harry. Harry didn't even respond. He went straight to the telephone and started to dial.

"Who are you calling?" she asked.

"I'm calling Dr. Thibodeaux."

"It's night," she said. "He's not at his office."

"I'm calling him at home."

"But, Harry, do you think it's anything?"

"It's probably not," he said, "but there's no use taking any chances. I wish you'd told me the minute you started feeling it."

She sat listening as he told the doctor what she felt, and the oncologist told them to be at his office first thing the next morning.

She went through another round of CT scans and blood tests, then endured another season of waiting. Her Gethsemane continued.

They returned to the doctor's office the next day to get the results. Sick of the place, she wished she could change the curtains and reorganize the furniture. Better yet, she wished the doctor would meet her and Harry in a restaurant that was crowded and bustling with activity and life, instead of in these offices full of other cancer patients waiting for bad news.

Dr. Thibodeaux had that look on his face again, the one that made her want to put her hands over her ears. "It's spread to your liver," he said.

Sylvia had expected crushing despair, but instead she just felt numb. The pain in her back had already convinced her that the treatment strategy was failing. The doctor was only confirming it.

He looked up at her, his eyes tired. She wondered if he'd been at the hospital late last night or early today. Oncologists carried such burdens. For the first time, she felt sorry for him.

"I'm so sorry, Sylvia," he said, "but this means that we have to change our approach. We have to get more aggressive."

Sylvia swallowed. "That would be because the liver *is* a vital organ as opposed to the skeleton. Am I right?"

"That's right."

She looked at Harry. The blood seemed to have drained from his face.

She forced herself to speak. "But what does more aggressive therapy mean? Chemo again?"

The truth was, more chemo was one of her greatest fears. Her dark night of suffering had finally come to an end. The thought of reentering it was more than she could bear.

"Yes." His voice was low, steady. She wondered how often each day he had to deliver this kind of news. "We'll have to put you on a more aggressive chemo this time," he said, "and you'll have to have tests after every three cycles. If it's not working, then we'll change the drug."

There it was, the crushing despair . . . the feeling that she had been kicked in the kidney.

"How long will you do this?" Harry asked.

The doctor cleared his throat, shifted in his chair. He met Harry's eyes across the table. "This time the treatment has to last until the cancer is gone."

She stared at him for a moment, dissecting his words. "You mean I could be on chemotherapy for another six months or a year . . . or two years?"

"We'll fight it as long as we have to."

She looked at Harry. His head was slumped down, and he stared at his feet. "You mean I could be on it until the day I die?"

"I'm not going to lie to you," the doctor said. "Liver cancer can be fatal. When the disease has metastasized this much, we're dealing with a lot bigger challenge than we've had before."

Harry took her hand. His was as cold as hers. Her breath was shallow, inadequate. *Breathe*, she told herself. *Just breathe.*

"Okay," she said. "Given this new development, what are my chances?"

He shook his head. "You know I don't do percentages, Sylvia. There's no point in that."

Her voice got louder. "But how many people die when they have what I have?"

"Some of them," he said. "But some of them live. And you believe in miracles, don't you?"

"Are you telling me it's going to take a *miracle* to pull me through this?"

His eyes looked almost as forlorn as Harry's. "A miracle would help," he said. "I'm telling you that we have good drugs and they work. It's going to be a struggle, but you're strong enough to take it. I know you are."

It sounded hopeful, even gentle, but Sylvia knew he'd just given her a death sentence.

Harry reached for her, but she sat stiff, unable to respond. "Harry, I don't know if I can go through with this."

"You can. Honey, you can. I'll help you."

She started to cry, and turned back to the doctor. "Will my hair fall out again?"

The doctor turned his compassionate eyes to her. "Probably. The side effects might be worse than they were before, but it's the best treatment we have. And, Sylvia, it often does work."

She wiped her nose and got up, looking helplessly for a Kleenex. Why didn't he have a Kleenex? "How long?" Sylvia asked. "How long do I have? I want to know."

He shook his head again. "I don't do that, Sylvia. I'm not going to tell you you have six months or a year."

"Six months or a year?" she asked. "Is that what I have?"

"I don't *know* what you have. You might have twenty years."

"Worst-case scenario?" she said. "If the chemo doesn't stop this cancer and it keeps spreading at the rate it has been, how long do I have to live?" She leaned over his desk, her hands balled into fists. "I need to know!"

He didn't answer, so finally, she turned and headed for the door.

"Sylvia, we still need to talk."

Sylvia turned back to the doctor. "Set everything up with Harry. I have to get out of here."

Then she ran up the hall, past the bookkeeper, out into the waiting room. She hurried out to the car and got in, and screamed out her rage, grief, and anguish. She could have torn the steering wheel off and slammed it through the windshield, broken glass all the way around, started the car and rammed it into a wall.

But she sat in the passenger seat, doubled over with her hands over her face . . .

My children, she thought. *How will I tell my children?*

It would shake their faith. It would shake everyone's faith. So many were praying for her. They all believed she would be healed. Why would God let them all down?

She had said it was a gift—this cancer, this archenemy that occupied her body. She had even believed it, when chemo was a temporary torture and the cancer hadn't found another home in her body.

But now . . .

The peace and joy she had once known had been banished, and stark fear took its place.

Where are you, God? Where's the victory in this?

She heard Harry at the car door and sat up, wiped her face. The sobs kept hiccuping from her throat, but she tried to get control.

He got in with several papers and the appointment for her first chemo treatment, twisted, and set them on the backseat. He looked at her, assessing her condition. She patted his hand, reassuring him that she had not completely fallen apart. But Harry looked old, frail . . .

They were quiet as they rode home, and when they were back in their driveway, Sylvia got out of the car. "I have to go ride."

She started around the house and headed for the barn. Harry followed her. "Sylvia."

"You don't have to come with me," she called. "I can do this by myself. I need to be alone."

"But I don't!" Harry cried. "I don't want to be alone. I want to be with you!"

He followed her into the dark stable, and she opened her horse's stall. Going in, she slid down the wall onto the hay and covered her face with both hands. The horse dipped his head and nudged her.

"I won't survive the treatments, Harry," she cried. "They'll kill me faster than the cancer. If I'm going to die, I want to do it with dignity, not with nausea and fatigue and sores and a bald head and yellow skin and all my joints aching like I'm a ninety-year-old woman."

Harry sat down next to her in the hay. "Honey, I know it's a lot to ask. I know you don't want to go through this again, and right now you probably don't even feel that bad, just a little pain in your side and back. But, honey, that pain is your enemy, and it's *my* enemy, and I want you to live. I want you to do the chemo because there's a chance that you'll beat it. I don't think God's finished with you yet. There's still hope. I haven't ever asked you for much, have I?"

She shook her head. "No, not much. The last time you asked for something really important, you wanted me to leave all my memories behind and traipse off to Nicaragua to save the world."

"And you did, valiantly. You gave it all up, and the next thing I knew you were more passionate about doing our work there than I was. And there's so much more for us to do yet. I want us to go back to León together. I want us to see the children again. I want to take care of those people who depend on me," he said, "but I can't do it without you. I need for you to fight. I need for you to go through this chemo. I need for you to suffer a little longer just for hope of the good outcome. Please, Sylvia. Don't reject the chemo. I'm begging you."

Her face softened as she looked at her husband and realized this was the most important request he had ever made of her, even more important than forsaking everything and heading off to the mission field. This was life or death. Her life. Her death. And she owed it to Harry to fight.

She reached for him and pulled him against her, stroked the back of his head and breathed in the scent of him. She loved him so dearly. She would do anything for him. Even this.

Finally she pulled back and looked into his face. "All right," she said. "I'll give it the fight of my life. For you. And for whatever fruit is left in me to bear."

That night she fell exhausted into bed and drifted into a shallow sleep. Harry lay next to her for a long time, but sleep didn't come for him. Finally, he slipped out of bed, quietly got on his clothes, and headed out to the barn. Once there, he got down on his knees, face to the ground.

"Please don't take her," he cried to God. "I've never asked you that much before. I've been very accepting of the things you've wanted for us. I've given you our lives and I've been obedient, and so has she. I'm begging you now, Lord, please don't take her. She's my helpmeet, my soul mate. You chose her for me. I'm begging you, Lord. I know that death has to come at some point in our lives, but not now. Please not now. Please, God, answer this prayer. Give us a miracle. Save her life."

He wept until the wee hours of morning and prayed and wrestled with God. Finally, around three A.M. he felt a peace fall over him. It wasn't a peace that he would have the answer he sought. God wasn't making that promise. It was only a peace that God would walk with them through this shadow of death, and that they should fear no evil. It was a tall order, Harry knew, and he wasn't sure if either one of them was strong enough to follow it. But he had committed to trying, just as she had.

CHAPTER
Sixty-Four

The next morning Harry and Sylvia were quiet as they started their day over breakfast with tired eyes and long faces. "We have to tell the children," Harry said.

"I know, but not yet."

"When?" he asked.

"I think I need to spend some time in God's Word," she said. "I need to soak up all the strength I can. I need to find verses about why God lets us suffer, about death and dying, about what the future holds and whatever else God decides to show me. I need to be ready for their questions."

Harry rubbed his eyes. "That's a good idea, Sylvia. I'll do it, too."

"I was thinking that, once I feel I have enough strength, I want to call the neighbors over and have a dinner party, and try to be upbeat and positive as I tell them. And I want to call the children and tell them the same way. I don't want them to see us like we were last night, or even like we are right now. I want them to see a godly woman continuing to serve God even in the dying season of her life."

"It's not your dying season," Harry said. "It's just a dark season . . . but there's going to be light again."

"There's going to be light again whether it's my dying season or not," she whispered. But she couldn't be happy about that just yet.

"I wish I didn't have appointments today," he said. "I don't want to see patients."

"I want you to go." Sylvia took her plate to the sink. "I'm just going to stay in today and study the Bible. By the time you come home I'm hoping I'll feel better."

She spent the day weeding through the Bible, searching for passages that would give her comfort, passages she could pass on to others to give them comfort, too. By that night she still wasn't ready to tell her children or the neighbors, so she and Harry spent the time in prayer.

Harry took the following day off, and he spent the day with her poring through the Word. Finally by early afternoon Sylvia thought she could manage the announcement.

One by one she called Cathy and Steve, Tory and Barry, and David and Brenda, and invited them over for a dinner party that night. Nothing in her voice warned them what was coming. She didn't want it to be some horrible surprise. She just wanted them to see a smile on her face, a positive attitude, hope shining in her eyes, when she told them the bad news.

She set about to cook for them. While the lasagna baked in the oven, she called her children.

Heartbroken, they both said they would drop everything and come to be at her side, but she told them it wasn't necessary. She would let them know if things got bad, but until then she would just be pressing on with the things she had to do. All she needed from them now was their prayers.

Then she and Harry set about preparing for the dinner party. They hummed praise songs as they worked, decorating the house with fresh flowers, putting out hors d'oeuvres, arranging the tables, buttering the garlic bread.

By the time the doorbell rang, she was quite sure that she was ready.

Tory and Barry were the first to come over. Barry and Harry sat in the living room watching a baseball game that was almost over, while Tory helped Sylvia in the kitchen. Then Brenda and David showed up and David joined the guys in the living room, rooting for the Atlanta Braves as the last inning of the game wound down. Brenda came in and picked up a celery stick to crunch on.

"So how's the job going?" Sylvia asked her.

"I love it. Since it's summer and we're not doing school, I'm getting the work done earlier every day. It's working out great. I owe it all to you."

Sylvia waved her off. "I didn't do anything."

"Yes, you did."

The doorbell rang and they knew it was Cathy and Steve. They waited a moment until Cathy buzzed into the kitchen with hugs for everybody.

"Cathy, Brenda was just telling us how great her job is working out."

Cathy slid up onto the counter and looked at Brenda. "Isn't Sylvia a genius for giving the doctor the idea?"

Sylvia laughed. "Common sense, my dear. Those doctors have their minds so busy with people's diseases that they can't focus on little things."

"How does David feel about it?" Cathy asked.

"Fine now." Brenda glanced out the door to the men congregated around the television.

Cathy pulled open the oven and peeked in at the contents. "Mmm, Sylvia. You outdid yourself. The bread is almost ready."

Sylvia pulled it out and set it on the stove.

They chitchatted until the game was over, and when they heard the guys cheering in the living room at the victory of the Braves, Sylvia decided it was time to take the food to the table.

"All right, guys. Everybody come eat."

They headed in and took their places around the table, and Harry led them in a prayer. His voice broke as he spoke to God. He asked God to bless the meal and the conversation, and to give them all the strength they needed to get through the coming week.

Finally, they sat down and began chattering all at once as they filled their plates and passed the bread and salad. When they'd finished with their desserts and were ready to leave the table, she asked them all to assemble in the living room. She had some news for them, she said.

Harry helped her clear the table as the others quietly assembled in the living room, whispering. Harry took her into the kitchen, pulled her into his arms, and held her tight. She told herself she couldn't cry. She had to put a smile on her face and say this with bright eyes so that they would not feel dismal about what she faced.

Harry held her hand as he led her back into the quiet living room. They sat together on the love seat, as all six of their guests stared at them.

"What do you have to tell us?" Tory asked her.

"I bet I know," Brenda said. "Sarah's pregnant again. Right?"

Sylvia shook her head. "No, not yet." She looked down at her hands and realized they were trembling. "It's medical news." Her smile faded and she knew that her face was giving her away.

"Medical news?" Cathy stood up. "Oh, my gosh, Sylvia. What is it?"

She brought her face up. "Well, we found out that the cancer has spread to my liver."

Dead silence.

She looked around from one pair of shocked eyes to another. Brenda's eyes were already filling with tears, and David's face was turning red as he gaped at her. Tory looked angry and shook her head as if this couldn't be true, and Barry put his arm around her as if to support her. Steve got to his feet and slid his hands into his pockets, and she could see his jaw popping under the pressure.

Cathy's mouth hung open. "Sylvia, what does this mean?"

"Well, it's all right really. It's not as bad as it sounds." She knew they weren't buying any of it. She tapped Harry's leg, passing the baton to him.

"She's about to start chemo again," he said. "It'll be a lot more aggressive and it will continue until the cancer is gone."

"Oh, no," Brenda whispered.

"Is it still in the bones, too?" Tory asked on a wavering voice.

"Yes, it is, and it just keeps spreading."

She knew they all wanted to ask her what the prognosis was, what her chances were, how long she had to live, so finally she decided to address those points one by one.

"The prognosis is very iffy, guys," Sylvia said, "and the doctor wouldn't give me odds. Some survive this and some don't. And as far as how long I might have to live, it could be anywhere from twenty days to twenty years."

Tory collapsed against Barry and buried her face in his chest. He held her tight and she could see the tears taking hold in his own eyes. Cathy backed against Steve, and he slid his arms around her. Brenda seemed frozen with a look of horror on her face. David looked down at his knees.

"I wanted to tell you like this, because I wanted you to see that I'm okay and that I'm willing to do what I have to do to live. But if I don't live, God is still in control, and whether he plans to pull me out of this or take me home, I trust him absolutely."

David looked up at her and she met his eyes. She could see the questions reeling through his mind. *How can you trust?*

She uttered a silent prayer for David. *Lord, help me to have enough trust to make a difference in his life before I go.*

She cleared her throat and went on. "Now I know how things are going to be after this," Sylvia said. "You're all going to be upset, grieving my loss before I'm even gone, praying for me constantly, bringing me food and books and articles on alternative medicines. And that's all fine. But what I really need from you, and what I'm asking from you now, is that you don't cut me out of your lives just because you think I'm too ill to hear the daily activities. I want you to come visit me even when I'm sick. I want you to tell me what's going on in your lives. I want to know about every one of your children and what they're doing and what they're thinking and how they're acting. Those things keep me going, guys. I love hearing them and I don't want to be left out. And I don't want to always be talking about cancer. In fact, if I never hear the word again, it will be fine with me."

She saw the pain on their faces. They grieved already. They would go home tonight and cry and lie awake and wrestle with God.

She had never felt more loved. Her heart broke for them.

"It's going to be okay," she said. "All my life, I've told others about the principles of God. That he is faithful. That he supplies all our needs. Now's the time for me to test those principles, and prove whether I truly believe them to be true. We talk big, until our own rough spots come. But I intend to be a testimony of those principles, whether God chooses to heal me or not. God will not fail me now."

Her eyes met David's, and she saw the questions, the amazement.

Cathy got up and came over, sat down, and hugged her so tightly that she thought she would break. Then Brenda came, then Tory.

She wished she could spare them the pain.

When the couples had finally gone home, Sylvia felt a surge of relief as she turned back to Harry. "There. It's done."

"You did well."

She shook her head. "Maybe I should have told each of them privately."

"No, I think you did it exactly the right way. They saw you smiling. They saw your hope, your strength. They saw what you're made of."

That night they fell exhausted into bed. There were no more words to exchange. Harry just held her as she fell asleep in his arms.

CHAPTER
Sixty-Five

Annie didn't take the news well. Cathy had taken her into her and Steve's bedroom when she got home, and told her what they'd learned.

Annie grabbed a pillow from the bed and hugged it against her. "No, Mom, it can't be. Tell me it isn't."

It was as if Cathy had just told her that she, herself, had been diagnosed with terminal cancer. "Honey, it's true."

"Mom, she's just got too many things to do. How could this be?"

Cathy pulled her into her arms and wept with her. "Honey, I know how much Sylvia came to mean to you when you were in Nicaragua, but she wants us to know that God is faithful and he's still in control."

"But I can't stand to see her suffer. I thought it was over. Oh, Mom . . ."

Cathy pulled back and looked into Annie's face. She hated seeing her daughter crushed like this. Her own grief was multifaceted. It wasn't just for Sylvia, but for herself and for the neighbors . . . for all those children who loved her from Nicaragua . . . for Annie.

"We're not going to give up hoping. We're going to keep praying for her and know that pretty soon this will all be behind us. This different chemotherapy she's going to try might really do the trick. We'll just have to have faith."

Annie grabbed a towel out of the laundry basket and wept into it, then flung it down. "This is worse than when Joseph was sick."

Cathy shook her head. "I don't think so, honey. I think it was horrible both times."

"But Joseph came out of it. God healed him."

"He sure did."

"Don't you think he'll heal her, Mom? Don't you think if we have enough faith that God will honor that?"

"God always honors faith, honey," she said, "but his ways are not our ways. And death is something that comes to all of us."

"But Sylvia's too young. She's just got too much to do. I don't think God would really want this." Annie plopped down onto Cathy's bed, grabbed a Kleenex out of the tissue box. "Mom, do you think this is something from Satan, that he's afflicted her, cast this disease on her somehow, just a form of spiritual warfare to keep her from doing the work she's supposed to do?"

Cathy thought that over for a moment. "I don't know, honey. I'm not smart enough to answer that question."

"I mean, God doesn't give people cancer, does he?"

Cathy looked up and saw Steve standing in the doorway. She hoped he could see how ill-equipped she was to answer questions like this. "Steve, come in. Annie has questions. We all have questions."

He nodded. "I have them, too."

"But you're the one who knows so much," she said. "You know the Bible way better than I do."

He got onto the king-size bed with them, leaned back against the headboard.

"I know what you're gonna say," Annie muttered. "You're going to say that cancer happens because of the Fall. But that doesn't explain anything to me. Why do people always say that?" She wiped her eyes roughly.

"I don't know if that's exactly what I was going to say, but that is part of it. The sin in the Garden of Eden did bring an awful lot of problems into the world."

Annie punched the pillow she held. "But it wasn't Sylvia's fault that Eve ate the apple. Why does *she* have to pay?"

Steve's face was compassionate as he looked at the forlorn girl. "We all have to pay."

"But I don't understand why that has anything to do with her getting cancer!"

"It's why cancer is even in the world," Steve said. "Before the Fall the world was a perfect place. No disease. No shame. No sin. And then when sin came into the world, all of a sudden we have death and decay. We have a world that gets worse instead of better. Things break down, *bodies* break down, people get sick and they die."

Annie slid off of the bed and slammed the pillow down. "Then it's better never to have been born at all."

Cathy got up and pulled her daughter into her arms. She felt Annie's sobs as she held her.

"Some people might think that," Steve said quietly, "but we're here for a reason, Annie. Sylvia has done a lot of good while she's here. You wouldn't suggest that the world would have been better off if she'd never been born."

Annie looked up. Her face was wet and raging red. "No, of course I wouldn't suggest that. But maybe to *her* she would have been better off."

"I don't think even she would suggest that," Cathy said.

Steve propped his arms on his bent knees. "The fact is, this world is not our home, and these bodies are not our home. Maybe God makes us real uncomfortable in them before he brings us home so that our new glorified bodies will be all the more exciting."

Annie still wasn't buying. "But what about us? The ones they leave?" She turned back to Cathy. "Oh, Mom, what are we gonna do without Miss Sylvia?"

Cathy didn't know.

"What am I saying?" Annie asked. "It's like I've given up on her. Like I've already buried her. I'm not giving up. I'm going to keep praying for healing."

Cathy nodded. "You do that, honey. I'll do it too."

They hugged again, and Cathy heard the bed creak as Steve got off of it and stepped across the room. He put his arms around both of them, and the three of them cried together.

CHAPTER
Sixty-Six

Sylvia's chemo treatment on the first day of August—almost a full year after her diagnosis—left her bed-ridden for three days. When she finally felt like emerging back into the world, Harry urged her to go to a cancer support group someone had started in their church. She had avoided it before, thinking it was a self-indulgent pity party.

But her first meeting surprised her. It wasn't a pity party or a place of sadness or despair. Instead, she met survivors of cancer, those in the throes of it like herself, family members and loved ones of those who had died.

They smiled and laughed and shared Scripture. And they shared strategies for coping with the various treatments and the fears plaguing them. By the end of the night, she had a little more energy to her step as she headed back home.

At the end of the week, Sylvia sat on the floor in the classroom as ten little Down's Syndrome children sat around her, two of them in wheelchairs, two propped in chairs, and the rest sitting on the floor with their legs crossed. They seemed glad to see her after she had missed several days.

They each brought their wordless book to the group, anticipating having her lead them through it again. Her hands trembled, and she felt so weak that the walk down the hall had forced her to stop and rest, but she was glad to be here. She picked up the wordless book and opened to the first page.

"What color is this, boys and girls?"

"Yewwo," Bo cried out.

Tory laughed and patted his head. "Very good, Bo."

"And can anybody tell me what the yellow stands for?"

"Heben," one of the children in the wheelchair muttered.

"That's right," Sylvia said. "You're so smart. It's heaven, because in heaven there are streets of gold. And the best part about heaven is that somebody we know and love very much lives there. Does anybody know who?"

"Dod," one of the children cried out.

"God. That's right," she said, "and the Bible tells us that God so loved the world that he gave his only begotten Son, that whoever believes in him should not perish but have everlasting life. Raise your hand if you believe in him."

Every one of them lifted their hands, and Sylvia laughed.

"Now tell me about Jesus. Who is he preparing a place for in heaven?"

"Me," one of the children cried out.

Sylvia clapped her hands with delight, and winked at Tory. The teacher who sat across the room working on the next project for the day laughed as well.

"But God is holy and perfect," Sylvia said. "And he can't allow anything into heaven that isn't perfect. So there's one thing that can never be in heaven. Can any of you think what that thing might be?"

The children got quiet. No one seemed to know the answer until she turned the next page. "What color is this?"

"Bwak," Bo cried out.

"Very good," she said. "And what does black represent?"

Bo raised his hand again, not wanting to be overlooked. "Bo, tell me what the black represents."

"My hawt," he said.

Tory turned her stricken eyes to the boy, then met Sylvia's eyes. It was working, she seemed to say. He was really getting it.

"That's right, Bo. Our hearts. They all have sin, right? We all do bad things sometimes. Everybody. Big or little, young or old. No matter where you live or who you are, you've done something bad at some point in your life. And we know that God punishes sin, doesn't he? He punishes all the bad things we do. But we don't have to be punished, do we?"

"No!" One of the children bound to a wheelchair spoke out, and Sylvia caught her breath. He rarely spoke at all, but lately she had watched him following along in his book. She turned the page.

"What color is this page?"

"Wed," someone cried out.

"That's right. And what does the red remind us of?"

"Deezus," Bo said.

"Yes, Jesus!" The energy was returning to Sylvia's limbs, lifting her spirits, reviving her body. "Because God sent Jesus to be born as a little baby and to live a perfect life. He never did anything bad, did he? But he took our punishment, so we wouldn't have to." She held up the cross they had made last week out of Popsicle sticks. "What is this?"

"Cwoss!" someone yelled out.

"Yes. Jesus died on a cross, to take our punishment. Isn't that right?" The children all nodded.

"And so now the heart that's in us that's black and bad can be replaced, can't it? We can have a new heart." She turned the page to the white page.

"The white reminds us of a clean heart, doesn't it? And how can you have a clean heart? You can ask God to take your black, dirty heart away, and give you a new heart."

The children hung onto every word, nodding their heads and looking down at the white page in their own books. She turned the page.

"And what color is this, Bo?"

"Gween," he said, proud of himself and grinning at all the kids around him.

"That's right," she said. "And green stands for things that grow, and when you have Jesus in your heart, you want to become more like him. Isn't that right?"

Bo nodded his head like he'd written the book himself.

"And so we pray, and we talk to God, and we read the Bible, and we tell others about Jesus, and we get our mommies and daddies to take us to church. Right? And whenever we do something bad, we can tell God we're sorry."

The children clapped their hands in pure delight, and for a moment, Sylvia forgot her cancer and the pain in her side and back, and her thinning hair, and the next treatment that would send her to bed. She forgot about her fears and her questions and her death. Because here, in this room, there was so much more.

Tory gestured excitedly as she drove Sylvia home. "I never dreamed these kids could learn colors this young," she said. "But you've not only taught them the colors, you've taught them the whole gospel message ... and they understand it. That's just a miracle."

"Well, God's in the business of miracles," Sylvia said.

Tory looked at Sylvia, her eyes bright with unshed tears. "I hope I can be like you, Sylvia. That I'll never underestimate the fruit I can bear in any situation."

"You will bear fruit, Tory. You will."

Exhausted, Sylvia lay her head back on the seat and closed her eyes, certain she would sleep all the way home.

CHAPTER Sixty-Seven

Two days after Sylvia's next chemo treatment, Tory took Hannah over, hoping the baby would cheer Sylvia up and get her mind off of her illness. Harry greeted her at the door and led her down the hall.

Tory stepped into Sylvia's room. The lamp was on, but darkness still hung on. Sylvia lay in bed, a skinny heap of bones. Her skin was a pallid color, somewhere between death and life, and the hair that had begun to grow back had fallen out again.

"Sylvia," Tory said softly, "do you feel like visiting with Hannah and me?"

Sylvia opened her eyes and squinted up. Tory could see by the look on her face that she nursed a headache, among other things. She thought of leaving, but Sylvia rose up.

"Give me that baby."

Hannah smiled and kicked her feet as Tory laid her next to Sylvia on the bed.

But the child didn't want to lie still. Instead, she rolled over and raised up on her hands and knees.

Sylvia gasped. "Is she crawling?"

Tory smiled. "Just about. That's what I wanted you to see."

"Put her on the floor," Sylvia said. "Let me see what she can do."

Tory set her on the floor and coaxed her to crawl. Hannah laughed and rocked back and forth on her hands and knees. "While she's been in the nursery without me, she's developed this awareness of the kids around her. And she's started trying to do what they do."

Sylvia forced herself to sit up, but Tory wondered if that was wise. She looked as if she might collapse if the air conditioner blew too hard.

"Crawl for Miss Sylvia." Sylvia clapped her hands. "Come on, sweetie. Let's see you do it."

Instead of crawling, Hannah grabbed the bedspread, and started to pull up.

Sylvia reached for her, and the child stretched up. "Tory!" she said. "She's going to stand up."

"No way," Tory said. "She can't stand."

"Watch." Sylvia took the child's little fists, and pulled her up carefully, until her dimpled little legs locked beneath her.

Tory squealed and began to clap, and Hannah looked over at her, surprised. Sylvia picked her up like an Olympic star, cheering and clapping.

Tory started to cry. "Sylvia, she stood up. She stood up!"

"She sure did," Sylvia said. "Who would have thought this little thing could make me feel better?" She set Hannah on her lap, and made the baby clap her own hands.

"Do you know what this means, Sylvia? She'll walk someday. She'll walk on her own two feet, and her legs will hold her up, probably without a brace. Don't you think so? Don't you think she'll walk?"

"I know she will." She set her back down, hoping she would do it again. Tory helped the child pull back up as Sylvia lay back and watched.

When the child did it one more time, they both cheered, and Hannah laughed and brought her own fat little hands together.

Tory knew better than to stay much longer. Sylvia was waning.

"Well, I'd better get her home before she forgets how to do it," Tory said.

Sylvia smiled. "Thank you for bringing her over, Tory. What a gift."

"And who knew she was going to give it to you? Now if she'll only do it for Daddy. When I tell Spencer and Brittany, they probably won't leave her alone for the rest of the night. They'll insist on having her walking by morning."

"Don't ever underestimate her." Sylvia reached out for a hug, and Tory bent down.

"I love you," Tory said. "You get better, okay? Call if you need me."

"I'll be as good as new in a couple of days."

"Good," she said. "Because our class is having their school program, and I don't want you to miss it."

Sylvia's face brightened. "I'll be there," she said. "Nothing could stop me."

CHAPTER
Sixty-Eight

The package from León came on a day when Sylvia desperately needed it. A week after her chemo, she hadn't bounced back, and the pain in her liver had grown more intense. Her back had begun to hurt so badly that she could hardly stand up straight, and she'd started having headaches that wouldn't let go.

The package made her get out of bed, and when Harry pulled the video out, she actually managed to get dressed and put on her wig.

"Call Annie," she said. "I want her to come watch it with us."

Annie dropped everything and hurried over. She sat on the love seat next to Sylvia, watching the children they had ministered to so diligently for the last year of her life.

Each child had a message for Mama Sylvia. Juan, her favorite who rarely left her side when she was there, smiled into the camera. In Spanish, he blurted, "Mama Sylvia, one of the new doctor men gave us Reeses. I saved half of mine for you."

He held up the half-eaten peanut butter cup. "Please hurry back. It smells very good."

For the first time in days, Sylvia laughed out loud.

"I have to go back there," she said. "I can't even fathom the thought that I'm never going to see them again."

"Me, too," Annie whispered. "As a matter of fact . . ."

Sylvia looked up at her. "As a matter of fact, what?"

Annie sprang to her feet. "As a matter of fact . . . I've told Josh so much about León and the children and the clinic. And he's studying to be a doctor, you know. And then we found out that some of the doctors at our church were getting up a medical missions trip to work at Dr. Harry's clinic, and he decided he wanted to go with them."

Sylvia brought her hands to her face. "Are you serious?"

"Yes. And I'm going, too." She struck a pose, then screamed. "Can you believe it? I'm going back! We're going during Christmas break this year!"

Sylvia got up slowly, her face glowing with delight. "Oh, Annie. That's wonderful. You can help so much, since you know where everything is. You can take presents to the children from me, and bring back news."

"Oh, yeah. I'm going for the kids. I mean, it'll be fun going with Josh and everything, but he'll be busy at the clinic. I just want to spend the whole time at the orphanage, and hug those precious children, and get to know the new ones."

"New ones," Sylvia said. "I guess there are new ones. A whole bunch of them who don't know anything about me."

Annie's smile faded, and her eyes rounded. "I'll tell them about you. And that you'll be coming back soon."

Sylvia hugged her. "Now don't you two fall head over heels in love and go off and get married in Nicaragua. Your mother would never forgive me."

Annie laughed. "Yeah, that'll be the day. Talk about giving my mom a heart attack. I'd never do that to her."

"Don't do it to me either," Sylvia said. "I want to be at your wedding."

"Whenever it is, and whoever it's with, you'll be there, Miss Sylvia. I wouldn't have it without you."

But that night, as she lay in bed, trying hard to sleep through her pain, Sylvia had the shivering, dreadful feeling that she wouldn't make it to Annie's wedding day.

She might not even make it to Christmas.

CHAPTER
Sixty-Nine

When Miva come back?" Bo's question came as he sat in the circle in their classroom, each of the children clutching the wordless book they kept in their cubbies. Tory looked around, wondering how much to tell them about Sylvia's decline. With each passing day, Sylvia grew more ill, but Tory could hardly speak of it without her throat tightening.

"Miss Sylvia's not feeling well. We've got to keep praying for her. And she would like it if we kept reading the book she gave us."

Carefully, Tory went through the wordless book, letting the students call out what each page meant, just as Sylvia had taught them. When she'd finished, she sent the children back to their desks. But Bo hung back, looking at her through the thick lenses in his glasses. She hoped he wasn't going to ask her about Sylvia again.

"What is it, Bo?"

"I wanna new hawt."

Tory's eyes rounded, and she bent toward him. "What did you say?"

"I want Deezus give me new hawt." He turned to the white page and pointed to it.

Tory got down on her knees in front of the child, and looked him in the eye. "You want a new heart? Why, Bo?"

He shoved his glasses up on his nose. "My hawt ditty."

Tears filled her eyes, and she touched his shoulder. "You're heart's dirty?"

He nodded. "Deezus give me *new* hawt."

Tory looked up and her eyes met Linda's. She saw the teacher grab the camcorder, cut it on. *Yes*, she thought. *This is one of those moments we'll want to remember.* She cleared her throat. "You can have a new heart, Bo. All you have to do is ask Jesus. Tell him to take your dirty heart out and give you a clean, new heart. And he will."

Bo grinned, and his eyes grew wider. "And he wive in me?" He tapped his heart. "In here?"

"That's right. He'll live with you in there. Right inside of you. Every day of your life."

"Den I go heben," he said.

"That's right. And then you'll go to heaven."

Tory struggled to keep herself from crumbling right in front of the child. What would Sylvia do now? she wondered. She would pray. Yes, she would pray with little Bo.

Her voice came out on a whisper. "Let's pray right now, Bo, and we'll ask Jesus to take out your dirty heart and give you a clean one."

The little boy knelt in front of her just as she had done, and folded his hands.

"Deezus," he whispered, and he began to pray his own Down's Syndrome version of the sinner's prayer.

When they came out of the prayer, Tory's face was wet, and she desperately needed a Kleenex. Bo went to tell his friends about his new heart, and Tory got to her feet. She looked at

Linda again. Still holding the camcorder, the teacher hugged Tory. "Do you realize what you just did?"

Tory laughed through her tears. "Do you realize what *Bo* just did? And all this time I thought these children weren't capable of making a decision for Christ."

"In Bo's case, you were wrong," Linda said. "I made this video so we could show it to his parents. I thought it would mean the world to them."

"Can we make a copy?" she asked. "I'd really like to show it to Sylvia. It's only right that she should see the fruit of her labors."

"You bet," Linda said. "I'll have you a copy made by the time you leave the school this morning."

CHAPTER *Seventy*

That night, Cathy, Tory, and Brenda got together to visit Sylvia. Pain twisted Sylvia's face, but she made a valiant effort to smile around it. When they showed her the video of Bo praying, she started to weep.

The other three passed a box of tissue around.

"You know something, Sylvia?" Tory got the video out of the VCR. "Other than Spencer and Brittany, Bo's the first person I've ever led to Christ, and you did most of the work."

Sylvia waved a hand, as if that was ridiculous. "Oh, I didn't. All I did was read him a book. God did all the work."

"But isn't it amazing," Tory said, "to think that a little boy like that with such a simple mind could grasp something so profound?"

Sylvia smiled. "God showed you this, Tory, so that you'd know that he'll be able to do the same thing with Hannah when she's older. This was God's way of telling you to instruct

Hannah in the ways of salvation, even though she'll always be so childlike. Let's watch it again."

Tory put the video back in and rewound it. While they waited, Cathy took Sylvia's cold hand. "Sylvia, you're my hero."

Sylvia frowned at her. "Why on earth?"

"Because even when you've been fighting the hardest battle of your life, you were out there teaching children about Christ."

Brenda concurred. "You were, Sylvia. Most of us would have been licking our wounds, but your mind has always been on everyone else."

Sylvia smiled. "If you only knew. I've thought about myself. Trust me."

They watched the video again, sniffling and wiping their eyes. Finally, when it was over, Sylvia said, "Let's pray. Come here, all of you. Let's get in a circle and pray like we used to on Brenda's front porch." The women came around her and held her hands.

"God showed Tory a miracle today," she whispered. "But I'm asking for one more." She knew they all expected her to ask for healing, but she had something else on her mind. "There's one more person that I want to see saved before I die."

"Who's that?" Cathy asked.

Sylvia looked at Brenda. "I want to see David come to know the Lord."

CHAPTER
Seventy-One

The cough that Sylvia developed in September was another clue that the chemotherapy wasn't working to stop the cancer. When the time came for her next round of scans, her fears were confirmed. The cancer had spread to her lungs.

The doctor changed the chemo once again.

Sylvia hardly noticed when Harry quit his job at the hospital. Suddenly he was with her every moment of every day, by her side when she retched into the toilet, helping her walk through the house when she was too weak to do so on her own. Every ounce of Sylvia's energy went into her survival. There was none left for conversation or thoughts of despair or worry of any kind. She just concentrated on getting through one moment at a time.

Soon her breathing got shallow and raspy, her fever spiked, and she lay for hours without the energy to open her eyes. She had a vague awareness of Harry bustling around her, putting cold compresses on her head and neck and arms and chest . . .

Harry's frantic voice into the phone . . . neighbors touching her and talking to her . . .

Limp as the doll that Sarah used to carry around as a child, she felt groping hands, stethoscopes, an IV going into her arm.

Then they rolled her into an ambulance. Harry held her hand and prayed over her for the long, jostling ride.

Sometime later, Harry sat helplessly in her hospital room, listening to her breathe beneath the oxygen mask. Urgently, he searched his Bible for some word from God, some sign that he was going to pull her out of this and heal her. It was God's way, he told himself frantically. Didn't he like making things look grim, so that it was clear a miracle had been done? Wasn't that what he'd done when Jonathan and his armor bearer had overtaken the Philistine army? God had thrust confusion into the Philistines' hearts, and they had killed each other. And when God was raising an army with Gideon as the leader, hadn't he sent everyone but three hundred men home, just to show the world that they hadn't done the work, but God had?

If cancer was their enemy—and it most definitely was—then maybe God was letting it look as grim as it could, so that he could do his miracle.

So Harry searched the Psalms for some word from God that he would deliver her, some sign that he would not make her suffer any longer, some indication that she would be restored.

But he found none.

When the doctor came by the room, Harry jumped to his feet and confronted him. "She's dying, isn't she?"

The expression in Dr. Thibodeaux's eyes gave him no hope. "She's very sick."

Harry wanted to put his fist through the man's face, grab him by the collar and tell him to get out of here and find a cure. He tried to keep his voice steady. "You've got to do everything you can to keep her alive. If you've heard of any kind of treatment that might work, any kind of clinical trials, I want to know about them. Alternative treatments. Experimental drugs. Anything."

"I've been looking, Harry, just as you have. But she's very, very ill, and this is an aggressive cancer that we haven't been able to stop. It's growing and spreading too fast."

Harry's lips compressed tightly across his teeth. "She can't die. Do you understand me? My wife cannot die. Not yet." But even as he said the words, he knew that the matter was out of the doctor's control. He might as well be waving his fist at God.

"We'll do everything we can for her, Harry. You have my word."

There was nothing more that Harry could demand of him. It was too late for medicine and science to work in Sylvia's body. It was going to take a true miracle. Only God could heal her now.

But for the first time, Harry had to face the fact that God might choose not to.

CHAPTER
Seventy-Two

From the depths of fevered unconsciousness, Sylvia felt as if she floated at the bottom of a warm ocean. There was no pain there, no drugs, no time ticking away ...

A bright light shone through the opaque depths, and she swam toward it, but as hard as she swam, she got no closer to the light. It wasn't time.

Still, that light shone like an escape hatch through which she would soon pass ...

And for the first time, there was no dread. Beyond that light her Father watched and waited ...

Home beckoned ...

She was not forsaken, but anticipated.

She was not abandoned, but summoned.

Soon, a voice seemed to say from that light, *but not yet. There's more for you to do.*

So she stopped swimming and floated there, limp and docile, as she began to rise to the top.

When they got the fever down and gave Sylvia a transfusion to get her blood count back up, she began to return to full consciousness. "How in the world did I wind up here?" she asked Harry.

Harry got onto her hospital bed and lay beside her, stroking her face. He'd spent the last two nights sleeping on the couch in her room, and fatigue had crept over him like a life-eating fungus. "An ambulance brought you." His eyes misted over. "I thought I'd lost you."

"That bad, huh?"

"Yeah, that bad."

She stared at him for a long moment. "Harry, I'm going to die."

The statement surprised him, and he closed his eyes and shook his head. "Don't say that," he whispered. "Please don't say that."

She touched his face, stroked her fingers across the stubble. "I have to, Harry. You know it's true."

He squeezed his eyes shut and pressed his lips together.

"Honey, it's okay," she whispered. "Don't cry."

This was all wrong, he told himself. He was supposed to be telling *her* not to cry. She was the one who hurt . . .

He steeled himself and forced his eyes open. "I'm supposed to be telling you that."

"But why? You're the one who'll be left when I go. The greater pain in this is yours. I'll just be going home." A tear rolled across her nose, and he wiped it away.

"Remember the night after we met with the surgeon, and we talked about the elders laying hands on me? Remember how we said that whatever happened, we would know that God had heard our prayers, and had chosen to answer according to his will?"

Had he really said that? Had he meant it? Had he even known what he was talking about? It had been easy then, at the beginning of this, when she wasn't so ill and there was so much hope. But now ... "Why is this his will?" he whispered. "It seems so hard."

She kissed his wet cheek. "It's not hard, Harry. Remember how you told me that, whatever happens, we know that God loves me even more than you do?"

He nodded.

"He does, you know. He's there making a place for me ... waiting for me ... He loves me, and he loves you. And I'll bet he's weeping with us. Hating that our hearts are broken. Hating that we can't see the big picture that he can see. But he loves us, Harry, and we can't doubt that."

"So what do we do?" His voice was rising in pitch ... he wasn't going to be able to hold strong for her. He felt like a brokenhearted child who'd just learned the meaning of death. "How do we handle this?"

"Medically, we keep fighting. Spiritually, we start accepting."

Harry let out a shaky breath. "I thought I could do that. But now I wonder how that's even possible."

Sylvia's eyes twinkled as her dry lips stretched into a smile. "When I take the chemo, I sing praises. It gets me through the fear and the sick feelings and the dread. It keeps me focused. So that's what I think we should do, Harry. I think we should sing."

No, not that. He didn't have a song in his heart. It was too heavy to work up a tune ... "I can't, Sylvia. I can't sing right now."

"Yes, you can," she whispered. "Come on ... sing with me."

He sighed. "I'm tired, Sylvia."

She stroked his thinning gray hair. "I know you are. You can rest in a minute. After you've sung one chorus with me."

He knew she wouldn't relent, so reluctantly he said, "All right. Pick a song."

He had hoped she'd, at least, pick a slow one ... one that reflected the sorrow in his heart. But she didn't. Instead, she chose the upbeat "Shout to the Lord," and started to sing softly, coughing intermittently as they went. He joined in weakly, trying to mean it, trying to make his mind focus on the Creator of the universe who could have healed Sylvia but hadn't.

By the end of the song, her eyes smiled with a serenity that he wished he had. But he feared he'd never know the feeling of peace again.

∽≈∾

David and Brenda came to the hospital as soon as they heard that Sylvia had emerged from the fog of fever.

Brenda held David's hand as they made their way down the hall to her room. She glanced at his face, and saw in his misty eyes that he, too, was struck with the memory of their child lying so close to death in this very building.

They reached Sylvia's door. "Let me peek in and see if it's a good time," she whispered, and David stood back, waiting. "I don't want to disturb her if she's sleeping."

She cracked the door open and saw that the drapes were open. Sunshine streamed into the room, and she saw Harry sitting on the couch and looking toward the bed.

Instead of the sick silence of machines, she heard a song. Sylvia sang quietly . . . in her thin, raspy, breathless voice. "When Christ's sweet face I see . . . the suffering shall flee . . ."

Brenda caught her breath and stepped back. She put her hand over her heart and turned back to David. "She's singing!" she whispered.

David took a step toward the door, and listened.

"My trials will be worthwhile . . . when His face I see."

Brenda stepped inside, and Sylvia began to laugh at the sight of her.

∽≈∾

David stood outside the door, unable to follow just yet. He stepped to the side and leaned against the wall, trying to contain himself.

How could Sylvia sing?

Joseph had been like that, too. As he'd grown closer to death, he'd grown closer to his God, and what seemed like passing into the end had only been a beginning to him. It was that way for Sylvia, too. He couldn't fathom how she could sing about cancer in her breast and bones and liver and lungs being worth it all . . . It was something he couldn't get planted in his mind.

But the truth of it was growing clearer every day. If there was ever a time in life when spiritual things were clear and the mind and heart were at their peak, he supposed it was when a person was about to die. He wondered how he would face it. He knew there wouldn't be a song in his heart. There would probably be anger and bitterness, helplessness and despair.

Unfamiliar tears trailed down his face, and he looked from side to side, then quickly wiped them away before anyone could see.

Then drawing in a deep breath, he made himself go into the room.

Brenda stood beside the bed, speaking to Sylvia in a soft voice. "Harry was your knight in shining armor," she said. "When you were so sick, you should have seen him spring into action. We were all there, trying to help him . . ."

Sylvia saw David entering the room. "Oh, David," she whispered, and reached out for his hand. "What a joy to see you!"

Again he found that it was too hard for him to speak, so he only held her hand with both of his and tried to smile.

She looked tiny in the hospital bed, with an oxygen mask that should have been over her mouth but now hung under her chin, an IV running out of her arm, and wires and monitors running from her body to machines around her bed.

He couldn't escape the certainty that Sylvia was dying, and there was nothing that medicine or technology could do about it.

For the second time in his life he wished he believed in prayer.

CHAPTER
Seventy-Three

The decision to stop the chemotherapy and put Sylvia into hospice care was the hardest one of Harry's life, but her body was too weak to accept the ravages of any further chemo, and her pain was too great. After many meetings with the doctors, he agreed to shift their focus from healing to comforting her and keeping her free from pain.

They set her up in a hospital bed in their bedroom, and a hospice nurse came to set up the equipment they would need to keep Sylvia as comfortable as possible.

Sarah and Jeff dropped everything and came to be with her. To Sylvia's chagrin, Sarah left the baby with Gary and showed up alone, looking like a porcelain doll with a dozen cracks just beneath the surface, waiting to shatter if it was jarred.

When Sylvia fell asleep, Harry took the kids into the kitchen and sat across from them. Jeff looked like a lost little boy, struggling to hold back his tears, and Sarah couldn't look at him.

"Sit down, sweetie," he told her as she gazed out the window toward the barn.

"I'm okay standing," she said.

He sighed. "I need to talk to you, honey. I need for you to look at me."

Slowly, she turned back around. Her face twisted with pain, and she covered her mouth. "Oh, Daddy, don't say it."

He forced himself to go on. "I have to. Your mother is going to die."

Sarah shook her head. "No, Dad! You're giving up! There are still things you can do! You can't just give in to this and let it have her!"

"I'm not giving up," Harry said softly. "I've just had to come to terms with it. She's going to die. She's suffering, and it's hard to keep her free from pain. It won't do me any good to lie to you and give you false hope. We need to prepare ourselves."

Jeff got up now, his hands hanging in fists at his sides. "How could he do this to her?" he asked. "How could God refuse to heal her after all she's done for him?"

Harry closed his eyes and swallowed back the tightness in his throat. "He will heal her, son." The words came hard, but he managed to get them out. "He's going to heal her in his way. Maybe even the best way. When she dies, she'll be with him and she'll be healthy and sound again."

"That's not healing!" Sarah said. "That's not what we prayed for. God knows what we're asking. He promised that if we delighted ourselves in him that he would give us the desires of our heart. Well, my desire is for her to live!"

Jeff turned his sister around and pulled her against him, and they held each other as they wept. Harry stepped around the table and put his arms around both of them. "She will live," he whispered. "Just not here, with us."

He knew it wasn't enough for them, not yet. They wept harder than he'd ever seen them weep before, and he wept with them, holding them and hugging them and reassuring them as the reality of their mother's life and death seeped into their spirits.

When Harry returned to her bed, he saw how still and life-less she lay. The morphine had knocked out her pain, but in her drug-induced state, he wondered if she would be able to sit up and have a conversation. Would she be able to pray? Would she sing again?

The morphine didn't last long, and each time it wore off, he heard the groaning in her throat and saw the pain on her face. He squeezed her pump, issuing more drugs into her blood-stream, knocking her out again until the medicine wore off and she gritted her teeth in pain . . .

That night, as he lay in the bed he used to sleep in with her, he watched the sporadic, labored pattern of her breathing in the hospital bed, and wondered if she'd make it through the night.

He lay there, exhausted from the struggle to keep her drugged before the pain took hold, and realized that he'd come to the absolute end of his hope. It was time to start praying according to God's will, and according to Sylvia's needs.

"I can't stand her suffering, Lord," he whispered into the darkness. "Go on and take her. It's okay with me. Just don't let this suffering go on."

Sleep didn't come for him that night. He just lay there near her, listening for every breath, every groan, every beep of every monitor, while the children slept in their childhood rooms.

He had never felt more alone.

Chapter
Seventy-Four

For the sake of the children, Harry convinced the doctor to pull back on Sylvia's morphine, just long enough to get her coherent to give closure to the children. She would want it that way, he was sure. He could just hear her spirit sitting up in bed and shaking her finger at him. *Harry, don't you keep me so drugged that I can't say good-bye.*

The pain soaked her in sweat and made her body tremble, but she tried to smile as Sarah and Jeff came to her bedside.

They sat on either side of her, each holding one of her hands. Sarah leaned in, and pressed her forehead against Sylvia's face. "Mama, don't go," she whispered. "Please don't go. I need you. I don't know how to be a mother without you."

Sylvia let go of Jeff's hand and stroked Sarah's hair. "Yes, you do, sweetheart. You're doing a great job."

"But that's because I can pick up the phone and call you. You can walk me through it."

"But you have everything you need," Sylvia whispered. She swallowed with great effort. Even her throat had begun to feel cancer ravaged. "I've taught you everything I know. And you'll still have your dad. And Gary is so precious. I have perfect peace about leaving you with him. He'll take care of you. He'll help you through this." She turned Sarah's face up to hers, and made her look into it. She remembered when Sarah had wept inconsolably over a boyfriend who had broken her heart. She must have been sixteen then, Sylvia thought. Her face had looked like this, and Sylvia had wanted so much to be able to dry her tears and say the words that could heal her heart. But there hadn't been words then, and there weren't any now.

"Sweetheart, you're going to raise a houseful of godly children who serve the Lord and bear bushels and barrels of fruit. And when they ask about their grandmother, you're going to show them pictures of me and tell them that I'm in heaven, waiting for all of you to come and join me. Home, where we all belong."

Sarah's weeping broke her heart, but Sylvia didn't have the energy to cry her own tears. She looked at her son. His face was red and wet. She hadn't seen him cry since he was ten years old. She wished he had a wife now, one who could help him through this time, comfort him and cry with him. But he looked so alone.

She touched his face with her cold, trembling hand. "Jeff... my sweet Jeff... you'll be okay, too."

He could hardly speak. "I know, Mama."

"I've prayed so hard for you. God's going to send you a wonderful, godly woman someday, and you'll be a precious husband to her. You'll be just like your father. And when you have children, they'll be the most blessed children in the world. There will be generations of blessings for your family. I know that without a doubt, because I've prayed it since you were born."

A pain shot through her side, and she sucked in a breath, then started to cough. Sarah got up and tried to help her, but she turned on her side and kept trying to clear her lungs.

Jeff put the oxygen mask back on her face, and she was able to get some air into her lungs. She lay on her back, her eyes squeezed shut, as the nerves in her back seemed to break into attack mode, shooting bullets of pain through her body.

One of the children went to get Harry, and he came into the room. She saw him grabbing the morphine pump, squeezing it. She would slip into oblivion soon, she thought on a wave of panic. She hadn't finished saying good-bye.

When he leaned over her to kiss her, she grabbed his shirt. "Harry," she whispered. "I want you to get me the tape recorder."

"Why?" he asked. "What do you want to tape?"

She didn't have the energy to explain it to him. "Please. I'll rest for a minute, but don't pump the morphine again. Let it wear off so I can talk. Then bring me the tape player. I have some things to say to the people I love."

Harry straightened, and she saw the pain pulling at his face. As painful as her decline had been, she knew that he suffered even more.

"I want it to be played at my funeral," she whispered.

He looked so helpless. "Sylvia, I don't want you expending energy on that."

The morphine was taking hold, pulling her under, dulling the pain, but also dulling her senses. "Honey . . ." She knew her speech was slurred. "I have no intention of letting my death be the end of my fruit-bearing. The Lord has been too good to me not to do this last thing for him. I want to minister in my death, just as I've ministered in my life. I want my death to glorify Jesus. And I want to say good-bye."

She touched his face, felt the tired stubble. "Please, Harry. I have to do this."

He sighed, the heaviest, saddest sigh she'd ever heard in all her life. "I'll get the tape player."

When the morphine wore off, and the pain sank its teeth into her again, Harry sat her up, tried to make her comfortable, and pinned the microphone onto her gown. Then he turned the tape recorder on and left her alone to say her final good-bye to the people she was leaving behind.

CHAPTER
Seventy-Five

With each day that passed Sylvia declined further, until finally those who loved her began to pray her home. No matter how much morphine they gave her, it wasn't enough. She flailed and jerked and trembled in bed. Days had passed since she'd been able to speak or look anyone in the eye.

In many ways, she was already gone.

Harry didn't want her to linger in this place between life and death for his sake ... or the sake of the children. Instead, he wanted her to go where she could shed the pain like an old garment she wouldn't need anymore.

He prayed for the Lord to take her, night after night after night ...

But when the time finally came that the doctor warned him she wouldn't make it through the night, he found that he wasn't ready. It was a funny thing. Sarah and Jeff had suddenly developed the strength they needed to make it through their mother's death ... but he ...

He didn't know if he could really let her go. The thought of her still being here in some form was preferable to having her disappear from the earth, no longer a part of his world.

He didn't dare pray for God to give her more time. That would be selfish. Instead he prayed for strength. He would need God's arms around him, propping him up, moving his feet as he walked through these final hours. He could not do it on his own strength.

He knew that the neighbors needed to see Sylvia one last time, and in some way, he felt that she would know they were there. Sarah called, and found them at Brenda's house, praying on the front porch. David called them in to the kitchen and they sat around the telephone listening to her stopped-up voice.

"They don't expect Mama to make it through the night," she said. "My dad said that it would be all right if you'd like to come over."

"We'll be right there," Brenda whispered.

They were at the door in moments, and Harry could see that they'd shed as many tears tonight as he and the kids had done. They came silently into the house, hugged everyone quietly, then followed Harry into the bedroom.

As they went in, Sylvia opened her eyes. Harry rushed to her bed. "Honey?"

Her eyes looked glazed, distant, but then she focused on him.

"Honey, the girls are here. Brenda, Tory, and Cathy came to say hello."

Sylvia felt as if she swam through Jell-O, fighting her way to the top where she could get air. She heard Harry's voice ... sniffing ... the whisk of tissues pulled from their box ...

" ... girls are here ... came to say ..."

She had to talk to them, she thought. She had to see them one last time. *Please, Lord, pull me up ... one last time ...*

And there they were, standing around her bed, Cathy on one side next to Harry, Brenda and Tory on the other. Sarah and Jeff stood at the foot of her bed. They looked like they hadn't slept in days.

She locked into Cathy's eyes, then turned to Brenda and Tory. "Best times," she whispered on a thin breath. "Tell me . . . best times . . ."

They had always done it. It was their ritual after an ordeal. When Joseph survived his heart transplant, when Tory had given birth to her Down's Syndrome baby, when Cathy got Mark safely home from jail. They had always run down the list of the very best moments . . .

There were so many.

In stark silence, the three women made herculean efforts to control their tears. She felt sorry for them, and wished she could touch them and impart some kind of peace.

Finally, Cathy spoke up in a raspy voice. "Watching when you came home with my Annie," she whispered, "and I saw how changed she was. That was a best moment."

Sylvia smiled. "Good one," she managed to say.

Brenda patted her hand and tried to put on that cheerful face that came so naturally to her. But it didn't look natural when her face was covered with tears. "When we went trying on wigs," she said.

Sylvia breathed a laugh. "So silly."

"Yeah, we were silly," Brenda said. "But it was definitely a best moment."

Tory squeezed her hand. "When little Bo accepted Christ."

She squeezed back. "Priceless."

"Yeah," Cathy agreed. "The look on your face as you watched the video of him giving his life to Christ."

Sylvia closed her eyes and remembered.

"The best moments weren't just in the last year," Cathy said. "They go back for several years. Remember when you realized you were supposed to go to the mission field, and surrendered to Harry's call?"

Sylvia opened her eyes, laughing weakly.

"And the moment I met Steve," Cathy said.

That was a good one, Sylvia thought.

"Barry," she whispered.

Tory nodded. "I was just thinking of that. When Barry came back home after we'd been separated. That was one of the best moments."

"And Joseph's heart." Sylvia almost couldn't get the words out. She hoped they heard.

"Yes." Brenda's voice wobbled. "When he woke up from surgery with all that color in his cheeks."

"Good moments . . . ," Sylvia whispered. "Best moments."

She started to cough, and they all gathered closer, as if their closeness could somehow help her clear her lungs. But it was no use. Harry put the mask back over her face, and she sank back into her pillow as the pain tightened its vice around her body.

She sensed the grief overtaking them all, and she wished she was a better actor, that she could pretend to be relaxed, serene, and pain-free. She tried to lie still, tried not to jerk or moan, tried not to wince with the shooting pain.

Then she felt the drugs sweeping over her, dulling the pain, relaxing her body, taking her out . . .

But she wasn't ready . . . not yet . . . she had to pray for them . . . they weren't ready. . . .

Lord, please . . . just another minute . . .

Cathy thought she would collapse in grief, but somehow she managed to leave Sylvia's bedside. Sarah was there to hug her, and she felt the young woman's racking sobs as she held her. Brenda hugged Jeff, and Tory clung to Harry.

"Don't go."

Cathy turned and saw that Sylvia was awake again, reaching for them. Sarah and Jeff rushed for her, taking her hands, and Harry grabbed that pump again.

"Want to pray for you," she said on a shallow whisper. "Come ..."

One by one, they took each other's hands, until they stood in a circle around Sylvia's bed, tears flowing and noses running and hearts moaning ...

And then she spoke as clearly as if she'd never been sick. "Lord," she said, "help them to see the joy in this ..."

Her words trailed off, and her eyes closed. Her raspy breathing settled and stilled ...

... and all grew quiet.

The monitor beeped out a warning, and Harry fell over her, shaking her and touching her face, trying to make her open her eyes.

But she was gone.

Sylvia had gone home to be with Jesus, with a prayer for her loved ones still on her lips.

CHAPTER
Seventy-Six

Silence hung over the Dodd house as they got dressed the morning of the funeral. Brenda moved by rote, ironing shirts and preparing breakfast. But her mind remained in that bedroom at the Bryans' house, all of them crowded around Sylvia's bed, receiving a prayer of blessing before she passed into eternity.

Sylvia had prayed that they would see the joy in this, but so far, Brenda only saw the tragedy of losing her mentor and closest friend.

What would she do without Sylvia? Who would teach her? Whose wisdom would she call on?

She took the boys' shirts to their room. Daniel stood in front of the mirror, combing his hair. He'd been crying, she could tell. His eyes were red and slightly swollen, but he would have denied it if she'd acknowledged it.

He took the shirt, stared down at it.

She stood in the doorway, and remembered when Joseph hung between life and death, how Sylvia had come to stay with Daniel and the girls. She'd told Brenda how Daniel had done the only thing he'd known to do. He'd come down in the middle of the night to wash his own sneakers, so he could take them to Joseph the next day. The child's feet had been too swollen for his own shoes, and Daniel imagined that his feet were cold.

She knew that he had bonded with Sylvia that night, and was running those moments through his mind. What had once been a sweet memory now burned with the bitterness of death.

She took the other shirt and headed to Joseph's room. Leah and Rachel were coming out of theirs, their eyes swollen and pink.

"Mama, tell Rachel she's supposed to wear black. It's rude to wear color to a funeral."

Brenda looked at Rachel's choice of the yellow dress she'd worn on Easter. "Mama, do I have to?"

Brenda forced a smile. "I think it's fine for you to wear yellow, honey. Miss Sylvia wanted us to see the joy in this. Yellow is a joyful color, don't you think?"

Leah crossed her arms. "Well, should I change into a color?"

"You look beautiful." She kissed Leah's forehead, then Rachel's. "Both of you do. I wouldn't change a thing."

She took the shirt into Joseph's room, and saw him sitting cross-legged on his bed in his T-shirt and pants, the Bible open on his lap.

He looked up when she came in. "Mama, look. The gates of heaven are made of one gigantic pearl on each gate. And there's a sea of glass, and there's no need for light, because God is so bright."

She put her fingertips over her mouth, and nodded.

"And the disciples are there, and the apostle Paul, and Moses and Abraham ... Do you think Sylvia's had the chance to ask them questions yet?"

Brenda forced her voice to remain steady. "What questions?"

"Like what Paul's thorn in the flesh was, and what Jesus wrote in the sand, and what was going through Abraham's mind when he went to sacrifice Isaac."

Brenda pictured Sylvia at the feet of the fathers of their faith, getting the story behind the story. The thought made her smile. "I think she probably has."

Joseph nodded. "Because it says that right now we see through a mirror darkly, but someday we'll see face-to-face. Seems like everything should be clear to her by now, huh?"

Brenda wished her youngest son could have been the one to preach Sylvia's funeral. He seemed to have the most perfect perspective of all of them.

She gave him his shirt, then went to finish getting ready.

David was putting on his tie. His hands trembled as he did, and she caught his reflection in the mirror. The lines around his eyes were deep. He hadn't slept much the last two nights. Last night she'd heard him get up in the wee hours of morning, and he had never come back to bed.

He was taking Sylvia's death harder than she'd expected. She thought of that prayer that Sylvia had prayed some time ago, for David's salvation.

It had not been answered, and the pain of that rose up high in Brenda's chest, twisting her grief and bringing her close to despair.

But she had no choice but to trust that God had heard that prayer, and had every intention of answering it . . . someday.

She wondered if Sylvia still prayed from heaven.

She went into the bathroom and sprayed her hair, put on earrings and her watch. Then she checked the time, and saw that they needed to go.

It was time to lay Sylvia's body to rest.

CHAPTER
Seventy-Seven

Next door, Tory tried valiantly to get her family ready. She had taken Hannah in to the school this morning, to be cared for while she attended the funeral. The faces of all the teachers had been grim, but the children, who had been told yesterday, played as though nothing had happened. They didn't understand, she thought. How could they?

When she spoke to Bo, he looked up at her with a smile. "Miva in heben," he told her matter-of-factly.

"Yes, she is," Tory said. "She's in heaven, all right."

"Bo see her dere."

"That's right. Someday you'll see her there."

There was no grief on his face, no crushing sense of loss. Only joy, pure and undefiled, as he imagined Sylvia's new situation. Time had little meaning to him. As far as he knew, he'd see Sylvia tomorrow, when Jesus returned for him.

As she left the school and headed back home, she realized that Bo had it right. There was no need for grief. Sylvia wasn't suffering. She probably had great hair in heaven, and a twenty-five-year-old body, and a brain sharper than it had ever been.

Still, the grief pulled at Tory like quicksand.

As she got Spencer and Brittany ready for the service, she struggled to keep from letting that grief suck her under.

"I'm choking," Spencer said as she knotted his tie. "I can't stand this."

"Spencer, you need to wear it. Now don't give me a hard time."

Barry stepped into the room and touched her shoulder. "Here, let me."

She stepped back, and watched her husband sit on the bed in front of the boy. "We want you to wear a tie today, Spence, because it's an important time, and we want you to look like the little man that you are."

Spencer seemed to stand taller. "And because Miss Sylvia might be able to see me?"

Barry met Tory's eyes. "I don't know," he said. "I don't really think so. The Bible says there are no tears in heaven. If she could see how sad Dr. Harry is, she might cry. So I doubt that she can watch."

"Yeah." Spencer stuck his chin out as his father straightened his tie. "She probably has too much to do, anyway. Checking out her new mansion, and talking to Jesus, and all that stuff."

Tory stood back at the door, listening to the quiet conversation. God was using the mouths of babes today, to show her the joy in Sylvia's passing.

Just as she'd prayed before her spirit left her body.

Come to me as little children, the Lord seemed to remind her. *See what they see. Understand as they do.*

She went to Brittany's room and saw her eleven-year-old, already fully dressed, struggling with her hair in front of the mirror. She'd grown so beautiful in the last year . . . still a child, but almost a woman.

Tory came to her rescue. "Let me help."

She pulled her hair up out of her face.

"What's gonna happen, Mom?" she asked. "Will we see Miss Sylvia?"

Tory shook her head. "No, honey. She asked Dr. Harry to have a closed casket. She wanted us to remember her as she used to be."

"She was *always* beautiful on the inside," Brittany said. "I think we can remember her all the ways that she was, even when she was sick."

Tory turned her daughter around and hugged her. "I'm glad you understand that, sweetie. Sylvia was never more beautiful than she was at the very end. Skinny and sick and bald . . . she was the most beautiful woman I knew."

"She's even more beautiful now," Brittany whispered.

Again, from the mouths of babes . . .

Barry stuck his head in the room. "We should go. It's getting late."

Tory nodded, but wasn't able to speak as she got her purse and headed out to the car.

CHAPTER
Seventy-Eight

At the Bennett house, Cathy tried to console her daughter.

Annie was already dressed, but her eyes were so swollen and wet that Cathy had brought her ice packs in hopes of making her look more normal at the funeral. But the girl couldn't stop crying.

"Mom, why did they ask me to speak, of all people? There's no way I can do it. Look at me. I'll fall apart."

Cathy shook her head. "Annie, you spent a year with Sylvia, doing what she loved most in the world. Who better to tell about her?"

"But I just don't get it." Annie held the pack against one eye, but her tears countered the work it did. "Why did she have to die? Aren't we all here to bear fruit? Why would God take somebody who bore more than anybody else I know?"

Cathy drew in a deep breath. "Last night I was reading my Bible and trying to find peace ... and I read something that

Jesus said. He said, 'Unless a seed falls in the ground and dies, it cannot bear fruit.' I don't think he meant that you can't bear fruit when you're alive, obviously, but I do think he was saying that sometimes death brings even more fruit."

"How?"

Cathy stroked Annie's hair. "Honey, there will be a lot of people at that funeral today. Harry's even having it videotaped for the memorial service they're having for her in León. Think of all the unbelievers who will hear the testimony of Sylvia's life, and embrace Jesus for the first time. Then they'll tell people, and they'll tell people . . . her fruit could keep reproducing for years."

Annie nodded and brought the ice pack down. "Generations even."

"That's right."

Her face twisted again. "But what if I let Dr. Harry down? What if I mess this up and make him more upset than he already is?"

"You won't, honey. Just read what you've prepared. If you cry, that's all right. We'll all be crying with you."

She left Annie alone to get her bearings, then checked on Rick. He had come home for the funeral, and stood in his room now, staring out the window at Sylvia's house next door. She stepped into his room. "You almost ready, honey?"

He turned around. "Yeah, Mom. How are you?"

The sweet question brought tears to her eyes, and she nodded. "I'm okay."

"Good."

"You okay with being a pallbearer?"

He nodded. "I think so. I'm a little nervous. This isn't the kind of thing they teach in college."

"You'll do fine." She walked into the room and reached up to kiss him on the cheek. "I'm proud of you. Dr. Harry chose his pallbearers well."

Rick shrugged. "I can see him picking David and Barry and Steve. But me and Mark and Daniel?"

"You're the men of Cedar Circle," she said. "Why not you?"

When she'd left him alone, she went to Mark's room and saw that he was already dressed. His cheeks were mottled pink, as they always were when he was nervous or upset.

"You ready, Mark?"

"Yeah." He looked up at her. "Mom?"

"Uh-huh?"

"I know the Bible says that we're not supposed to grieve as those who have no hope. But do you think it's a bad witness if we cry at the funeral?"

Cathy breathed a sad laugh. "Of course not, sweetheart. Jesus wept at Lazarus's funeral, even though he knew that he was going to raise him from the dead."

"Yeah," Mark said. "I've wondered about that. Why do you think he cried if he knew it was going to have a happy ending?"

"Because his heart broke for Mary and Martha . . . just like it's probably breaking for us." Her voice broke off, and her own tears rushed to her eyes. She tried to hold them back.

Mark hugged her, and she clung to him, so proud that he had become a young man who cared about God's Word.

"Mom, I know this is gonna be hard for you," he said as he held her. "Miss Sylvia meant so much to you."

She swallowed. "I owe her a lot." She pulled back and wiped her tears. She had to get herself together. With Annie as upset as she was, one of them was going to have to be strong.

"I'm worried about your sister. She's so upset."

"I could go in there and torture her a little bit. Make her forget her troubles."

"Generous offer." Cathy laughed softly. "But I don't think so."

He looked at his watch. "We'd better get going."

Cathy drew in a deep breath. "Yeah. Let's go."

She went down the stairs, and found Tracy in the kitchen, loading the last of the breakfast dishes into the dishwasher.

"Tracy, look what you've done. Thank you, sweetie."

Tracy got a sponge and began wiping the counter. "I got ready early. It was something I could do."

Cathy kissed her cheek. "That was very thoughtful."

The girl turned her face up to Cathy, and gazed at her with big, round eyes. "I'm sorry you're sad, Cathy. I wish I could make it better."

"You just did," she said.

She found Steve in their bedroom, sitting in the rocker with his elbows on his knees, his head bowed, his eyes closed.

She knew he was praying, so she stood quietly in the room, watching him, so thankful that she had married a godly man who knew where to turn when he hurt.

After a moment, he looked up at her. "You ready?"

She nodded, but those tears rushed her again. He stood and took her into his arms, held her for a long moment.

"I miss her," she whispered. "I miss her so much."

"Me too." She felt his tears on her neck, and clung tighter to him.

A knock sounded on the door, and Annie stepped into the doorway. "I'm ready, Mom," she said.

Cathy wiped her face. "All right then. Let's do this."

And quietly the family piled into the car.

CHAPTER
Seventy-Nine

The casket at the front of the church was closed, and on top of it sat a lovely picture of Sylvia, before she'd gotten sick. Her eyes laughed in the framed photograph, and her smile spoke of love and joy. A bright spray of autumn flowers lay across the casket, proclaiming life rather than death. It was just as Harry had ordered it.

The neighbors of Cedar Circle gathered with the family in a back room as the church filled with mourners. Harry led them in prayer, and asked that this funeral minister in her death just as Sylvia had ministered in her life.

"Lord," he prayed, "let this funeral not be a time of glorifying Sylvia. She wouldn't have wanted that. Let it glorify you, from its beginning until its end."

His voice broke off, and for a moment he struggled to get the knot out of his throat and finish the prayer.

"Lord, we have so much to be thankful for. Thank you for healing Sylvia in the most complete way possible. Thank you for all the years we had with her. Thank you for what she taught us, how she loved us, the way she modeled you. Thank you for letting her touch our lives. And thank you for assuring us that we will see her again, when we see you in all your glory, and we're all finally home."

Harry waited as the family and neighbors filed into the first few rows of the church. All three of Sylvia's closest friends huddled close together, holding hands. Their husbands and sons who would serve as pallbearers sat in the front row, their faces grim.

As Harry walked in, he met David's eyes. He was the only one among the pallbearers who didn't believe. How sad, how crushing that grief must be, Harry thought. And as he took his seat, he prayed the prayer that Sylvia had prayed until her dying day.

Lord, save him.

CHAPTER *Eighty*

As the funeral began, and the full choir of the church sang "Because He Lives," anger swirled up in David's heart. The funeral was supposed to be about Sylvia, a woman so many in this room mourned. He couldn't fathom why they would put so much emphasis on Jesus. The fact that Harry had prayed for that very thing baffled him.

When Annie got up to speak, his anger faded. He knew that she would talk about Sylvia rather than the God she believed in.

She looked as if she'd been crying for days, but as she got behind the podium, she stood like a portrait of poise and maturity.

"I spent a year with Miss Sylvia and Dr. Harry in Nicaragua," Annie began, her voice wobbling. "And as I was trying to decide which things to tell you about her, and which to leave out, I realized that there was too much for me to choose. We'd be here all day. So instead I e-mailed León, and asked that the children of the Missionary Children's Home, the orphanage where she worked, e-mail me back with the things they wanted you to know about the woman they called Mama Sylvia. Here's what they said."

She began to read the heartfelt notes—translated into English—from children of all ages, telling how Mama Sylvia had taken them in when they were alone and frightened, how she'd loved them when they grieved over parents killed in the hurricane, how she'd taught them and nurtured them. Every single note spoke of how she had led them to Jesus, and how they knew they would see her again. The final note, dictated by a six-year-old boy named Juan, came like a blow to David's heart.

"All I can say now is, 'Please, Jesus. Hurry up and come. Take me there, too, so I can see Mama Sylvia's smile again. And you, because you're the reason for her smile.'"

Tears stung David's eyes, and he looked back at his wife. Brenda sat between Tory and Cathy, holding their hands and weeping. Her heart was broken, but the tears weren't angry or bitter. She grieved without despair, just as Harry did.

When Harry got up and went to the podium, David sat straighter, watching, listening.

"My wife . . ." Harry stopped and cleared his throat. Finally, he went on. "My wife planned her funeral. She told me who she wanted to preach it, who she wanted to speak, who she wanted to sing. She had very specific instructions."

He stopped and brought a handkerchief to his nose. "A few days before her death, she asked me to bring the tape recorder to her room. She had some things she wanted to say to all of you. So here . . . in her own voice, and her own words, is my wife's message."

He went back to his seat and wiped his eyes, stuffed the handkerchief back into his pocket.

David glanced at Brenda again. Her face looked stricken as she waited for the tape to begin.

Then David heard the hiss of the tape. He stared down at his hands, listening.

"Hello, friends."

It was as if she stood in the room with them, standing at the microphone, her smile lighting up the place.

"When you hear the rumors of my death, don't you believe them."

He looked up, frowning, and locked eyes with the picture of her on her casket.

"By the time you hear this, I will be in the presence of Jesus. I'll be free of this sick, earthly body, and I'll be laughing with more joy than I've ever known on earth. And I've had lots of joy. John 16:22 says, 'Now is your time of grief, but I will see you again and you will rejoice, and no one will take away your joy.'

"So don't cry for me. Remember the happy times, the times when God worked in our lives, when he taught us precious lessons, when he used us together. Remember the best moments."

David met Brenda's eyes, and wished he could be beside her.

"And think ahead to that day, not so far from now, when I'll be there to greet you, as you come home, too.

"Harry, I can't express how much I've loved you. God chose you for me when we were very young, and you have been a model to me of how much Christ loves me. My love for you has not died. It remains and lives on.

"Sarah, what a beautiful daughter you've been, and what a precious mother. You're my treasure, and my hope. Everything I had I put into you. I can't wait to see all your crowns when you get here. Gary, take good care of her and little Breanna, and all those other children that you and Sarah will have.

"Breanna, know that your grandma loves you. You won't have memories of me, so let me tell you what's important to know, and what I want you to tell all the other grandchildren yet to come. Tell them that my life was worth it. Everything, all of it, was worth it, because of the unsurpassed joy that Christ has on the other side.

"Jeff, my son, my precious boy . . . You're a man after God's own heart, and I'm so proud of you. Someday you'll marry and have children, too, and though I won't be there to see them, I'll be ready to make up for lost time when they get here.

"To my dear neighbors, and my very closest friends in the world, I've loved you so much."

David felt tears ambushing him, catching in his throat, pulling at his face. He closed his eyes.

"Cathy and Steve, God has brought the two of you together, and joined your two families. You've been joined for a purpose, all of you. I pray that you'll learn the art of dying to yourself, living for each other, and bearing much fruit for the Lord who gives you everything you need.

"Annie, you were right all those months ago. When God lit up our path that day, he was telling me that he would light my way. I know you're thinking that my prediction didn't come true, that I'll never dance at your wedding. But when Christ comes to get his Bride, I'll be with him. I'll see you in that white gown, after all."

Annie covered her face and pressed a wad of tissue to her eyes.

"Mark and Rick, you're turning into such godly young men. You'll be wonderful fathers and husbands some day. I'm so proud of both of you. And Tracy, what a precious child. I know you'll grow into a godly woman.

"Tory and Barry . . ."

Next to David, Barry leaned his elbows on his knees and dropped his face into his hands.

"Your faith has grown so much in the last few years. The Lord has done mighty things in your lives. I know he'll continue those mighty works. I know that your children will grow to become people of God—Brittany and Spencer, and even little Hannah, who will one day invite Jesus into her heart. There's no doubt in my mind. Always remember to have the simple faith of that little child, and you can't go wrong.

"And Brenda and David . . ."

David looked up, staring through his tears at that picture again. It was as if Sylvia's eyes were fixed on him.

"What a dear family you have, and God has done amazing works in your lives. I expect multitudes to know Jesus, because of Joseph's sweet, priceless heart, and Daniel, Leah, and

Rachel's abiding faith. Brenda, you've done a wonderful job with them. Never let the worries of the world interfere with your life's work.

"Joseph, I want you to have Midnight. Dr. Harry and I have arranged for you to keep her at a stable nearby. Her rent and food are paid for for the next five years. I think God meant her for you all along . . ."

David smiled and looked at his son, saw that Joseph smiled through his tears.

"And David . . ."

He snapped his gaze back to the picture.

"David, I want you to know that God does exist, and he loves you. I want to see you in heaven, David. I want to see the joy in your eyes as you walk down the streets of gold and behold the light of the Lord's glory. All of your family will be there. David, don't be left behind."

It was as though a stake had been driven through his heart, killing something inside him, crushing the core of who he believed himself to be. From Sylvia's perspective, he was an incomplete man, a man who hid from obvious truth, a man with a void the shape of hope in his heart.

He couldn't stop himself as grief—for Sylvia, but even more for himself—conquered him completely. He set his elbows on his knees and dropped his face. Barry straightened beside him and touched his shoulder. Daniel patted his knee.

The rest of the service went by in a blur, as the preacher gave a message that once again pointed to Christ rather than Sylvia.

Someone sang, someone read a poem . . .

But none of it registered in his mind. All he could hear was Sylvia's voice ringing in his ears. *David, don't be left behind.*

He pictured that day, when his family went to heaven and greeted Sylvia again. Joseph, running and jumping in some divine meadow, Leah and Rachel glowing like angels, Daniel rejoicing, Brenda laughing and laughing and laughing . . .

But he was not in that picture. Like the night they had all headed off for the program at church, the program that he'd almost missed, he would be left out.

David, don't be left behind.

The pallbearers stood, and shaking himself out of his reverie, he stood with them. Leaving the casket where it was for now, they filed out of the room. Harry and the family, and Brenda, Tory, Cathy, and the kids all lined up behind them and left the room.

He couldn't talk to anyone, couldn't look in their eyes, couldn't make small talk about what a wonderful service it had been. Instead he went into the rest room, bent over the sink, and splashed water on his face. Slowly, he dried it off, and looked at his reflection in the mirror.

David, don't be left behind.

He left the bathroom, and went back into the sanctuary. It was empty now, except for the casket. Sylvia's picture had been taken down, but the autumn flowers still draped across its lid.

Tears that seemed to come from some aged place in the deepest part of his soul rushed up to drown him, and he twisted his face and let it go.

Slowly, he fell to his knees at the altar behind the casket.

"David?" It was Harry's voice behind him, and he looked up at the man who should have been the one doubled over in grief.

He started to rise up. "Harry, I'm so sorry . . ."

"It's okay." Harry knelt beside him. "Talk to me, David."

David tried to stop the slide of his anguish. "What she said on that tape . . ."

Harry smiled. "Tough stuff, huh? It was very serious business to her. Your salvation has been on her heart for a very long time. Just as it's been on Brenda's."

David didn't know how so many tears could be pouring from his eyes, while his throat seemed so dry. "Harry, I saw a picture of heaven in my mind during the funeral. And I wasn't there." He sucked in a sob and wiped the tears from his face.

Finally, he looked Harry in the eye. "Harry, I don't want to be left behind."

Out in the church foyer, Brenda searched the faces of the departing mourners for David. Soon they would be loading the casket into the hearse, and the cars would line up for their procession to the grave site.

She knew he was upset. She'd watched his profile as Sylvia spoke directly to him, and she'd seen the pain on his face. As much as she wanted Sylvia's words to penetrate his heart, she hated the thought that he was hurting or embarrassed, somewhere alone.

She found Daniel standing with the other pallbearers. "Honey, where's your dad?"

"I don't know," he said. "Somebody said they saw him go back into the sanctuary, but I don't know why he'd do that."

Frowning, Brenda hurried down the hall. As she neared the sanctuary, she saw the funeral director standing just outside the door.

"Is anyone in there?" she asked him.

"Yes," he said. "I was going to roll the casket out, but Dr. Bryan and another man are having a private conversation."

Another man. She knew it was David. She bolted through the doors and into the large room. She saw her husband kneeling at the altar, with Harry beside him.

She stood silently as he prayed. She couldn't hear the words, but her heart soared with hope. *Lord, are you answering my prayer?*

After a moment, the prayer came to an end, and David looked up. Harry hugged him tightly, and both men came to their feet.

As David turned to her, she saw the tears on his face. "Brenda," he whispered.

She ran into his arms, and clung to him with all her strength.

"I'm so sorry, Brenda."

"So sorry? For what?" she asked. "What have you done?"

"I've failed you all these years," he said, "by not believing the truth that was so obvious. The truth about Jesus Christ. He's real. I've seen it so many times, but I chose to reject it. All the things you've stood for all these years are right, and I don't know why I've been so blind."

He broke down, and Brenda kept holding him. "It's okay, honey. It's okay."

Harry put his hand on both of their backs. "Tell her what you did, David."

He pulled back and looked down at her. "I asked Christ to forgive me and change me," he said. "I want to live for him from now on, like Sylvia did . . . like you do. When I die, I want to leave good things behind. And I want to be a spiritual leader in our family, because you deserve that. I want to be a new person."

Brenda suddenly knew the joy that Sylvia had prayed for. There *was* joy in her death. Fruit had come from it. David was a believer!

As she wept and pulled Harry into their circle, she saw that Harry had that joy, too. All of Sylvia's prayers had now been answered.

CHAPTER
Eighty-One

❧

The Lord seemed to have adorned the world for Sylvia's burial. The autumn trees wore an explosion of colors, from yellow to bright red, and the early November breeze whispered gently across the hills.

The neighbors of Cedar Circle stood hand in hand at the burial, their husbands behind them. Next to Cathy stood Annie, Rick, and Mark, each struggling with their own open grief. Brenda and David stood on the end with Joseph, Leah, Rachel, and Daniel beside them, and Tory and Barry had Brittany and Spencer standing quietly in front of them.

When the burial service was finished, all of the funeral attendees went back to their cars. Harry and the kids stood near the cars, talking softly to the mourners.

"It was a beautiful day," Brenda whispered. "Sylvia would have liked it."

"Yeah," Cathy said. "She would have been clipping leaves to use as Thanksgiving centerpieces."

"Riding Midnight," Tory added.

A gentle wind whipped up, blowing their hair and drying their tears. But more came.

"I can't do this," Tory whispered. "I can't say good-bye."

"Yes, you can." Brenda squeezed her hand. "We said it when she went to León. We knew we'd see her again. It's no different now."

"It feels different," Tory said.

Harry came back and gave them each a flower from the top of the casket. One by one, he kissed their cheeks. "We'll go on," he told them. "It seems impossible now, but we will. There's work to do."

Cathy took his hand. "You're going back to León, aren't you?"

"Yes," he said. "I want to be back for their memorial service next week. The kids are joining me there for Christmas. I think it'll be good for them to see the results of their mother's work."

"We'll miss you," Brenda said.

He couldn't answer. His eyes strayed to the casket, still sitting beside the grave it would be lowered into after they were gone.

"She would tell us to sing," he whispered. "Don't you think she would?"

There was a long silence . . .

Then Brenda began to sing. "It will be worth it all, when we see Jesus . . ."

Cathy joined in . . . then Tory picked up . . . and Harry followed.

The song lifted on the breeze, carried across the grave sites, rose up the hills on the other side . . .

From the depths of their grief came a fragile joy . . . and from the hollow of their good-bye . . .

. . . A distant hello.

For their story would not end, until they met again.

Seasons Under Heaven

What does a child's life-threatening illness cost the neighbors of Cedar Circle? What joys can be hidden in life's greatest tragedies? As the women of Cedar Circle band together to save a dying child, they learn that each moment is precious in every season under heaven. Gently uncovering the inner struggles, stresses, and joys that surface among neighbors living in a quiet cul-de-sac, the authors show us the power of ordinary lives being knit into a strong, many-textured fabric of family and friendships.

Softcover: 0-310-23519-7

Showers in Season

On the quiet cul-de-sac of Cedar Circle, where neighbors are close friends, fierce winds of circumstance threaten to sweep one couple away. Their Down's Syndrome pregnancy is shattering news for Tory and Barry Sullivan, but the option Barry proposes is abhorrent to Tory. It will take a wisdom and strength greater than their own to carry them through. That, and the encouragement only a loving, close-knit community can provide.

Softcover: 0-310-24296-7

Times and Seasons

More is at stake for Cathy Flaherty than her son, who has been arrested for selling drugs. With Mark in juvenile detention, the single mother of three finds herself struggling over whether to marry Steve Bennett, a man she truly loves. It will take strength and wisdom for Steve to see Cathy through this time of family conflict. Fortunately, he is not alone. Other lives, each with concerns of their own, weave together in a strong show of mutual care and support. And through the hands and hearts of this loving community, God moves.

Softcover: 0-310-24297-5

We want to hear from you. Please send your comments about this book to us in care of the address below. Thank you.

GRAND RAPIDS, MICHIGAN 49530 USA

WWW.ZONDERVAN.COM